WHOSE BUSINESS IS TO DIE

Also by Adrian Goldsworthy

FICTION

Run Them Ashore

All in Scarlet Uniform

Send Me Safely Back Again

Beat the Drums Slowly

True Soldier Gentlemen

NON-FICTION

Augustus: From Revolutionary to Emperor

Antony and Cleopatra

The Fall of the West: The Death of the Roman Superpower

Caesar: The Life of a Colossus

In the Name of Rome:
The Men Who Won the Roman Empire

The Complete Roman Army

Cannae: Hannibal's Greatest Victory

The Punic Wars

Roman Warfare

The Roman Army at War, 100 BC–AD 200

WHOSE BUSINESS IS TO DIE

Adrian Goldsworthy

Weidenfeld & Nicolson
LONDON

First published in Great Britain in 2015 by Weidenfeld & Nicolson,
an imprint of The Orion Publishing Group Ltd,
Carmelite House, 50 Victoria Embankment,
London, EC4Y 0DZ

An Hachette UK company

1 3 5 7 9 10 8 6 4 2

A CIP catalogue record for this book is
available from the British Library.

ISBN (Hardback) 978 0 2978 7186 6
ISBN (Ebook) 978 0 2978 7187 3

Typeset at The Spartan Press Ltd,
Lymington, Hants

Printed and bound in Great Britain by
Clays Ltd, St Ives plc

The Orion Publishing Group's policy is to use papers that
are natural, renewable and recyclable products and made
from wood grown in sustainable forests. The logging and
manufacturing processes are expected to conform to the
environmental regulations of the country of origin.

www.orionbooks.co.uk

For Thomas Atkins Esq., past, present and future

How stands the glass around?
For shame, ye take no care, my boys,
How stands the glass around?
Let mirth and wine abound,
The trumpets sound!
The colours they are flying boys,
To fight, kill or wound,
May we still be found,
Contented with hard fare, my boys,
On the cold, cold ground

Why, soldiers, why,
Should we be melancholy boys?
Why, soldiers, why?
Whose business 'tis to die!
What, sighing? Fye!
Damn fear, drink on, be jolly boys!
'Tis he, you or I,
Cold, hot, wet or dry,
We're always bound to follow, boys,
And scorn to fly.

'Tis but in vain;
(I mean not to upbraid you boys),
'Tis but in vain,
For soldiers to complain.
Should next campaign,
Send us to Him that made us, boys,
We're free from pain.
But should we remain,
A bottle and kind landlady
Cures all again.

• • •

'Why, soldiers, why?' was featured in the 1729 play *The Patron*, and was very popular during the Peninsular War. It was often called 'Wolfe's Song' and may well have been sung by the army in the Quebec campaign of 1759. There was also a story that General Wolfe sang the song the day before he was killed at the moment of victory, but this is almost certainly apocryphal.

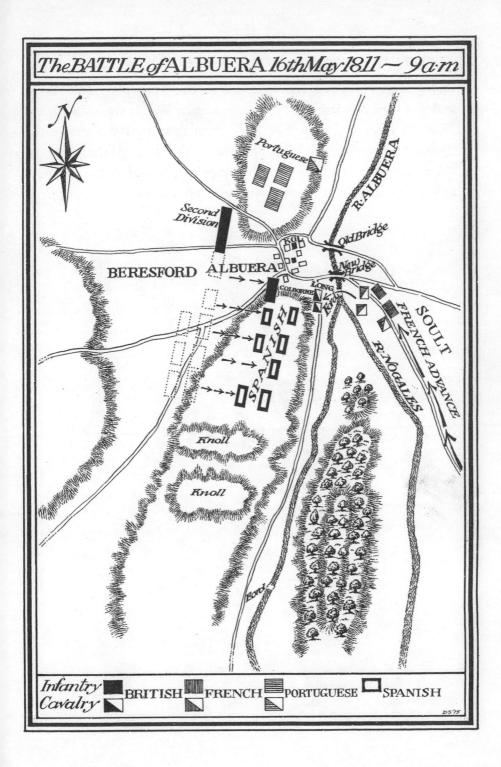

The BATTLE of ALBUERA 16th May 1811 ～ 9 a·m

N

Portuguese

Second Division

R. ALBUERA

Old Bridge

KGL

New Bridge

BERESFORD   ALBUERA

COLBORNE   LONG

Ford   SOULT

FRENCH ADVANCE

SPANISH

R. NOGALES

Knoll

Knoll

Ford

Infantry   BRITISH   FRENCH   PORTUGUESE   SPANISH
Cavalry

DS'75

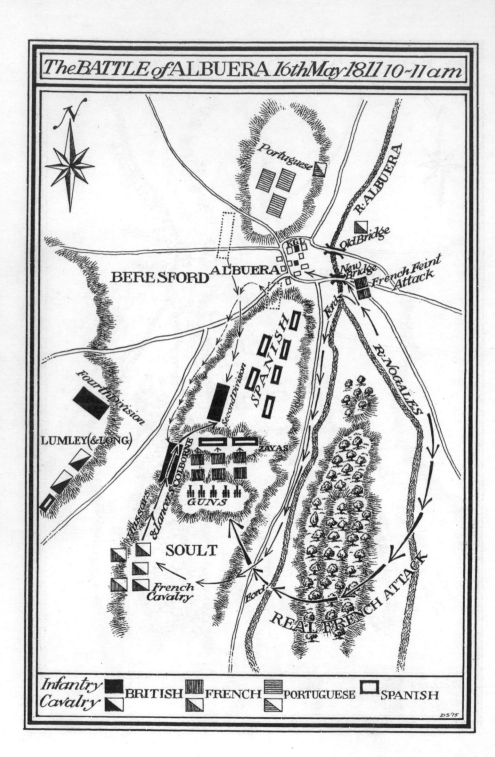

The BATTLE of ALBUERA 16th May 1811 10-11 am

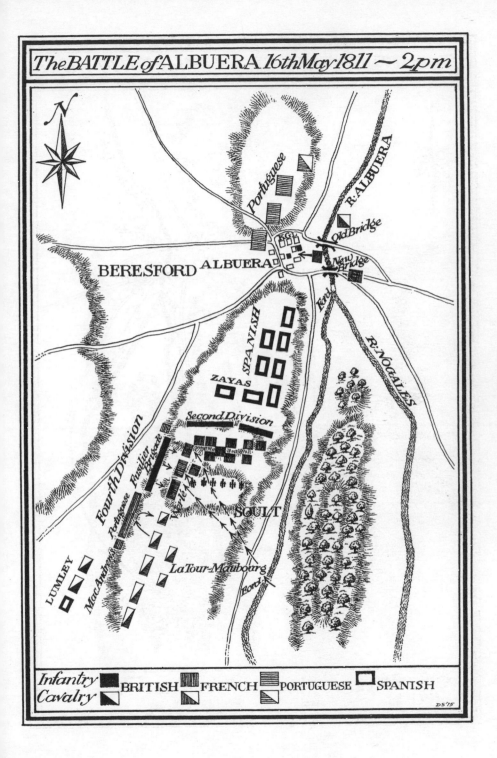

The BATTLE of ALBUERA 16th May 1811 ~ 2pm

I

As soon as he saw the tree the officer knew that he had come the right way. The twisted shape was distinctive, its trunk shattered by some winter storm, and while once again he wondered why the farmer had let this one grow outside the walled orchard, that did not matter because he had not led the column astray. The colonel had found this route during the night, riding ahead of the army, and then sent him back to bring on the brigade so that they approached the open country through this stretch of shallow valleys and hills dotted with vineyards and gardens. Everything looked so different in daylight, and the slower pace of a marching column compared to three staff officers and a couple of dragoons on their own had made the trip seem far longer and fed his worry that he had made a mistake. That had set him thinking, trying to remember each change of direction and work out whether he had gone wrong. Yet there was the tree, and that meant that he was right and there was barely a quarter of a mile to go.

'Well done, girl.'

Lieutenant Hamish Williams patted his grey mare on the neck and then arched his stiff back. An inch or more over six foot, he was a big man and powerfully built, and this impression was reinforced because the horse was a short-necked, clumsy-looking beast of barely fifteen hands. Yet for all her ill-favoured looks, Francesca had proved a good purchase, for she had plenty of stamina and was showing herself to be uncommonly sure footed. His other horse, a chestnut gelding with the graceful lines of an

Andalusian, was proving less good, and had already gone lame in its offside front leg.

Williams reached inside his heavy boat-cloak and pulled out his watch. It was almost ten minutes past twelve on the morning of – and this took a few moments of calculation in his weary state – the twenty-fifth of March in the year of Our Lord Eighteen Hundred and Eleven. The watch, like the horses and the new uniform he wore under his cloak, was one of his Lisbon purchases, part of those wild two days when he had spent more money than ever before in his life. The only thing he had failed to find was a good glass, to replace the one the French had taken last year. Intended to be mounted on a stand, it had been a clumsy, heavy weight to carry strapped to his pack, but the magnification was so wonderful that it had seemed worth it. More than that, it was a present – and one she could not really afford – from his mother when, much against her wishes, her only son had gone for a soldier. He still had not had the heart to write and say that it was lost.

Williams looked back over his shoulder, but there was no sign of the leading company. If they did not appear in five minutes then he would have to ride back to find them, but he had not long left them and they should not have gone astray. He really ought not to have to wait long. Looping the reins over his left hand, Williams plucked off his oilskin-covered bicorne hat and ran his other hand through his fair hair, blinking as the fatigue washed over him. His chin felt as rough as sandpaper, although in truth only the closest observer would have seen that he had not shaved. Three years of campaigning in all weathers had given just the slightest dark tinge to his fair, freckled skin, although there were a few black flecks of powder encrusting his right cheek from where he had fired a musket more times than he could remember. Even so, with his bright blue eyes and fresh face, the lieutenant still resembled an overgrown schoolboy more than a veteran soldier.

The infantry did not appear, and to stop himself from hurrying back to search for them and risking appearing nervous, he unclasped his cloak and rolled it up to fasten behind his saddle. He would have to remember to shake it out and dry it later on – or ask his soldier servant to do it. Having a servant was as much a new experience as possessing a watch and two horses, so such thoughts did not come naturally to him.

'Ah, better late than never,' he said out loud as a rank of soldiers marched over the rise a couple of hundred yards behind him. 'Earth has not anything to show more fair,' he added, and then tried to remember where he had read the line. Not Shakespeare, of course, but someone modern. It was probably something a gentleman should know, although literary knowledge – indeed knowledge of any sort – was scarcely the boast of many good fellows, let alone the thrusters, in the army. Williams felt his want of education keenly, and wished one of his particular friends from his own regiment were here to ask. Pringle, Hanley or Truscott would no doubt have known – and would not mock him for his ignorance.

There was an officer walking to the right of the front rank, and when his cloak parted for a moment it gave the briefest glimpse of his scarlet coat, but that was almost the only dash of colour. The men were a drab sight in their grey greatcoats, shoulders hunched and heads bowed as they walked. They had been marching for seven hours, with only the usual short rests every hour, and most of the time they had faced driving rain and a road churned to mud by the cavalry who had preceded them. Their trousers, which were almost any shade of brown, blue, grey or black rather than the regulation white, were uniformly red-brown from mud, and more mud was spattered on the long tails of their coats. Muskets were carried down low at the slope, an affectation of the light bobs that he had always found less comfortable than slinging the firelock from his shoulder.

Williams doubted anyone back home would see the little column as fair in any way, the dark figures marching across muddy fields on a grey day. Many Britons rarely thought about their soldiers, save perhaps to puff themselves up when news came of a victory, and there had been few of those for some time. If they saw them at all it was in the shining splendour of a parade or field day, or in coloured prints where neat lines of men directed by officers on prancing horses fired or charged through the smoke. The soldiers in those pictures were as immaculate as their formations, and fought their battles in picturesque landscapes with mountains rearing in the background. Williams had seen prints of Vimeiro and Talavera and had seen nothing that reminded him in any way of those grim fights.

The officer watched the column come closer, and saw the head of the second company following on behind. He did not know these men, for he had arrived with the brigade only three days ago, but he knew plenty like them. Back in '08 he had joined the army as a volunteer, a man considered a gentleman but without the influence to secure an officer's commission or the money to purchase one. He had carried a musket, worn the uniform of a private soldier and done duty in the ranks while living with the officers. Those had been strange days, ending only when he survived Vimeiro and was rewarded with an ensign's commission, and they had left him with a deep respect for the redcoat as well as an affection almost idolatrous in its intensity.

'Anything to show more fair,' he repeated under his breath. Was it Byron? It sounded sufficiently overblown for the aristocratic poet, but he did not think that was right. His taste stretched far more to the classics. Miss MacAndrews would know, and would tease him for not knowing. The thought of the girl brought back the familiar pangs of anger and despair. Keep occupied, he told himself, work until exhaustion blots out all feelings and thoughts. Think about poets or any other nonsense when there was nothing else to do.

Well, whoever it was would no doubt have raised a perfumed nosegay to shield himself from the sight and the wet earthy smell of the approaching light infantrymen. They were small men in the main, many young but aged by wind and weather, trudging along, not wasting any effort on unnecessary movements or chatter, not even thinking very much about anything. Williams had been on plenty of marches like this one, had known the discomfort of the issue pack which always hung heavy and too low so that its straps burned into the shoulders and pulled at the chest. Just keep going, place one foot in front of the other, loosely in step, not for the look of it, but because it was unconscious habit and made it easier not to tread on the heels of the man in front.

No one back home would ever see them like this, dirty and dishevelled, the locks of their muskets wrapped tightly round with rags to keep out the damp. Like the rest of the army they were bound to be infested with vermin from living in the fields or sleeping on filthy straw in dirty houses and barns. All too many of them would drink themselves senseless at every opportunity, duty and suffering alike forgotten for the moment.

No one back home would ever see them standing in ranks as friends dropped around them, ripped to shreds by shot and shell, or watch as they went forward into the smoke, faces pale but determined not to let each other down. He had seen such men fight and win when all seemed lost and, if they were not pretty, then they were magnificent.

Maybe it was better that Britons never saw them like this, he thought. No one at home had earned the right.

'Morning,' Williams called as the officer led the first company up to him. The man nodded in acknowledgement.

Williams turned in the saddle and pointed. 'Bear right at that tree, follow the wall of the orchard and then cross the stream and form in column at quarter-distance on the slope beyond it. An orderly dragoon is waiting there to mark the spot.' The only response was another nod. Williams was new to the brigade and not yet one of the family.

He nudged Francesca and set her trotting back past the column, before veering off up the side of the valley.

'Goddamned dandies!' Someone swore as he passed and he realised too late that he must have flicked mud up over the marching men. He regretted his lack of care and laughed at the thought of being dubbed a dandy. Any officer on a horse who was not from their own battalion was always treated with suspicion. Men might wonder what folly had been cooked up for them by the powers on high, but they would not wonder for long because there was nothing that they could do about it.

Williams reined in at the top of the slope and looked back, pulling down the tip of his hat as he squinted into the distance. The last of the four companies at the head of the brigade was just beneath him. About three furlongs beyond them was the dark mass of another, larger column. He wished he had his old telescope, but did not bother to fish out the cheap replacement from his saddlebags. He did not need to see the slightly greater detail this would offer. Everyone was where they should be and now he needed to report this to his commander.

Riding back the way he had come, Williams took care to pass the marching men at a safe distance. Even so he half heard a flurry of comments, and was pretty sure that he caught a cry of 'Missed us this time, yer booger!' in a North Country accent. A good officer knew when not to hear things. He could tell that the men were in good spirits, and guessed that they realised the march was almost over. They always seemed to know, even before the formal orders had reached their officers.

They would be happy at the prospect of halting, hoping for the chance to rest – veterans like these could make themselves comfortable very quickly. They might be called upon to fight, for the French were close, but that was something they could worry about if and when they were sent forward. At least the rain had stopped. Only a fool or a cavalryman wanted to fight when it was wet. Just a few drops of water seeping into the frizzen pan of a musket turned gunpowder into a dirty sludge no flint would spark into life. So the light infantrymen were glad it was dry – their very lives might well depend on it.

Tired, uncomfortable in their sodden greatcoats, these men were nonetheless indeed in good spirits, and Williams knew that the same enthusiasm spread throughout the entire army. For once, for the first time in years, they were advancing and the French were going back. At this rate there would soon be scarcely a French soldier left in Portugal, save for the prisoners crammed in the transport ships off Lisbon. Spain was another matter, but at long last the inexorable advance of Napoleon's legions seemed to have slowed and then stopped. They were retreating for a change, and Williams had enough grim memories of the long retreat to Corunna to know how rapidly confidence faded into despair, and just how easily an army of brave soldiers could fall apart.

Five minutes later the grey mare cantered up the last slope and Williams joined two other officers sitting on horseback overlooking the wide plain.

'The Light Companies are up, sir,' he reported. 'The Sixty-sixth are half an hour's march away and the guns just behind them.'

Lieutenant Colonel Colborne nodded. He was a slim, handsome man in his early thirties. At six foot he was just a little shorter than Williams and in many ways he was a slighter version of the Welshman, his darkly fair hair flecked with grey.

'Look, sir, they are moving.' Captain Dunbar was pointing at the French column formed little more than half a mile away on the old highway running east towards the Spanish border. Beyond it was Campo Major, its medieval walls showing the scars of cannon strikes. Its defences were old, in poor repair, and not designed to deal with the assault of a modern army, and yet an elderly Portuguese officer and a garrison of volunteers had held it for a week before being forced to surrender. 'They deserved a better fate,' Colborne had said, but no aid could reach here until several days too late. Now three divisions of infantry and a strong force of cavalry had come to take the place back, less than a week after its fall.

'Perhaps seven or eight hundred horse and two or three battalions of foot,' Dunbar said, 'so two thousand all told?' The French were formed with cavalry in the lead, then a darker, denser mass of infantry, and more cavalry bringing up the rear.

The colonel nodded. 'That is my estimate.'

'Cannot blame them for not wanting to make a fight of it in that old ruin,' Dunbar added.

When they had all arrived, the British and Portuguese would number more than eighteen thousand men, and so the French column was lost, but only if enough of the Allies arrived in time.

For the moment they could almost match the enemy numbers, but not with a balanced force. Williams saw the colonel lower his glass and glance at the two regiments of redcoated heavy dragoons formed up to their left. Beyond them, almost a mile away, there was a dark smear moving slowly over the rolling ground, following the path of a little river. The colonel did not need to use his telescope to know that these were the British light dragoons and the Portuguese cavalry – everyone said that Colborne had the best eyesight in the army.

Until last summer the lieutenant colonel had commanded only the second battalion of his own regiment, the 66th Foot, one of four battalions in the brigade. Then the divisional commander had moved to higher things, and their brigade commander had in turn moved up to lead the whole division. Colborne's rank as lieutenant colonel had been gazetted before that of the men leading the other three battalions, so overnight he had jumped to lead the brigade. The post was not permanent, but in the last seven months no general had appeared from Britain to take over. A few days ago Williams had arrived to replace his aide-de-camp, who had got his step to major and gone back to his own corps. The Welshman was now acting ADC to an acting brigade commander and had no idea how long this would last.

In the meantime Colborne kept his two staff officers busy. Dunbar as brigade major was given the greater responsibilities, but often both men found themselves trailing along behind the colonel, who slept little and employed every hour of the day to the fullest extent.

'We must do everything within our power, Mr Williams,' the colonel had told him when he first arrived, 'and not spare ourselves if a little more effort helps to ensure victory and spare the lives or preserve the health of our men.'

It was Colborne who had led the others on the reconnaissance to find the route the main column would follow, looking for the easiest path, but also the one offering best protection from prying eyes. They had not seen a single French outpost, but then that was no surprise. The French kept their patrols and sentries

8

close for fear of the vengeance of local peasants on any man caught on his own. They tended to stay especially close when the weather was so foul.

While the stormy night had lasted the lieutenant colonel led the vanguard of the army, with his own brigade and some attached Portuguese cavalry. When dawn broke – even the grey dawn of a gloomy day like this – that responsibility passed to the commander of the Allied cavalry, although he was now under the eye of Marshal Beresford, who had come up with his staff. The marshal was in charge of this southern force detached from the main army under Lord Wellington. Regardless of rank, it was clear that Lieutenant Colonel Colborne remained eager to spur his seniors into swift action, before the French column escaped.

'Captain Dunbar, ride to Marshal Beresford and inform him that the First Brigade has arrived, and that I hope to have Major Cleeves' brigade of guns up soon.'

The brigade major nodded and set off at a canter. Williams noticed that he had changed to another horse from the one he had ridden during the night. An ADC could not perform his duties without at least two good mounts, but he doubted that the chestnut would recover for a week or more and might well prove prone to the same failing in the future. Williams suspected that he was a poor judge – certainly an unskilled buyer – of horseflesh and had been fleeced. Up here near the frontier there was little chance of finding another mount for sale. That left one obvious source, and it was clear that the colonel's thoughts ran along a similar line.

'Mr Williams, ride to Brigadier General Long and his cavalry and tell him that the infantry are up so he may press as hard as he likes. There is no reason for a single Frenchman to escape.'

'Sir.'

'And, Mr Williams, I do not require you back for a little while, but take care, for it would inconvenience me if you did not return at all.' Colborne's eyes sparkled.

Williams grinned, and set the grey off at a trot to preserve her strength. The British army was advancing, its spirits were high, and he was going to steal a horse from the French.

2

'Bills! Bills, you old rogue!'

Williams had hoped to pass Marshal Beresford and his staff without attracting attention. Then annoyance turned to pleasure when he recognised Hanley riding over to him and waving his hand in greeting. They were both officers in the 106th Foot, and had served together in its Grenadier Company when the army first came to Portugal.

'I did not know you were here,' Williams said after they had shaken hands.

'Ever elusive,' his friend replied, 'flitting from shadow to shadow.' Once an artist, then only with great reluctance a soldier, Captain Hanley was now one of the army's exploring officers, riding behind the French lines – at times more the spy than became any gentleman. A few weeks ago Williams had sailed up from Cadiz with him, but the two had gone their separate ways after Lisbon.

'Any news of Billy and the others?'

'Yes,' Hanley answered. 'The battalion has come north and is to be attached to the Fourth Division. They may already have joined for all I know.' Hanley had spent years in Madrid before the war, and with his black hair and tanned complexion readily passed as a native. 'More than that I do not know. I fear my omniscience is waning!'

'And the major?' Hanley was an old friend, often a confidant, and no doubt guessed far more than he had ever been told, and yet even so it was difficult for Williams to broach so delicate a subject.

Hanley grinned, his teeth very white. 'Major MacAndrews is well as far as I know, although still waiting for the promised brevet promotion to be gazetted.' He paused for a moment. 'And I believe it more than likely that his family will accompany him – to Lisbon at least, if not up to the frontier. You know the determination of Mrs MacAndrews.' Major MacAndrews' tall American wife was a formidable lady, held in awe and a good deal of affection by those around her, and she followed him to garrisons and on campaign alike. Only one of the couple's children had survived to reach adulthood, and Williams was the devoted admirer of the girl – a secret shared only by the entire regiment. Jane MacAndrews was small, fiery of hair and character, and in his view the most perfect woman he had ever met. Just when he had dared to hope, it appeared that all must be over. Williams felt despair engulfing him again, something the constant activity of recent days had kept at bay.

'Look, Bills, I really should not worry...' Hanley began, only to be interrupted. A rotund civilian escorted by four hussars from the King's German Legion had joined them.

'Mr Williams, it is a pleasure to see you. I trust that you are enjoying your duties with Colonel Colborne?' Mr Ezekiel Baynes was fat and red faced, the very image of the stout English yeoman beloved of cartoons. Before the war a trader in wines and spirits, he had become a master of spies for Lord Wellington. His voice was gruff, his speech rapid so the words tumbled out one after another like coals poured from a sack. 'You are looking well, sir, indeed you are. I see that you are quite recovered from your wound. Splendid.'

'Thank you, sir, I am pleased to say that it no longer troubles me.' Williams had been shot in the hip back in the autumn, which had undoubtedly saved his life since it pitched him over and meant that a second bullet aimed at his head merely grazed him. Left behind by the army, he had spent weeks lost in fever and then even longer recovering, sheltered by a band of *guerrilleros*, partisan fighters who fought the bitter 'little war' against the French. Those months already had a dreamlike quality, and he knew that he had not yet made peace with himself for all that he had seen and done. As with so much else, not least the matter of Miss MacAndrews, there had not been time. It was typical of Baynes to parade his knowledge, while giving the impression that he knew much more than he said. Given the man's rapid intelligence and his occupation, it was quite possible that he did.

It seemed that Hanley, Baynes and their escort were also seeking out General Long. 'A happy chance,' Baynes declared. 'We shall be most glad of your company, and perhaps your assistance.'

Williams was very fond of Hanley, but had serious doubts about his judgement. His friend was a gambler to his core, a man who enjoyed cleverness for its own sake, his thrill growing with the size of the stakes, and so was all too ready to risk the lives of those around him in elaborate schemes to outwit the enemy. Baynes' bluff and open manner veiled a sharp, ruthless mind, judging the benefit and price of every venture in the war with as calm a manner as he had once run his business. Together the two men were likely to prove dangerous company.

As they rode along, Williams confessed to his true errand, prompting a benevolent smile from Baynes and a snort of amusement from Hanley.

'Pringle was right,' his friend said, 'you have turned pirate!'

The previous year Hanley, Billy Pringle and Williams had spent months in Andalusia working with the partisans along the coast, carried ashore and retrieved each time by the Navy. One night Williams had taken part in a cutting-out expedition, capturing privateers and merchantmen from an enemy harbour. As a result, he later found himself the surprised recipient of six hundred and twelve pounds, seventeen shillings and thruppence prize money, paid into his account at the regimental agents of Greenwood, Cox, and Company, agents to the 106th as they were to half the army. It was only this fortunate event which permitted him to accept the invitation to become a staff officer. More than half had gone on equipping himself for the field, since Lisbon prices were grossly inflated after four years of war and with the entire army wintering near the city.

'It appears the simplest solution to my want,' Williams said in his defence. 'There is no prospect of purchasing a replacement for some time.'

Baynes chuckled, his face bright scarlet. 'Clear, reasonable thought,' he said. 'The world is often so unfair when it dismisses the intellect of soldiers!'

Williams bowed as far as it was possible in the saddle.

'Yet, though as a mere civilian I may be mistaken,' Baynes continued, 'is it not the rule that captured horses are to be offered for sale to the commissaries, so that the entire army and the wider cause may benefit from their capture?'

That was the rule, and although Hanley's expression betrayed his lack of concern for such regulation, Williams had feared that this would prove an obstacle and so had hoped to avoid anyone too senior from finding out about the business. The justification that the rule was often ignored, and that a horse taken from the foe was the only plunder considered acceptable for an officer to take, seemed weak.

'It is for the good of the service,' he ventured, disliking the pomposity of his claim and hoping that the unmilitary Baynes would not pursue the issue.

'I have no doubt of it, so perhaps we should leave it at that, and leave you, my young friend, with the more pressing problem of dividing an unwilling Frenchman from his horse. Of course,' he went on, 'though I am no real judge, I am told that our own cavalry officers ride finer horses than the French. Indeed, it is said their comrades garrisoned in France write to friends asking them to capture such a beast, with the promise of rich reward. Perhaps for the pure good of the service you should look elsewhere?'

Williams grinned, and a few moments later Baynes chuckled again to demonstrate that it was – almost certainly – a witticism.

'I doubt in the circumstances that the Army will be much inclined to examine the details of your acquisition, since part of our purpose today is to arrange theft on a far grander scale. Damn the man, will he not sit still for a moment!' This last was presumably directed at General Long and the light cavalry, who had set off forward again, just as they were coming up to them.

Hanley waved a hand at the corporal in charge of their escort to show that they would keep at a walk and not race forward to catch up.

'Don't want the horses tired,' he explained to Williams.

'Indeed not, indeed not,' Baynes mumbled. 'And no doubt they will halt again soon enough.' He stared at Williams for a moment and then turned to Hanley. 'Your friend is not the most curious of fellows, is he, William? We confess a conspiracy to rob and he says nothing. Too caught up with plotting his own act of brigandage, no doubt.'

'It is for the good of the service,' Captain William Hanley agreed.

'Since manners or disinterest prevent you from asking,' Baynes began, 'I shall declare that our interest is with cannon – at least one of our interests. Does that stir your curiosity?'

'The French siege train?' Williams ventured.

Baynes turned back to Hanley and gave a nod of exaggerated approval. 'Your Mr Williams may not be inclined towards curiosity, but at least his mind works quickly. Yes, Lieutenant,' he continued, smiling now at Williams, 'the enemy brought some fifteen or sixteen heavy guns to besiege Campo Major.'

'They left just before dawn,' Hanley added. 'The Portuguese cavalry saw them. They must be three or four miles away by now. It would be better for us if they did not reach Badajoz.' The big fortress town protected the Spanish side of the frontier.

Baynes' face became serious for the first time. 'It really is all about Badajoz. Are you familiar with the place?'

Williams nodded. He had seen the fortress back in '09, when the army was forced to retreat even though it had beaten back the French attacks at Talavera. Those were bad times, with sickness rampant and claiming almost as many lives as the battle, and perhaps those bad memories shaped his recollections for to his mind there was something sinister about the place. Built in a naturally strong position, the King of Spain's engineers had done a fine job, following the most modern principles of military science to fortify it. Its defences were as far removed from those of Campo Major as a rifled musket was from the flint-headed spear of some primitive tribe.

'It is formidable,' he said, trying not to think of the horror that would come when regiments were thrown against its walls. The French had had trouble taking the place, and it was only the death of its tough old commander and his replacement by a weaker man which had taken the heart out of the Spanish defenders.

'The French have held the place for two weeks,' Hanley said. 'The longer they hold on to it then the more chance they have to repair the damage inflicted on the walls by their own guns. So our best chance is to attack soon, and for that we need a siege train.'

'We do not possess such a thing.' Baynes spread out his palms and then calmed his horse when the animal stirred. 'Or to be more accurate I should say that we do possess one, but it is sitting on board ship somewhere off Lisbon and it would take a month or more to bring it all ashore, and even longer to fetch it up here.

'And since we cannot hope to purchase siege guns up here on the frontier, we are left with Mr Williams' simple solution. If you soldiers can overcome the French rearguard in the next few hours, it should be possible to catch their cannon before they reach safety.'

The plan appeared sound, the prospects of success good, and then Williams had an idea which might help in some small way. Leaving the reins in his left hand, he used the other to unfasten the top of his saddle-holster.

'Good God, you really have turned pirate!' Hanley gasped as the Welshman pulled out a naval boarding axe.

'If you do overrun the siege train, it may be wise to cut the traces,' Williams suggested, offering the axe to his friend.

'Won't we need the harness to pull them away?'

'Just in case they have to be left for a while. It will mean that the French cannot carry them off, whatever happens.' Williams moved to replace the weapon. 'It was merely a suggestion.'

'And a good one, I am sure, although let us hope it does not come to that.' Mr Baynes was beaming again. 'Take it, my dear boy, take it. And I do believe that we should let the lieutenant more fully into our confidence.'

'Badajoz fell too easily,' Hanley said, his face doubtful as he took the short heavy staff of the axe. Ahead of them the cavalry column had halted again, and they were getting closer. 'It is all too likely that French agents were at work, and French gold helped to open the gates of the fortress. Do you remember Sinclair?'

Williams stiffened at the name. Major Sinclair had posed as a British officer, riding among the partisan bands in Andalusia gathering information. The group sheltering Williams had been surprised by French soldiers led by the Irishman, who was in fact a member of Napoleon's green-jacketed Irish Legion. For a moment he saw again the burning farm, the *guerrilleros* dead or in flight, and remembered the feel of Guadalupe clinging to him.

'I remember Sinclair.'

'He serves on Marshal Soult's staff, helping him to gather intelligence – among other things. And then, of course, you know Dalmas. He is now also a major and serves in a similar capacity.' Williams remembered the big cuirassier officer, but felt less distaste for him than for Sinclair. He had first met the Frenchman when he had gathered a tag, rag and bobtail group of stragglers left behind by the army as it slogged through the snow to Corunna. Dalmas was trying to find a way around Sir John Moore's army to cut the British off from the sea, and Williams and his little band had stopped him, holding a bridge long enough for reinforcements to arrive – reinforcements led by Colborne, who was then one of Moore's ADCs. Since then their paths had crossed more than once.

'Dalmas is a proper soldier,' he said in the Frenchman's defence.

'Aye, right enough, but he is more than that,' Baynes concluded. 'And one of our sources says that a man from Soult's staff came to Campo Major with the French, and they do not believe he has left – at least not before today. Whoever it is, but especially if it is one of that pair of rascals, it would be a handy blow for our cause if he never leaves.'

'You wish him dead.' Williams kept his tone level to make it clear that he was not asking a question. Yet he could not keep the distaste from his voice.

'We wish them all dead or to the Devil,' Hanley cut in quickly, 'but it would be better to take whoever it is. If we cannot, then he would be less of a threat to us if killed. They are dangerous men.'

Williams did not presume to point out that the same might be said of someone who talked so readily of deliberate killing.

'For the good of the service,' Hanley continued. 'Or at least for the good of the cause.' The last words were in a whisper, for they had come up with the rear of the cavalry. Closest to them were the 13th Light Dragoons, wearing their tall crested tarleton helmets and with buff facings and braid on their blue jackets. Orders were shouted and the front of the regiment wheeled to the right and went over a hump in the ground. The light dragoons deployed smoothly, the horses going at a brisk walk, scabbards, carbines and other equipment bumping and the harness jingling with the motion.

'The French must be close,' Williams said. Even after all these years he was unsure how well his friend could read a battlefield. His hand slid across and took the grip of his sword, lifting gently to make sure that it would be easy to draw if he needed it.

They waited for the cavalry to deploy before following. The enemy were indeed close, and when they topped the small bank they could see that the five small squadrons of Portuguese cavalry were formed on the left. From this distance their uniform was similar to that of the British light horse, with dark blue jackets, grey trousers and black helmets. If he went close, a man would see that the coats were plainer and without braid, although the red plume in each helmet offered a flash of colour brighter than anything in their allies' appearance. Even from this distance their horses were clearly small, ill-fed beasts, and alongside the fine chestnuts and light bays of British light dragoons the appearance was most ill.

'Looking for your mark?' Hanley whispered, having seen Williams observing the cavalry.

'They are not sufficiently close,' he replied. Almost five hundred yards ahead of the 13th Light Dragoons was a line of French horsemen – to Williams' eye it looked a slightly longer and more numerous line than that of the British regiment. The enemy were dressed in dark green coats and even without a glass he could see the warm orange fronts of the jackets. Most of the men had baggy brown trousers, and only a few wore the regulation grey breeches above their high black boots. All wore brass helmets in Grecian style, decorated with brown turbans and trailing black horsehair plumes.

'Dragoons,' Williams said.

'Probably the Twenty-sixth Regiment.' Baynes smiled as the others looked at him. 'They were reported to be with the French force which came here.'

'Those are the Chamborant Hussars.' Hanley pointed to a couple of squadrons of men dressed in brown some way back behind the left flank of the dragoons.

Williams did his best to look like a proud parent as his friend spoke with such confidence.

'Well, we have seen them before,' Hanley said in an apologetic tone.

Beyond the hussars there were a few more still on the highway, leading the infantry off. Williams saw two distinct battalion columns marching steadily along the road, with more hussars bringing up the rear. The dragoons and the supporting squadrons must have been drawn from the advance guard and deployed to threaten the British and Portuguese light cavalry.

'They must have hoped to show a front and keep the Portuguese at a distance,' Williams told them. 'My guess is that they formed in two bodies so that if we dared to charge one of them then the other would sweep in around our flank. Would probably have worked if the Portuguese were on their own. I'll wager they were none too pleased when the Thirteenth appeared. Their dragoons have wheeled to face them, regiment against regiment, so there is not much chance of striking at our flanks. They will still be hoping to get away without a fight.'

'There are plenty of them,' Hanley ventured, but with rather less confidence than his earlier pronouncements. Williams wondered whether his friend was thinking back to that dreadful day at Medellín, almost exactly two years ago and not too far away, when the Spanish cavalry had broken, and these very French regiments swept down to massacre the abandoned infantry. Much the same had happened time after time as a long succession of Spanish armies marched off to defeat – the most recent when the army protecting Badajoz was cut to ribbons by the blades of the French horsemen. From the very start of the war, the enemy cavalry had ruled these plains. 'Will they not fight? To drive us back and give themselves more time to escape?'

Williams shook his head. 'Only if they have to. They want to get away, for if they stay the numbers will turn more and more in our favour. The heavy dragoons should be coming up so that will make their situation precarious. All they want is to hold us for a quarter of an hour and then they will retire and face up to us again only when they wish to slow us down. That is if General Long does not call their bluff.'

'Do you think he will attack?' Baynes asked.

'I should be most surprised if he does not.' Williams reached to check his sword again.

'Bloodthirsty pirate,' Hanley whispered in a low tone.

'Then we had better speak to the general without delay,' Baynes said, and kicked his horse into a trot.

Brigadier General Long proved to be a compact man of middle years riding a dragoon's horse. A single staff officer attended him, but as they rode up the man cantered off towards the Portuguese.

Hanley saluted. 'General Long, sir, may I present Mister Baynes of the political service attached to Lord Wellington's headquarters. We have papers, sir.' He held out a letter.

Long stared at it as if it were the oddest thing he had ever seen. 'This is no time for reading, sir.' His heavy-lidded eyes flicked across them and then fastened on Williams. 'I know you, Lieutenant, do I not?'

'It is gracious of you to remember, sir, for it was now two years ago, although I have no doubt that the sorrow remains fresh for us all.'

'Ah, yes, I recollect.' Williams had been beside Sir John Moore when he took his mortal wound. He could remember the pieces of bone sticking out from his mangled shoulder, the melancholy procession as the Highlanders carried him back to the town, the general's lucidity, concern for the fate of the day and of his own staff. Long had joined the men attending him in those last hours, as had Colborne, watching the man they admired above all slip away. 'He was the best of us,' Long said, as if to himself. The brigadier looked pale and sallow. 'Well,' he added in a firmer tone. 'What is it you want of me?'

Hanley explained their concern to secure the French siege train.

'Well, as to that, sir, perhaps you should direct your petition to Marshal Beresford. He commands here and appears eager to instruct us all in every detail of our duties.' Long frowned, perhaps concerned that his comment was indiscreet.

There was a strange gurgling sound, quite distinct, and clearly emanating from a human or animal body. The brigadier general pursed his lips, but said nothing. His eyes looked at each of them in turn as if in challenge.

'Go to the marshal, sir. I have no time for such matters now. First we must beat these fellows before I can concern myself with capturing convoys miles away along the road. Let the marshal worry about that for you.'

'Would you object if we stayed to watch?' Baynes ventured, with none of the usual assurance in his voice.

'You may do as you please, sir, but do not get in my way.' The general shifted slightly in his saddle and at that moment broke wind, the sound amplified by the leather.

No one betrayed any sign of noticing.

'Good day to you, sir,' the general said. 'And it is good to see you again, Lieutenant.'

As they moved away, Williams did his best to maintain an impassive expression. A stout old fellow who tended to sit in front of his family in church back in Bristol had been prone to similar eruptions, almost always in the moments of silence during a service. His sisters would giggle whenever it happened, and it was hard not to join them. Their mother, the stern, devout, unyielding Mrs Williams, who never let anyone forget her pride in being born a Campbell, would have reproved them with a look, and then once they were home gone off to a room on her own and laughed out loud.

His head snapped round as movement flickered all along the line of dragoons. The French cavalry had drawn their long straight swords.

'It may be only a threat,' he said quietly, 'or they may have decided to see us off their land.'

Brigadier General Long trotted over to speak to the commander of the 13th Light Dragoons, and they were close enough to hear the exchange.

'Colonel Head, there's your enemy. Attack him.' Long's voice was calm and confident, no doubt meant to be heard by the light dragoons. Fortunately there was no repeat of the recent emissions. 'And now, Colonel, the heavy brigade are coming up on your rear, and, if you have an opportunity, give a good account of these fellows.'

'By gad, sir, I will,' was the simple soldier-like response. Lieutenant Colonel Head walked his horse round to the front of his regiment.

Williams and the others stopped some fifty yards or so behind the line.

'The Thirteenth will prepare to advance,' Head shouted in a high, clear voice. 'Draw swords.'

This time they heard the grating sound of steel blades scraping free of their scabbards. An old troop sergeant had once told

21

Williams that the noise broke his heart every time he heard it because the metal rubbing against metal took a little off the finely honed edge. Even so it was invigorating, a hint of firm purpose like screwing a bayonet on to the muzzle of a musket.

His horse's ear flicked forward in excitement. He patted her neck, noticing that the King's German Legion hussars were calming their horses as instinct took over and they wanted to join the rest. Williams reached over to draw his sword and then felt Baynes' arm on his.

'Not yet, if you please. I would prefer you to stay back with us and watch,' the plump man said. 'We will follow, but not get too close for the moment.'

Williams wondered whether for once the self-assured merchant and master of spies felt that he was not in control. He had no sword, in fact appeared to be wholly unarmed. The Welshman was surprised that Baynes had not left them and gone back to the marshal and his staff.

'Walk march.' The 13th Light Dragoons went forward.

'Wait a little before we follow,' Baynes said.

'Have you ever ridden in a cavalry charge, Bills?' Hanley whispered.

'We are only watching, are we not?' The irony was forced, and then he realised his friend was anxious. 'No need to worry. Stay close to me and even closer to those fellows.' He jerked his head towards the corporal and the three hussars. The King's German Legion were widely held to be among the finest cavalrymen in the army and these men looked very capable. 'Apart from that, just try to stay on.'

They started to walk their horses forward.

3

The 13th Light Dragoons were formed in two ranks, with subalterns, some NCOs and other file closers dotted along behind the rear rank. They were in loose files, with some six inches between each rider rather than the close order where a man's knees almost touched those of the riders on either side. With five troops present, two pairs were formed into squadrons with the fifth, orphaned troop on the right. Hanley tried to count in groups of five as Williams had taught him, and reckoned that there were around one hundred men in each rank, with perhaps thirty or so file closers. He could not see past them all that well, but thought that they must just about match the length of the main French line, if not their flanking supports.

'I am not sure that you will find that suitable at the moment,' Williams said to him in a low voice.

Hanley realised that he was still holding the axe. Part of him wondered whether his friend was wrong. There was a primitive feel to the weapon, so much like the sort of thing one imagined a Red Indian wielding, and it seemed fitting for there was something very ancient, almost primal, about being so close to all these horses and men with swords. His own mount was stirring, wanting to run, and even if he could not tell whether it wanted to go forward or back, he could sense that it felt part of a herd. When infantry marched forward to mow each other down with musketry it did not feel like this.

Williams looked calm. The man always did, and it was hard to know what he really felt. For all his piety and sober disposition, Williams was a sensitive, intelligent man with a lively imagination, so must be as plagued by fears as everyone else. Hanley remembered MacAndrews drumming it into them that as officers they must always appear fully confident of success and survival in any situation. Hanley was unsure how convincing he was in this act.

The light dragoons were still walking, their heavy-bladed, curved sabres resting on their shoulders. Then they went into a trot. Hanley had not heard the order, so intent was he on the scene. He watched the men as they sat in their saddles, backs swaying with the motion.

'Far enough for us, I think, gentlemen,' Baynes said. Williams glanced at the corporal and there was doubt in both their faces.

'It may be better to follow or go back a little,' he said. Hanley was inclined to take his friend's advice when it was a matter of the battlefield, but Baynes did not appear worried.

'We will stop here, so that we can see. I dare say we can run away in plenty of time if it becomes necessary. Forgive me, Mr Williams,' he continued, a fresh smile beaming, 'I did not intend to imply anything by that. I speak merely as a fellow of too many summers and too many joints of beef to desire to make the acquaintance of any sword-wielding Frenchman. We need to be able to see in case one of those rogues is about.'

Hanley was not really listening. The light dragoons had gone into a canter – again he had missed the order. He stood up in the stirrups, trying to see past them, but could not.

There was a spattering of shots – individuals popping away rather than an ordered volley.

'The squares,' Williams said. Hanley had forgotten the French infantry on the road. He had not seem them form from column to square, but had not really been paying them much attention.

'*Vive l'empereur!*' He had heard the shout many times before. This time it was a little more ragged, although just as determined as when a column of infantry came on.

'Charge!' He heard Colonel Head's shout this time, and then the light dragoons were yelling – not a cheer so much as a roar. Sabres came off shoulders and were raised high, points towards the enemy though turned slightly to cover the face.

The line looked solid, men and horses only slightly shifted from their places. Hanley still could not see the French, but their cry had suggested no lack of spirit. They must be very close, and the British cavalrymen did not show any signs of checking or hesitation. He knew that horsemen would not charge home against a solid square of infantry, but he suspected that it would be different when cavalry met cavalry. Horses barged each other readily enough at the best of times. His mind tried to picture the French dragoons galloping straight at the British horsemen, and imagined the two lines getting closer and closer before slamming into each other in a collision that must surely shatter bones and tumble horses and riders.

'Bless me!' Baynes sounded like a parson noticing a fly in his soup. The light dragoons had broken up, the files opening to more than a horse's width between them. It took only an instant, and then suddenly the regiment was spread out and Hanley could see French dragoons in green coming through the gaps, like passing the fingers of one hand between those on the other. Swords flashed as men went by each other, slashing and jabbing. In a great scything cut one of the Frenchmen was chopped from the saddle. Another took a slice that opened his mouth to his chin. Hanley saw one of the Thirteenth jabbed in the sword-arm. The man slumped, arm limp and sabre hanging down by its cord. Then they were through, a loose crowd of green-coated dragoons coming on in a swarm towards them. It was one of the strangest, most unexpected things Hanley had ever seen.

'Back! Back!' Williams shouted. The Welshman yanked at Baynes' reins to turn his tubby horse and then slapped the beast on the rump to send it running off. 'Move, you fool!' he yelled into Hanley's ear, breaking the spell.

Hanley kicked his horse into a canter and then urged it into a gallop, following the others. The four hussars were clustered protectively around Baynes, and Williams was trailing a length behind, looking back to make sure that he was following.

They did not go far, and when Hanley was able to turn he saw that the mass of enemy horsemen were wheeling round. It was no longer a neat formation, but a crowd, each going about at his own pace. No one had followed them, although if they had stayed where they were they would have been in the middle of several hundred Frenchmen.

Officers urged them on, waving their swords in the air and shouting. Hanley heard another big roar, knew that it was the light dragoons, and then the French were answering with their own cries and spurring their horses back the way they had come in a new charge. The two crowds merged into one, not flowing through this time, and then green jackets and blue were locked in hundreds of little duels. Sabre clashed against sword, blades struck ringing blows on helmets or bit into cloth and flesh with a dull sound. Even from this distance Hanley was amazed at the amount of noise. As a boy he had often gone to watch the coppersmiths at work. This was like that noise magnified a thousand times. Men fell, horses reared and screamed.

'You should go back to General Long, sir,' Williams said to Baynes, 'for I must borrow your escort for a moment.' The words were quietly said, and just as evidently a command. The Welsh-man turned to the German corporal. 'Follow me.' Then he was trotting forward.

The corporal glanced at Baynes, and gave a crisp instruction in his own language before he and his men followed. Williams drew his sword, a light, well-balanced blade with a gentle curve. The hussars copied him, each carrying the heavy 1796-pattern sabre like the light dragoons.

Hanley followed.

'You don't have to come,' Williams said, and then grinned.

Hanley gripped the handle of his own sword and pulled. The blade was unwilling to come. He yanked, tried to turn it back and forth, and with an effort it came free, and his arm swung out high and wide.

'*Scheiße!*' hissed one of the Germans as the tip of the blade swept within a few inches of his face.

Williams laughed, then pointed. 'On the left. We hit them there and cut our way through.'

Hanley saw that the French were crowding around the British right, and it was only there that the light dragoons were outnumbered and looked to be giving way.

Dear God, just six of us to sway the balance, he thought, but then Williams yelled and charged. Hanley's horse lurched as its stride changed. He had his sword up now and stared at it. There were spots of rust dotted along the blade. The weapon felt clumsy and awkward in his hand. He had rarely held it and never used it before and wondered why he had come and not stayed with Baynes. Just in time he remembered to loop the rather grubby red sword-knot around his wrist.

The last twenty yards vanished under them, the sound of their horses' pounding feet adding to the other noise. One dragoon turned to face them. The man wore a tall bearskin cap instead of a helmet and had red epaulettes on his shoulders, so must be from the elite company. Like the grenadiers in an infantry battalion, such men were meant to be the tallest and best soldiers.

Williams rode straight at him, the Frenchman kicking his heels to stir his own mount forward. The Welshman's mare was much the same size and moving faster, and perhaps that was why the Frenchman's horse flinched. Williams lunged, beating the man's guard and striking just above the collar. Dark blood gushed on to the orange front of the man's jacket as momentum carried the lieutenant on and he jerked his blade free. Williams closed with another man, coming from behind. The Frenchman turned, wheeled away, and his thrust changed into a slash that ripped through the dragoon's sleeve and gashed his bridle arm. Williams kept going into the mass.

The German hussars followed, striking with cold fury as they caught their opponents unaware – the corporal chopped another member of the elite company from the saddle, and then one of the privates sliced down hard to sever the wounded arm of the man Williams had struck. No longer feeling pressure on the reins, the Frenchman's horse turned and bolted, coming straight at Hanley, who sawed at his own reins as he tried to get out of its way. Instinct made him flinch away and he leaned to the left, lost his right stirrup and was half falling as his own horse started running again into the crowd. A Frenchman on a bay ran into him on that side, helping him back up, but his grip on his sword loosened and he let go. He ducked as the dragoon launched a cross-bodied cut at him, felt the wind of the blade as he swayed away from it and it sliced through the air, thankful that he was on the man's wrong side. The Frenchman had his cheeks gashed open so that the flesh flapped as he moved and his cries were horribly distorted.

Hanley's sword was heavy as it hung by the cord of the sword-knot and he fumbled for the grip and then swung his arm at the dragoon just as the Frenchman raised his blade for another cut. His own weapon slapped his horse on the neck and it bucked, kicking out behind and breaking the leg of another animal, which fell and pitched the dragoon riding it on to the wet grass. The Frenchman with the slashed face screamed at him, spitting gobbets of blood and saliva through the gashes in his cheeks. He had checked his last blow and now raised his blade to lunge. Hanley's horse bucked again, flinging him high and bringing him back down to slap hard against the saddle. The Frenchman watched him, taking careful aim, determined to make no more mistakes.

One of the 13th appeared, Tarleton helmet gone, spatters of blood dark on his face and over the buff braid on the front of his tight-fitting blue coat. The Frenchman shifted his blade in time to parry the man's first cut, giving Hanley time to regain his lost stirrup and then get hold of his sword. He saw sparks as the Englishman and Frenchman's blades met again. The light dragoon was red faced and breathing heavily from the effort – the Frenchman's mangled face made his state hard to read. Hanley pushed his horse forward and without really thinking thrust straight into the dragoon's body. The tip of his sword was not very sharp and pressed the heavy cloth of the man's jacket back for an instant before punching through and sliding between two of his ribs. Hanley was a big man and the blow had all the added strength of his fear. The dragoon made more odd noises, but his eyes fastened on the British officer as they widened. Hanley watched them, saw them flicker as the life faded from them. The man slid from the saddle, his weight dragging at Hanley's sword because he could not pull it free. Only when the dying man was almost on the ground did the steel slide out with a ghastly sucking sound Hanley heard over all the other noise.

'Bloody good, sir!' the private from the 13th said, and then tugged his horse around to seek new prey.

The crowd of horsemen was thinning. Hanley took one last look at the Frenchman he had killed and then pushed on to escape him. He sensed that the dragoons in green were starting to go back a little. Yet they were still fighting, and he was relieved when the corporal and another of the hussars closed on either side of him, sabres held at the guard save for when they actually delivered an attack. There was blood on the corporal's sabre, and yet when he looked there was little on his own and that puzzled him. He struggled to accept that he had just killed a man – something he had never before done even after four years of campaigning. It did not seem real.

There was a fresh shout and three French dragoons were spurring forward, urging the others to rally and return to the attack. Williams rode at them, beside him a squat, broad-shouldered man who wore the blue jacket of the 13th with the buff chevrons of a corporal on his sleeve. The Welshman was a little ahead, his normally simple, almost innocent expression, contorted with savagery – Hanley wondered whether he had looked like that a few moments ago, but doubted it.

Williams took the attack of the first Frenchman on his blade, deflecting it and then flicking his own sword quickly to jab at the man's face. His opponent went back, leaning away to avoid the blow but losing his balance for an instant and making the mistake of bending his arm. Williams got inside his guard and jabbed again, pricking the man on the inside of his elbow. A second dragoon closed with him, and the lieutenant hurriedly parried this fresh attack until one of the hussars appeared alongside him and evened the odds. The third Frenchman made for the corporal from the 13th, who feinted left but went right, and opened the man's throat to the very bone with a strong and very well-directed cut.

'*Vive l'empereur!*' A French officer surged forward, his deep voice raised in anger as much as challenge as he went for the corporal. There were the gold epaulettes of a colonel on his shoulders, and his helmet had a leopardskin turban rather than the usual plain brown. The corporal pulled away and avoided his first attack, and then the two men began to circle, a wide space having opened around them. There were still plenty of other fights raging, but it was almost as if they no longer mattered. Hanley stopped, guarded by the hussars, and watched.

The French colonel was a slim, elegant man, he and his horse so well-practised that they seemed to move as one, stepping carefully, waiting for the moment. Unlike those of his men, the colonel's sword had a gentle curve to the blade, and was polished to such a high sheen that it glinted even on this drab day. With no visible signal Hanley could see, the horse bounded forward, and the sword lunged at the light dragoon's face. The corporal parried the blow with a careful flick of the wrist, using the heavy sabre as if it was as light as a feather. Sword and sabre clashed once, twice, and then the horses were apart again, stepping lightly as if in a riding school. The corporal lacked the colonel's elegance, but matched his skill. Neither man spoke, and their eyes never left the other for a second.

Hanley's horse shifted beneath him, and he looked down to see a good part of an arm lying beside him, still partly covered by a green sleeve, the gloved hand holding on to its long sword. There were several light dragoons on the ground, even more wounded and making their way to the rear. He was not sure that there were so many French dead, but there were many more wounded and they were horribly mutilated. The British sabre was a clumsy, scything weapon that in well-trained and strong hands worked butchery on the enemy. The colonel and the corporal closed again, and their blades met, each probing the other's defence. Not far away Williams had again wounded his opponent, this time higher up near the shoulder, and the man's arm was so weak that he could barely hold his sword up to defend. Beside them the hussar and dragoon defended more than they attacked. Hanley sensed that all of them were half watching the struggle going on near by.

With a cry of victory the colonel lunged and the light dragoon only just had time to block the blow, then recovered faster than Hanley would have believed possible and raised his sabre. He cut down hard, the blow ringing against the Frenchman's brass helmet like a cracked bell. The officer swayed, struggled to bring his own sword up to parry, but was not fast enough to stop a second cut which snapped the scaled chinstrap and sent the helmet spinning off. With a grunt of immense effort the broad-shouldered corporal sliced down a third time, the heavy blade passing through scalp and skull. The colonel slumped to the left, and his corpse dropped down, blood and grey matter spilling from the great gash in his head. Hanley saw the corporal nod, as if in approval of his victory, and then say something in what sounded like Gaelic. The officer was not sure whether to exult or vomit.

The French were fleeing, the spirit gone with the death of their colonel, and the British were starting to follow, chasing after the dragoons and striking at their backs. Williams and the hussar with him took their opponents prisoner. The one Williams had wounded was a sergeant old in war, who knew when it was time to fight and when to quit. The other one was a young officer, nominally his leader, who seemed more confused than anything else. There were other prisoners guarded by a few lightly hurt men from the 13th, for the rest were haring off in pursuit.

Baynes appeared, and Hanley wondered how far away the man had gone during the fighting. If he had been killed or taken then it would have been a serious loss – perhaps a critical one if he was taken and the French realised who he was.

'You should not have come,' he said to the smiling merchant, who did not appear appalled in any way by the sight of the carnage around him. Instead his expression was one of curiosity.

'I fear it must be my insatiable spirit of adventure. Dear God, look at that man!' Baynes had noticed the corpse of the French colonel. 'That must have taken considerable strength,' he went on, impressed, but not moved to any other emotion. 'You seem to forget, William, that you and I have ridden battlefields before.'

Shouted orders drifted towards them. Brigadier General Long was forming two of the Portuguese squadrons into columns to follow the 13th Light Dragoons and act as a solid support should the French rally.

'Ah, it looks like our lieutenant has won his prize,' Baynes said as Williams came towards them, the two prisoners behind him and the hussar bringing up the rear. The man's horse was limping from a gash on its hindquarters. 'What is that fellow's name?' he asked the corporal.

'Becker, sir.'

'Well, Becker, you will take these men to the rear, but remember that one of their horses belongs to Mr Williams, here. You will take the officer's, I presume?'

'I should prefer the sergeant's,' Williams said. 'Only let it carry him to have his wounds tended first.' In response to Baynes', questioning look, he offered an explanation. 'I have generally found that an experienced sergeant will be better equipped than a young officer, sir.'

The statement amused Baynes. 'That does have the ring of truth − the old servant oft-times eats and drinks better than his lord! Well, you must stay with me and we shall keep one of the hussars. Corporal, choose another man and stay with Captain Hanley.'

'Sir.'

'Hanley, follow on with those stout fellows' − Baynes gestured at the Portuguese as they set off after the light dragoons. 'Do everything you can to ensure that we secure the guns and the rest of their train. I dare say more soldiers will be coming along behind you?' The question was directed at Williams, who looked for a moment at the two French squares and the supporting hussars on the highway.

'The heavies are not far behind us, and part of my brigade not much farther behind them. We should be able to force the column to surrender. Though perhaps we should attend General Long to discover his intentions.' From where they were, they could see the French around the road, but could not see much behind them of their own supports. There was no sign of the heavy brigade, although it must be close.

'In a moment perhaps. Go, Hanley, be off with you and do not come back without plenty of cannon!' Baynes dropped his voice. 'And better yet one of those rogues for me to talk to. I'll keep Williams so that he can recognise Sinclair or Dalmas if it turns out that they are with the column. Now, off with you.'

Hanley cantered towards the Portuguese, the corporal and the private just behind him. He exchanged greetings with the English colonel leading them, who showed no particular interest, but was happy for them to tag along. They dropped to a trot to match the two squadrons as they went steadily on, the ground rising a little before again dropping away. They passed a couple of bodies stretched on the ground, Frenchmen with their heads badly cut about, and a wounded light dragoon leading along some bloodstained and battered prisoners.

Once over the rise they could see the light dragoons chasing after their quarry, both now spread out.

'View halloa!' said the English colonel softly. Without any order the trot quickened and Hanley could feel the exhilaration stirring all of them. More to his surprise, he felt it himself, the sense of power as the horses surged forward. He realised that he still held his sword and then the thought came to him that he had killed a man, and yet the world did not seem so very different.

'View halloa!' he said, and laughed out loud.

4

Williams took a rag from one of his saddle holsters and wiped his sword clean before sliding it back into the scabbard. He sat on his horse beside Baynes and the remaining hussar, as they waited at a polite distance for Brigadier General Long to give a message to an ADC.

'Tell Marshal Beresford that I have lost sight of the Thirteenth Light Dragoons and the Seventh Portuguese under Colonel Otway, but I have the First Portuguese with me. If the Heavy Brigade comes up then we can complete our victory. Go.'

'Yes, sir.' Williams caught the hint of an accent before the man galloped off.

'That is Baron Tripp – a Dutchman, although he now holds the King's commission,' Baynes said as if passing the time of day. 'General Long has been less than a week with the army, and his own staff and camp equipment have not yet arrived.' That explained why the general was riding a troop horse.

Baynes edged a little closer, but the general's expression was scarcely welcoming.

'You may follow if you wish, sir, but I have no time for you,' Long said, the force of the rebuff weakened by a sudden rumble from his stomach. Without looking at them, he trotted over to the head of the remaining three squadrons of Portuguese horse, with white collars and cuffs to their dark blue tunics. Riding beside the regiment's commander, he led them forward, veering towards the road. The French column had begun moving again almost as soon as the 13th Light Dragoons had chased away their opponents. The infantry were still in square, which made marching a slow business, yet even so they were making clear progress along the highway. The rearmost squadron of French hussars was several hundred yards away, with just a few skirmishers out covering the withdrawal. They were dressed in a faded light blue and had carbines in hand, although as yet none had fired.

General Long halted just short of the highway and stared at the retreating enemy. Then he looked round to the rear past Williams and the others. The Welshman followed his gaze and realised that the heavy brigade had not followed them. He could see the two regiments, formed in column some distance away, but to the south of the road. They looked to be almost half a mile away, and at this distance their dark horses looked black, topped by a streak of red from the jackets of the men.

'Mr Williams.' Brigadier General Long did not shout, but had a carrying voice. 'Would you be so good as to join me.'

Williams reached the general and saluted. Long looked even paler than before, the red rims around his eyes standing out against his pale cheeks.

'Mr Williams, I do not have all my staff with me today and so I must ask you to carry a message for me.' It was politely done, even if neither man could possibly imagine a lieutenant refusing the request of a general.

'Find Marshal Beresford. I think it likely that he is with the heavies. Give him my best compliments and tell him that the Heavy Brigade must advance to support me. If it does then we have these fellows trapped. If the artillery is up then all the better. Tell the marshal that the Thirteenth and the Seventh Portuguese have gone, and I have only the First Regiment still with me, and so I need the heavy dragoons to finish the job. Have you got that?'

Williams repeated the message, even after a few days used to the routines of staff work, and the solemnity of the moment passed without any more unfortunate eruptions from the general's stomach.

'Good,' Long said, 'then go, and better take that fellow with you.' He nodded in Baynes' direction, his voice raised so that the merchant would hear. Williams glanced at the French column and saw that they were still moving, and then turned his horse, pretending not to notice a fresh churning gurgle from the general's innards.

'It seems my presence is not wanted,' Baynes said drily once they were out of earshot. Williams put Francesca into a canter, and the others matched her pace. Baynes was a better horseman than his looks suggested. 'Still, the poor man appears most unwell. And he is a twin, of course, and it is always interesting to see how a twin copes without his sibling. Some are not good on their own.'

Williams said nothing, not caring to discuss a senior officer, especially one he scarcely knew. He was surprised to learn that Long was a twin. Williams had three sisters, the middle one already married and widowed, but, growing up as the lone male in a female household, he had often felt that a brother would have been welcome company. The idea of a twin was a strange one, a fellow like himself in looks and much of his character. A gloomy thought, probably inspired by his mix of Scots and Welsh blood, made him suspect that the brother would have possessed all the charm, confidence and poise he felt lacking in himself. Bet the swine would have had better luck in love, he thought.

'Are you acquainted with Marshal Beresford?' Baynes' question thankfully interrupted the inevitable despair concerning Jane MacAndrews.

'I have not had the good fortune to meet the marshal.' Beresford was a general in the British Army and a marshal in the Portuguese. Appointed to command Portugal's land forces, in the last few years he had thoroughly reorganised and retrained them, fighting battle after battle with a sclerotic bureaucracy in a country whose resources had been drained by French invasion. He had brought in officers and sergeants from British regiments, giving some of the latter commissions, and mingled them with the Portuguese. The results were promising indeed. Williams had seen Portuguese infantry fight well alongside their redcoat allies, and had heard of other similar incidents. They were said to have done very well at Busaco the previous year.

'Well,' Baynes continued after a moment, 'the marshal has a formidable appearance. He is a big fellow, bigger even than you. One of his eyes no longer works – I believe a shooting accident when he was young, although how anyone could mistake that tower of a man for a pheasant escapes me. Nevertheless, I tell you this for it can be disconcerting when you meet him for the first time. As to the rest, he is not the most mannered of gentlemen, quite the Goth in fact, and no doubt you know about Buenos Aires? No? Well, the marshal captured the place back in '06 when we tried to steal the Spanish Americas, and then had to surrender when the Spaniards – rather impudently you might feel – decided they would take the city back. You would know better than I, but such a thing might well prey on a soldier's mind.'

The disastrous expeditions to South America were a source of continued shame and anger in the army, not least because they were so woefully mismanaged. Williams knew little of them and had not realised that Beresford was involved.

There was no time to reply because they were almost there. Closest to them was a squadron of heavy cavalry who sat on their horses and waited, a low murmur of conversation coming from them since they were obviously at ease, swords still in scabbards. Several of the horses were cropping the grass, only half-heartedly restrained by their riders. The men wore red jackets of similar pattern to the infantry, although in this case they were as faded and patched as any he had ever seen. Their collars and cuffs were green, and so these must be the 4th Dragoons, which meant, reasonably enough, that the senior regiment, the 3rd Dragoon Guards, was in the place of seniority over on the right. The 4th had been in Portugal and Spain for years now, and showed every sign of hard service. Most still wore their bicorne hats, but often so misshapen by the weather that they were barely recognisable. The sergeant on the end of the rear rank had a large chunk missing from the front of his hat, the hole ragged where it had

37

been. Beside him was a man in a forage cap, and next to him another with a tall hat more like an infantry shako. Perhaps it was this raggedness, perhaps the reassuring red jackets, but somehow Williams felt more akin to a regiment like this than to the light dragoons or hussars, fine fellows though they were – at least for cavalrymen.

They rode past the squadrons of the 4th Dragoons and saw a cluster of horsemen in capes, cloaks and neat cocked hats behind them. Marshal Beresford stood out for his bulk, and because it was clear that he was at the centre of things. Williams slowed his horse to a walk, and as he made his way forward saw a familiar face.

'Ah, Williams, it is good to see you.' Colonel D'Urban's smile was genuinely warm, but there was no time for other pleasantries. 'You are with Colborne, I understand.' D'Urban was Marshal Beresford's quartermaster general, and so the head of his staff. The colonel noticed Baynes and raised a gloved finger to the peak of his Tarleton helmet, his smile remaining warm, if a little wary. 'Ah, something is afoot, I gather. Well, I am sure we can speak privately later. Now, Williams, what does Colonel Colborne have to say?'

'I am in with Colborne, sir,' Williams said, at last able to get a word in to interrupt the flow, 'but I come now with a message from General Long.'

D'Urban's smile faded. 'Ah, then that is important. Come, you must report to the marshal.'

Beresford proved as formidable in appearance as Baynes had suggested, his milky white left eye looking as if it stared off at some distant object. Williams struggled to resist the urge to follow its gaze. There was also a glumness about the man, his heavy features giving a sense of despondency.

'General Long's compliments, sir,' Williams began, 'and he asks that the Heavy Brigade advance to support him. If it advances then he says that we will have trapped the French column on the highway, especially if our artillery has arrived. General Long reports that the Thirteenth and the Seventh Portuguese are gone, and that he has only the First Regiment with him, hence his need for the heavy dragoons to complete the victory.'

Beresford stared at him, the dead eye no longer focused on the far distance, but now seeming to bore into him. He did not seem pleased by the report.

'No, sir, it will not do.' The marshal shook his head, as if to reinforce his conclusion. In his heavy cloak there was something immense and bear-like about the man. 'Where is Brigadier General Long?'

'On the far side of the road by now, about three-quarters of a mile to our front,' Williams said, and wondered why the staff were here behind the heavies. If they moved just a little to the side then Long and his Portuguese would be clearly visible.

'He has the First Regiment with him. How steady are they after such losses?'

'Losses, sir?'

'Do you not know the meaning of the word, young man?' The marshal's voice was gruff and getting louder.

'The First Regiment appeared steady, sir, and our losses are trifling.' Williams used the word before thinking. It was the way of things to speak of such matters in this manner, but a little voice inside his head murmured that it would not be so very trifling to bleeding men waiting for the surgeons, or to the families of the dead. The wound in his hip began to ache for the first time in weeks.

'Trifling, sir, trifling!' The marshal's face blazed red. 'Damn you, young man, do you call a whole regiment taken a trifling loss!' Men stirred in the rear rank of the 4th Dragoons at the scale of the marshal's anger and the dreadful news. 'The Thirteenth are lost. Surrounded by French cavalry and taken. You have just told me that they are gone, have you not, sir? Yet you see this as a mere trifle. Now, out of my sight, sir!'

Williams was dismissed and for the moment stunned. As he walked his horse away to join Baynes, the marshal was issuing an order to one of his own aides, telling General Long to halt where he was. Williams could not believe it. Yet if the 13th Light

Dragoons were gone, what of the Portuguese and Hanley? Was his friend in French hands or dead?

'I do not believe it,' he said aloud, before realising that D'Urban was still beside Baynes. Now that he had spoken, there seemed no point in hiding his views, especially since the colonel had always struck him as a shrewd man. 'The French were broken and the Thirteenth following in pursuit. The Portuguese went after them so they have supports. There was no sign of any reverse.'

D'Urban was sympathetic, but unconvinced. 'We have certain word that the Thirteenth were faced with overwhelming numbers of French cavalry and forced to surrender. Such things can happen so quickly with cavalry. After such a reverse we must be cautious. If the guns come up in time then we may still achieve something.' There was little trace of confidence, and then the colonel was called away.

'Best if we move off a short way,' Baynes suggested.

'They are wrong, utterly wrong,' Williams told him.

'They are also far more senior than a lieutenant,' Baynes said quietly, 'and although a civilian, I believe it is not considered proper behaviour for a lieutenant to tell generals that they are wrong.'

'Even if they are.' Williams' anger was fading a little.

'Especially when they are.'

Clear of the 4th Dragoons, Williams fished out the cheap telescope he had bought in Lisbon and studied General Long's Portuguese squadrons. They had formed in line, facing not the road, but to their left. He moved the glass and saw a dark line of horsemen opposite them. Once again he regretted the loss of his old glass, for he could not be sure about the numbers, although evidently these were French. Their appearance placed Long in a difficult position, for he had been moving parallel to the road. He was level with the infantry squares as they slowly made their way to safety, and the rearguard of French hussars was almost behind him.

There was sudden movement on the edge of the lens, and Williams shifted the glass, found the Portuguese squadrons, lost them and found them again. He just glimpsed a little red speck on a dark horse ahead of the lines of dark blue as Long led them in a charge against the hundred or so Frenchmen. Smoke blossomed from the side of the square as they passed and the Portuguese line staggered, men and horses falling. It wavered, became ragged, and then broke up into many little figures as one after another the cavalry turned and sped to the rear. The red dot on the dark horse was left on its own, and then followed as French horsemen hurried towards him.

'Oh dear,' he said. 'The Portuguese cavalry are put to flight,' he explained. Baynes had been watching with one hand shading his eyes and had probably not seen clearly.

'Do you then fear that things are as bad as the marshal believes?' the merchant asked, for once uncertain.

'No. Perhaps a squadron or so of French cavalry have rallied – their hussars were not much engaged by the Thirteenth, but I do not believe there would have been enough to change the fortunes of the day. And if the heavies had advanced as requested, none of this need have happened.'

'I doubt very much that this would be an appropriate moment to express that view to the marshal or his staff,' Baynes said, patting Williams on the arm. He had not realised that his fingers were clenching and unclenching in frustration.

'Oh, for Lord Wellington,' Williams sighed.

'Oh, indeed,' the merchant agreed. 'But since he is up north keeping an eye on Marshal Masséna, we must do as best we can in other hands. And "oh" again, for we appear to be moving.'

The heavy brigade walked forward for almost two hundred yards and then stopped. The French continued their stately progression along the highway.

'At last,' Williams said as two teams of horses came at a slow trot from behind them. There were four to each team, pulling a limber and a six-pounder cannon, the KGL gunners jogging along behind. They passed the heavy cavalry and then wheeled off to the left of the road. The artillerymen were well trained and experienced, working smoothly as a team, and Williams knew that no one could have deployed more quickly, and yet even so he resented every second. At long last – in fact after only a couple of minutes – each gun captain raised an arm to show that his piece was loaded and laid on the target.

'Fire!' Captain Cleves shouted, and the guns belched flame and smoke and leaped back a good six feet. Williams was watching the French and saw one of the shot strike the stone of the road, then skip up to shatter the legs of two of the hussar horses from the rearguard squadron. The French did not stop.

'Fire!' The second salvo came not much more than a minute after the first, which was testament in itself to the practised skill of the German gunners. Williams did not see the strikes this time, but the hussars wheeled away to each side of the highway, leaving a dark bundle behind them.

'Why do we not move?' Williams said to Baynes. He realised that once again his hand was restless and he clenched it into a fist and held it shut. Marshal Beresford had come forward to watch the guns play on the French, but there was no sign that he planned to advance.

'Fire!' Cleves shouted again and again. The guns could see the rearmost square now that the hussars had moved. Williams saw the ranks ripple as the shot struck home and could well imagine the carnage. Yet the French did not stop and the British did not seem inclined to chase them. The British cavalry were fresher and far outnumbered the remaining French squadrons, and were heavier than the hussars, for they were bigger men on bigger horses. They could expect to drive them off with ease and leave the two squares on their own. It was a shame that there were only two guns – where the rest of Cleves' brigade was baffled Williams – but even so they could pound the squares while the cavalry watched. When the French infantry started to waver the dragoons could charge and ride down the broken squares. It would take an hour at the most – half an hour if someone had the sense to bring forward the 2/66th and the Light Companies from his own brigade.

'I do not understand this,' he said, loud enough to make D'Urban turn and glare at him.

'Nor so I, but I am a mere civilian.' Baynes spoke softly, with only a little of his usual amusement at the folly of others. 'However, it is clear that we have nothing to do here. I ought to stay just in case, but I do not believe that I will need you to identify any French rogue for me. Best go back to your own duties. I will make sure that the horse is sent to you.' He chuckled. 'Better to take the sergeant's rather than the officer's! You are a bright fellow, Mr Williams, but best not to linger here.'

Williams rode off, the noise of each discharge from the guns getting quieter as he cantered away. Colborne was still on the hilltop with Dunbar, the Light Companies and the 2/66th sitting or lying in formation in the valley behind. Williams suspected quite a few were asleep.

'Where have you been, sir?' Colonel Colborne's manner was surprisingly brusque. Williams noticed that Dunbar was avoiding the gaze of either man. Unsure of how to respond, he hesitated. 'Well, sir, what have you to say for yourself?'

The truth was simplest, and as Williams explained what had happened he could see the colonel's mood soften. The frustration remained, but was no longer directed at him, and by the end he was able to smile.

'Did you get what you wanted?'

'Yes, sir,' Williams replied, 'a good steady beast, I think, if not perhaps able to meet Captain Dunbar's standards for the aesthetic.' Dunbar was free in his distaste for Francesca's ungainly looks.

'Well, at least someone has achieved something today.' Colborne spoke bitterly. 'Fools or knaves, I cannot decide which, but the harm has been great.'

The French column was far away and the guns had gone silent. The heavy cavalry had not moved.

'I do not understand why everyone has become convinced that the Thirteenth are taken by the French,' Williams said, feeling his own frustration bubbling up again. Dunbar was gesturing for him to stop, and he guessed this was already a well-trodden theme, but he could not desist. 'There was no sign of it, none at all, and yet they are all so convinced.'

'Fools.' Colborne steadied himself, breathing hard for a few moments. He had a reputation for never swearing – an attribute Williams greatly admired and did his best to match, but a rare one in this army. He suspected that he had come very close to seeing the habit broken.

'Fools,' the colonel said more softly. 'We saw the charge from here – the most beautiful thing I ever did see – and the French were swept from the field. An aide tried to tell me that they were surrounded, but I sent him back to assure Marshal Beresford that they were not. We saw it all as plain as day, and yet we were not believed.'

'The marshal did not have clear sight of the action,' Williams offered, knowing that it was a weak justification. A general in charge of an army should find the best spot from which to survey the field. Moore would have done, and so would Lord Wellington.

'Fools or knaves.' Colborne repeated the phrase. There was something rueful about the way he spoke the next words. 'There was a most brilliant *coup de main* staring us in the face and we threw the chance away.

'Well, I had better ride and see what our lords and masters want of the brigade, since they have not deigned to inform us.' Colborne kicked angrily at the side of his horse and cantered off down the hill.

Dunbar sighed. He had removed his cloak to show the silver epaulettes and green facings of his regiment, for like the colonel he served in the 2/66th and the two men knew each other well. Williams found the captain to be a friendly man and a good soldier, and was sure that without the latter quality he would not have held this post regardless of his affability.

'The colonel has had a trying day,' Dunbar said. 'He cannot abide mismanagement or lack of spirit, and unfortunately he expressed himself fully when the marshal's aide came to us. Sadly, General Stewart was with us and he took the criticism as a personal insult – though I have no doubt that none of it was directed at him.' Major General Stewart had commanded the brigade until he was moved up to have charge of the entire Second Division. He was a slim terrier of a man, well liked and well respected.

'Stewart demanded a retraction. The colonel would only say that a brilliant opportunity had been squandered. The general looked at him coldly and said, "Well, then, in future, Colonel Colborne, I shall only address you in the most official manner." Just like that, and then he galloped off. It is sad for they have always been good friends. I have heard the colonel say more than once that General Stewart is the bravest man he has ever known. So sad.' Dunbar shook his head.

The French were now a dark smear on the landscape, almost at the horizon. No one was following them, and the heavy dragoons had dismounted to rest their horses. Williams wondered where Hanley was, and where the cavalry had gone.

'We are such a happy army,' Dunbar said, half to himself.

5

The horses pounded over the earth. The grass was wet, but the soil had been so dry that now they were on the plain it had simply sucked up the rain and was still as hard as rock. Hanley felt his horse excited by the sheer joy of running with so many others, a herd rushing it did not matter where so long as they were running.

At the start the Portuguese cavalry had kept to formation, moving no faster than a trot. Then they saw a dozen dragoons forming up – they must have fled off to the side and avoided the onslaught of the 13th Light Dragoons.

Swords scraped on scabbards as they were drawn and without orders the leading squadron charged, the others following. They did not cheer, but shrieked like excited children. Hanley gripped his own sword tighter and drove his horse forward, its longer legs stretching out and soon passing the smaller animals ridden by the cavalry. His mouth was open and he was whooping with delight.

The French ran. Before the deluge of blue-coated cavalry and the redcoated officer at their head reached them their horses went about and they fled. Hanley saw their backs and realised that he was yelling with delight as he gave chase. The French scattered, but their horses were already weary and a couple of them tried to flee straight back. Hanley closed with one, a trumpeter in an orange coat laced with green. He looked to be barely eighteen, fresh faced and terrified as he turned and stared back at his pursuers.

Hanley grinned and urged his horse on, reaching back to slap the flat of his blade against it to make it run faster. He was closing quickly, saw another hurried look of terror from his target, who reined in, and then he was passing so fast that he simply slashed backwards and knocked the wind from the trumpeter and the trumpeter from the saddle. The man looked shocked as he lay on his back with his booted legs in the air. Hanley had meant to use the edge, but had forgotten to tighten his grip. He looked back and saw the trumpeter push himself up only to be hacked on the shoulder by a passing cavalryman and flung down again.

They rode on. Hanley looked and saw that the two hussars were still with him, the corporal looking a little bemused. All three of them slowed their mounts, for they were running away from the smaller and poorly conditioned cavalry horses. They went at a comfortable easy canter, which matched the little Portuguese horses' gallop. A few more French stragglers were caught and cut down, others lay on the grass, and after a couple of miles they saw the 13th Light Dragoons, still haring across the plain and spread out as they hunted the enemy down.

Hanley found it all intoxicating, but as the time passed he began to think for the first time since they had set off. He had wanted to kill the trumpeter, and thought the man's desperate fear amusing as he had run him down. The urge to kill again, so soon after he had killed for the first time, was disturbing. Hanley thought himself a peaceable man. He loved Spain and the Spanish people, admired the Portuguese, although with a lesser acquaintance, and he had found the closest friendships of his life with men like Pringle, Truscott and Williams. For all those reasons he devoted his energy and passion to driving the French back across the Pyrenees. His war was fought away from the battlefield, using stealth and deception to outwit the enemy.

Hanley knew that his successes often meant that the enemy were brought to the field at a disadvantage. Men died when they were beaten, perhaps more of them than if he had done nothing, but it was all at a distance. In his service with the 106th he had never taken a man's life, and as far as he knew the same was true of Pringle, if not of Williams. The Welshman killed with a chilling fluency. Now he had run a man through and was puzzled because he felt no revulsion. It was almost as if there was now more honesty in what he did – not with the world, but with himself. Still, he wished one of the others were here and there was time to talk. Williams would have been hard to draw forth, Pringle would have joked, and Truscott looked to philosophy, so he was not sure how much they would have helped. Since he was being honest in his thoughts, perhaps it was better to say that he wanted them here to listen.

They rode on, the Portuguese mingling with the British. Many of the light dragoons rode horses white with sweat, and yet still they ran on, eating up the miles. Hanley and his escort edged further and further forward, and so were among the leaders when they raised a shout at sighting new quarry. Ahead of them on the road was a long procession of wagons and heavy guns pulled by horses and mules. Soldiers walked alongside, but there was no sign of any formed escort.

'Tally ho!' The shout came from an officer riding a light bay horse which looked as if it had scarcely even warmed up.

'Come on,' Hanley said to the corporal. He felt his heart quickening again, realised he still had his sword in his hand, but fought down the urge to thrust it into another Frenchman. Now that he had some purpose to achieve, it was much easier to think.

The British light dragoons were scattered. Two of the Portuguese squadrons were in more or less dense masses, if not formation, but it did not matter. The French gunners and other soldiers fled as soon as they heard the shouts and saw some four hundred horsemen bearing down on them. A few muskets popped from far too great a distance, and then the men dropped their weapons and joined the rout. The British were first among them, slicing down with their curved sabres. Hanley saw the officer on the bay run down one of the fugitives. The man had lost his shako and had his hands clasped protectively on top of his head. The officer braced himself in his stirrups and raised his sabre, with its ornate oriental hilt. He waited for the precise moment and then sliced down, cutting through the gunner's wrist with such force that the blade sank into his head. Momentum carried him onwards and he swung his arm so that the sword came free as his victim dropped.

'The guns!' Hanley shouted at the man. 'We must secure the guns!' The man did not turn or appear to have heard. There were screams as more light dragoons caught up with the running French and heavy sabres slashed. Some of the blades were blunt now from use, so that Hanley saw more than one Frenchman bludgeoned to the ground by furious light dragoons, only to get up moments later, bruised and dazed, but not seriously hurt.

'Sir!' He saw the colonel of the Portuguese. 'We must secure the French siege train. It is vital for the army.'

The man blinked at him, then seemed to comprehend, realising that an officer in a red coat like Hanley would be here only if he was a staff man. The colonel began shouting orders to rally his men. Many of the Portuguese were already swarming towards the guns and caissons, chattering to each other excitedly. There was no more resistance, as the surviving French were either in flight or huddled as prisoners, looking down at the ground and trying not to draw the attention of their captors. Many were wounded, with deep cuts to the head and shoulders, or gashes on their arms from where they had tried to protect themselves. Some could not stand, and from the look of their wounds Hanley wondered whether they would ever leave this place. He did not know how much time had passed, but most of the light dragoons paused for only a few minutes, before giving fresh chase to the stream of fugitives, led by all those with beasts to ride.

There was a wagon some way ahead of the main column, and that seemed odd. There was a knot of riders around it, and men moving about on the canopy. He saw a flash and a puff of smoke as one of them fired, bringing down the horse of the closest light dragoon. It took seconds for the sound of the shot to reach them.

'Come on,' he said to the corporal, and was not quite sure why, but the guns were secured and he was puzzled. His horse resisted the prod of his heels for a moment, shook its head, and then lurched awkwardly into a canter. Another man fired from the wagon, missed, and two light dragoons were there hacking at the men. One fell, and even from this distance Hanley could see that he no longer had a head. The riders sped away, abandoning the vehicle and the men in it. A white cloak was bright as it streamed behind a tall man on a big horse. Then Hanley saw a rider in a green coat – not the dark green of the dragoons or the olive shade of chasseurs, but a vivid light green. He glimpsed another man in the same uniform, who appeared and then disappeared behind someone in a dark coat and a smaller figure in turquoise.

'Sinclair!' Hanley shouted, and he felt his blood racing again, but this was with a much more familiar excitement. Baynes' informant had been right. Light green was the colour of the Irish Legion, and he had seen Sinclair in this uniform before. He kicked his horse hard, hit it again with the flat of his sword and yelled 'Come on, lad!' The gelding picked up the pace, leaping across the grass. With a scrape the two hussars drew their sabres – Hanley had not realised that they had sheathed them.

They passed the wagon, the headless corpse lying next to the wheel and another man draped over the tailgate. A light dragoon was inside, another holding the reins of the man's horse.

'Empty bloody boxes!' came a shout from under the high canopy. 'Get the mules, Tom, at least there's prize money there!' The Army did not pay out rewards on the same scale as the Navy, but there would be a little for captured animals.

Hanley kept going. They were among the leading light dragoons now, the knot of Frenchmen only three or four hundred yards in front of them. Just one of the 13th was ahead of the pack, closing rapidly on the fugitives. It was the officer on the bay, and the beast raced on. Hanley saw the man raise his sabre high and yell with sheer delight.

The man with the bright white cloak looked back, and then spun his big black horse around with remarkable ease. He had a helmet much like the dragoons', but steel rather than brass, and as he turned and flicked back his cloak, Hanley saw a gleaming cuirass.

Dalmas! Hanley had never seen the man close up, but knew

that this was surely the cuirassier officer, and if he and Sinclair had both come to Campo Major then there was certainly something dirty going on.

The light dragoon officer gave a flourish of his sabre as he and Dalmas sped towards each other at a gallop. His opponent already had his straight sword at the charge, arm raised in front of him and the point spearing forwards. The Frenchman was silent.

They closed so fast that Hanley did not see clearly what happened. The light dragoon was screaming out a challenge; his sabre glinted as it cut and glanced off the Frenchman's armour. There was a grunt and the officer arched his back. Dalmas was already past him when the Englishman slid from the saddle, sabre hanging from his lifeless wrist. He fell to the left, but his foot caught in the stirrup and so he was dragged along, head bumping on the ground as his terrified horse ran on. Dalmas raised his sword above his head and was turning again, no more than a hundred yards away. The closest light dragoons growled in anger and urged their mounts on to catch the Frenchman.

A shot erupted, the noise of the discharge sudden and loud. One of the French horsemen dropped, and two of the others, the man in the dark uniform and the one in light blue, had turned and were rushing towards the British. Someone shouted. It was Sinclair, and Hanley could see the Irishman clearly as he turned and came after the other two. Another man in a plainer version of his green coat stopped his horse and jumped down, unslinging a firelock from his shoulder.

'*Prisonnier! Prisonnier!*' shouted the leading rider as he flung his empty pistol back over his shoulder. He was dressed in very dark blue, breeches and jacket alike, with his cocked hat tied tightly around his chin. Hanley guessed he must be an engineer or artillery officer, and one who lived well given his plumpness. A few strides behind him was a slim figure in a hussar-style uniform of tight breeches and dolman and a round fur cap. The turquoise fabric was so covered with silver lace that he must be an ADC. The face beneath the cap was smooth and young, so no doubt this was a relative of some important man. Dalmas was still turning away, unable for the moment to change direction again.

Another shot, this time from Sinclair, who had stopped and aimed his pistol with care. The turquoise hussar's horse staggered and then sank to its knees, throwing the rider, who tumbled into the grass and fell, cap rolling away and long fair hair shaken loose. The other man glanced back, but only for a moment.

'*Prisonnier!*' he shouted. 'I surrender. I am prisoner!' The words were clear even if the accent was strong.

'Stop, man!' Hanley yelled at a light dragoon who was lifting his sabre ready to cut. 'He is surrendering.'

The Frenchman reined in beside him. Hanley struggled to stop his own horse, and the gelding went round one side of the engineer officer's mount and halted behind him. He smiled. 'I accept your surrender, sir,' he told the man, repeating the words in French.

'*Merci, monsieur, je suis Major Bertrand et je...*'

Something hummed past inches from Hanley's ear and he heard the crack of a shot a moment later. The left lens of Bertrand's glasses shattered, his eye vanished in a smear of red as his head jerked back and the man went limp. Some of his blood flicked on to Hanley's cheek.

There was a little cloud of dirty smoke in front of the kneeling figure of the man in the green jacket.

'Get him!' Hanley yelled at the nearest light dragoons, pointing at the man on foot. 'Kill the bugger! Kill him! You two, stay with me,' he added to the hussars. 'Come on.'

'Mister Hanley.' A familiar voice called out to him, but not a voice he would expect here. Bertrand's name rang a bell, but for the moment he could not place it. Dalmas and Sinclair were fleeing as more and more light dragoons headed for them. The man on foot was running, but his horse had decided to trot away. 'Kill him!' Hanley yelled again, for he knew who the man was.

'Mister Hanley.'

The man in green threw his rifle away — the sharper noise could only have come from a rifle — and ran, grabbing the reins and scrambling on to his horse with a light dragoon only a few yards away.

'Bloody hell, Mister Hanley, have you got cloth ears?'

He looked down, and there was Jenny Dobson looking up at him with her big brown eyes, dyed blond hair dishevelled and loose from the fall. The turquoise hussar uniform clung to her, so tightly tailored that it cannot have been easy to put on. Even with her sash and hessian boots there was nothing remotely military or masculine about her looks.

'Well I'm damned,' he said, wondering why he had not recognised what and who she was more quickly.

'If you like,' the girl said, and winked. Only Jenny would wink in the middle of a battle.

'Jenny,' he said, still not quite believing his own eyes.

The girl reached back to rub her behind. 'Bugger me, I'm sore,' she said.

It was definitely Jenny, daughter of Sergeant Dobson from the Grenadier Company of the 106th, who had fled from the army to the enemy to become a whore and then a mistress. That was why he knew Major Bertrand of the engineers, for he was the girl's keeper, and last winter she had stolen secrets from him and sold them to the Allies.

Yet there was no time to linger with reunions. 'We'll talk later, Jenny,' he said. 'Corporal, give the lady the major's horse and look after her. Take her back to that wagon. I will meet you there. If you can, stop it from being looted.'

'Private,' he said to the other hussar, and wished that he had taken the trouble to learn the man's name. 'You follow me.'

'Lady,' he heard Jenny say softly as he bullied his horse into running again.

6

It was more than a mile before Hanley and the hussar caught up. There were not many French fugitives still running along the road to Badajoz. The slow ones had been caught and were cut down or captured. The gamblers had split off to the side, giving the pursuers more chance of catching them for a minute or two until they got out of the way. Only the determined ones on the best horses were still there, some fifty or sixty dragoons and a dozen or so from the convoy. Hanley doubted there were even a hundred light dragoons left in the chase and half as many Portuguese. No one was yelling any more, or calling out hunting cries. Men and horses alike were panting, struggling with the effort, and pursuers and pursued went as fast as they still could in silence apart from the drumming of the hoofs. They were spread out, each going at his own pace and without the slightest order.

After another mile the land began to rise gently up to a ridge. Hanley was about to give up, and go back to find out what he could learn from Jenny, when he spotted something white far ahead among the leading French. As he rode on he stared ahead of him, searching for men in green, and saw one not far from Dalmas, and another among the last of the French.

Brandt, he thought, and wished Williams were here. Brandt was a soldier who had served in a foreign regiment recruited from prisoners and deserters. Williams caught him trying to rape the wife of a partisan chief, but the man had escaped, deserting again and fighting for the enemy. The man was an excellent shot, especially with the British Army's issue rifle. Sinclair must have enlisted him in his own regiment, hence the light green coat, the latest in a long succession of uniforms the man had worn.

The French reached the crest of the ridge and spilled over, vanishing for the moment. Hanley's horse revived as it went up the slope, bounding ahead, so that he was one of the first to reach the crest.

'Bugger,' he heard the light dragoon next to him say.

To their left was a small fort, little more than a tower, but perched on a hillock and surrounded by ditches. Back some way from that was a much larger and more formidable fort, the San Cristoval, guarding this bank of the River Guadiana. Ahead was the defended bridge, crossing the great river on high Roman arches, and on the far bank, looming up on its hill, the great fortress city of Badajoz.

They must have chased the French for almost eight miles, although Hanley could scarcely believe it. The sight of sanctuary stirred the French on to a last great effort. Some of the British and Portuguese slowed and stopped, but more did not, and pulled on their last resources of strength to catch the enemy.

'Try to get the one in green.' Hanley pointed at Brandt, whose horse was slowing and who was trying to get to the San Cristoval. 'Kill him if you cannot take him.'

The German nodded and set off. Dalmas and Sinclair were further off, probably too far to catch as they made for the bridge, but Hanley felt that he ought to try. His horse was trotting now, and the motion was uncomfortable after so long in the saddle. He tried to rise with each step, but got out of rhythm and bounced in the saddle before he sat, rocking with the motion and regaining his balance. There were light dragoons ahead of him, their horses foamy with sweat, the men bright red in the face.

A gun fired, a big gun from the San Cristoval fort, and perhaps it was to sound the alarm because Hanley did not see a shot land. The dull boom echoed along the valley and in its wake British and Portuguese cavalry alike slowed or stopped. Hanley saw men slump in the saddle, weariness overcoming them as at last the all-absorbing elation of the chase faded away. He sheathed his sword, forcing it with all his strength when it started to stick.

'Thirteenth, rally on me!' Colonel Head of the light dragoons was waving his sword in the air and shouting at his men. 'Form on me!'

Other officers and NCOs were calling out to their men. Hanley saw the Irish corporal who had killed the French colonel gather a handful of men together. His own horse had stopped before the last echo of the cannon shot died and the gelding was hanging its head down and breathing hard. A few light dragoons still followed the enemy, but he could see Dalmas and Sinclair reach the gateway of the *tête-de-pont* protecting the bridge and knew that it was over. Muskets squibbed from the rampart and the leading light dragoon's horse sank down on its knees, flinging the rider over its head.

More guns thundered from the San Cristoval fort and he heard the cannonballs tearing through the air over his head.

'Time to go, boys,' shouted Colonel Head. He gestured with his sword back towards the ridge and the little groups of horsemen started to walk up the slope. It was over. Guns fired again from the Cristoval fort, and Hanley saw a shot graze through a bunch of cavalry, ripping off a man's arm and shattering the skull of the horse beside him. The walk turned into a trot, even a canter for those still able.

Hanley searched for the hussar and saw a horse cropping the grass not far from the ditch outside the fort. Beside it, still clutching the reins, was a bundle of blue and grey clothes. It did not move. Either the man was dead or so badly wounded that he could not be carried off. Hanley felt flat, wondered whether he should go and retrieve the valuable troop horse, but then a trumpet sounded from the far side of the valley. The gates had opened and French dragoons were coming out of the *tête-de-pont*. It looked to be no more than a squadron, but the Allied horsemen were spent and in no state to fight. A few infantrymen appeared from the San Cristoval and spread in a skirmish line.

The first shots punched through the air, one of them so close that Hanley could feel the wind of it passing his head.

'Time to go, come on, man!' Colonel Head was shouting at him and gesturing for him to follow. Hanley obeyed. There were cries as some of the men who had gone too far or who still did not want to go back were caught and shot down or taken.

Hanley's horse responded. Perhaps the beast sensed somehow that it was going home, for it sped up the slope. He would have to remember to give Baynes' groom something, for the man kept their horses in excellent condition. The gelding was eager to go, and so he gave it its head and was soon passing the ragged groups of light dragoons and Portuguese cavalry. Since he had failed here, at least he could get back to Jenny Dobson and that wagon and start to find out what was going on. The cavalry paid him little attention – staff officers were always rushing around without rhyme or reason.

It took longer going back, even though his horse was eager, and at least that gave him time to think. He had last seen Jenny in Salamanca and still was not sure whether she had betrayed him to the enemy. The girl may have had little choice, and the business had worked out well, but now almost a year later she appeared with Bertrand. Was the man trying to desert or surrendering out of fear and to protect his mistress from harm? Something was certainly going on, if both of Marshal Soult's heads of intelligence-gathering were here. Bertrand might be a traitor or pretending to be one. The man was dead, so Hanley would see how far he could work the whole business out.

The wagon was ahead of him, with the horses standing beside it, but the mule team had gone. Jenny sat hunched up in the driver's seat, with a blanket around her, while the corporal leaned against the wheel. Hanley was about to go to them when he saw something on the ground and leaned back, urging his gelding to stop. It was Brandt's rifle, and on a whim he dismounted and picked it up, slinging it over his shoulder. Then he led his horse over to the wagon.

'Took your time,' Jenny said cheerfully, but he ignored her

because the corporal was pointing. The retreating British and Portuguese were closer than he had thought, which could only mean that the French were chasing the tired men. There might not be many of them following, but it did mean that he had little time.

'Look at this, sir,' the corporal said, and hauled himself into the wagon. Hanley followed. The bed of the cart was full of boxes and chests, most of them open and empty. The German moved aside two which were filled, but not excessively heavy.

'Here, they're mine,' Jenny said. Hanley ignored her, for the corporal was struggling to pull out another small chest, the lock already broken open. From it he produced two heavy bags and threw one to the officer. It clinked as he caught it and had the unmistakable feel of coins. Undoing the tie, he poured silver dollars out on to his gloved hand.

'Bloody hell!' Jenny said, eyes staring in astonishment. 'Mean sod never told me.'

There must have been a couple of hundred coins in the bag, and a dozen bags in the chest, so it was far too heavy and cumbersome for them to carry away.

'Take one,' he told the corporal. 'Better you have it than the French.'

'What about me!' the girl said.

'If you like.' Hanley tied up the bag he was holding and tossed it to her.

Surprised by the weight, Jenny fumbled the catch, letting her blanket go and uncovering her turquoise uniform. Cleary the cold could not compete with greed. Hanley fished out another bag.

'Leave the rest,' he said. 'We need to go.'

'How about my clothes?' The girl looked at the two locked boxes.

'I'll get you all you need.' Hanley spoke lightly.

She grinned. 'I might need a lot.'

'Well, have this cloak for a start,' Hanley said, reaching up to take the rolled cloak off the back of his saddle. 'Best if you do not attract more attention than is necessary.' She stuck her tongue out at him, and for a moment he saw the sixteen-year-old woman-child he had first met three years earlier. 'Take this as well.' He plucked off his cocked hat. 'Tuck in your hair.'

'Yes, Mr Hanley, sir. Thank you, Mr Hanley, sir.'

The foremost of the light dragoons were not far, coming on steadily. Hanley could see a dark column some way behind them and guessed that it was the French. They were not gaining, but they kept pace, and no doubt were already picking up anyone whose horse gave out.

The three of them set off, Jenny swathed in his cloak and hat. The other two horses had had time to rest and his was still going well, and so they soon lengthened their lead. An officer of the light dragoons came towards them, his right arm bandaged.

'Have you seen Colonel Head?'

'Behind us,' Hanley said. 'What is happening?'

'There is a strong enemy force coming up the road from Campo Major, and I am sent to warn him.'

'What of our supports?'

The officer merely shook his head and rode on.

They pressed on, but Hanley kept them to a steady canter in case they had to escape again. Ten minutes later they sighted the French siege train and there, half a mile beyond, just as the officer had said, were French cavalry with infantry behind them. He realised that this was the force marching from Campo Major, but could not understand how the rest of the army had let them get away. There were a few British cavalry guarding the guns and their prisoners, and they rode over to them.

A captain was in charge, his head bandaged, and he was trying to get a couple of teams together to pull off at least some of the guns. 'The Portuguese had the rest. Had them out of their harnesses and off before you could say kiss my foot. Don't blame the poor devils, the way they are mounted anything would be better, but it does present a problem.'

They had got two guns moving, with light dragoons riding

on the trace horses and doing their best to lead, when Colonel Head arrived.

'Where are the heavies? Where indeed is everyone else?' he asked of no one in particular.

Hanley could see the leading French squadrons clearly now, as they wheeled to form, one on either side of the road. Both wore the brown of the Chamborant Hussars and carried drawn sabres.

'Leave 'em,' Head said wearily. 'Quickly now! Get back on your own horses.'

'The prisoners, sir?' the bandaged officer asked.

'Leave them as well. It cannot be helped.'

The French hussars walked their horses forward, the lines neatly dressed, but the threat was obvious. Head still had almost as many men, but none had the energy to charge or fight and the French were fresh, as well as backed by two battalions of infantry and more squadrons behind them.

They left guns and prisoners alike and trotted as fast as they could manage to the north of the road, making a wide loop to take them around the French column. There were distant shouts as the French coming from Badajoz saw the others.

Hanley wondered whether, if the rest of the army came on quickly, they might recapture the guns and so gain the siege train they lacked, but his heart told him that it would not happen. Something had gone wrong, badly wrong, and though he did not know what, he doubted that it would soon be remedied.

Failure weighed him down. He had not helped secure the guns, and had let Dalmas and Sinclair escape. Brandt was not important, although it would have been nice to deal with the man. Bertrand was dead, and he kicked himself for having forgotten to stop and search the body for papers. Perhaps Jenny carried something for him.

Hanley looked at the girl as she rode beside him. She rode well, and unconsciously or not she had let her cloak part, revealing her well-filled uniform. There were plenty of glances from officers and soldiers alike, but he rebuffed any attempt to secure an explanation or introduction. Jenny was not her usual flirtatious self and ignored the attention. She had grown, he thought, perhaps an inch or so in height, but a vast amount in knowledge of the world. Hanley thought back to when he had drawn her portrait, a sixteen-year-old girl, knowing and innocent at the same time, wearing the new dress bought for her wedding. She had been pretty then, and was prettier still now, whether in her tight uniform or better yet in something more feminine. Ideas began to take shape in his mind, some of them professional and some thoughts and needs of his own.

Jenny must have become aware of his scrutiny. She looked at him, her face sheepish, which was unusual for her. She was well used to men looking at her and usually responded with brazen confidence. Instead her eyes met his for only a moment and then flicked down modestly. A moment later she glanced back and smiled, not so much with challenge as with satisfaction. She was performing, no doubt about it, but it was a different role to her usual one. Hanley felt his raw ideas strengthen.

'Stay with the lady, corporal, I shall only be a few minutes,' he said, noting another smile at the word 'lady'. He turned his horse and threaded his way past the weary light cavalymen.

The French were not chasing them. Instead the cavalry from Badajoz had met up with the column on the road. The sound of cheering drifted towards him. He took out his glass and watched as infantrymen were divided up into groups and began hauling the guns and caissons along. No doubt messengers were already on their way to the fortress to summon draught animals, but the French were not inclined to wait just in case the British resumed their advance. Hanley could see no sign of that, and the highway back towards Campo Major was empty as far as he could see.

'Damn,' he said, for they had failed utterly and the army would not easily find another siege train. Hanley had lost everything they had come here for, and yet he had unexpectedly found a girl and a design was growing in his mind. Perhaps it was not all for nothing after all. He turned his horse and followed the others.

7

The sounds were soft, far fainter than the slamming of the door in the little house set back from the road, and yet Billy Pringle and the other old hands knew instantly what they were.

'That, my young griffs, was a cannon,' Lieutenant Derryck announced to his audience of two ensigns and a volunteer, all of whom had arrived with the small draft which reached the battalion just before they left Cadiz. 'Two cannon, if I am not very much mistaken.'

The three Johnny Newcombes strained to listen and a little while later there were two more gentle coughs.

'Yes, two guns, most certainly,' Derryck declared. He was not yet twenty and had become a lieutenant just a few weeks ago, after Barrosa. The promotion was not yet confirmed, but that was a formality, for he was the senior ensign and battlefield losses among officers were always replaced by promotion within the regiment.

'French, of course,' added Ensign Messiter, who had first smelt powder at Barrosa and since then had assumed the airs of a veteran.

Pringle watched the pair of them baiting the newcomers, without paying too much attention to their nonsense. It was well past noon and the 106th Foot were about ten miles away from Campo Major. They had been marching all day, knowing that they were catching up with the main force. This was after the long journey from Lisbon, first in barges along the Tagus and then marching through the mud.

'How can you tell the guns are French?' The question came from one of the new ensigns, a small, thin youth, whose uniform jacket and hat were far too large for him. He had large, trusting brown eyes, but what was visible of his face between silk stock, stiff collar and the tip of his hat had erupted in blemishes as vividly scarlet as his jacket.

Pringle noticed his friend Truscott stiffen as the youngster spoke. He had his back to the little group, and was making a conscious show of not listening, but he was also reaching up to run his fingers over the cuff where his empty left sleeve was pinned to the front of his jacket. That was the telltale sign of worry, one his friends knew well. The young ensign was his brother, Samuel, newly joined and a constant source of concern.

'Ah, my lad, it is a simple matter when you know how,' Messiter informed his audience. 'But you must listen very carefully.' He held up a finger and they waited in rapt silence for the next discharges. Around them was a low hubbub of conversation, but few of the men had much inclination to talk. The battalion had come up with the rearmost column of the Portuguese Division. Sensing that there was little point in following closely and stopping every time the regiments ahead of them halted for some unknown cause, the colonel had ordered the 106th to halt for an hour and so the battalion had removed packs and spread out on either side of the road.

'I believe you have frightened them off,' Derryck said.

'Most unreliable, your average Frog.' Messiter held his hand up again for silence, and a moment later came the two faint discharges. 'There, did you not hear it?'

Samuel Truscott shook his head, and the other two simply looked blank.

'It is quite distinct, I do assure you, and your ears will become attuned to it in time,' Messiter insisted. 'The French guns speak with a high-pitched voice, almost an effeminate note. Just what you would expect, of course. When John Bull's cannon fire it is with a deep, manly roar. Even at such a distance the difference is quite distinct, I do assure you.'

The audience appeared deeply impressed.

'And how far away are they?' Ensign Truscott asked, his words beginning as a gruff bass, but breaking into soprano halfway

63

through. Sixteen years and seven months old, his voice had lately broken and so such sudden shifts were frequent, but even so it made him sound nervous. His older brother's fingers ran up and down his empty cuff with greater force.

'Have no fear,' Messiter was generous in his reassurance, 'there is nothing to worry about, although the enemy has great guns able to shoot for three or four miles. They are drawn and fought by blackamoors that Boney picked up in Egypt, for only they are strong enough to work them. Why, I once saw …'

Billy Pringle decided that his friend needed to be distracted from listening to subalterns making game of a younger brother.

'I have been thinking a lot of late,' he began.

Truscott blinked, and shifted his attention to his friend. 'Well,' he said, 'I am sure we are all relieved to hear it.'

Pringle gave a slight bow.

'Do the enemy have many of these great guns?' Young Samuel's words drifted towards them. 'And are they so much more powerful than ours?'

'Perhaps now you understand why he did not follow me to Clare College,' Truscott said. He was a Cambridge man, and Pringle had attended Oxford, making them fairly rare birds in the Army. For Billy Pringle those days seemed more than a lifetime ago, when his family still cherished the optimistic hope that he might become a parson. The Army suited him far better and he had never regretted the change.

'I have been thinking a good deal of matrimony,' Pringle resumed.

'Why, Mister Pringle, this is all so sudden.' Truscott fluttered his eyes and then looked demurely down. 'Is this the letter again?' he asked, but then Billy saw that his attention had drifted back to the subalterns.

'You are being made game of,' Derryck announced. 'Although I suspect that these stout young men are simply being polite to you, Messiter! They can see that age and drink have addled your wits. I shall tell you why we know that those are French guns and not our own. That is if you care to learn the truth?'

'Perhaps we could take a short walk,' Pringle suggested, as

64

the youngsters assured Derryck that they were eager to learn. He felt it better to draw Truscott away, for the captain could not really interfere unless he wanted it known that his brother could not cope on his own. The older subalterns would play on the youngsters, just as they always did and always would. It had happened to them when they were freshly joined and done no real harm.

'It is absurdly simple,' Derryck began with a flourish. 'Those are French guns because we never have any of our own, and even if we have them the Board of Ordnance refuses to permit our gunners to fire them. And do you know why?'

'They should get very dirty, I suppose,' Samuel suggested, and Pringle felt Truscott relax at this sign of humour. He led his friend away off into the fields. Sergeants Dobson and Murphy from his own Grenadier Company were sitting around a fire with some of the men, tending to the contents of a camp kettle. The tantalising scent of bacon came from it. Officers and men alike managed to avoid noticing each other and hence the need for any formality.

'Probably best not to ask where they found that,' Pringle said.

Truscott agreed. 'Or the wood to burn. Although sometimes I wonder whether we are no better than the French.' Since they had arrived in Lisbon they had heard stories of Marshal Masséna's retreat and the barbarity of his soldiers, worse even than things both men had seen in the past. 'We are in Portugal, after all, and these are our allies.'

'True, though I suspect the men feel that since we fight and risk our lives for them they should not resent the loss of the odd chicken or bits of fence for fuel.'

'That was no chicken,' Truscott said, 'but what would you expect of the "bacon bolters"!' It was an old nickname for the grenadiers, traditionally the largest soldiers in a battalion. They tended to claim that they were also the bravest, although the other companies were apt to say that they were merely the least intelligent.

'The difference is that the French would take everything, and hang the farmer and ravish his wife. They would do all that whether or not their officers were there, indeed often under orders. At least our fellows make sure we never catch them stealing, and expect no leniency if they are taken.' Lord Wellington was very strict in punishing plunderers, and if it did not stop the men, at least it placed limits on their abuses.

'Well, that is a difference, I suppose.' Truscott's tone was grudging.

'It is a great difference. If we are not saints then at least we are far from being the worst sinners.'

Truscott smirked. 'As I have said before, it is doubtful that the established Church appreciates what it lost when you laid down the Good Book and picked up the sword – what sermons you might have delivered to shape the morals of your parishioners! Theft to supply your own wants entirely justified, regardless of the dire consequences for those robbed. Our reading from the Book of Pringle, chapter one, verse one.'

'Amen.'

They were far enough away for gentle conversation not to be overheard, and yet still close enough to answer the summons of the drum when the battalion started to move again.

'I take it that the letter is preying on your mind,' Truscott said.

Pringle had charge of a letter from Miss MacAndrews to Williams, given in the hope that their paths would cross. The major's family were in Lisbon and it was not yet clear whether they would join him and the regiment. Much depended on where the 106th were sent and, with the prospect of months of manoeuvring and fighting, they might not come up until the autumn and more settled times.

'It is. And I truly wonder what it contains.'

The letter was sealed and its contents a mystery, so it was hard to know how his friend would react if and when it was delivered. Billy liked Jane MacAndrews, and not simply because she was a beautiful, lively young lady. He liked pretty women, a subject which blissfully occupied his mind for most of his waking hours. In the case of the major's daughter prudence and inclination ensured that he had never acted upon the attraction, save for some vividly imagined scenes. There were plenty of other pretty girls, so he saw Jane as a friend and no more.

Williams loved Miss MacAndrews with a devotion which had only grown stronger with the passing years – and that in itself was another reason for never attempting to win favour with the girl. A friend was a friend, after all. Billy felt closer to Williams, Hanley and Truscott than he did to his own brothers, all naval officers and so rarely seen in recent years. He was unsure of the details, but it had seemed in Cadiz that Williams' dedicated courting was at last beginning to bear some fruit. The girl was almost of age, and perhaps a little more ready to consider a permanent attachment. She was also now of independent means, following a legacy from her mother's American family. That had placed Williams in a quandary, for he dreaded earning the name of fortune hunter. Even so, the pair appeared closer.

'I am convinced the news cannot be so very bad,' Truscott said. 'I do not quite know why, but I have always felt that one day Bills and the lady would marry. They would surely be very happy, or bicker like cats and dogs.' He considered this for a while. 'Most likely both at the same time!'

Pringle had felt much the same, and had become surer of it all last summer. Then they were sent on that disastrous expedition to take Malaga, and Williams was shot down and left behind on the beach. As the months passed without word it became more and more certain that he was dead. The regiment did not return to Cadiz, and so Pringle had not seen the girl, but Hanley visited whenever he was sent to report there. There were also frequent calls from Pringle's older brother Edward, a naval officer whose brig often visited the port. Ned was only lately a widower after his wife died along with the child she had just brought into the world. His brother appeared to have recovered his spirits with remarkable speed, or perhaps, as Hanley thought, it was the grief which had drawn the two of them together. Ned was a personable fellow when he wanted to be, and as enthusiastic an admirer of the fair sex as Billy, especially when flush with prize money.

'Edward writes with confidence, if not quite openly, speaking of good news he hopes to share with the family when he next returns home.' Only six weeks ago Ned had been made post captain, given a frigate and sent to the East Indies. It was unlikely that he would return for a year or more. 'Yet I am certain there is no engagement.'

Truscott agreed, as he had always done when they had discussed this before. 'MacAndrews was not there, so at the very least he has no permission.'

'It is to be hoped that there is not even an understanding. At least not on her part. Ned was always inclined to take anything but a direct and brutal refusal as full assent. I cannot see Miss MacAndrews as a sailor's wife, left alone on shore for most of her life.'

Truscott said nothing. Pringle had raised the subject so many times that there was nothing fresh to say. Yet it was not really of his friend and the major's daughter that Pringle had wished to talk. In the last weeks he had been inching towards a decision, a truly important one, and oddly the distant sound of the guns had brought it to the front of his mind.

'Do you believe it is right for a soldier to marry?' he asked.

'The wives help the men a good deal,' Truscott said, his face relaxing since he obviously believed that the serious conversation was at an end. 'It amazes me again and again how resolutely they follow the battalion through all weathers.'

'What of officers?'

'Oh, I misunderstood, and I would judge that the enquiry is not of a general nature, but specific.' Truscott watched him closely. 'Indeed, something of personal import?'

Pringle nodded.

'Dear me, and I feel that I have failed in the duties of a friend since I have taken insufficient interest in your affairs to know the identity of the lady. Would she be of the Roman faith?'

Pringle wondered whether his friend had heard about Josepha, the lover he had taken when he was on detached service up on the border a year ago. The poor child was fleeing from an unwanted betrothal, and he had given her protection for a short while, but not the permanent union she wanted. For a moment the guilt came back, marring the warm memories of having the girl in his bed. The last he heard she was living with a commissary, but heaven knew where she was now.

'No,' he said, for he had not spoken of the Spanish girl. 'The lady is English, albeit a Methodist.'

'The letters!' Truscott roared loud enough to make faces turn towards them from the nearest cluster of soldiers. 'Why, you cunning file,' he added in a lower voice. 'You mean Williams' sister! But you have only met on a few occasions and then not for a year and a half.'

'That is true.' Anne, the oldest of the three Williams sisters, was a golden memory of his last visit home, and over time the place and the person had merged into a dream of peace and happiness.

Truscott whistled softly through his teeth. 'You do realise that Bills is the head of the household, and so you would have to seek his consent?'

'Yes.'

'He does know you very well,' Truscott said, his tone hinting that this might not prove altogether to Pringle's advantage.

'I am touched by your high opinion of me, truly touched. But this is all to run ahead of ourselves. My concern is whether it is fair to ask a lady to bind herself to me when I do not know when I shall return to England. Or if I ever shall. Would you consider marriage, assuming you formed an attachment?'

Truscott did not reply for a while. Pringle noticed that he was again touching his empty sleeve and hoped that he had not caused his friend distress. Did he worry that no lady would be eager to accept the proposal of a man who had lost his arm.

The drums began to beat, and all around the road the men of the 106th stirred themselves. Fires were doused, and as much of the contents of the kettles saved as was possible.

'We had better go,' Billy said. 'Though I notice that you have not answered my question. Is it fair for a soldier to marry when he might any day be killed?'

'Or maimed…' Truscott's voice was sad. 'Lately, with the boy come to join the battalion, I have come to know what it means to worry. The fear that he will fail, for I do not believe him to be robust or quick witted. Will he become a laughing stock, or still worse be disgraced? And yet most of all I dread having to write home and tell our parents that he has fallen. I suspect they naively believe that I can keep him safe.'

'You will do all that can be done, and your friends will help,' Pringle said, aware that it was little consolation.

They walked in silence, and were about to part to go to their companies when Truscott whispered, 'I know that I have not answered you, my dear Pringle. It is because I do not know what the answer is.'

Formed up on the road in open column, the 106th stepped off at the stentorian command of the sergeant major. They marched for another five hours, stopping for breaks after each hour, and twice more held up by regiments ahead of them. It rained a few times, if never again the deluge of the early morning. The showers fed the already deep mud on the road, and by the time they reached Campo Major every man's white trousers were covered in filth. The 106th had come out to Gibraltar with new uniforms, and had spent months in garrison. Even so the brief campaign of Barrosa and the march from Lisbon had already begun to take their toll. Pringle noticed that several of his grenadiers had the soles of their boots flapping as they walked, and made a note to have that attended to when they stopped.

As they marched past the town the sun dipped beneath the frayed canopy of clouds and bathed the world in light. It had little warmth, but Pringle felt cheered. The sky to the west was a glorious canvas of pinks and gold, and he felt that no one could see such a sight and not feel hope growing within him.

The battalion was led by a guide to a field beside the road and ordered to bivouac for the night. There was something very familiar and comforting about the routine of the camp, even if for the first time in weeks they were not alone, but had battalions all around them. It was the Grenadier Company's turn to provide pickets so it would be a while before he had leisure

to rest. Doing the rounds he passed an open space to the left
of the camp, and noticed some of the subalterns staring at scattered white boulders. Spotting the diminutive shape of Samuel
Truscott, distinctive in his immense hat, Pringle wandered over
to see what they were looking at.

Young Sam suddenly leaned over and Billy heard the sound
of retching.

'Oh, Truscott, you have covered my boots!' squealed one of
the others.

The boulders were corpses, stripped naked before they were
cold, the way he had seen the dead on so many fields. Coming
closer he saw the pale bodies rent about the head and arms with
dreadful cuts, the blood looking black in the fading light.

'This was where the light dragoons broke the French,' Derryck
told him. They had heard rumours ever since they approached the
town, accounts of a heroic charge and of bungling by generals.

Samuel Truscott stood up, looking paler than the bodies, but
then sight or smell struck him again and prompted another loud
burst of vomiting. The boy sank down on to all fours.

'That one is the French colonel.' Derryck gestured at a body
with its head terribly mutilated. 'They say an officer came across
with a flag of truce to find him and then wept by his side. It was
his brother, do you see. Poor fellow.' The sympathy was brief, and
in a moment Derryck's usual exuberance returned. 'Come on,
you fellows, enough of this ghoulish interest. There is a bottle
or two waiting and food as well, so come along. Help Truscott
up if he cannot stand.'

Brothers were a concern, thought Pringle. He had heard that
the Second Division were here as well as the Portuguese and
their own Fourth Division, so he might be able to find Williams,
and perhaps even learn what damage Ned had wrought on his
friend's hopes.

The sun went down, not with the slow grandeur of home,
but still moving enough in its way. Pringle sighed and made up
his mind.

8

'Well, at least we know that they are up to something,' Baynes concluded after listening to Hanley's story and questioning many of the details. 'From what I am told of his activities in the south, Sinclair is fond of besieging fortresses with gold. Which reminds me.' The merchant fished in his pockets for a note. 'That ship your friend Williams helped capture last year, the gold found in it is confirmed as lawful prize and will be distributed. This is the sum your friend is due.'

Hanley took the proffered note, read the columns and was suitably impressed. They had found half a dozen chests hidden beneath a cargo of cotton bales. All had contained gold, and it was suspected that the money was intended to be used to bribe prominent men to accept Joseph Bonaparte as their king. The discovery had been kept secret in the hope of catching some of those involved.

'It will be paid before the year is out, and perhaps sooner,' Baynes continued, 'so our young friend may have less need to continue his career of brigandage, though some would say that the best way to remain rich is to spend only when absolutely unavoidable. You may tell him or not, as you wish.' He took the note back.

The merchant sat down and poured them each a glass of port. He tasted it, winced. 'Heaven knows how I sell this muck,' he muttered, and drained the glass. 'Now then, what do you think is afoot?'

'It looks very much as if Soult has sent Dalmas and Sinclair to gain more *afrancesados* whether in Spain or Portugal or both,'

Hanley suggested. 'They would either pass the money over directly, or more likely provide it to pay agents who would suborn others. It may be simply to win over as many influential men as possible to supporting France, or they may have some specific end in mind.' He sipped the port, found that it was very good and let the warmth spread from his throat to his chest. It had been a long day. 'Do we know of any agent living in Campo Major or near by?'

'No one we thought was important, and the only other one was arrested and taken to Elvas weeks ago. There may be others. There are men willing to turn traitor for pay in every place and every country. I have little doubt that there are plenty of them in London, Lisbon, Cadiz or anywhere else you care to name.'

'So we will leave aside the question of why here for the moment. What of Bertrand?' Baynes refilled his own glass and topped up Hanley's. The room was lit by a large fire and a couple of candles. They were in one of the houses near the walls. Owned by a haulier known to Baynes, the place was empty apart from a couple of servants.

'He was an engineer – quite a good one by the sound of it – so he may simply have come to direct the siege. He was at Ciudad Rodrigo helping to lay out the batteries last year.'

'Odd to bring his mistress.' Baynes produced a loaf and some cheese.

'Yes. That may have been the reason he was ordered here, but there must be more to it. He had debts, very large debts. It appears that he hoped to recover his situation by selling information to us. Perhaps he guessed what Miss Dobson has been doing, or she may have encouraged him.'

Baynes smiled. 'Miss Dobson – how very proper that sounds. Though is she not really the widow Mrs Hanks?'

Hanley could barely remember the big, quiet, rather dull grenadier Jenny had married. A match arranged by her formidable father when it was widely believed that she was already pregnant by someone else. He could not remember telling Baynes about that, although perhaps he had years ago. 'Either, as you like. But I

73

am sure she encouraged him. She says that he had papers, listing the strengths and disposition of all three corps in the south.'

'Useful,' Baynes said, 'if unlikely to make us willing to pay off "very large debts". I sometimes suspect that we are almost as well informed of such things as Marshal Soult himself.'

'The most valuable material was supposed to be in his head,' Hanley explained. 'At least that is what she says.'

'Unfortunate. Most unfortunate, since his head has such a large hole in it. And does she know what he was holding back?'

'No, she says that she does not. Nor is she sure whether he planned to desert or to send her across to us and commence negotiations.'

'Bertrand appears to have been a cautious man,' Baynes said with a measure of respect.

'Not cautious enough, though. Dalmas appeared suddenly – though she does not admit it I am sure Miss Dobson and he know each other – and from then on never left his side. Brandt stayed with them as well. They were not formally under arrest. That was why he made a run for it when he saw the chance.'

'Well, forget him, forget the girl too if you can, at least for the moment. Would you care for cheese? No. Saving yourself, eh? You will find what you asked for in the basket over there, and in the bag. That is for later. As I say, for the moment forget them. In my case I wish that I could forget the execrable dinner provided by Marshal Beresford. Not an experience I can recommend, so perhaps it is all to the good that he rarely issues invitations. However, perhaps I should be grateful for the chance of witnessing the true artistry of his cook – it must take considerable care to ensure that half the food is too hot and half too cold, while at the same time presenting the burnt and the raw in the same dish.

'The marshal's headquarters is not a happy place this evening, not at all, save for the delight they took in finding others to blame for all that went wrong. Well, I am no soldier, not at all, but it causes concern. The peer has given the marshal very strict instructions, and I wonder whether they tie his hands too tightly, rather than guiding them to the task. If only Daddy Hill had not

gone home – at the very least I should have got a better dinner!'
Lieutenant General Hill had fallen ill and returned to England
back in the autumn, and his command was entrusted to Marshal
Beresford. 'With Hill gone, and Craufurd too – now there is a
man who knows a thing or two about bad dinners – we have
to make do with men of lesser capabilities, and the peer cannot
be everywhere at once.

'Well, that is something we cannot govern, so perhaps we
should turn our minds to what we can achieve. So, what do the
French want?'

'They wanted Lisbon,' Hanley said.

'Aye, they did, and they would have taken it last year had it
not been for Lord Wellington and the fortifications prepared at
such cost and effort.' Baynes knew that Hanley had been in the
south when all this happened. 'Masséna ran up against them in
the autumn and then stopped. He stared at them for months,
living in country stripped bare, and stayed far longer than we
believed possible, but somehow he managed it. He must have lost
twenty thousand men, and most of his animals, and then at long
last he went back and has been chased all the way into Spain.
He tried his damnedest to stay in Portugal, but the peer forced
him out. It should be a few months before his army recovers,
although even after all those losses his reinforcements mean that
he will still match or even surpass our numbers. It will not be
so very long before they could try for Lisbon again.'

'What of the fortifications?' Hanley asked. 'Will not the same
thing happen again?'

'Perhaps, but merely stopping them from taking the city last
year cost His Majesty's Government over nine million pounds.
Dear God, nine million! And from all I see this year will be even
more expensive. All that to save a tiny piece of Portugal and then
evict the French from the country for a while. The Whigs do
not like this war – or perhaps it is better to say that they see it as
making the government vulnerable, and party advantage counts
for more than the benefits to the country, so they rant against
it and condemn it at every opportunity. If the Prince Regent

75

decides to dismiss the government and ask his old friends to form a new one, then Portugal and Spain may well be left to their fate.'

Hanley was surprised by Baynes' pessimism. 'Can they not see that defeating the invasion of Portugal was a great victory?' he asked.

'Perhaps, but I do not believe they would see that as of any account. A man who lives in Westminster rarely has much sense of the world beyond. Wellington is a Tory and so they detest him, and disbelieve anything to his credit. And there was no great battle. A victory in the field with masses of enemy shot down and enough of our own poor fellows killed to convince them that it was a hard fight – though not enough to upset them or their dear little consciences – would be harder to ignore. Englishmen, whatever their political inclinations, greatly love reading about a moderately bloody victory.'

'Perhaps we should seek to give them one?'

Baynes beamed. 'The same reasoning that has led so many Spanish armies to attack the French at the first opportunity. It is also why there are scarcely any Spanish armies still in the field. Come, come, dear boy, you know better than that.'

'Well, of course, I am a soldier,' Hanley replied, mocking the merchant's often repeated claims of military ignorance. 'Badajoz, then?'

'If we can, but I dare say the French will not be idle. They have held Ciudad Rodrigo and Almeida since last year and so they control the north road from Spain to Portugal. The lands there have been plundered as Masséna passed, but once he has recovered there is little to stop him advancing again by that route. Lord Wellington hopes to blockade Almeida and starve the garrison into submission – he cannot assault without a siege train, especially since the French have repaired the city's defences.'

'Which means the enemy hold the north road,' Hanley said. 'And in the south we keep Elvas, but they have Badajoz.' There were only two routes into and out of Portugal usable by an army. On each one Spain and Portugal had constructed their own fortress by the border.

'That should make it harder for either side to attack in the south,' he continued. 'If we can take Badajoz then at least we could seal one road.'

'Soult surprised us at the start of the year,' Baynes said, his voice filled with regret, 'and so I have not been doing my job.' The admission was painful. 'It was not that he attacked in the south to support Masséna – the wonder was that he had not done it before – but the speed with which they took Badajoz and the lesser towns along the border – Campo Major scarcely a week ago. Soult's main force has retired to restore control of Andalusia, but a corps remains here, only half the size of Marshal Beresford's forces or perhaps a little larger, but directed with clearer purpose. What are their intentions?'

Baynes refilled their glasses and they drank in silence.

'Foul,' the merchant muttered after a while and then drained the glass. 'Quite foul.'

'I wonder whether the best guide to that might be to consider what we would least like them to do,' Hanley began. 'They are spreading money like water, purchasing support. Is that to ease the path of a new attack, perhaps at Elvas?'

Baynes rubbed his chin, and then slid his fingers inside his collar to scratch.

'That would be a blow without a doubt,' he said. 'It would give them the southern road and permit them to attack again either in the north or south or even both. They still have six or seven times as many soldiers as us and if they had the sense to give up parts of the country and concentrate even a third of those men to move against us then no fortifications in the world would stop them. Even if they do not do that then they keep us boxed in. England will not indefinitely spend so much gold simply to preserve Portugal while Spain is lost.'

'Bertrand as an engineer may well have known of designs on Elvas, and perhaps that was what he planned to sell us?' Hanley wondered.

'Or perhaps they have designs much deeper into Portugal?

Either way, we need to find out anything we can. Do you think the girl knows more?'

Hanley nodded. 'Probably more than she has said, though I doubt too much more.' He thought for a while, and then decided that his vague idea was worth explaining. The thoughts ordered themselves as he spoke and Baynes listened.

'Well, it could be arranged,' the merchant said at the end of it all. 'May I presume that your acquaintances who form part of this scheme remain wholly ignorant of it all? Yes, I thought so. I can arrange it, and it may have considerable merit. It will take a while, but then so will this war. Yet the whole business begs one obvious question.'

'Many, I should have thought,' Hanley said, pleased at Baynes' acceptance.

'Perhaps, but one should come first. Do you trust the girl?' The merchant was studying him intently.

'Jenny Dobson is clever,' Hanley said. 'She has supplied us with a good deal of useful information.'

'And appears to have been caught – perhaps not for the first time given what happened to you last year. Anyway, are you answering a different question to the one I asked?'

'I believe she has some loyalty to her country, but ultimately her efforts are directed at making her own fortune.'

'A whore, then, in every respect,' Baynes said, his tone flat. 'That at least lends a degree of predictability. Sad to say that agents who work for their own gain are often more reliable than the idealists, unless their ideals are consistent and wholly in agreement with our own aims. Yet it does pose the danger that we may be outbid.'

'As you say, that ought to be predictable.'

'My dear William,' Baynes said, 'it does appear a worthy experiment and so I will do what I can.' He refilled his own glass and raised the bottle in Hanley's direction.

'No, thank you. I ought to be going.'

'Yes. Well, there is one last question, and I do not expect an answer because the words would mean very little. I speak merely as a friend.' He drank again, licking his lips. 'It is simply this. In this matter, my dear boy, do you trust yourself? No, as I said, do not bother to answer.'

Jenny sat on a chair beside the fire, a blanket wrapped tightly round her shoulders. She was reading and that surprised him. In the past he had received written reports from her, so knew that she could write a fair round hand, but for some reason Hanley had never thought of the soldier's daughter as even vaguely interested in books.

The girl looked up and glared at him. 'Took your bleedin' time.'

'My humblest apologies,' Hanley said. He nudged the door shut behind him and walked over to the table. Apart from another chair and the simple bed it represented all of the furniture in this attic room with its steeply slanting ceiling. They were in the house Baynes had taken, and Jenny had been left here on her own for more than two hours. 'How are you?'

'Hungry and cold.'

Hanley put a basket down on the table. 'There is some food here, although we will need to cook it.'

Jenny snorted. 'When a man says that he means I'll need to cook it for him.'

'It might be better. There are also some clothes.' He gently put a laundry bag down. 'All I could get for the moment. There will be more and better when we reach Elvas.'

'Bloody well hope so,' she murmured, but did not get up or even look up from the book.

'I have something else which you may like to have returned.'

Jenny slammed the heavily bound book shut and laid it on the floor. The blanket came loose, showing a couple of the buttons on her hussar jacket glinting red in the firelight before she pulled the covering tightly around herself again.

'An interesting read?' he asked.

'Bloody awful. Some old French fart talking about fish, but

there was nothing else here and I like to practise.' The boldness faded, and Jenny looked shy after making the admission.

Hanley felt fresh surprise at this reminder that the girl spoke and read French, still more at this desire to learn. He opened the basket and took out an envelope which he gave to the girl.

'I tried to keep it as flat as I could.'

Jenny frowned in suspicion, but took it and pulled out the single sheet of paper. She looked at it for a while and said nothing. 'That's me,' she said, and began to cry.

Nothing surprised him any more. It was the sketch he had drawn of her back in England before the regiment went to Portugal in '08. It had been a present to mark the girl's wedding, and Jenny had slipped it to him while he was unconscious and a prisoner of the French. He had kept it ever since, not quite sure why.

'Don't cry, Jenny,' he said for want of anything better. He was unsure whether the girl was acting or genuinely moved.

'Is Da all right?' she asked, eyes and cheeks still moist. 'And the others?' Jenny never mentioned her abandoned son, Jacob, who was being raised by Major MacAndrews and his wife.

'Yes, when I last saw them. The battalion is camped outside the town if you want to see your father.'

'No.' Jenny seemed to have hunched down and for once looked small. 'Doubt he'd want to see me.' She raised the picture again and stared at it in silence for a long while.

'You were very pretty, even then,' Hanley said.

Jenny swayed her head a little from side to side, as if considering. 'Too skinny,' she concluded, and stood up, letting the blanket drop down in a fluid motion. That, at least, was certainly a practised gesture. He thought of Cleopatra coming before Caesar, but did not think of it for long.

'Don't you think I look better now?'

Her figure was certainly fuller, something made very clear by the snug-fitting hussar uniform. She was a little taller as well, certainly straighter in her carriage, and a good deal more confident.

'Those clothes must be damp,' he said. 'I am surprised that you have not removed them.'

'Oh yes,' she snorted. 'And what was I supposed to wear? You have only just turned up.' She came over to the table, close to him now, and her hair brushed against him as she inspected the contents of the laundry bag. There was another snort.

'It was the best I could obtain at short notice.'

Jenny looked up at him, her eyes big. 'I'll need help.'

'Thought you were a big girl now,' Hanley said.

She turned around, leaning against the table, and ran a finger along the middle of the three rows of pewter buttons on the front of her tight dolman jacket. Hanley watched. He had not been with a woman for a long time and her performance was a good one.

'This get-up was Bertrand's idea. The Prince up north had his mistress dressed up like a young officer.'

'I know.' The stories about the elderly Marshal Masséna and the young wife of one of his staff had reached the British many months ago. It was said that officers were offended, and the wife of General Junot outraged by her presence.

'Bertrand and a few of his friends wanted the same. I only chose the colour.'

'It was a good choice.'

'Bloody uncomfortable.' She unfastened the top button. 'The breeches are the worst. Every time I had to wear them Bertrand would get his philistine to sew me into them. Couldn't put them on otherwise.'

'I'll wager he enjoyed that.'

'Henri? No, not him. Don't think he cared much for women, but the bugger was a dab hand with a needle.'

A second button was undone, then a third. Jenny held his gaze and then flicked her eyes down. 'You'll need to help with the breeches,' she said softly. 'The seams have to be cut and I can't reach.'

Hanley gently brought his hands up to the girl's shoulders. She quivered at the touch, looking up again.

81

'Why do they call them philistines? It's from the Bible, isn't it?'

He nodded and said nothing. French officers used the nickname for their servants, but he did not care why they did so.

Hanley moved quickly, hands grabbing the sides of her jacket and tugging it open with all the force he could muster. There was a soft sound of tearing and the next three buttons snapped from their threads and fell away. The girl was right, the stitching was good, for he had hoped to rip the jacket open. He tried again, but it took a third violent rip to complete the job.

'I said I needed help with the breeches.' There was challenge in her eyes and a smile on her lips.

'No wonder you are cold,' Hanley said, for Jenny was bare underneath.

'There is no room to wear anything. At least, that's what Bertrand said, but I think he just liked it that way.' She noticed him glance down at her breeches and her smile broadened. 'Yes,' she said. 'Or rather, no, there isn't.'

Hanley peeled the jacket off and then lifted her in his arms. Left in only breeches and boots, she clung to him and responded when he kissed her. He felt strong and alive, a thrill akin, if not quite the same, to the exhilaration of riding in the cavalry charge. With one hand he started to fumble with the buttons on her breeches. They were stiff and hard to move. He gave up, contenting himself with letting his hand feel her shape through the material, and still they kissed.

They went over to the bed.

''Bout time,' she said.

9

It took a long time for the ensign to dry out, so it was just as well that it took another seven trips to ferry the rest of the battalion and its baggage over the river. Samuel Truscott sat by a fire lit by soldiers of the Light Company, while his uniform was stretched over a triangle of branches to make the most of the heat. It was one of several fires as the two companies of the 106th made themselves comfortable and waited.

'How on earth did it happen?' Williams asked.

Pringle shrugged. 'Goodness knows, although it would not surprise me if my young fool was not part of it. A wager, probably – see whether they could walk along the side of the pontoon without falling in.'

'Well, I suppose at least we know the answer to that question.'

They were on the east bank of the River Guadiana, almost two hundred yards wide at this spot and at least chest deep after the recent rains. Marshal Beresford wanted to surround Badajoz, which meant getting across the river, but there were not enough pontoons to build a bridge. Instead the engineers had rigged up a system of ropes and pulleys so that a single boat went back and forth, carrying about one hundred men on each trip.

'We came across yesterday morning,' Williams said. 'Wholly dry,' he added with a smile.

'If Dobson and Evans had not acted so fast to fish him out then we would not all have got across at all,' Pringle said sourly. 'Poor Truscott is worrying himself half to death about the lad.'

'Hard, I should imagine. Still, if Sergeant Evans thought he was worth saving then that is a good sign.' Williams had served with the Light Company at Barrosa and knew Evans to be a good soldier, but an angry, ill-disposed man. 'Dobson would bother regardless of who it was, but Evans...'

Only the first boatload of the 106th had crossed, carrying all of the Light Company and most of the Grenadier Company, both sadly depleted after the desperate fighting at Barrosa. Williams was waiting for the next load to arrive, for he needed to cross back to the far bank.

'Some of our ammunition mules have gone astray,' he explained. 'I expect it is those rascals in the Fourth Division, thieving again!'

'No doubt about it,' Pringle replied cheerfully. 'Rogues to a man. I am sure that we will fit in.' The 106th had joined the Fusilier Brigade, the senior brigade of the Fourth Division under Sir Lowry Cole. There were two other battalions, the 1/7th or Royal Fusiliers and the 1/23rd or Royal Welch Fusiliers.

'How do you find your new comrades?' This was the first time Williams had seen his own battalion, or any of his particular friends, apart from Hanley, in the ten days since the 106th had reached the rest of the army.

'A little sullied by the introduction of a mere battalion of the line into their august company.' A century earlier fusiliers had been the first regiments in the army to carry flintlock muskets instead of the old matchlock, and they clung jealously to this ancient distinction. All companies wore shoulder wings like the flank companies of other battalions, and on parade in England the men sported fur caps like old-fashioned grenadiers.

'There is the usual more or less concealed and mutual suspicion,' Pringle continued, 'with occasional acts of open hostility. I do not recall ever having served alongside other corps without much the same things happening. In this case one might feel that their own self-esteem ought to have been punctured by the simple truth that when we joined neither of the other battalions possessed a single pair of shoes to their name. Now they have ugly local ones, of dull buff leather and with seams on the inside. Poor devils have enough to worry about hobbling along in those without bickering with us. I remember a few of the Seventh from Talavera, so acquaintances have been resumed and some introductions made.'

They watched the pontoon coming closer to this eastern bank.

Pringle sighed. 'About two more minutes I should think. Then I shall have to tell friend Truscott that I nearly managed to lose his brother.'

'Billy,' Williams began, and hesitated. 'Is the major well,' he said after a moment, 'and his family?'

'Pringle, you are a numbskull!' His friend started patting his jacket. 'Now where did I put it.' Eventually he found what he wanted in a waistcoat pocket. 'They are all well, so far as I know, but I have correspondence. A letter from your sister and another from a certain lady.'

Williams felt his heart quicken, excitement and fear both rising, and it took an effort not to snatch the letters.

'Thank you,' he said, marshalling himself. 'Has my sister also written to you?' Williams was aware that the pair corresponded, although he remained unsure what significance to attach to this. It might be no more than friendship and gratitude on Anne's part, since Pringle had fought a duel to defend the reputation of his second sister, putting a ball through a young cavalry officer who had abandoned her and helping to arrange their subsequent marriage.

'She has, and so I am happy to tell you that your family are all in good health. Mrs Garland's infant caught a chill some time ago, but has been nursed back to health.' Williams suspected more by Anne's hands than those of the child's mother, but this might have been unfair. 'In all other respects they have passed a pleasant enough winter.'

Pringle took off his glasses and polished the lenses with the fringe of his crimson sash. It was a familiar ritual, one he never cared to have interrupted, and so Williams did not speak. The pontoon was almost across, and soon he would have to go. He was still holding the letters, and so used this opportunity to put them into his sabretache – the waterproof case fixed to the scabbard of his sword. All cavalrymen carried them, but as

85

a staff officer he also found it useful and had acquired one. He wondered what Miss MacAndrews had written, dreading the final destruction of his hopes. Hanley had told him that he had more prize money to come, several times greater than the award he had already received. It was not true wealth, his friend had warned, but still a sum of several thousand.

Williams had never possessed so much in his life – that was assuming his friend was correct, and Hanley usually knew about such things. Not a fortune, then, certainly not on the scale of Miss MacAndrews' let alone that of a nabob, but if not quite her equal it would have made it possible for him to seek her hand without disgrace. It was a bitter irony for this to have happened when it must surely be too late.

Pringle coughed. 'My dear fellow,' he began, 'there is something…' They were interrupted by a screech. Sam Truscott was hopping about, one boot on and the other half off, yelling in horror. Men laughed as he passed, and then dodged when he flung the loose boot away. Something green-brown in colour leapt from it. Captain Truscott was on the newly arrived pontoon, leading his company off, and his face was grim as he stared at his younger brother.

'Who would have a brother,' Pringle said.

'I dearly wish that you did not,' Williams said under his breath, although he feared that his friend caught either the words or the sense. 'I had best be off,' he added out loud, ashamed of himself, and walked over to unhitch Francesca's reins. He led the mare towards the pontoon. 'Steady, lass, steady,' he whispered to the horse as she shied a little at the sight of the wooden ramp propped against the boat. He and Truscott exchanged pleasantries, although he could tell that all the time the captain was really watching young Sam.

'Visit us again soon, Bills,' Pringle called, his voice no longer serious. 'It is well known that staff officers never have anything useful to do!'

Williams coaxed the mare into the pontoon. The only other person going back across the river was a commissary, a sallow-faced little man with prominent yellow front teeth, who gabbled away for the entire trip, barely pausing for breath. Williams made appropriate noises, but paid no real attention. If on his own he might have been tempted to read the letter – and that from his sister as well in due course, but he could not pretend that this absorbed his thoughts. It was not something to be done in company, for he feared its contents and his own reaction. Instead he tried to think on other matters.

'Do you know how quickly an army eats up stores of food, sir?' The question broke through his musings by its sheer volume. For just a moment the commissary looked abashed.

'I understand it to be very swift,' Williams said. He wondered whether the man judged him to be fresh in the country from the newness and quality of his jacket. Staff officers were so often friends brought out fresh from England with little knowledge of the country or of war.

'You are most correct, my dear sir, and so is it to be helped if there is not always sufficient when many thousands of soldiers arrive at short notice? Why, a man can only do so much if he is not informed, and is it my fault if some then go without...'

Williams suspected that the man was preparing his excuses for higher authority. No doubt he had made some error – gross even by the low standards of commissaries – but it did not appear to affect his own brigade and so he once again tried to ignore the flow. The army was bigger these days, there was no doubt about it. With two British divisions and one of Portuguese along with the cavalry, Marshal Beresford commanded more men than had fought under Sir Arthur Wellesley at Vimeiro, and almost as many as the British had fielded at Talavera. Yet this was only a part, and the smaller part, of the army, and the same Sir Arthur was now Lord Wellington, and led another six divisions further north, watching Marshal Masséna. The war was becoming less intimate, and there were far more officers and whole corps that Williams simply did not know, even by sight or reputation.

★

The sun was low in the sky by the time Williams recrossed the river, having waited for forty minutes until room was found for him. The 106th and their brigade had gone when he reached the far bank, in a pontoon filled with Portuguese infantry. He came without the missing mules and their drivers and escort, who seemed to have crossed during the afternoon while he was looking for them at the brigade's former campsite. Williams did not understand how he had passed them, but there was no longer any doubt about it, and he found them already on the east bank and half a mile from the crossing. Telling the sergeant in charge to wait there because he would send back for them, Williams rode on to find the brigade.

They were not where they were supposed to be, but a brigade of KGL guns was there, watering its horses and settling down for the night. They had arrived only an hour ago, but the German captain thought that the infantry had been moved further down the road.

'*Ja*, the first brigade. If not there, then they have gone to the left.'

That was the opposite direction and seemed unlikely. Francesca was tired, so he kept her to a walk as he followed the road. There was no sign of anyone else. Half the army, perhaps more, were across the river, and yet here he was riding past fields that seemed to be empty. As the sun set he saw the roofs of a village a quarter of a mile away. That must be Villa Real, where the marshal and his staff were, but he had no desire to ride in there and ask where his own brigade was – not unless he had to. Williams was glad that he had left the sergeant and the mule train behind. It was bad enough wandering about on his own, but at least he was not dragging unwilling pack animals and drivers with him.

Williams rode on, and wondered what was in the letter, for he had been in company or moving all day, and there had been no opportunity to read it. He tried to force the thoughts down. He was riding in the dark and seemed to have lost the army. Williams could not afford to let his concentration wander. By now he must be near the outposts of the army. Perhaps Colborne's brigade had been given this task, and perhaps not, but someone would be out here watching the French. Men got nervous at night, especially when the enemy were near. It was eleven days since the charge at Campo Major and the French had been unusually quiet. The slow crossing had meant that for the first day less than a third of the army was stranded on its own on the east bank. They were vulnerable, outnumbered by the French and with nowhere to run if driven back. It was a risk, perhaps even a mistake, and yet either the French did not realise what was happening or they chose not to act. That did not mean that they would remain idle for ever.

Francesca stopped and sniffed the air. Her ears twitched and she arched her neck, stepping back, and then turning when he tried to calm her. Williams scanned the fields around them, silvered by the light of the moon and stars. He caught the faint smell of wood smoke and, listening, heard soft voices on the air.

Williams nudged the mare on, cutting away from the track in the direction of the sound and smell. They splashed through a little stream, and then he saw a darker patch against the night. Closer he saw the outline of a wood, the red glint of fires coming from beyond it. He checked that his sword was loose in its scabbard, and went on carefully. No one challenged him, and he saw no signs of sentries or pickets. He stopped, waited for his breathing to steady, and listened again. The voices were stronger, and he heard someone roar with laughter. He could not catch the words, but struggled to believe that he could have ridden through his own army and ended up in the enemy lines. Williams patted the mare on the neck and they walked on.

'Clumsy sod, look where you're going!'

This time there was no doubting the words or the language. He pushed on with more confidence, but still with caution. Passing round the edge of the copse he saw a couple of huts, and beside them lines of tethered horses, half a dozen campfires, and men either sitting by them or rolled in their blankets.

He saw the sentry standing carbine in hand just as the man challenged.

'Lieutenant Williams, One Hundred and Sixth Foot, on the staff of Colonel Colborne,' he replied.

'Advance, friend.'

'Major Morres, Thirteenth Light Dragoons,' the officer in command said when Williams was introduced. 'Do you bring us new orders?' he asked, the voice weary, but resigned to the ways of the army.

'No,' Williams said, and saw the look of relief.

'Thank God. This is the first food we have had for two days and the lads need a rest. Would you care to join us, Mr Williams, or do you have pressing duties? You must be tired, out and about at this late hour, and your horse certainly appears in need of a rest.' Morres peered at Francesca, and the mare chose this moment to stick out her splayed teeth and roll her long tongue. 'That is a horse, I take it?' the cavalryman added.

Williams explained that he was searching for his brigade.

'God knows where they are.' Morres and his squadron had been on picket duty for a day and a half. 'We were only just relieved by the Portuguese a couple of hours ago and sent back to rest. So there is nothing beyond us apart from their outposts – oh, and Johnny Crapaud beyond that, I suppose. There have been hussars lurking about all day, but they did not seem inclined to try anything. We still have a picket on the far right near the river, but the rest of the front is covered by the Portuguese.

'So I would guess the Second Division and your lot will be back towards the river somewhere. No sense blundering off until you have rested. Join us in some food and a pipe and then be on your way. There is plenty of time for you to get lost again before the night is out!'

The major and three other officers shared one of the huts.

'Keep something for Macrea,' Morres told the soldier who brought them their stew. 'I sent the cornet back to report to General Stewart. If he returns he may be able to tell you where your brigade is placed. That is if the fellow can find his way back in the dark!' A cornet was the most junior officer in the cavalry, ranking with an ensign.

Williams asked them about the outpost duty, and as he listened to the explanations remembered another night, visiting the greenjackets of the 95th when they had watched the border country up north.

While they were eating, one of the lieutenants looked at Williams. 'I know you, do I not?' The man rubbed his chin. 'Yes, you were with us at Campo Major. Near Logan when he chopped down the French colonel.'

The news caused Morres to become even more hospitable, especially when Williams praised the boldness of the 13th and the success of their charge.

'It was most gallant, and I believe that the whole army shares in my admiration.'

The cavalrymen smiled, exchanging glances.

'That is what all the fighting soldiers say,' the lieutenant who had recognised him said. 'They know that the fault in exploiting the success was not our own.'

'The marshal blamed us to Lord Wellington, who wrote a stiff rebuke and ordered that it be read to us on parade.' Morres waved his spoon in barely controlled anger. '"Undisciplined ardour!"' His voice grew louder. '"Their conduct was that of a rabble, galloping as fast as their horses would carry them over the plain!"' By now he had stood up and was shouting. 'Threatening to dismount us and set us to guarding stores! God damn them all. Take our horses, would they!' The major looked around wildly. 'You must excuse me,' he said in a more controlled tone, and went out of the room.

'It is an understandably difficult matter for us,' the lieutenant explained. 'It is to be hoped that when Lord Wellington learns the truth he will alter his opinion.'

'I am sure that is true,' Williams agreed. Privately he had his doubts. From all he had heard and the little he had seen, the commander of the army was a shrewd man, but not one inclined to make public admission of a mistake.

'Brigadier General Long paraded us and read out the rebuke as ordered,' the lieutenant continued. 'Then in front of us all he ordered that it would never be entered in the records of the regiment.'

Morres reappeared. 'Please excuse my passion,' he said gruffly. 'The injury is still a fresh one.'

Williams stood and offered his hand. 'I most earnestly believe that every corps in Portugal holds the Thirteenth in the highest esteem.' He smiled. 'Though I suspect in the case of the enemy that esteem is mixed with fear!'

Morres took his hand with a grip like a vice and pumped it vigorously while the subalterns stamped their feet and called out 'Hear, hear!'

'Will you stay the night, Mr Williams? It is well after half past two in the morning, so I doubt that you will get any rest if you do not take it with us.'

'Thank you, you are most kind, but I must get on. I have come to suspect that Colonel Colborne has little need for sleep and expects similar unceasing exertion from his staff!'

'Well, goodnight to you.'

One of the lieutenants accompanied him out and called softly for a soldier to bring Williams his mare. Most of the squadron were asleep, huddled around the dying fires. Deep breathing and more than a few definite snores mingled with the shuffling of the horses. Williams noticed that they had taken the bridles as well as the saddles off and asked about this.

'Worth taking any opportunity to give the beasts some relief,' explained the lieutenant. 'The Portuguese are ahead of us, so if the alarm is given we should have an hour's warning. Half that time would be enough in a pinch.' He grimaced when Francesca was brought over. 'I trust she has a good nature.'

'Well, goodnight to you.' Williams hauled himself into the saddle and reached down to shake hands.

'Good luck finding your missing brigade!' came the reply.

IO

A tall French officer on a big horse watched as Williams bid his farewell to the lieutenant, but was too far away in the darkness to recognise a man he had once fought. Not that it would have mattered or changed his actions in the slightest, for he had the enemy at his mercy and had no intention of showing them any.

Jean-Baptiste Dalmas lifted the heavy helmet up for a moment and adjusted it. After all these years the major no longer paid much heed to its weight or for that matter to the awkwardness of the back- and breastplates of the cuirass he wore. The makers claimed that it would stop a bullet, but he had seen too many fellow cuirassiers shot down at close range to believe their lies. It would stop sword or lance, but since that was no protection to arms, legs or face it did not make a man safe. Yet there was something about the gleam of the steel armour that frightened opponents, and a frightened enemy was always easier to beat.

Dalmas did not wear his regiment's uniform for that reason. Most cuirassier officers dispensed with helmet and armour when they were not in action or on parade, let alone if detached to the staff. Marshal Soult's ADCs paraded about in hussar uniforms. Dalmas was an unofficial member of the marshal's staff, but was sure that no one would question him if he aped them, or simply adopted a smart but simple and practical undress uniform. Instead he remained a cuirassier, and he knew that it was mainly through pride. The cuirassiers were an elite, the heavy horsemen who had ridden over all the armies of Europe, and he was proud to wear their uniform. More than that, it showed the world that he was no pampered headquarters man, but a fighting soldier.

'Draw swords!' he hissed without turning around. Behind him came a series of faint scrapes as the hussars drew their curved sabres. Dalmas glanced to his right and could just make out the darker shadow of the other squadron about a hundred yards away. There were faint gleams as the sabres were drawn. The 2ième Hussars were a good regiment.

'Walk,' he said softly, and walked his horse up the low bank beside the lane and down into the field. Harness creaked and bits and buckles gave off soft metallic noises as the squadron followed him.

Dalmas wondered whether he would ever understand the English. They fought well – take them head-on and they would pound away at you and not give up – and sometimes they were clever. No one had guessed that Lord Wellington would fortify the approaches to Lisbon as he had done and then just wait for the French to starve. It was not very glorious, but it was effective, and Dalmas, like his Emperor, admired such ruthless calculation.

The English were tough. Not tough like the Russians, who fought like tethered bears – strong, ferocious, but unthinking in their rage. The Austrians made war scientifically, organised everything, and then lost scientifically because they never coped with chance or the enemy failing to do what was expected. Back in '06 the Prussians had been brave, but so badly led that they never had much of a chance. Dalmas had fought and beaten them all, and since then ridden down Spanish and Portuguese armies more times than he could remember.

The English could fight and they could be clever, and then they did something like this. He had been with the cavalry outposts for the last few days, growing ever more angry because no one senior would take the decision to attack when the enemy were divided as they crossed the Guadiana. Until this afternoon the English light dragoons had done a good job of watching the French on the roads to Olivenza. Then a fresh regiment took over – Portuguese by the look of them, but surely English-led.

94

Dalmas had watched them riding along opposite their outposts until he was sure. There was a gap, a great wide empty space of more than half a mile, on their left. As the sun set he took two hussars and rode in for a closer look. The fields were dotted with copses and woodland, offering plenty of cover, and there was not an Allied soldier to be seen.

At midnight he led this raid, moving carefully, for part of him still struggled to believe that the enemy could make such a mistake. Once again he rode ahead with only a few men, and let the squadron columns follow. They found a campsite, embers still glowing and warm.

'Six hours,' was the verdict of a corporal with drooping moustaches, a pigtail and braids or *cadenettes* on either side of his forehead.

They went on, and still no challenge came. An hour later, they spotted the fires, and then he and the corporal walked close enough to see the enemy camp. It took time to go back and bring up the main force. Even this little expedition had tired the horses. In Spain and Portugal the French cavalry never got any rest from patrols, outpost duty, escorting convoys and chasing *guerrilleros*. Weeks went by without the chance to unsaddle, for all too often the squadrons slept at the ready. The horses were tired, badly fed, plagued with sores on their backs. The 2ième looked after their horses better than some, but even so the animals were small, unhealthy beasts compared to the fine mounts regiments like this had ridden in Germany and Poland just a few years earlier.

Dalmas halted. 'Form line,' he called. The English were two hundred yards away and no one stirred. He could see the officer on horseback talking to the one on foot, but it would have been hard for them to see past the firelight into the dark night beyond.

Glancing back, he saw that the hussars were ready, with one company of fifty men in two ranks and the second company of the squadron behind them. He could not see much detail, could barely make out the silhouettes of the men in their flat-topped shakos, let alone see the fat grass bellies of their little horses.

Dalmas turned back to face the enemy camp. There was no point waiting for they were perfectly placed. His job these days was to help outwit the enemy, seeing through their deceptions and fooling the English with lies of their own. For the moment, it was mainly a matter of delay – slow the enemy down and so allow just a little more time to repair the walls of Badajoz and be ready to resist their attack.

Yet at heart he was a cavalryman, a schoolteacher turned soldier who had discovered that he was very good at his new profession. The Emperor rewarded talent and so the conscript cavalryman had become an NCO and then an officer. Dalmas longed to be given his own regiment of cuirassiers and let loose against the foes of France.

He raised his sword above his head.

'Charge!' he yelled, and before he nudged its sides his big gelding was cantering.

'*Vive l'empereur!*' The cry split the night air.

In battle a cavalry charge should start slowly, gain speed by stages to keep the ranks in order and only for the last short stretch reach an all-out gallop. That was against a formed enemy ready to meet the attack. Here his enemies were helpless, taken completely unaware, so all that mattered was speed to complete their destruction.

Men stirred in the camp. He heard the first shouts, then a challenge.

'*Vive l'empereur!*' The hussars were surging around him, all order gone, but it did not matter.

The shouts became louder as drowsy men in the camp woke to the horror rushing towards them. A man sprang up from behind a bush, his bare bottom very white in the darkness as he clutched at his trousers. He fled, lost grip of his pants and then tripped and fell, saving him from the slash of a hussar's sabre.

Dalmas reached the camp, thrust at one of the enemy, driving the tip of his sword into the man's neck and then riding on. He saw the shape of another man appear and this time cut down into his skull. All around him he heard screams and the grunts of the hussars as they swung their blades and drove them through flesh, muscle and bone. There was a shot, just one, the flame appallingly bright in the gloom, but few of the enemy showed any signs of fight. In the glow of the firelight he saw the mounted officer waving a pistol, as the one on foot leapt barebacked on to a horse. Dalmas spurred towards them, but a knot of men were in his way. One had a sabre, the blade glinting red, so he pulled on his reins and kicked the sides of his horse so that it rose in a well-practised move, hoofs flailing in the air. The men spilt up, and Dalmas cut down, slicing through the man's eye and cheek. His horse was back on all fours, and as the soldier screamed and clutched his face, Dalmas thrust neatly into the man's chest, feeling metal grate on rib before it slid past.

A shot punched the air and ripped through the epaulette on his right shoulder. Dalmas swayed with the impact, saw that it was the officer who had fired, and cut down at another of the soldiers near him. The two British officers turned their horses and fled, the man riding bareback with hands gripping the animal's mane. A screaming figure ran into the neck of his horse, and he had raised his sword to strike when he saw the long hair and terrified face of a woman looking up at him.

Men raised their hands and shouted out that they surrendered. Many of the hussars still sliced with their sabres.

'They're English, take them prisoner!' a hussar captain shouted, his deep voice carrying over the chaos of the captured camp.

'Get those horses!' Dalmas yelled, pointing with his sword. 'Don't let any get away.' The animals were a far more valuable prize than any prisoner, useful though those might be. The British had the best horses in the whole Iberian peninsula – some said the best in the world. They were certainly better than any remount ever likely to come the way of the 2ième Hussars.

'Stop, man!' Dalmas passed a sergeant grabbing the sword-arm of one of the hussars. 'It's over.'

A flurry of shots rang out as the other squadron fired into the night.

'Some of them are hiding in a marsh,' their captain explained. 'Can't follow them, but we might get lucky and hit a few.'

'Any losses?' Dalmas asked.

The man grinned and shook his head. It was the same with the other hussar squadron.

'Are we going on, sir?' the captain asked.

Dalmas felt the temptation. It had all been so easy, and here they were inside the enemy outpost line. They could ride on, seeking more prey while the English still had no idea what was happening.

'No,' he said. They were only two squadrons and could not take on an entire army, no matter how surprised. 'Secure the horses and the prisoners, and let's get away before they realise we are here. Who is this?'

Two hussars were leading along a figure on foot, a bareheaded British officer with his jacket undone.

'And you are, sir?' Dalmas' English was clear if accented and slow, learned years before from Jenny Dobson.

'Morres, sir, major in the Thirteenth Light Dragoons.'

'Then, although I regret to say that you are now our prisoner, I am otherwise pleased to make your acquaintance. My name is Major Dalmas of the Thirteenth Cuirassiers.' There was no harm in courtesy to a beaten enemy. 'If you will give me your word not to try to escape, you may have your sabre.'

Morres' eyes flicked from side to side. There were still three or four hours before dawn, and in the darkness a man might be able to slip away. Dalmas knew that the man was thinking about it, just as he would have done in the same position.

'I cannot, sir.'

'I understand.' Dalmas switched back to French, 'You two, keep a close guard on him and the other officers.'

Dalmas walked his horse away to join the two squadron commanders.

'Gentlemen, a very good night's work. These are the Thirteenth Dragoons, so we have some vengeance for Colonel Chamorin and his dragoons.' The hussar officers both smiled. 'Well done, all of you. Now let's make it a better night still by slipping away without being seen.'

Dalmas wiped his sword on his horse's mane and slid it back into its sheath. Reaching up, he felt the damage to his epaulette and wondered whether the Englishman had been aiming at him for any reason other than that he was leading the charge and bigger than anyone else. There had been that fellow at Campo Major – the one Sinclair said was the elusive Captain Hanley. It was hard to be sure in the darkness, but he did not think this was the same man.

Well, for the moment it did not matter. Such thoughts could wait for tomorrow, when he went back to scheming. Enjoy tonight, he thought to himself, and relish the sheer joy of leading cavalry into battle and crushing the enemy.

Around him the two squadrons had formed up, with hussars detached to lead strings of captured horses and escort the prisoners. The captured woman was bandaging her husband's arm and would go with them. Three of the British were so badly wounded that they would have to be left.

'Right, lads,' he said, 'let's go home.'

'Two officers, a sergeant major, five corporals, two each of trumpeters and farriers, and forty private soldiers. In addition sixty troop horses, a brace of mules, and about a dozen horses owned by the officers.' Williams finished reading out the list and folded the paper away. He had noted the figures down because he could still not quite believe what had happened.

'Dear God,' Captain Dunbar said. 'That's a whole troop of cavalry gone.'

Colborne sat in silence on the camp chair, staring up at the roof of their tent.

'So soon after Campo Major, as well,' Dunbar went on, 'when the same regiment put the fear of the Lord into the French. All those men, and all those horses.' The captain's lip curled. 'Notice they did not take that ugly brute of yours, though!'

'I did not wait around to present them with the opportunity,'

Williams said, knowing the mockery was well intended. He thought back to the night and the desperate ride to escape. 'The situation was hopeless, and it seemed the best thing to raise the alarm, and especially to warn Villa Real. It was no more than half a mile away, with no troops in between.'

Dunbar gave a low whistle. 'What a chance the French missed there. They could have snapped up Marshal Beresford and half the senior officers of the army.'

'It may not have been too great a loss.' The colonel spoke in a whisper, probably unaware that he had voiced the sentiment.

Dunbar looked embarrassed. 'Who is to blame?' he said to Williams. 'That is what I should like to know.'

'The Thirteenth thought that they were screened by the Portuguese cavalry, but there was a big gap in the line of vedettes,' Williams explained. He and the dragoon lieutenant had given the alarm in Villa Real, and then watched as various senior officers and staff men ran about half clad and shouting. It took a good twenty minutes to achieve any sort of order. Marshal Beresford's hulking figure was in the middle of it all, and he gave Williams a splenetic glare when he recognised him. Later, as things grew calm, the marshal was moderately civil when he asked the two lieutenants to report.

'Well, sirs, you have done well,' he told them in a gruff voice.

Williams had waited in the village until dawn, with little to do. He saw Hanley and was able to tell him that he had seen Dalmas before his friend was summoned away. Later, as the sun rose, Baynes passed, bid him good morning, and then hinted that the senior officers were now busy blaming each other. 'You may as well go,' he suggested. 'This is probably not the best place to be at the moment.'

Williams took his advice, having already found out where his brigade was encamped, a spot almost four miles from the site chosen the day before. On the way he roused the sergeant and the mule train and led them back as well.

The brigade had no orders to move today, so he had found

the colonel and the captain taking breakfast. That was half an hour ago, and a warm welcome was followed by many questions.

'A blunder, a truly bad blunder,' Dunbar concluded.

'The fault is not with the men,' Colonel Colborne spoke aloud this time, looking at each of his companions in turn, 'but the higher powers who gave poor instructions and then did not go to confirm that all was in order. And so the army is humiliated – a whole troop taken without a fight. 'That is why we must never neglect the least thing. Never.' There was silence for a while.

'You know, Williams, my dear fellow,' Dunbar said, 'you do appear to have the knack of finding trouble!'

'That is no bad thing for a soldier, no bad thing at all.' Colborne gave a thin smile. 'Now, you look all in and are no use to anyone half asleep. Your tent is not set up, but I have no need of this. Dunbar and I are going to visit the picket line.' Unseen by the colonel, Dunbar grimaced. 'Sleep, Mr Williams. I shall not require you until noon. Make use of my camp bed.'

After they had gone Williams lay down. The letter from Miss MacAndrews was in his hands, still unopened, and he stared at it as he lay there, suddenly overwhelmed with weariness. His eyes clouded, and the letter dropped to the floor as he went into a deep sleep.

II

The yellow-brown walls of Olivenza looked almost as old as Major Alasdair MacAndrews felt as the noon sun blazed down on him. His throat was as dry as sandpaper, and thanks to a ball from a French sharpshooter up on the battlements he had nothing to drink. Obviously it was better to have a shattered flask than shattered bones, but it was certainly a nuisance. To cap it all the young pup of an ensign did not seem to understand that he had done anything wrong.

Another ball smacked into the boulder above them, flicking up a puff of pale dust. Samuel Truscott moved to look over the edge of their little hole in the ground and the major grabbed him firmly by the shoulder. An officer was not supposed to manhandle another, even one so junior, but there were moments when convention could go and hang itself.

'Stay down, sir, stay down!' MacAndrews almost spat the words. The hole they were in was none too deep, the stones around the rim on the side closest to the walls smaller than he would have liked. Two more musket balls pinged off them. The French were watching, no doubt mightily amused and taking bets on who would be first to bag a redcoat officer. Shots came back in the other direction from his own men, but he doubted it would be enough to prevent more Frenchmen from having a go at the two British officers cowering in their tiny cover so close to the rampart.

'Sit still,' he repeated as the ensign wriggled. 'We wait for the battery to open up before we move, do you understand.'

'Yes, sir,' came a muffled voice. MacAndrews realised that he was pressing the ensign's head into the earth, but was not inclined to slacken his grip for the moment.

'Now, Truscott,' he said in a gentle tone, as if talking to an infant. 'We must wait for the great guns to practise on the wall and then we may have the chance to get back to the rest of the men. Do you understand?'

'Yes, sir,' came the faint reply.

'Well, then, I am going to let you free, but you must not sit up, not even a little. Is that clear?'

'Yes, sir.'

MacAndrews let go, and shifted to be more comfortable, head ducked down to his shoulders, and leaning against the largest of the boulders. His hat was gone, somewhere out there, plucked from his head by another shot as he ran to grab the ensign. Exposed, his white hair wafted in the breeze – his wife always claimed that it was like heather, incapable of being tamed by any comb.

Sam Truscott managed to roll over, so that his excited face looked up at the sky. MacAndrews could see that he was itching to move again, and wondered whether to let him go, and see if the fool's luck held. The boy was sixteen, and to him looked to be more like ten, and still too much of an infant to be away from his mother's apron strings. MacAndrews was a little younger when he had landed on Long Island back in '76 – an age ago and only yesterday. He wondered whether the experienced officers had seen him as a mere child and had watched him take absurd risks. There was no memory of having done anything quite so foolish. MacAndrews was sure the boy's brother was watching through a glass and could only guess at his feelings.

This was the first time the young ensign had really smelt powder. They had been outside the walled town of Olivenza for over a week, watching the small French garrison and waiting for heavy guns to be fetched from Elvas. The rest of the army had gone on further south, and all the land around Badajoz was now in Allied hands, apart from this place. Along with Campo Major the French had taken it in March, and like the other town

Olivenza had only obsolete old walls. Thus it was probably fitting that the Allies had only six obsolete old guns dragged here from Elvas to besiege the place. MacAndrews had seen them arrive on their clumsy carriages, less powerful and twice as heavy to move as modern cannon, so that it took a big team of mules an hour to pull them a mile.

The rest of the army had gone on, and only the Fourth Division been left to take this place. Until the guns came up last night there had been little to do. The other brigades spent the night digging an emplacement for the battery, with the Fusilier Brigade told to prepare to assault the next day. Just before dawn, he was sent forward with the three Light Companies, one from each of the recoated battalions, and an attached company of riflemen from the Brunswick Oels Jaeger. These Germans were a grim bunch, with their dark uniforms and the skull-and-crossbones badge on their French-style shakos, but he was glad to have them, for their short rifles were far more accurate than the smooth-bore muskets everyone else carried.

In the darkness they had crept towards the walls, listening all the time for cries of alarm from the town. MacAndrews had done his best to make sure that the men carried only what they needed. Packs were left, canteens kept full so that they made less noise, and no one was to have a loaded firelock in case they tripped and the weapon went off. Even so the noise seemed deafening, every footfall, every scrape of bayonet scabbard on the ground, every stumble, every muffled curse magnified until he was sure the French must be waiting for them, watching, and letting them come into close range.

There was no challenge, and when he guessed he was one hundred and fifty yards away from the walls, MacAndrews whispered the order to halt. The supports would wait here – there was a convenient gully where they could kneel down in cover until needed. The other half of each company crept forward in pairs, told to find the best shelter as close as possible to the rampart and then wait. He had listened to the little sounds as the men loaded.

MacAndrews was given this command because he was the

senior major of the brigade. He knew Captain Headley of the 106th's Light Company well. The other men were strangers, but all seemed capable and the men were experienced. In truth this mattered far more than any orders he had given. When the sun rose the men were in place. He was with the supports, ready to commit them as and when they were needed, but from the gully he could see little red figures crouched behind bushes or in dips of the ground. The Germans were harder to spot in their dark uniforms, and because they were good, and that was encouraging. It ought to be much harder for the French to see them.

The sun rose, setting the cloudy sky aflame in the east – a warning to sailors and shepherds, but he hoped not to soldiers, unless they were French. A shout came from the wall almost immediately, followed a moment later by the first shot. It was answered by the cracks of several rifles, and MacAndrews heard a scream from the ramparts – whether of alarm or pain he could not tell. His men were doing well. Only the few with a clear target and a couple of the more nervous had fired. The rest waited.

MacAndrews saw movement on the wall, soldiers filing to their places, and then more puffs of smoke. His own men replied, the duller booms of muskets mingling with the distinctive snap of rifles. The wall on this side of the town did not have battlements except in a few places, and the embrasures for the light cannon mounted on it were poor. Head and shoulders were in plain sight whenever one of the French soldiers bobbed up to look or to shoot. His own men were better protected, for the fields close to the walls were full of little hollows, stretches of dry-stone wall, gardens, bushes and trees.

They fired for twenty minutes, and even in that time the return fire from the wall slackened. Then MacAndrews stood up on the bank in front of the gully and blew his whistle three times.

'Cease fire!' he shouted, waving his cocked hat from side to side. There was another crack and then silence. He saw a Frenchman gingerly peer over the parapet, but at this distance it would be the worst possible luck to be hit by anyone shooting at him with a musket, and so he stood unconcerned. Thank the Lord that the French were too stubborn to adopt the rifle.

MacAndrews watched the little party ride forward under a flag of truce to summon the French governor to surrender. The man was an infantry colonel, a good soldier by all accounts and from what they had seen of the defence so far, so there was no surprise when he saw them ride back after only the briefest of parleys. A runner reached him just as the batteries opened fire, the great cannon sending out gouts of flame and noise. There were lesser booms from the field pieces mounted in separate positions and aimed at the French guns on the wall.

The major gave a long blast on his whistle and then waved his hat again, this time in a circular motion. His men resumed their fire – a good scatter of shots whenever a target appeared. At first this was often. The French replied manfully, with musket and with the four cannon able to bear on the attackers. They were light pieces in the main, save for a twelve-pounder which could just hit one of the flanking batteries. Both sides spent plenty of powder to little result. None of his men came back wounded, and he saw no corpses. Their own shooting kept the French nervous and seeking cover more than it struck home. Over time the enemy fire slackened.

MacAndrews drew his glass and watched the stretch of wall being pounded by the main breaching battery. Already there was a cloud of dust around the spot, but he thought he could see pieces of stone shattered with each strike of shot. Fire on both sides slowed as the morning drew on. The Allied gunners were growing weary and took longer to reload and point their pieces. The French were nervous of appearing on the wall unless the target was excellent, which in turn meant that his men had fewer good marks.

At eleven o'clock a white flag appeared above the main gate. The Allied guns ceased fire, and MacAndrews gave the same order by whistle and gesture. It took longer this time for his men to understand. He knew that many would be locked in their own little world, which extended no further than the patch of cover hiding them and the stretch of wall they watched for the chance to strike an enemy and for any risk to themselves. There were several more shots before all was quiet.

Half an hour later the guns resumed, and another runner brought him a message to say that an assault party was forming for the attack. MacAndrews had already heard the drums beating and had guessed as much. Obviously they wanted the French to know what was coming in the hope that this would convince them to surrender even at the last minute. If the plans were serious then everything possible would have been done to conceal the Allies' purpose.

By now many of his skirmishers were no doubt running low on ammunition, and on top of that it would add to the pressure on the French to see them being reinforced.

'I want half of each platoon extended as a chain,' he told the captains waiting with the supports. 'I will lead them. Be prepared to commit the rest as soon as the assaulting party begins to advance. We must give them all the support we can.' The men, stiff from waiting for so long, stood up, and half of each reserve line doubled forward and spread out in pairs.

'March on, boys!' he called cheerfully, and strode off.

The French saw them coming, and a few bobbed up to fire at long range. MacAndrews saw a puff of dust flicked up by a ball striking a few yards ahead of him, but nothing came closer. The appearance of the Frenchmen on the wall prompted a great flurry of firing from his own skirmishers. A heavy shot from the breaching battery thrummed through the air over his head.

MacAndrews stopped after about fifty yards. 'Edge as far forward as you can, boys, but take care to find what cover you may.' There was no need to say more, for the men knew what to do. He saw that rogue Sergeant Evans jogging forward with his number two, heading for a clump of bushes.

Then a little figure in a scarlet jacket popped up from cover among the skirmishers and started capering in the open, waving his curved sword and his hat in the air. The lad was shrieking in excitement, and MacAndrews could not catch the words.

'Get down, you damned fool!' Captain Headley shouted from his station with the remaining supports.

The boy did not hear or did not care, and began to advance towards the wall. Frenchmen appeared, fired and ducked down. Young Truscott danced through it all, little fountains of dust thrown up as bullets hit the ground around him. An arm reached up to pull him down, but the boy kicked it away.

'Mr Truscott, get back into cover!' MacAndrews called the words as an order, hoping that habit might make the idiot respond in spite of his elation. He wondered whether the boy was drunk. The other subalterns had filled him with puggle one night back in Lisbon, but otherwise he seemed a sober fellow.

The ensign continued his caper, shaking his sword at the French. A bluecoated infantryman rose above the parapet, taking careful aim, but a rifle cracked and the man was pitched back before he could fire.

'Down, you fool, down!' Headley was shouting, and Mac-Andrews glanced back to see the captain running forward, moving slowly and awkwardly because his leg was still not right after the wound he had taken back in Portugal in '08.

'Oh, hell,' MacAndrews said, and set off through his chain of skirmishers.

There were shouts from the wall, as more Frenchmen appeared. A few fired at the ensign, but a tall man in scarlet coat with the gold epaulettes of a field officer was a far more tempting target. MacAndrews felt the first ball whizz past inches from his cheek. He held his sword high to stop the scabbard from tangling up his legs, and ran as fast as he could, breathing hard because he had not expected this exertion. In a desperate attempt to make himself a more difficult mark, he zigzagged as he went.

His hat was plucked off, the long tails of his coat twitched by another ball, and then there was a blow to his hip and dampness spreading. His legs were still working and there was no pain so he kept going and with his hand he felt the moist material and realised that his water bottle had been shot through.

MacAndrews ran on, dodged to the side and felt the wind of another ball which would most surely have struck him if he had not changed direction. The ensign was close now, the young idiot spinning as he danced a jig.

'Oh, sir, is it not glorious!' The boy was grinning from ear to ear, his eyes wide with enthusiasm.

MacAndrews saw the boulders and the hollow in the ground behind them. He ran at the ensign, hit him at waist height, prompting a satisfying gasp, and flung them both down into cover.

A minute later, the Allied guns fell silent, but the French muskets on the wall did not. His men replied now and again. Ten minutes later – or so MacAndrews' watch told him, although he could have sworn that it had been hours – his own men stopped shooting. After a last flurry of shots around their little shelter, the defenders also stopped. Both officers were covered in dust, for they were little more than a pistol shot from the stretch of wall worked on by the breaching battery.

They waited, and MacAndrews tried to think of any words which might actually sink in to the boy's empty head. He and his wife had buried three children as infants, and he wondered how he would feel if one of the boys had survived and gone into the army. How would you tell a young lad to act with a sense few possessed at such an age? He worried enough about Jane, the only survivor, and now come of age. At least in her case there was no fear of shot and shell, but this business with Pringle's brother was concerning. As far as he could tell there was sympathy on her part, without deep affection. Now Esther wrote to say that she and Jane were travelling to Elvas to be nearer him, and 'to do their duty'. The phrase had puzzled him ever since he first read her letter.

Young Truscott's eyes were closed and with a shock Mac-Andrews realised that the boy was sleeping. There was no trace of liquor on his breath, and at least the fool had stopped moving.

It was a while before MacAndrews dared to peer over the top of the boulders. No one fired, but there was movement through the thinning cloud of smoke and dust around the breach. Figures were coming down. For a moment he thought they were French, come to kill or capture the officers hiding so close to the wall. Then he saw that they were civilians, carrying bundles of possessions.

Well, at least the breach was practical – the engineer's term for when the artillery had knocked a hole in a wall and brought down enough rubble to create a ramp the infantry could climb into the fortress. The civilians seemed to be picking their way down without any trouble, which suggested that it was as easy as any breach could ever be.

A trumpet sounded from within Olivenza, and MacAndrews dared to raise himself further and glance around. The French were on the parapet, leaning in comfort and showing no signs of hostility. His formed supports had come up and were standing around in a similarly casual manner.

'They have surrendered!' Captain Headley had cupped his hands around his mouth to shout the news. 'We are to secure the town.'

MacAndrews shook the ensign awake and stood up, waving to acknowledge that he understood.

'I'll take the Seventh and the Owls up the breach,' he called back, using the nickname the redcoats had given the Brunswickers. 'Lead the rest in by the main gate.'

The ensign stood beside him, yawning like a cat, his face burned almost as red by the sun as the violent heads of the spots infesting it. MacAndrews sought for some words of reason that might teach the lad wisdom.

'Do that again, and I shall shoot you myself,' he said, and cuffed the boy's curly hair. 'Now, Mr Truscott, go off to your company.'

Olivenza had fallen, and on the whole MacAndrews felt that the civilians inside had been spared for there was little damage to the houses and they had not had to face a storm when even the most disciplined soldiers were likely to run riot. He watched as the garrison paraded, and counted fewer than five hundred men, including the wounded. Up on the walls, most of the cannon were propped up on rotten carriages or none at all, incapable of firing with any sort of useful charge. The garrison had managed to keep the entire Fourth Division, almost ten times their numbers, occupied for well over a week when they might have been doing something useful. MacAndrews felt that the French colonel could feel well pleased with himself, and no doubt Marshal Soult would be delighted.

Two hours later, as he was posting sentries at the gates, on public buildings and to guard the prisoners, Ensign Truscott came running up.

'Beg to report, sir, but Captain Wachholtz of the Owls has been taken prisoner by the Portuguese, and says could you come at once to sort it out?'

MacAndrews sighed. Von Wachholtz was proud of his uniform, but had before now complained that British and Portuguese alike seemed incapable of telling it apart from the French. Somehow going to release a man arrested by his own side was a fitting end to this whole pointless business.

'Lead on, then, Mr Truscott,' he said wearily.

12

Hanley shifted slightly to bed the butt of the rifle more firmly into the fold of his shoulder, waited to steady himself and let his breath out halfway. He pulled the hammer up to full cock, waited again, and only when he was ready squeezed the trigger. The flint struck down, the sparks set off the powder in the pan and he felt a fleck of it on his cheek. He made himself keep still for that little delay before the main charge went off and the rifle pushed hard against his shoulder. A cloud of dirty smoke blotted out the target. He let out the rest of his breath and lowered the rifle, walking forward through the smoke.

'You are getting better, sir,' said Corporal Scott from the 5/6oth Foot, who was tutoring him.

Hanley looked at the fresh hole, off centre, but only by an inch and within the smallest of the concentric rings on the circular target.

The corporal stuck his little finger through the hole in the pasteboard and grinned. 'Another year, and you might be half decent, sir.' In spite of his name Scott was English, a very rare thing in a battalion recruited mainly from Germans, and he was in the hospital in Elvas rather than with his company because a wagon wheel had run over his foot and broken a bone. It was healing well and in a few weeks he might be able to march and catch up with his company. For the moment, he was happy to receive sixpence for each day the officer was in the fortress and wanted to practise firing the rifle.

It was the one the turncoat Brandt had dropped, and Hanley had decided that it would be no bad thing to learn to use such an effective long arm. His duties often took him off on his own or with only a small escort, so it made sense to take more care to be well able to defend himself. That at least was what he told anyone who asked, including Pringle when he spotted his friend with a rifle on his back. The truth was that he enjoyed learning something new, and a secret part of him liked the idea of being able to take a life from two hundred yards away. Hanley remembered the expression of the dragoon he had killed, and the terrified face of the trumpeter he had knocked down, the images coming to his mind again and again with a surprising, even disturbing, amount of pleasure. He also remembered coming face to face with Sinclair in the woods near Barrosa Hill, and the fear he had felt as the Irishman raised his pistol. A rifle might not have helped in the circumstances, but he doubted that carrying one could do any harm.

An hour later Hanley met Baynes for the second time in the day.

'We were right,' the merchant began, after a servant had left them coffee and then departed. 'Gutiérrez is passing information to the French.' They were in a comfortably furnished room in a big house just behind one of the great bastions in the wall. It belonged to another of Baynes' connections, and in this case came with a full staff.

'You are certain?' Hanley had met the man twice, and rather liked him. Gutiérrez owned a small estate and kept cattle. He had sold some to the French, and never concealed it, but for the last year and a half the grey-haired little man had brought regular reports of what he had seen of French numbers and dispositions, and useful gossip about the community of French sympathisers in Estremadura and even large parts of Andalusia. The man lived near Olivenza, but knew Seville well.

'There can be no doubt.' Baynes handed him a captured dispatch. 'This was in the packet that arrived at noon.' A bundle of documents acquired by the partisans along this stretch of the border had not arrived in time for their meeting earlier in the day. 'The source is not named, but you will see that it repeats our message word for word.'

The British wish to discover how much is known about their forces in Cadiz and Gibraltar. These are to be reinforced, with the intention of exploiting their recent success by launching a much larger attack in the south.

Doubts had grown about Gutiérrez, whose recent information was proving of little or no use. At the same time it was clear that the French were better informed. Instead of reinforcing the south the Allies were drawing troops away and bringing them north. Two Spanish divisions had sailed from Cadiz, landing on the coast and marching overland to link up with Marshal Beresford's army. The French did not know, and the hope had been to trap several regiments between the two forces, but the enemy were warned in time and escaped. In that case Gutiérrez was not their source, for the man was ignorant of the whole affair. Several messages were intercepted before they reached the French, which gave some idea of how many agents and informers they possessed. At least one must have reached them.

Gutiérrez was not to blame, but he was false. That was now clear. Baynes had come up with the idea of testing the man with this misleading request, which he had written and Hanley had delivered several weeks ago.

'I am sorry that we were right,' Hanley said.

'And how often can we say that? From what I have learned, he has taken some money from the French, but that is unlikely to be the chief reason for his change of allegiance. The man's daughter was taken and is held in Badajoz. An officer and a soldier came and took the girl, who is only seventeen and his only remaining child since both his sons were killed in battle. Gossip claims the girl is in love with the French officer, but expresses surprise at the speed of the seduction as he had not visited Olivenza before – at least to anyone's knowledge.'

'The gossips appear well informed.'

'They usually are in a small country town, even if they are not always accurate.'

'I trust your investigations have been discreet,' Hanley asked, for the slightest hint that Gutiérrez's activities were known by the Allies would render that knowledge useless – apart from any consequences it had for the man and his child.

'My dear boy,' Baynes' lips parted in his usual great smile, 'I am not a raw hand at this game, allow me some credit. There is also one more thing, and I doubt that it will come as too much of a surprise.'

'The officer and the soldier wore pale green jackets.'

'Precisely. Sinclair is at the bottom of this. As far as we can tell he went south after Campo Major, to help Marshal Soult stamp out the embers of rebellion in Andalusia. Dalmas stayed here – well, your friend Williams saw him that night. What a pity his shot missed! Still, that cannot be helped, and my feeling is that Dalmas is still at heart a soldier, and whatever he does will aim at advantage on the battlefield. Sinclair is by far the bigger rascal, for his instincts are political and so he may strike far deeper.'

Hanley rubbed his shoulder, which was sore from firing the rifle, especially at the beginning when he failed to couch it properly. 'I am inclined to doubt that Gutiérrez's treachery is the sole end of Sinclair's mischief, or even a major part of it.'

'Certainly, I suspect it offers no more than an indication of their methods. If they have reached one of our men then I would be most surprised if they have not found others. Bribery and threats may have turned others as well. I doubt Gutiérrez's daughter is the only hostage in Badajoz, indeed I am sure of it, although I cannot learn their identities.'

'There is more,' Hanley said. 'There has to be more, some greater game, given Bertrand's secrets, the money, and all this.'

'As I said before, we must work out what the French want. We want Badajoz, and now at last we have the place surrounded and have driven the French back, at least for the moment. One thing they wanted was time to repair the defences of the place, and since it is three weeks since we advanced I believe they have gained plenty of that. Or perhaps it is better to say that they have been handed it on a silver platter.

'Lord Wellington is on his way, and it is to be hoped that he creates more sense of urgency before he has to return to the north.'

'Can we take Badajoz?'

'You are the soldier, my dear fellow, you tell me.'

'I doubt it will be easy,' Hanley said.

'It is hard to contest such simple wisdom.'

Hanley got up and went to the fireplace, lifting the tails of his coat to warm himself. 'Sinclair would know what the French want,' he said.

'Once again, I am not inclined to dispute the claim. And since we cannot simply ask the man and expect him to tell us, I presume you have something to suggest.'

'A trap. Draw him out, and then do what we failed to do at Campo Major – catch him or kill him, or Dalmas or both if we are lucky. Let us use Gutiérrez, feed him some information to reassure them of his trustworthiness, and then dangle the bait before them.'

'The bait? I presume you have something – or is it someone in mind.' There was a knowing look in the merchant's eyes. 'I see,' he added after a moment. 'It is a risk, a considerable risk.'

'And a considerable prize.'

'Perhaps. Yes, I believe you may have something. It will take very careful judgement and we must not rush anything, so let us think on the problem.

'Now,' Baynes said with a smile, 'it is growing dark and I imagine you do not care to waste your night in Elvas talking to me. I understand that the Dobson girl is responding well?' There was more than one way of taking that, even though Baynes' expression did not change. 'Her tutors are satisfactory. I have arranged for Major MacAndrews' wife and daughter to take part of a house when they arrive. They will be near Colonel Dalbiac and his wife. The colonel is ill, and his wife cares for him, and I believe the ladies are known to each other, so friendship will

116

explain their presence here as well. I leave it to you to explain matters to them – to one or both as you see fit – and convince them to assist us. Is there anything else you require?'

'Not for the moment.'

'I should think not! Let us hope there is some gain to be made from all this in the months to come. Well then, goodnight to you.'

He had reached the door before Baynes spoke again. 'Oh, and Hanley, do try to get some sleep. You look quite fagged, old man.' Ezekiel Baynes was beaming even more brightly than usual. 'Thank God I am too old for such exertions!'

Jenny was reading when Hanley arrived, and this no longer surprised him. The dye had almost wholly washed out of her hair, which was back to its old rich brown – less striking perhaps, but he felt more becoming. She did not look up, but continued to read, frowning at the pages.

'I don't see that it is so very funny,' she said after a moment.

Hanley peered over her shoulder. It was a copy of *The Rivals* bought when they auctioned off the effects of a captain in the 43rd who had died of fever. The Light Division was always staging productions.

'It helps to see it being performed,' he said. 'Helps even more if you have drunk a fair bit. It is a well-known principle of the theatre that a comedy's success relies a good deal on the extent of inebriation in the audience.'

'Mrs Malaprop makes me laugh,' Jenny admitted. 'Not as funny as Bottom and the others, though.' There was a collection of Shakespeare among the books he had managed to obtain, and the girl had surprised him by preferring it to everything else, even Fielding and Richardson. 'Too slow,' she told him. 'Nothing much seems to happen for chapter after chapter. With Shakespeare they're more like real folk you meet, frightened or jealous and foolish.' Hanley wished that he could take her to see a play performed. He asked her about the day's lessons.

'My feet hurt.'

'Dancing is hard work,' he said.

'It's these ruddy shoes,' she replied, and Hanley reflected that in some spheres there was a good deal left to do.

'The new pairs are being made, but this is not a big town, nor a wealthy one. I have had to have the last sent away. Are you happy with this place?'

'It is nice,' she said, and then thought for a moment. 'Thank you.' Hanley was renting a small house in one of the narrow side streets. He had hired a maid and a cook, who shared a room next to the kitchen on the ground floor. Jenny had a large and almost empty sitting room as well as a bedroom to herself. 'There is a man watching us,' she added.

'Just to keep you safe,' he said, and was relieved that she had noticed only the one man, no doubt the fellow with the limp, harelip and tall hat hired because he would draw attention away from the real guardians.

'And to keep me here.'

Hanley walked over to the open wardrobe, and felt the muslin of a dress. 'Do you wish to leave?'

'No.'

'I'm glad. Now show me what Monsieur Lafayette has been teaching you.'

'My feet are sore.'

'A lady would never mention such a thing. Take off your shoes if they are uncomfortable.'

Jenny did not bother, but rose and walked to face Hanley. He bowed, and she curtsied, a little too deeply for perfect modesty.

'Do you like the clothes?' he asked.

The girl stood upright again, making her neckline less revealing. 'Some of them are pretty. Not sure about this one. It's rough on the skin.' The gown was of cheap cotton, but at least was shaped to the modern style, as far as Hanley could judge. Many of the other garments Baynes had obtained were old fashioned, or styled for local taste.

'I shall try to get you better. There is also a simple answer if you are uncomfortable,' he suggested.

'Huh.'

'Then shall we begin with a quadrille?'

'Lots of imagining to do,' she said. 'And hard without music. Monsieur always counts out loud.'

Hanley did his best to keep calling out the rhythm and to act as her partner in an imaginary line of dancers. It had been some time since he had attended a ball, and his memories were vague.

'Wrong way,' she said more than once to call him back. 'And again.' Three times they collided, and twice they met when they should not.

When he started to laugh Jenny looked offended.

'You wanted to do this,' she said, trying to continue.

'Ten, eleven, fifteen,' he called out, as he staggered happily against her.

'Daft sod.' Jenny stopped, glaring at him, so he took her by the waist.

'Oh yes,' the girl said, eyes bold.

Hanley ran a hand up her back. The other went lower, both feeling the cotton of her dress and the body underneath. 'This is rough.'

'Told you.'

'It must be uncomfortable.' He pressed open the highest of the hooks at the back and began working downwards.

Her eyes never left his. 'Is this how gentlemen behave?'

'When they get a chance.' Hanley finished his task, and his fingers spread around the young woman's bottom. Jenny pulled herself closer to him.

'I know this dance,' she said, and they kissed.

13

Williams woke with a start when the drums beat. The dream, a wondrous, lustful dream, was already fading. He had been in Cadiz again, watching as Jane MacAndrews climbed a long stone staircase and was caught in a swirling storm of wind, her skirts flying high, exposing the glorious curves of her legs sheathed in white silk stockings. The cherished memory was often in his mind, preserved as best he could manage, but in his dream it was vividly real, and he had run after the girl, as he had not dared to do at the time, swept her up in his arms, kissed her, and... He was not an experienced man, knowing little of such things, and yet the dream carried on and felt real, even if part of him knew as he was dreaming and that it was no more than that.

There was a basin on a folding stand beside his cot, once more part of his recently purchased camp equipment. Williams got up and cupped his hands in the water left there from the night before and threw it over his face. His back ached and he felt even more tired than when he had lain down some four hours ago. Colonel Colborne kept his brigade busy, and his staff even busier, and Williams had thought himself exhausted and yet deep sleep had not come. He had dozed, dreaming and waking time after time. Some of the dreams had been nightmares – twice he relived the panic on the beach at Fuengirola, and the slam of the ball driving into his side, and then the burning pain as the second shot gouged his scalp. Even worse was watching as a woman died – he could not now remember whether it was Jane or one of his sisters. Such horrors were familiar, common whenever he did not sink down into real slumber, and he hoped that he had not cried out loud enough to be heard by anyone outside.

A shave would have to wait until later – one of the advantages of having fine, light-coloured hair was that no one was likely to notice. He had slept in his overalls and boots, and now pulled on his jacket and began to fasten it up.

Another dream was more disturbing than all the others, for all the pleasure of the moment itself, for it too had been erotic. Williams sometimes dreamed in this way of women other than Miss MacAndrews, but the faces were never of people he knew. This time he had dreamed of Lupe, poor hurt Guadalupe, the sister of the wife of the partisan leader El Blanco. Little more than a child, she had been ravished by the French, and then Williams had failed to save the sister from being raped by a British officer. That man was dead, his throat slit from side to side by Lupe, for the two women fought alongside the men, and they were brave and skilful.

Lupe had nursed Williams back to life after he had been shot and had fallen in love with him. He was grateful, admired her, but there was no love, and yet one night she had come to him and he had taken her in his arms. It was only the fear in her eyes and the trembling of her body which had made him pull away, a decision made simpler minutes later when the French launched a sudden attack on the band's camp. In his dream he had not pulled away. Once again he had watched as Lupe danced in the wild, passionate southern fashion, and in his dream he had gone to her. Trembling and afraid, Lupe cried out as he tore off her clothes and flung her to the ground.

Then he had woken up, his back soaked in sweat.

Williams fastened his sash around his waist, buckled on his sword belt, and put on his cocked hat. That dream had not faded so quickly and it worried him. He did not like to think that he could be unfaithful to his love for Jane MacAndrews, even if there was little hope of fulfilment. Worse was the fear of violent, predatory demons lurking inside him. Williams confessed himself to be a sinner, unworthy of the salvation offered by his Lord. He knew that he was a mere man, weak and wicked in his instincts, and tried to do his poor best. It frightened him to think that he might be capable of acting in this way.

He picked up his gloves and bent down to leave his little tent.

'You look fresh and rested,' Captain Dunbar told him, the irony heavy in his words. It did not look as if the brigade major had managed to get much sleep either. He stamped his feet to fight off the cold of the early morning.

'Bright as a spring flower, ready for the burdens of the day,' Williams replied, pretending to hobble like an old man.

'That is good to hear, for I am sure that I can find plenty to keep the pair of you occupied.' Lieutenant Colonel Colborne gave the impression of having slept twelve hours in a feather bed.

It was nine minutes to six o'clock and an hour before dawn. The brigade was not due to move today, and so, just as they did every other day, along with every British corps in the field, the four battalions stood to arms in case of attack. Each company paraded and then marched to form with its battalion at its alarm post. The time just before dawn was when men felt low in spirits and drowsy, making it a good time for the enemy to attack.

'All ready, sir,' Dunbar reported. An officer had come from each of the battalions to report.

'Good, then let us be off.' Colborne strode to their waiting horses.

'Morning, sir,' Corporal Stiles said to Williams. 'I think he will do you proud.' He was leading the captured gelding, now much slimmed down after weeks of gradually replacing his green fodder with grain.

'I've made another couple of holes,' he whispered as Williams put his boot in the stirrup. Yesterday he had tried the horse out, and when he rose to trot the saddle had shifted under him, rolling to the right. It had not happened quickly, and so he had slid sideways, managing to free himself and jump down rather than fall. The girth had been as tight as it would go, but with the horse so much thinner than when he had taken her it was simply not enough. Captain Dunbar had had hysterics, and almost fallen from his own mount, and even the colonel had laughed.

Williams felt the leather strap, could not get a finger underneath it, so swung himself up. Stiles was a small man, and when he had taken the horse out his weight was not enough to make the saddle shift. As a corporal he should not really have been a soldier servant. He had been wounded in the hand and thigh at Talavera, serving with the 23rd Light Dragoons, and was still in hospital when the shattered regiment went home to recruit. His leg remained stiff, and with the fourth and fifth fingers on his right hand gone he could not really wield a sabre.

'Only be pensioned off if I go home,' he had explained when Williams met him in Lisbon, where he had spent the last six months looking after the horses of a senior surgeon. 'Be happier out in the field.'

The man knew horses, understood how to be comfortable in camp, and was reliable and – mostly – sober. Colborne winked at the breaking of regulation and permitted him to be kept on the establishment at his existing rank, since Williams would as usual be paying him the supplement given to a man acting as servant to an officer.

Williams patted the animal on the neck. 'I am sure he will do splendidly, Stiles.'

They set off, riding first to the paraded battalions just a short distance away and then out to check on the picket line. There was no sign of the French, who had rarely been sighted in the last few days and then only the smallest patrols. Even so Williams remembered the sudden onslaught of hussars against the slumbering camp of the 13th Light Dragoons, and was glad to be serving under a commander who took every precaution, no matter how safe they appeared to be.

'All quiet, sir,' said the lieutenant at the first picket. 'The same for the Steelbacks, over to the left.'

Colborne nodded, and Williams knew that he was pleased because the subaltern had made sure to make contact with the picket line of the brigade next to them. He did not even reprove the lieutenant for using the 57th's nickname. Their colonel was a noted flogger, routinely forming the battalion for punishment with offenders tied to a triangle of sergeant's pikes. For all that, the 57th were a fine battalion, and their commander popular with the men, who at least knew where they stood with him.

The entire Second Division and much of the cavalry were down near Zafra, cutting the old royal road that led to Seville, where Marshal Soult had his headquarters. Badajoz was surrounded, and there was little doubt that the siege ought to begin soon. When it did, they would no doubt be called north to take part, but for the moment it was their task to keep the French at a distance. They were acting in concert with two Spanish forces. One was the remnant of the army routed when the French took Badajoz earlier in the year. Its men were ragged, poorly equipped and drilled, and yet like so many armies they kept coming back from defeat after defeat. The other, under general Blake, consisted of two divisions from Cadiz, smartly uniformed and well-trained.

'I believe them to be good soldiers and well led,' Williams said when asked if he had seen anything of these regiments while he was down south. Colborne liked to chat as they went on their rounds.

'That will make a change,' Dunbar said, but did not sound convinced. 'I can remember thousands of the rascals running away at Talavera, scared witless by their own volley. Ran back miles and pillaged the baggage. I lost half my clothes, a hairbrush and a pearl necklace.'

Colborne was much amused. 'Pearls?'

'A present for my sister,' Dunbar murmured, clearly regretting mentioning the matter and probably reluctant in case he was asked to explain how he had acquired the gift in the first place.

'I have seen Spanish soldiers fight with great spirit,' Williams said.

'As have I, and if they had been better led from the start they would surely have enjoyed some success.' Colborne smiled. 'Oh, I know they call me an enthusiast and that so many disdain our allies, but we could never remain in the country without their aid.' He led them down a bank into a field where the next picket stood on a hill topped by a stone cross. The light was growing.

'One thing I must say,' he continued after a moment. 'I doubt very much that an English army would still exist if we had suffered as many bad blows as the Spanish.'

The officer in charge of the outpost had nothing to report, and so they went on, hearing the same reassuring thing each time. Williams was pleased with the gelding, which had plenty of energy and was proving sure-footed.

'Have you decided what to call him?' Dunbar asked as they rode to the next picket.

'I thought a solid, martial name would suit best,' Williams explained, 'and so have chosen Musket.'

That prompted a chuckle from the colonel. Dunbar grinned, so must have heard the story before.

'I knew a Captain Musket once, who came to us from the militia,' Colborne began. The colonel liked to tell stories from his years with the colours. 'A regular dashing fellow he was, with great side whiskers and a perpetual ferocious expression. Arrived one day when we were in Holland, saw his first Frenchman the next day and ran all the way back to the sea. Never saw him again. They let him buy himself out rather than have a scandal.'

Williams laughed and reached forward to rub the gelding's ears. 'He seems to possess a stouter heart than that – even if it was pledged to Bonaparte until recently!'

'Then let us take his measure.' Colborne pointed at a stone wall some three or four foot high and only a little out of their path. Then he was off, straight at it. Dunbar followed. Williams would have preferred to get to know Musket a little better before attempting even so modest an obstacle, but would not refuse the challenge. The horse was steady, his canter good. Williams urged him on, rose in the stirrups and gave him another flick with his crop just to be on the safe side. He had misjudged a little, but only a little, not yet used to the gelding's stride. The horse jumped a fraction too soon, and its rear feet clipped the top of the wall, but he cleared it and landed well.

'We need some practice,' he said happily when he joined the others.

There was no sign of the French. For a while their cavalry patrols were familiar, if distant, sights, but a couple of days earlier General Long and his cavalry had caught up with a brigade of hussars. The 13th Light Dragoons charged and broke them – by happy chance the same enemy horsemen who had captured Major Morres and his men. A few were cut down, more of them taken, but most of the two hussar regiments escaped because they could not be caught. The heavy brigade was supposed to have got around behind the French, but did not move with sufficient speed. Even at brigade level, Colborne and his staff had heard of the bickering over blame between the marshal and the brigadier general ever since.

The brigade was ready and waiting to receive an attack or, if ordered, launch one of its own, but the enemy was not there and so they waited as the sun came up. After about an hour, when, according to regulation, a grey horse could be seen at a mile's distance, Colborne ordered them to stand down and take breakfast. He was already confirming the orders for today's parades and training. His brigade would never stand idle. Relations with the general remained cold, but Colborne was still fond of quoting Major General Stewart. 'Hound the officers, and the common soldiers will take care to perform their own duties, for they will never believe that they will be treated less harshly than their seniors.'

After the morning drills, Williams spent most of the day writing, compiling lists of rations and effective strengths, confirming the receipt of orders and reports, and the orders for the overnight pickets and alarm posts – the last unchanged, but still this needed to be confirmed. He spent time with the battalion adjutants, the quartermasters and on his own, scratching away at a little chair and writing-desk, his head touching the canvas of his low tent. It reminded him of dull days working as a clerk in the office of a shipping chandler, a life he had enlisted to escape, but which now came back to haunt him. The paperwork required to run a company was bad enough. This was on a far grander and duller scale.

As he worked he wondered whether he ought to have declined the offer to become Colborne's aide. The 106th was short of captains, with only six available to lead companies. If he was back with the battalion he would surely have been placed in charge of one of the remaining four.

Yet there was never any real question of refusing such an honour. Lieutenant General Graham had recommended him to Colborne, who was an old friend. Williams had met them both on the road to Corunna, when they came to relieve his little force holding the bridge. They had taken him to Moore, who had spoken then of the need for a serious soldier to serve on the staff as well as with his regiment. Moore had arranged his step from ensign to lieutenant, and even from the grave appeared to be helping his career.

The day wore on and Williams wrote lists and checked them, checked lists brought to him and wrote more in consequence. All the while he would have preferred to write something else altogether, a letter long delayed and still not in any sense composed in his mind. It was not until well after dark that he got a chance, and his thoughts came back with more focus to the girl. Although it might have been more pleasant to picture Jane with her dress blowing in the wind, it was Miss MacAndrews' short note that kept coming into his mind. He remained unsure what it meant and hence did not know how he ought to reply – or if indeed a letter was proper.

Sitting on his own he took the letter from his inside pocket, not because he did not know the words off by heart, but to see her handwriting and know that she had touched it.

Dear Mr Williams, it began with sad formality. A few times in the past – he knew it to be three, for each stroke of the pen was valued – she had ventured as far as *My dear Mr Williams,* but it seemed those days were gone.

I trust that this finds you in good health. Mother and I are well and in Lisbon, having taken a fine house near the river. Young Jacob delights

127

in the place – that was Jacob Hanks, Jenny Dobson's abandoned child. *It is not yet decided whether we shall follow the major farther into Portugal or remain here. If we do follow him, then it seems likely that we will first arrange for someone trustworthy to take care of the child while we are away.*

Now I have supplied you with our little news, it is time to speak of more serious matters. It is much to be regretted that we did not part as friends. The meeting had been brief, for the day after Barrosa Williams received the invitation to join Colonel Colborne in Portugal, and General Graham, assuming his acceptance, had arranged for him to take ship immediately. He passed through Cadiz itself from the Isla only briefly, chanced upon the girl and her mother, exchanged pleasantries and then had only a couple of minutes to speak with very little privacy to Jane.

Sir, your anger was not becoming of a gentleman of your kindness of spirit, and marred what would otherwise have been a happy reunion. We had all believed you fallen in battle and lost for ever. It was the cause of great sadness to us all and in particular to your intimate friends.

There is no engagement between Captain Pringle, RN – Williams wondered whether she thought he might confuse Edward with his brother – *and your correspondent. What follows I tell you in the strictest confidence and trust you as a gentleman not to abuse this trust. Captain Pringle asked me to marry him. He did it with great courtesy and is a gallant gentleman. I have not given him an answer.* That had been the spark for his rage. When Williams proposed at Corunna she had turned him down in a brusque, even an insulting, way. He had said sharp words, and the fiery girl had replied in kind.

My true friends will know without being told the only answer I could give.

I remain yrs. Jane MacAndrews

He wanted to believe that her sense was that she did not and could not love Pringle or consent to the union, because her true affections rested with Williams, or at least were not yet settled. Yet her words could mean something completely different, and perhaps she wished to prepare him for the news that she would wed her courteous and gallant sailor.

He ought to apologise. That, at least, was certain, even if it was harder to say whether such an apology could be sent in a letter rather than made in person. Yet when would he see the girl? It might not be for many months, perhaps not even this year. Did she believe him still angry? Before he had been sent on the expedition to Malaga they had met and affection had burned so strongly that he wished somehow he could undo all that had happened since then.

Williams took out a paper and pencil and stared blankly into space. He was not even sure how to address the girl.

Dunbar's head appeared through the flaps of the tent.

'We are summoned to General Stewart,' he said. 'I fear it will be another short night for we poor functionaries!'

Williams sighed and put down the pencil. Perhaps it was for the best, for any words might only make matters worse.

14

Lord Wellington studied the walls with his glass and did not speak for a good ten minutes. Then he dictated a few notes, rode on to another spot and began to scan the defences once more. He was dressed plainly in a blue civilian coat, white breeches and hessian boots, and still managed to stand out in the cluster of staff officers. It was obvious that he was at the centre of everything, and everyone, from Marshal Beresford down, behaved just a little differently. Hanley could sense purpose in all that was done today. The general had ridden down from the border near Almeida and arrived at Elvas the day before, more than one hundred and fifty miles in only four days. An admiring ADC from the Fourth Division assured Hanley that the general had killed two horses through sheer exhaustion and lost two of his escort in a flooded river on the way.

It was well into the afternoon, and they had been observing the fortress for most of the day, coming up from the south on the Valverde road. At first the French did not appear to mind, for they were escorted by Portuguese cavalry and two battalions of King's German Legion Light Infantry, dressed in green much like the 95th and some armed with rifles. At Baynes' suggestion, Hanley had not brought his own rifle with him today.

'The peer prefers his officers to look respectable,' he said. 'Their adherence to uniform is a small matter, but he values men like you for their judgement rather than any capacity for slaughter.'

The merchant had stayed in Elvas, so Hanley rode instead with Colonel D'Urban. Just a few days ago he had helped the quartermaster general read a captured dispatch written in cipher. It had taken them a while, working through the page of numbers and symbols written altogether without gaps. The code proved simple, so they had searched for patterns – the frequently repeated 6= they guessed to be 'et'. That gave them two letters as a start, and as they put these into the sequence they started to guess at other words. In all it took them ten hours, closeted in a room with another staff officer, but by the end they had the whole text, which proved disappointingly bland.

'That they bothered shows that they are becoming wary,' Baynes concluded when they explained the system to him. 'And I doubt discovering the code will prove so simple a task next time.'

D'Urban was good company, and for the moment had little to do, something that would change as soon as Lord Wellington completed his reconnaissance and issued orders for the siege.

'There,' he said, pointing. 'Look at the lighter-coloured stone. That is where the French made their breach. I doubt that the work is good or yet settled, but you must admire them for repairing it so quickly.'

Hanley looked at the stretch of wall next to one of the great bastions, but this sign of recent fragility offered little encouragement. Badajoz depressed him more each time he looked at the brooding fortress. He hoped the general and the engineers and gunners saw something that he did not.

'Will that same spot be the focus of our assault?' he asked. 'If the mortar on the repairs is weak then it ought to be easier to knock down. And from what I saw at Ciudad Rodrigo the French engineers are good judges of the weakness of a place.'

'Aye, they are, but then they have the luxury of far greater resources and plenty of time. The ground on this south side is open, as you see, which means that we would have to start our trenches a long way back, and then dig forward. At the very least that would take several weeks, for I dare say the French would not make it easy for us.'

They moved on again, Lord Wellington leading them at a gallop towards the Picurina fort. It was one of two outworks on the southern side, both smaller than the San Cristoval, but still formidable.

There was a puff of smoke from the rampart, a moment later the boom of a gun and almost immediately a shot kicked up a spray of dirt some fifty yards ahead of the general. Lord Wellington turned off to the right and rode up to a gentle rise about half a mile from the outwork.

'It appears that we are not welcome,' D'Urban said as they followed.

The gun did not fire again, which suggested that they were too far away for good practice.

'Time is not on our side, Hanley. Badajoz has a strong garrison and enough food to keep them going for months. We may have hurt Marshal Soult's pride by driving him back, but merely surrounding the place will not do much more than that. We have to take it, and take it quickly, because the very moment we cut the first trench you can be sure the news will be carried south. Once that happens Soult will undoubtedly not let us alone. So how much time will that give us?'

Hanley thought before answering. 'Three or four days for the news to reach Seville, then a week to gather an army together from the garrisons. Less than a week to march here.'

D'Urban was pleased. 'Our thoughts are similar, and you will be pleased to hear that Lord Wellington has reached much the same conclusion. He judges that we will have at most sixteen days to take the place. By that time at the latest we will have to draw off all our troops from the siege to face Soult. We do not have enough men to prosecute the attack here and be sufficiently strong to meet the French army should they wish to force a battle.

'So sixteen days is likely all we have, and perhaps not even that. Unless a clever fellow like you can devise some scheme to get us in without a formal siege ... No. I do hear that marching round and round and blowing trumpets has worked in the past, so that may be a line worth pursuing!'

Hanley stared at the main wall and the two bastions protecting the nearest corner – the Santa Maria and the San Trinidad. Earlier on one of the engineers had voiced the opinion that the quality of work on the whole fortress was poor, but crude or not it would not be easy to take. The castle – it was a Moorish citadel if he remembered correctly from visiting the town some years ago – had high old-fashioned walls not designed to protect against cannon. It might have formed a weak spot were it not so hard to approach, with only a narrow spit of land before a river, dammed and flooded to make a wide lagoon, fed into the broad Guadiana. Hanley could see no quick way in.

Time was precious, but from all he had seen Marshal Beresford had not so far acted as if this was the case. That was not an opinion he dared express in his present company, for although D'Urban was a smart fellow, he was also fiercely loyal to his chief and Hanley worried that this clouded his judgement.

'Brute of a place, though, is it not?' D'Urban said when several minutes had passed and Hanley made no response. 'Oh, by the way, I have spoken to the cavalry and to the Germans and none of them saw either of your fellows this morning.'

By chance the reconnaissance force's advance had cut off a French foraging party. Suddenly two battalions had come rushing out of the gates to rescue them, one heading straight at the general and his staff and another at a company of the KGL. The senior officers evaded with ease – Lord Wellington's expression scarcely changing – although sadly the Germans were overrun and dozens killed or taken. Hanley had wondered whether Sinclair or Dalmas was behind the sally. He did not think it likely, since the attackers made no real attempt to catch the general, but he had mentioned the thought.

'No one saw a cuirassier or an officer in a pale green jacket,' D'Urban explained, and then grinned. 'Of course, the fiendish devils may have done something truly clever like changing their uniform!'

'Sometimes the enemy can be most unreliable,' Hanley replied, and soon staff and escort alike galloped off to stare at the fortress from another angle. 'They seem to have vanished,' he said when they stopped again. 'Perhaps they have both gone south to Seville?'

It was dark by the time the general, his staff and escort returned to Elvas. Hanley was tired and saddle-sore, having forgotten the pace at which Lord Wellington did everything. His meeting with Baynes was blessedly short, and the prospect of joining Jenny Dobson for the night brought on a thrill which easily overcame his weariness. Each visit to Elvas and encounter with the girl was becoming more pleasurable in every way.

Hanley made sure that he and the girl talked a good deal, along with eating, drinking and making love.

'You remember Major MacAndrews,' he said as they lay side by side on the bed at the end of a more than usually vigorous bout.

'Dad thinks a lot of him.'

Hanley reached over and stroked her cheek. 'Do you remember his family?'

'Tall wife, getting on a bit, but still quite good looking and dressed well. Bit of a busybody, but meant it kindly and always wanted to play with everyone's babies.' Hanley liked the way Jenny summed people up.

'And Miss MacAndrews?'

Jenny sat up and half turned to face him. 'Her? Pretty, if you like ginger hair, which I can't say I do, but all the officers sniffed after her like tomcats. I caught you looking at her a couple of times like she was a full bottle of gin and you were dying of thirst.' She cuffed him lightly, leaning so that her breasts swayed in front of his face.

Hanley grinned, reached up and after a few happy moments Jenny lay down again.

'Anything else?' he asked.

'Lovely clothes. Bit silly in some ways, but smart and kind. Had that Mister Williams dangling on a thread and kept playing with him like a cat. Are they wed now?'

'No.'

'Shagging?'

Hanley shook his head, and thought about how much work he still had to do.

'Bloody fools. Dad reckons Williams is the bravest, best and daftest man he's known. Think he thinks of him as a son.' Dobson had been Williams' front-rank man when he was a volunteer, standing in front of him in formation, and the old veteran had taken to the eager young Welshman.

'Do you like her?'

Jenny was surprised, and took a moment to answer. 'She helped me when I was having the baby. That means a lot.' It was the first time she had mentioned her son. 'It wasn't really up to me to like her or not, but she's all right.'

The girl sat up again. 'I like you, Mister Hanley.'

'I do get that impression,' he said, and made a lunge.

'I'm serious,' she said after a few minutes of giggling struggle. 'Always did like you because you're not like all the other officers. You're different from everyone else, just like me.'

'I really am quite delightful,' Hanley said happily. Jenny cuffed him again and he grabbed her and this time it was a while before they spoke again.

'You are like me,' the girl said in a little voice. She was not looking at him and just stared fixedly at the ceiling. 'We don't mean anyone any harm, but in the end we only care about ourselves.'

Hanley sensed she did not want to be interrupted, so lay beside her in silence. Here was another surprise.

'I won't ever be in love – not like in the books and plays,' Jenny went on, and there was sadness in the words, but no trace of pity, unless for others who had more fanciful views of the world. 'I like some men, may even one day want to be with just one, but I won't love.

'Never told anyone that,' Jenny added after a moment. She gave a little laugh and kissed him on the cheek. 'I can tell you because I like you, and I know you'll never fall in love with me.'

'Well, I might, just out of spite,' he said. The girl rolled against him and he folded his arm around her.

'So what about the major's wife and lass?' Jenny asked after a while. 'You never ask about anyone else from them days.'

'They are coming to Elvas. Should be here tomorrow if all goes well and will be living in a house not so very far from here. I want you to meet them – well, Miss MacAndrews certainly. There are some things I cannot teach you – the ways ladies behave, how they speak and act. Learn from them.' That was the start of his plan, to shape the girl so that Jenny the whore and mistress became polished enough to be Mrs Hatch the courtesan. That way she could move in higher circles and be far more useful. From the beginning the idea delighted the girl, who longed for a life of silk rather than one of cotton and wool.

'Do they know about this?'

'Not yet,' he confessed. 'But I think they will help. I shall not explain everything. Enough to spark their sense of duty and no more. Young Jacob has been left behind in Lisbon under the care of a kind family in case that was worrying you.'

'It wasn't,' she said, and for a while they simply lay in silence until Jenny burst out laughing.

'Just thinking,' she explained in answer to his puzzled look. 'I'll wager I could teach her a thing or two that would half kill Pug Williams on their wedding night if ever they have one.'

Mrs and Miss MacAndrews arrived early in the afternoon on the next day, having travelled the last stretches under the protection of a supply convoy. It was another drab day, with rain falling steadily, and overnight the Guadiana had risen so much that it was too deep for the temporary bridge planned to be placed near Badajoz.

'More delays,' Baynes told Hanley, 'but at least this is one time that it is not anyone's fault. The plans for the siege are being written as we speak, and the peer is off north tomorrow in case Masséna starts stirring again. There are some worrying reports coming in, and Colonel Murray writes that we may have badly underestimated the speed with which a French army can recover. At the very least that means that no reinforcements will come here to join us.'

Hanley sensed that there was something else and waited.

Baynes handed him a letter. 'There may be some good news. The third paragraph is the important piece and will give you all the details we have, but in essence this is it. Some partisans have captured an officer in French service masquerading as a British officer. He says he is an Irishman and gives the name of O'Keefe.'

'The description could be anyone,' Hanley said.

'Agreed, but it might be Sinclair up to his old tricks in an area where he is not known. The rogue has vanished after all. He may have gone north instead of south. It is far easier for Soult's army to send detachments or messages to Masséna at Salamanca than it was while he was in Portugal.'

'Odd to send a man from the area and army he knows well.'

'Yes,' Baynes agreed, 'which would suggest that either they have not done it and this is mere chance or they have done it for some very good reason. I am inclined to doubt that it is him, but I might be wrong and we do need to know.

'I am sorry, my friend, but I must ask you to go with Lord Wellington and his escort when they ride north tomorrow. There is no one up there who could recognise Sinclair if we can reach the *guerrilleros* or persuade them to bring him in.'

'Am I not needed here?'

'By me or by the girl!'

Hanley gave a dutiful laugh. 'I meant that we still do not understand what the French are doing.'

'I will miss you, I most surely will,' the merchant said. 'But the siege will not begin for several days and you should be able to return here before it is resolved or before Soult marches against us. If it is Sinclair then find out what you can and then have him brought here. Come on ahead if it takes time to arrange an escort. I need you back, but we cannot ignore the chance of catching the rascal.'

Hanley understood, and saw the reasoning, even if he did

not relish the prospect of a hard ride at Lord Wellington's rapid pace. He called on the ladies to welcome them, thank them for travelling all this way, and assure them of the good health of the major. It took longer to explain his request for their help. He had planned to speak first to the daughter, but Mrs MacAndrews insisted on staying.

'We know Mr Hanley, Mama,' Jane MacAndrews said, 'it is not necessary for the sake of decency.'

'Stuff and nonsense, child, I do not care too much for that, but I have not ridden so far in wind and rain to miss out on hearing of this secret.'

In the end they agreed, at least to make an attempt, and arrangements were made. After that he went to see Jenny Dobson, determined to make the most of his last chance to visit for some time.

'Keen, aren't you,' she said, as he came in and took her in his arms.

15

Williams heard the news when he visited his friends in the 106th. It was a fleeting opportunity, seized when he was sent back to Marshal Beresford's headquarters with a report and was told to return in three hours to receive new orders to carry back. The Fourth Division were near by, had been dismissed from morning drills, and so he found Pringle and Truscott ready to take lunch.

'One may suspect a friend who only appears when food is on offer,' Truscott said without looking up.

'One might also suspect a fellow who clears off just before the regiment is to be set to labouring,' Pringle added happily. 'Oh, not to loaf about on the staff like others I could mention. No, it is simply that the gallant Captain Truscott is to serve as an assistant engineer, and so the real work is left to poor silly fellows who lack the learning or connections to seek higher callings.'

'I suspect it will be an arduous and dangerous task,' Williams suggested.

'Not the way Truscott will do it, I'll be bound.'

'Friendship is such a rare and precious thing,' Truscott said. 'In truth I had forgotten putting my name forward many months ago, but the colonel remembered when the request came round. It should be of interest at the very least, for unlike you fellows I have never witnessed a siege.' Pringle, Hanley and Williams had all been on detached service in Ciudad Rodrigo when the French took the place in 1810, but Truscott had remained in England with the battalion.

'You can have my experiences and welcome to them,' Pringle

declared, 'but since we were inside rather than outside, they may not be of much help. I can tell you one thing of profound importance that will guide your hand at every stage, for it is the secret road to success.'

'Then I lend you my ears.'

'Thank you, I am sure they will prove indispensable. For the moment it will be sufficient to listen. You too, Bills, for this is the voice of wisdom and maturity, and all the lore of the ancients. So are you listening?' Pringle was going red in the face, a sure sign that he was revelling in his own wit. They nodded.

'Good. Well, this secret way takes ten years, and once you have waited that long you must ... find a good supply ... of wood ...' Pringle was struggling to get the words out as he chuckled with delight. 'And then ... and then ... you must set about building a great horse ...'

Williams groaned. Truscott flicked hot stew from his spoon and Pringle swayed out of the way, lost his balance and fell off the camp stool, still roaring with laughter and somehow keeping his own plate level.

'I have missed listening to you fellows,' Williams said.

'Our intellect is surely far greater than that of mere staff officers.' Pringle was rolling as he tried to get off his back without spilling his meal. His glasses had slipped up on to the top of his head.

'Dear God, I hope not,' Truscott said, and then looked at Williams. 'Sorry.'

'You know I never complain,' he replied.

'Yes, that is why I apologise, my dear Williams.' Truscott had always been a serious-minded fellow for all his jollity.

'If you have quite finished a comrade in arms requires your aid,' Pringle called, having failed to work out how to get up without dropping his food. 'Anyway,' he added, as Williams took the plate and gave him a hand up. 'I shall be left here to keep an eye on things, and attempt to cope with whatever havoc young Mr Truscott can wreak.'

Williams had already heard about the ensign's folly at Olivenza.

'He broke the main pole on the colonel's tent last night,' Truscott added. 'He has taken to drinking with some of the other subs and fell against it.'

'Heaven knows how he did it,' Pringle said. 'The thing was twice as thick as your thumb. I could not have snapped it if I tried with all my strength.'

Williams shared their meal, and they chatted happily about the affairs of the 106th and of people they knew. Apart from the antics of Truscott's brother, and the usual minor accidents and misadventures, all seemed to be well – and Williams tried not to be too excited by the discovery that Miss MacAndrews was not so very far away after all.

'Mary Murphy is as big as house,' Pringle told him, 'and the surgeon says that the child should be born in about a month.'

'And more to the point the women of the regiment agree,' Truscott cut in, 'and they are far more likely to know about such things than that old drunk.' Williams was pleased, for Sergeant Murphy's wife had lost a baby to the bad weather and fever a few years ago.

'I am hoping to make sure that she is in a house when the time comes and has plenty of chance to rest afterwards.' The sergeant was in Pringle's Grenadier Company. 'Mrs Dobson is keeping a close watch on her. And yes, she is well, and so is old Dob.'

An hour and a half went by in stories and nonsense before any of them noticed.

'I must go,' Williams said.

'Eats up our poor meagre fare and then bolts once the larder is empty.' Pringle shook his friend firmly by the hand. 'Off to find an excuse to go to Elvas, no doubt.'

The thought had certainly occurred to Williams, and at the very least he felt that he must write after all, since then his apology could be followed by the pledge that he would soon be able to repeat it in person. He did not know where he stood, whether any hope at all was left, but as always even the possibility of meeting Jane thrilled him and made him forget his fears and despair.

'I doubt that I shall be so fortunate,' he said, and then had a thought. 'However, if either of you should be sent to the place and have the time to call on Major MacAndrews' family, then I trust that you will give them my very best wishes.'

Pringle patted him on the arm. 'Of course we shall.'

The orders were not ready when Williams returned to the marshal's headquarters in a big farmhouse. The commander himself passed while Williams stood outside waiting and filling the time by talking to a captain in the deep blue uniform of the Portuguese service. Beresford noticed him, and glared – although with his one good eye his expression may have seemed more hostile than was intended. Colonel D'Urban gave him a friendly nod.

'Our fellows are splendid,' the captain went on. Like all the British officers who had transferred to a Portuguese regiment he had received a step in rank. 'It is quite splendid how they have come on. But they are not big men. Half my regiment is barely an inch or two over five foot and they are slightly built – strong for their size, but then, as I say, their size is not great.'

The captain had received an issue of spades, picks and other tools and been asked to see how well his men worked with them. 'The shafts were all too long for them, far too long, and the tools themselves simply too heavy,' the captain told him. 'They did their best, but worked clumsily and were soon tired out. I cannot see us being of much use unless someone finds us something better made and more suited to their size.'

Williams declined the offer of a cigar, and after a while the captain was drawn away by a rather harassed-looking engineer, with black facings on his navy blue coat. He got the impression that this was simply one more piece in a long stream of bad news.

After half an hour he was summoned and D'Urban in person gave him a heavy sealed envelope. 'We shall be keeping you all very busy,' he announced with a smile. 'And I shall hope to meet you more than once.' There was no verbal explanation to accompany the instructions, and so Williams saluted and went outside to where Musket was tethered. He had noticed a basket of pears, so took one and offered it to the gelding. It vanished in just a couple of large bites, so he patted the horse's neck and climbed into the saddle. He was growing fond of the animal, almost as much as he was of Francesca. The chestnut remained a fragile beast, even if Stiles promised to fix him in time.

Lieutenant Colonel Colborne took the new orders and went alone to study them for a good half-hour, working with a map spread out on his little table. When he called Dunbar and Williams in, he had the eager, predatory look that the Welshman had not seen since the early morning at Campo Major.

'We have a job to do,' he announced. 'One that will keep us all fully employed and should prove amusing, but the key will be to march hard and fast and never give the French a chance to regain their balance. Gentlemen, we are going south.'

It was to be a raid, launched by the brigade supported by a couple of Portuguese squadrons and a pair of light field pieces provided by the Spanish. There would be other Spanish detachments moving parallel with them in the first few days, but after that they would be on their own.

'"The object of this movement",' Colborne read from the orders, '"is to check the inroads of the enemy's parties of pillage, to give confidence to the people of Estremadura, and to cover the collection of our own supplies, while it would announce in Andalusia the neighbourhood of a British force by showing troops on the frontier." Just that, and no more, so as you see we have considerable freedom to act. All told it is believed that there are eight or nine thousand French soldiers still in Estremadura, but they are dispersed, and we must not let them concentrate or realise how few we are by comparison.'

The colonel chuckled. 'As you can see, we shall have plenty to do to prepare, so we had better begin now.' They worked for the rest of the day, taking a brief dinner in his tent, still gathered around the map. Distances were measured, routes discussed and plans made for each possible occurrence. Dunbar rode out to visit the four battalions and give warning of the move so that they could ready themselves, repairing shoes, and drawing any food and ammunition they lacked. Only a small baggage train of mules would accompany them, for ox carts were too slow.

The next day it was much the same, as every detail was set out. The guns arrived, little four-pounders drawn by teams of mules, commanded by an eager young captain who looked as if he knew his business. Williams rode out with Colborne and Dunbar to inspect the battalions, to welcome the newcomers, and to take a look at the first stretch of road they would follow. Then he rode out on his own for a longer reconnaissance. The rest of the day was spent in copying down orders. In the sole, very brief lull, he forced his stiff fingers and aching wrist to write the long-delayed letter.

Dear Miss MacAndrews

I hope that you are well, and that the same is true of your good mother.

Please accept my most sincere and deepest apologies for my outburst at our last meeting – I shall beg your forgiveness in person at the earliest opportunity.

Miss MacAndrews, you cannot be under any illusion as to my sentiments. They have not changed, nor do I believe them capable of change.

yrs in haste
H. Williams

30th April 1811

He handed the letter to a commissary who was heading back to the Fourth Division and promised to find someone going to Elvas if he did not go there himself in the next few days. Williams was too tired and too busy to spend much time reviewing the composition. Part of him wondered whether the girl ever spent hours puzzling over his phrases from their meetings or their correspondence and trying to see beneath the surface. Somehow, he doubted it.

The next morning the drums beat and the Light Company bugles sounded at a quarter to five, an hour and a half before dawn. Each battalion mustered at its alarm post, then marched to form up, right in front, ready to move.

Colborne and Williams visited the picket line, confirming as expected that there was no sign of the enemy, and gave orders for them to return to their units. Dunbar was waiting for them as they rode back to the head of the paraded brigade.

The captain saluted. 'All present, sir.'

'Very good.' Colborne turned to the Portuguese major in charge of the cavalry. 'You may advance, Major.'

Dunbar went to his station with the advance guard, a company of the 1/3rd. The rest of the battalion was formed ready to follow. Behind them were the guns, then the 2/48th with buff collars and cuffs, the 2/66th with their green facings, and with the 2/31st, apart from one company, bringing up the rear of the main force. The baggage was behind them, with the women, children and other followers, at least as far as they could ever be regulated. All that could be ensured was that they were not permitted to walk with the formed companies. The rearguard was provided by the company from the 2/31st. Like the other battalions apart from the 66th, these men had buff facings, even though they had not yet the antiquity of this distinction or the seniority of the 3rd Foot or 'Old Buffs'.

'By sections of three, march!' Dunbar called out the order a half-hour before dawn. It was already growing quite light and the intention was to cover a good stretch of ground as early as possible in case the day proved hot. At the moment there was no sign of rain, and the roads they were to follow were baked dry and not seas of mud.

The advance guard moved off. Colborne said nothing as he watched them march, ranks neat and arms sloped on the left shoulder, each man stepping as close to the regulation thirty inches as was humanly possible. Williams could sense the colonel's pride and contentment. The entire procedure was a familiar one, and yet there was something of near-mystical satisfaction in watching all their efforts and those of others fuse together, and seeing the brigade move like some great machine.

'Earth has not anything to show more fair,' he thought, as the Buffs came past, and then each battalion in turn.

Five minutes later he heard Dunbar shout the order, 'March at ease,' and listened as it was repeated down the column. The men relaxed, and he caught the murmur of conversation as they knew that they would be given their first break after only half an hour. That would give time to adjust uncomfortable equipment and for those inclined to take a few puffs on their pipes.

'Well, Mr Williams, let us go and give the French a scare!' Lieutenant Colonel Colborne put his horse into a canter and sped towards the front of the column, looking like a delighted schoolboy. Williams realised that he was grinning as he followed.

16

'So the king happily settles in the best bedroom in the house. It's a fine night, he's a sprightly fellow with plenty of energy for everything save work, and so he strolls out on to the balcony and spies the governess looking after the duke's children. She's a pretty little thing, spots him up there, so bobs down and gives a little simper as she looks modestly away.' The colonel put his head on one side, lowered his gaze and fluttered his eyelashes. He was a stocky man, with thick and unruly eyebrows, a creased red face and huge hands. 'Well, of course, that was all the encouragement he needed. As I say, King Joseph is a sprightly fellow.'

Dalmas had heard the story several times before, but had nothing else he wanted to discuss, so let the man talk. The colonel was the senior officer of the artillery train in Soult's army and good at his job. Like so many he had begun in the ranks, and even now would happily get off his horse and help to repair a carriage or push to shift a bogged-down caisson. As for just about everyone else of his rank and above, the war in Spain was making him rich, and apart from court gossip he was fond of picking up paintings and statues – not on the same scale as Marshal Soult, it was true, but then few could match the marshal's energy in this sphere.

'Well, it was the work of a few minutes for him to pen a sweet little love note inviting the lass to attend upon his royal person,' the colonel continued. 'A flunkey delivers it, and an hour later, this Venus is shown in, all dressed up in her finery, such as it is.' He paused in his flow, rather brusquely putting out one hand to stop Dalmas, while raising his cocked hat in the other.

'Good day to you, señorita,' he said, 'and to you, my dear.' Two

147

local ladies in brightly coloured dresses and with mantillas over their heads and shoulders, gave curt nods in acknowledgement and passed on, a couple of older chaperones and a manservant attending them. Dalmas saw no hint of a simper from either of them, but that did not appear to dampen the spirits of his companion.

'Oh, I do so love Seville,' the colonel said, striding off and making a couple of men step back to avoid him. The streets were getting busier by the minute, for today was a market day and this afternoon a bullfight was to be staged, courtesy of Marshal Soult, Duke of Dalmatia. Food was short after last year's bad harvest, and in some of the poorest areas of the city people were dying from hunger or the illnesses its weakness brought. When he had ridden into the city the night before, Dalmas had seen carts piled high with bodies being driven off for burial. Today none of that seemed to matter, and rich and poor alike thronged the streets dressed as gaily as their pockets allowed, and all filled with the spirit of festival.

They stopped frequently as the colonel paid compliments to any half-decent-looking and moderately young woman. Most were tall, although perhaps handsome was a better word than beautiful, all were lively and some were willing. Dalmas knew that the colonel kept a mistress in his commandeered house, but from the look of the man he was still eager to explore other possibilities.

'We ought to press on,' Dalmas said, 'or we shall be late.'

'The Duke is always late,' the colonel said airily, and gave a great wink at another group of women, evidently in from one of the villages judging from their dark dresses and brightly coloured scarfs.

'Marshals of France can afford to be late. We poor mortals are expected to be early. Anyway, the Duke was not late at Austerlitz – and neither were you!' It did no harm to praise a man for past glories.

'Ah, that was a day,' the colonel said, obviously pleased with the compliment. 'Now, where was I,' the man said after yet another halt to salute a lady, a genuinely pretty little thing who had shot Dalmas a generous smile when the colonel was busy greeting her companion. It made the cuirassier officer wish that he was staying longer in Seville, for it was a special place. Nowhere else in Spain, not even in Madrid for much of the time, could French officers walk without escort amid a busy crowd. Dalmas saw bright uniforms dotted among the sea of heads, plumes, helmets and other finery, making them stand out. It was not just that soldiers could walk without fear of the assassin's knife, here in Seville the people seemed friendly, especially and gloriously the women.

'Ah yes, so little Miss Governess comes all dressed up to be honoured by an audience with the king. Of course she doesn't need clothes for what His Majesty has in mind, so he has her out of those in a trice and they spend the night doing their best to break the legs off the bed. She gets a nice necklace, some money – and if she's unlucky the bigger gift in nine months time of a little squealing Bonaparte. And everyone's happy, except, as it turns out, the duchess. The next morning the governess gets a beating and His Majesty gets a note. His hostess declares herself insulted that he should invite a mere governess to his chamber.' The colonel paused, building towards his big surprise.

Dalmas liked the man enough to pretend not to know what it was. 'Well, I would guess an aristocrat does not wish to see their staff seduced – especially with such ease.'

The colonel laughed. 'You would think that, would you not? Especially here where the fine ladies go to confession so often. But no, what the duchess's note said was that she was offended that His Most Catholic Majesty had chosen to approach a servant when the mistress of the house was at his royal disposal! Can you believe it! The next night old Joseph was bouncing the duchess around. Must have been good, because he took her with him when he moved on to Madrid, and her husband – gave him a plum job at court as well as horns to wear.'

The colonel shook his head ruefully. 'Pity we don't all have brothers who can make us kings. If I was a king I doubt I'd ever get out of bed – don't think I'd be able to after giving audiences to all the well-bred ladies!' The man's whole body was shaking with mirth, a curiously animal gesture.

They turned off the main street, where the press was lighter, and walked towards one of the big town houses taken over by the army. The shape of the cathedral loomed behind it. There were sentries from the Carabineer Company of a light infantry regiment standing on either side of the main gateway, and they presented arms as the officers saluted. An ADC was waiting for them, and ushered them off to a side room where several other officers were gathered. There was no sign of the marshal who had summoned them.

'Told you,' the colonel whispered, and then went over to talk to a gunner who was a good friend. Dalmas was the most junior officer present, and was largely ignored until the appearance of a *chef de battalion* who had some responsibility for gathering intelligence. The men found a quiet corner and exchanged some recent news.

'No Sinclair?' the man asked.

'Not yet returned.'

'Probably better. From what I hear Marshal Victor is passing some of the blame for Chiclana on to him.' Sinclair had arranged a deception plan to provoke the British and Spanish in Cadiz to risk a battle. The result was the bloody defeat of two of Victor's divisions by the British. At the time Dalmas was up north, aiding the capture of Badajoz.

'The British call the battle Barrosa,' Dalmas said. 'And it achieved very little, for they retreated that same night and the siege of Cadiz was resumed almost immediately.

'Still was not a victory. Now, how is this new scheme of yours working?' The *chef de battalion* had lowered his voice to a whisper, but even so Dalmas considered him indiscreet.

'Too early to say – and if it works we may never know,' he replied as vaguely as possible, and moved the conversation on to other matters, for he had no wish to discuss his doubts openly. Sinclair was enthusiastic and clever, and they had worked well at first, but in the last months he had begun to wonder whether the man's ideas were too elaborate.

'That is a convenient answer. If things work out you can take the credit, but if it all falls to pieces then you can say that it was nothing to do with you.'

It was forty minutes before the ADC reappeared to say that the marshal regretted the delay, but that he would be a little longer. Well over an hour had passed by the time Soult appeared. Dalmas knew some generals and great men who would make others wait merely to demonstrate the superiority of their own position. He did not think Soult was one of them, and suspected that this was simply one in a succession of long meetings. Waging war was just one of the tasks that fell to the Duke of Dalmatia, for he was to all intents and purposes also the governor of Andalusia. If there was famine in some parts of the city this was not for want of effort on Soult's part, and Dalmas knew how much time had been spent gathering what surplus wheat and barley there was, carrying it in army wagons to feed the towns as well as the garrisons. The cuirassier also knew – and in this case was aware that even the Emperor did not – that Soult approved a covert trade with merchants in Cadiz and even England to foster commerce and obtain food and materials that would otherwise have been unavailable.

'So, what have you to tell me today?' Marshal Soult had marched to the head of the table, where he stood so that everyone else would have to stay on their feet and so be less inclined to pad out their reports.

One by one the senior officers reported on the strengths of the three corps under the marshal's command. There was little mention of the Emperor's wishes – Dalmas knew that orders from Paris were usually either altogether out of date or so impractical that they could not be considered. King Joseph was not mentioned at all, for there was little love lost between Madrid and Seville, and apart from that His Most Catholic Majesty had gone to France. Ostensibly this was to congratulate his younger brother on the birth of his son and heir, the King of Rome. Dalmas had heard – and was inclined to believe – that in reality this was another effort to persuade the Emperor to let Joseph leave Spain for some simpler responsibility. It seemed that few of the French leaders in Iberia were very happy at present.

'Marshal Victor respectfully requests that he be sent the regiments taken from him earlier in the year, and at least two others.' The colonel making the report did everything to make clear that the words were not his.

'Huh,' the marshal grunted. 'Well, perhaps he should look after the ones he has rather better.'

'Indeed, Your Grace.'

Dalmas had heard that Marshal Victor had been incapable of getting up from his bed when a staff officer rode down to hear his report on the defeat. There was little love lost between Soult and Victor, even though their current mistresses were sisters. Oh yes, thought Dalmas, it is a grand life for the French in Andalusia, and as so often he wished that the Emperor would come back to Spain, for only he could bring the marshals to heel.

There were more reports on the state of garrisons and the few troops currently in the field, before they came to the central question.

'Marshal Beresford has around twenty thousand men, two-thirds of them English and the rest Portuguese.' The *chef de battalion* did not need to read from his notes to supply the figures. 'Less than two thousand are cavalry. Beresford may gain another five thousand from General Castaños, and ten thousand more under Blake. Those are the regiments that have come up from Cadiz.'

'Have the Spanish joined Beresford yet?'

'No, Your Grace, they are keeping several days' march away so that they can control more of Estremadura.'

'Why are the British waiting?' Soult scanned the faces until he found Dalmas.

'They are not ready, Your Grace, and the rains have made the Guadiana too high to bridge,' he suggested. 'Otherwise there is no good reason for them to linger.'

'Are they waiting for reinforcement from Wellington?'

'The London *Times* says that Wellington is blockading Almeida and watching Marshal Masséna. The marshal's army is still strong, larger than Wellington's force and more experienced. The British cannot afford to weaken their numbers there and send any more regiments to join Beresford.'

'The London *Times* tells you this.' A smile flickered across the marshal's jowly face. Seville was adding flesh to his already solid neck.

'It tells me where the English army is, Your Grace – the rest I have to deduce.'

'Just so.' Soult chuckled. 'What would we do without the English papers!' With so much of the country plagued by partisans and plain bandits, it was hard for the French commanders in Spain to communicate with each other, even when they wanted to do so. It was widely known that the Emperor relied on the London papers for the most up-to-date news of his armies in Spain and Portugal.

'I can take twenty-five thousand men and lead them north, but only for a few weeks at the very most, so I cannot go there and wait for the British to attack. Badajoz must hold out on its own for two weeks. Can it do that?'

'Yes, Your Grace,' the *chef de battalion* replied.

'Then I will need you to give me news as soon as possible when Beresford begins his siege. With twenty-five thousand men I can beat him well enough, or drive him back, which will achieve the same thing. It would be better if the Spanish do not join him, for that will make the matter far less certain. I want a close eye kept on them – especially on Blake, who has the greater numbers and the freshest troops. Well, I think that is that.

'Gentlemen, be prepared to move at just three days' notice. I will let you know by tomorrow which units are to muster and how they are to be organised. For the moment, I suspect we all having pressing duties.'

Soult gestured to his chief of staff, who in turn nodded at the *chef de battalion* and Dalmas indicating that they should stay. Most of his officers were used to such behaviour by now, but even so a few of the more senior men glared at them as they filed out, boots echoing on the polished floor.

'I wish to repeat how important it is for you to watch the Spanish,' the marshal told them once the door to the room was closed. 'I need to know instantly if they join with Beresford. Now, what do you make of this Beresford?'

The *chef de battalion* gave a brief summary of the man. 'He is the bastard son of an Irish aristocrat, an excellent organiser who has reformed the Portuguese army, and he has some experience of higher command, although this is the largest force he has ever led.'

'He is hesitant, Your Grace,' Dalmas added, when his colleague had finished. 'Like all the British he will fight like a lion if you attack him head-on, but he will be slow to manoeuvre and reluctant to attack.'

'Huh.' The marshal's grunt could mean anything or nothing. 'And where is that rascal Sinclair?'

'He has not yet returned, Your Grace. We have learned the names of more enemy spies and so he has taken a party out to catch them and persuade them to work for us.'

'Hmm.' Another grunt, and this time more obviously annoyed. 'Does that mean that you will be asking me for more money?'

'No, Your Grace. There should be sufficient for our needs in what you have already given us.'

'I should damned well think so.' Marshal Soult's mood improved with the news. 'So there will be other persuasion?'

'Yes, Your Grace.'

'Make sure it is nothing unnecessary. We have won the goodwill of many people because we protect them from the bandits, so we cannot afford to behave as badly ourselves. And what is all this money you have had buying us?'

'More information than we would otherwise have had, Your Grace, much more, and our friends increase in number.'

'You cannot buy Marshal Beresford's friendship, can you?'

'Sadly, Your Grace . . .' Dalmas had used generous gifts to

weaken the resolve of some of the Spanish leaders in Badajoz and so helped the marshal to take the place. Then he and Sinclair had been given a smaller sum, much smaller, and had used it to deceive the British at Campo Major. The wagon they had abandoned was mainly filled with empty chests, and only one held silver. Sinclair had come up with the scheme, wanting to sell the British the idea that a fortune had already been spread to win over sympathisers. 'Make them doubt all their friends,' the Irishman had said.

Dalmas had liked the idea, but then the Irishman had come up with the whole scheme of using Bertrand and Jenny Dobson, and he had been far less keen. The engineer was desperate to escape his creditors and it did not take much to hint to the English girl that he might save himself by deserting. In a carefully arranged accident they let Bertrand have some of the most recent orders sent from Paris and other secrets and then waited. At Campo Major they did not arrest him, but insisted on accompanying him everywhere and so let the man worry until he made his bid to cross over to the enemy. It had worked, after a fashion, but Sinclair saw outwitting the enemy as a game, and sometimes became so caught up in it that he lost all sense of what it was for in his longing to win a hand. Dalmas was beginning to think him too elaborate. He had not been able to get a straight answer from Sinclair over whether or not Brandt had meant to kill the engineer officer or to shoot the Englishman Hanley, or simply to fire close to them and make it all look real.

'I thought as much,' Soult said. 'In that case I must bring him to battle and smash this one-eyed Irishman, and you two must make sure I know when is the best moment to hit him. Dalmas, you go back to General La Tour-Maubourg and help him watch the British and Spanish. I need to know as soon as Badajoz is invested, and then we need to hit them sooner than they expect, so do everything you can to stop them watching us.' The marshal flicked a hand across the tail of his heavily decorated coat and turned on his heel, ready to bustle off to the next meeting of the day.

'Your Grace?' Dalmas saw the flash of irritation in the marshal's face as he turned. 'I wonder if you have had a chance to consider my application.'

Soult frowned, and looked at his chief of staff. 'Major Dalmas has made several requests to go to his regiment.'

There was another grunt, of amusement as well as annoyance. 'Want to leave us, eh? Well, not at the moment, because there is too much to do. If you help me win a battle then I will consider the matter. Now, good day to you both.'

Dalmas was not surprised by the answer, but even so felt low in spirits as he left Seville later that day. For all the good he had done at the meeting he might just as well have stayed watching the British. Something was stirring, and it would be better to get the earliest possible warning of what it was. He wondered when Sinclair would turn up. The man had taken a dozen soldiers all dressed in the uniform of the Irish Legion, although in truth they were rogues from half of Europe. There had been no word for two weeks, and if that was not so very unusual it was inconvenient at the moment. He would need Sinclair's help to discover the enemy's plans and conceal the French advance, but sensed that the Irishman's failure outside Cadiz made him reluctant to get involved in another campaign. Instead he was retreating to the more distant prospects and possibilities of the wider war – important, without a doubt, and difficult, but also worth nothing if the army was defeated.

Major Dalmas was weary of intelligence work and hoped that he would soon be free of it. At least for the next few weeks he would be with the cavalry outposts. It was not quite the same as being back with a regiment, better still leading his own regiment, but it was simple and he was good at it. He would go and help the marshal to win his battle.

17

There was still no sign of the rising sun, and although the grey light was growing, it was hard to see very far in the lingering mist. The air was damp and cold, and when Hanley ran a hand through his hair it felt dirty. They were a good three miles away from Fuentes de Oñoro, where the French had attacked with such determination the day before yesterday, and so far the enemy had shown no interest in this, the extreme right of Lord Wellington's position.

'There, Don Julian, see the shadows under the trees!' Captain Brotherton of the 14th Light Dragoons was pointing to the spot, one of the many stretches of sparse woodland around the village of Nave de Haver.

Hanley knew the area well, having spent months in the country near Almeida before Masséna launched his invasion. The fortress, with its French garrison, was surrounded by Lord Wellington's army, and Masséna had come back with all his might to open the road and take a great supply convoy to the city. If he succeeded, then the place would fall only to a regular siege of the sort the Allies were not well equipped to mount.

'Are they your men, Don Julian?' Brotherton asked. He was a bluff, eager fellow, quite short and stocky like a lot of light dragoons. He was experienced in the country, but it was clear that the man was suspicious of the Spanish in general and especially irregulars like Don Julian Sanchez.

Hanley peered at the dark shapes on the edge of the wood. The men looked to be on foot, and he thought he glimpsed a flat-topped shako, but that meant very little, since Don Julian's band of *guerrilleros* sported all sorts of captured uniforms. El Charro, as he was known, was a former sergeant in the Spanish line whose peaceful civilian life was shattered by the French invasion. He had raised a band of fighters, and harried the French for years, making it difficult for them to move in this border country unless they came in force. Hanley had ridden with the band many times and both liked and respected its leader. These days El Charro led some fifteen hundred men, infantry as well as cavalry, and had been granted the rank of general in the Spanish army.

'That is one of my pickets,' Don Julian said, his tone level. For all his reputation, El Charro was a calm man, who picked his fights with care and never wasted effort.

The sun broke through the clouds, its light pale, but growing, and the mist grew thinner almost immediately. Birds, perched in the stunted oak trees behind them, redoubled their efforts to welcome the dawn.

'There are a lot of them.' Brotherton's voice was filled with doubt.

'My dear captain, you may depend on it.' Don Julian remained courteous. 'That is one of our pickets.' The partisan leader turned general was tasked by Lord Wellington with watching the far right of the Allied position. A little behind him, and stretched for more than a mile to the hamlet of Poco Velho, was the Seventh Division, recently formed and composed mainly of foreign corps and battalions new to the country. Brotherton's two squadrons from his own regiment had arrived during the hours of darkness to reinforce this wing, but it was a small reinforcement, and at the moment they were dismounted and cooking breakfast. Hanley had caught the tantalising scent of chocolate as he passed them.

The disposition made it clear that Lord Wellington did not expect a serious attack in this area. For all their ferocity and skill in harassing an enemy, El Charro's men were unsuited to fighting in the line of battle. Yesterday the French had done little, apart from staging a grand parade with bands playing to welcome the arrival of some regiments of cavalry from the Emperor's own Imperial Guard. Marshal Bessières had come to reinforce Masséna and since the two men did not care for each other, Hanley wondered whether this explained the enemy's lethargy. Yet they could not simply sit facing the Allies indefinitely, and Lord Wellington suspected that today they would either withdraw or attack. The last seemed most probable and so the only question remained where they would advance. A threat to his right seemed less likely than elsewhere, for it did not offer a good approach to Almeida, but even so he had sent Hanley to ride up to Nave de Haver.

'You know Sanchez as well as anyone,' Colonel Murray had told him. 'Just keep an eye on the fellow for us. Partisans like that can almost sniff the French long before they see them. Just make sure he gives us plenty of warning.' Murray was Lord Wellington's quartermaster general and with Baynes helped to direct the gathering of intelligence.

Hanley was due to ride south again, but was too useful to be allowed to leave until the battle was over. By the time he had arrived, Murray learned that the prisoner taken by the *guerrilleros* was dead, killed by his captors when they were attacked by a French column and he had made a bid for freedom. At least that was the story they maintained, and it would be hard to prove otherwise. They had left the body behind, so it was not even worth going to visit the band. Perhaps it was Sinclair, but more likely it was not, and his whole journey was wasted. They might not know until the fellow did or did not turn up again. Hanley wanted to be back in Estremadura, for he needed to speak to Baynes. There was something not quite right about the whole business, about the French money, the attempted desertion of Bertrand and the capture or turning of their sources. He could see plenty of smoke and not enough fire to cause it, and wondered whether his suspicions were getting the better of him. Murray did not know enough of the situation further south to feel himself able to judge, but did wonder whether they had all been humbugged.

'Are you sure, Don Julian?' Brotherton's words snapped Hanley from his thoughts. The mist was even thinner now, the sun turning red, and he caught glints from the dark shapes amid the trees. 'It looks like fifty or more men to me, with others behind. Look! There on the left. Those fellows are holding horses.'

Once again Hanley was not sure what that proved, for many of the *guerrilleros* were mounted.

'*Madre de Dios.*' El Charro gasped the words. For a moment the wind blew and wafted away even more of the mist. They could see lines of men under the trees. They were in uniform, not odd pieces of many different uniforms, but all in the same dark tunics and trousers and with light covers on their shakos, and all of them held the reins of a horse. Hanley did not hear the order, but the figures moved, all climbing into the saddle.

'Oh, damn,' Brotherton said softly. 'I knew it,' he added, speaking loudly and looking more at Hanley than the partisan leader, 'they are chasseurs. I must go to my fellows,'.

The French line sparkled as the chasseurs drew sabres. Brotherton sped away, and Don Julian glanced at Hanley before putting spurs to his own horse and heading for the houses.

Hanley watched the French come forward at a walk. There must be seventy or eighty of them in two ranks, and another squadron appeared in the gloom of the wood behind them. He wondered about drawing his rifle and taking a shot, and went so far as to reach back to the long leather scabbard he had got made and fitted to the back of his saddle.

'Come on, Englishman,' Don Julian shouted back at him, and he realised that he was being a fool so followed. Nave de Haver was small, but the garden walls of the grey stone houses were thick and at least shoulder high. El Charro's men were spilling out of all the buildings, pulling on clothes and carrying their weapons. The *guerrilleros* knew how to move quickly, especially when the enemy was near. This time they had been surprised, but these were not easy men to catch.

'Go! Go!' El Charro bellowed at his men, his deep voice echoing in the narrow lanes. His men did not need more orders than that. They bounded on to horses and mules and set off away from the enemy.

'Will you not hold the village for a while?' Hanley asked as he caught up with Don Julian. 'They are only cavalry and will not find it easy to winkle your men out of this place.'

The partisan general looked annoyed and baffled that anyone could be so foolish. 'No,' he said, and then his expression softened. 'No, my friend. The infantry will not be far behind and so they will charge in here and we cannot stop them.'

'You might give the army more time to prepare.'

'I might, but what of my men? If your soldiers are taken they will be prisoners. If we are taken then we will hang. Is a little time worth that!'

More of the men rushed past them. El Charro spoke to one of his officers, and then gave an approving nod. 'We are away. Will you come with us?'

Hanley considered for a moment. 'I had better find Lord Wellington,' he said.

'Then go with God, my friend!'

'You too.' Hanley watched El Charro trot away, keeping pace with his men on foot. There was no sign of the French, and so he walked his horse through the village and set out back towards the Seventh Division. Threading his way down the narrow lanes and between the walled gardens he began to hear isolated shots, muffled by the woods and the still-lingering fog. The path led into a little gully, and although the sides were not steep, he stayed in it to keep out of sight. A bugle sounded the alarm, so the Seventh Division was beginning to react.

The gully ended in some trees, and then the ground rose as he went through them. There was no hint of sunlight in here, the mist still thick and cold, but when he emerged on to a low rise it was as if a veil was pulled back, for suddenly it was bright and he could see well. A quarter of a mile in front Brotherton's two squadrons had formed up. They were facing French cavalry, and, although it was hard to tell, Hanley did not think that they were the men he had seen before. For a moment more regiments

161

could just be glimpsed behind them, and then the wind wafted in a bank of fog and they were gone. The attack was clearly a big one, involving at least a couple of cavalry brigades, but that did not mean that it was not a grand feint. So far he had not even glimpsed any enemy infantry. Yet if it was a major attack then it would strike home against a division too spread out to offer much resistance.

One of Brotherton's squadrons charged, sending a French formation back some way, but then a supporting line came up and it was the British who were going back. The second squadron of light dragoons made a bold front and stopped the enemy pursuit, so that after just a minute or two of action, both sides formed up once more and returned to watching each other warily. Perhaps it was the damp atmosphere, but as he watched them Hanley felt none of the excitement of joining the charge at Campo Major. He pressed on, heading for Poco Velho and keeping well behind where he thought the fighting was going on. Shots were coming more often now, and he heard at least one concerted volley, so the Seventh Division were presumably becoming engaged – unless the French really did have infantry with them.

'Hanley! Hanley!' He had only just emerged from the thicker fog in one of the folds in the plain when the voice hailed him. Murray was waving at him from a little knoll, and beside him was a group of mounted officers. As he trotted up to join them, he saw Lord Wellington, who gave him a curt nod.

The general came straight to the point. 'What is the situation at Nave de Haver?'

'French chasseurs approached at dawn – at least a regiment and probably more,' Hanley reported. 'Don Julian Sanchez did not believe that he could hold and has retreated. The Fourteenth Light Dragoons are doing their best to delay the enemy.'

Lord Wellington gave an abrupt snort of a laugh. 'That cunning old fox,' he said, 'he is turning my flank. Well, we must not permit him to succeed. Thank you, Captain Hanley.' A gesture summoned a staff officer and the general dictated an order to him as Hanley walked his horse over to join Murray. The knoll offered a decent view of the plain, but the mist had still not broken and every now and again blotted large areas from sight.

'They've caught us on the hop,' Murray said, without any trace of worry. 'We must get the Seventh back to the main army and form a new front, so the task is simple enough – it is merely accomplishing it that will take some delicate handling.' There were infantry behind the French cavalry, but still some distance away.

'At least a division, and perhaps two or three,' Murray said, and then the whole staff was off, following Lord Wellington as he rushed to another vantage point. They passed more light dragoons and the 1st KGL Hussars moving up, but the French chasseurs were joined by regiments of dragoons and outnumbered their opponents by three or four to one. The British and German horsemen charged, retreated and rallied again and again, delaying the enemy, holding them back for a little while, but all the time they were edging backwards.

Hanley followed the general and his staff and heard the reports come in. A British and Portuguese battalion were driven out of Poco Velho by French infantry, and then cut up by cavalry as they retired.

'They have rallied, but have lost heavily,' an ADC told the general.

Just after eight o'clock, a distant rumble came from the direction of Fuentes de Oñoro.

'That must be their guns,' Murray commented as if discussing slightly less clement weather. 'I dare say they will hit the village again soon.'

The cavalry kept up its bold front, and now and again the half-dozen guns from the troop of Royal Horse Artillery supporting them fired and for a brief moment blotted out the persistent murmur of the French cannon.

'I cannot understand why they do not press us harder,' Murray said, as the British moved back again. 'We could not stand against such numbers if they all came on at once.' There had been no more reports or glimpses of French infantry. 'They are either very clever or bungling the whole thing.'

The words were ill chosen, for as they watched a squadron of light dragoons charged and found themselves fighting against a much larger body of enemy cavalry. Men fell, and others were taken, before the British cavalry fled back, but once again they rallied in the shelter of a supporting line.

The battalions of the Seventh were formed, but scattered over too long a frontage.

'Ah, the Light Division!' There was obvious relief in Murray's voice as he peered back over his shoulder. A battalion of infantry in dark green was doubling up behind them, and beyond the riflemen a column of redcoats marched up with colours flying. Hanley saw a Regimental Colour of a red cross on a white field and a union flag in the corner flapping lazily in the still air. It reminded him of his own regiment, even though this battalion had white facings and not the red of the 106th.

'Thank the Lord, Craufurd is back,' Murray said, for the irascible commander of the Light Division had returned from leave only the night before. Lord Wellington rode to confer with the general, but spent only a short while with him before galloping away.

'Oh, we're off again, and back to Fuentes no doubt. Stay with the light bobs, Hanley,' Murray told him. 'Ride to us or send word if anything requires Lord Wellington to return.' The colonel used his crop to speed up his horse as he hurried to catch up with his chief.

The arrival of the fresh infantry seemed to slow the French down for a while. Craufurd formed his men into six squares – three from the redcoated battalions, two of Portuguese lights in brown, and one of the greenjackets of the 95th, with the rest of his riflemen acting as skirmishers wherever there was enough cover to hinder the French horsemen. Each square was four deep, with the first and second ranks kneeling. There were wide gaps between them and through these the weary units of the Seventh Division, some very low on ammunition, retreated.

Craufurd remained in place and watched, letting them go for more than half a mile behind him. To Hanley's amazement so did the French, even when the Allied cavalry and horse guns retired to station themselves in or just behind the same gaps. The enemy simply watched, and he could only think that they were drawing breath for some great effort. He did not ask General Craufurd, for apart from a curt acknowledgement the general had made no attempt to speak to him. Hanley knew Black Bob of old and expected nothing less.

They waited and still the French did not press on, save for a few companies of voltigeurs who appeared and began to squib away at the skirmishers from the 95th. The mist had cleared enough for them to see columns of enemy infantry, but these were standing over a mile away and showed no sign of advancing.

'I want the First Battalion of the Fifty-second, and both regiments of Portuguese to about-face in column at quarter-distance,' Craufurd said to one of his ADCs. 'Have them wait for my signal and then go back two hundred paces, halt, and about-face once again.'

'If they do not attack us now then it will be a miracle,' whispered one of the staff to Hanley, who looked on in amazement because it seemed that the plan was simply to turn their backs and walk away.

Orders were shouted, and three of the squares split apart as the companies re-formed into column facing away from the French. The redcoated battalion completed the movement first and began to march off.

'God damn their bloody hides, they are to stop until my signal!' the general bellowed in rage. The staff officers were near the square formed by the greenjackets and Hanley saw two of the riflemen nudge each other and laugh.

The redcoats halted, and the general waited for several minutes before he raised his arm and pointed back. Hanley was watching the French cavalry, and saw three squadrons of dragoons in brass helmets and green coats walking their horses forward.

'Make ready!' The riflemen in the third and fourth ranks

pulled back the hammers on their rifles. Unlike the kneeling men in front of them, they had not fixed their sword bayonets, for the heavy blades made the short-barrelled rifle awkward.

The French were trotting, riders bobbing with the motion, the black horsehair crests on their helmets streaming behind them.

'Present!' The riflemen brought their rifles to their shoulders and levelled them at the enemy. The French were still two hundred yards away, and a volley at this distance might empty a few saddles, but would not stop a determined charge.

'Steady, lads, wait for the order.' Officers and sergeants paced up and down in the hollow inside of the square.

'*Vive l'empereur!*' The dragoons cheered and surged forward.

'Steady, lads! Wait!'

At eighty yards the cavalry stopped. They had not provoked the square to fire and any volley at so close a range would most likely be devastating. A few skirmishers fired from a thicket and a dragoon was plucked from the saddle. The rest turned about and went back. Men in the square started to jeer.

'Quiet, damn your eyes, or I'll have the skins of your backs!' barked the general. The riflemen stopped shouting, but most were grinning. By now the other three columns had reached their station and formed back into square.

Cavalry squadrons, a little fresher after their brief rest, walked forward to occupy the gaps between the squares and then these changed into column and – waiting for the order from their cursing general – marched back through the three other squares until they too halted and formed up. The French made as if to charge, but stopped when faced by a British squadron or the steadiness of the infantry, who would not waste a precious volley at too long a range.

'By God, a ruddy miracle.' The staff officer sported a disbelieving grin as he spoke to Hanley. 'There must be four or five thousand of them out there, and they are letting us get away.'

There were three thousand eight hundred men in the Light Division, and perhaps twelve hundred horsemen supporting them. The French cavalry threatened, and sometimes charged, but whenever they did they either baulked at the prospect of the steady squares or were driven back by a charge from the British and German horsemen. Apart from the voltigeurs no enemy infantry came up to support their cavalry, and so stage by stage Craufurd's men withdrew. A few French horse guns appeared and tore holes in the squares, but none dared to come close enough to inflict real damage.

To Hanley it all looked more like a field day than a battle. The Light Division went from one formation to another with precision. For a while they did not bother to form square and remained in column, simply turning about to face the French. Then the enemy became bolder, and so for twenty minutes they marched in square. That was never easy, for the danger was that gaps would open up as the sides and rear stepped out at different speeds, and yet the men in green, red and brown did it as smartly as on a parade ground. Hanley wished Williams was here, or old MacAndrews, for he was sure their military hearts would have warmed at the sight.

After two miles, the French began to hold back a little further. Hanley realised that they were back near Fuentes de Oñoro, and that Lord Wellington had formed a new line, extending the old one at a right angle. In the early hours it had taken him twenty minutes of leisurely ride to reach Nave de Haver. It had taken the Allies all morning to retreat.

The French did not launch a serious attack on the new position, instead sending battalion after battalion into the narrow streets of Fuentes de Oñoro. Hanley had ridden through the village many times, and never thought it in any way remarkable. It seemed absurd that so many men were dying to capture the modest stone houses and little church.

'They nearly took it,' Murray said when Hanley rejoined Lord Wellington's staff. 'And if they had, then perhaps they would have launched a more general assault. But we hurled them back across the stream in the end.' It was afternoon, and apart from desultory skirmishing and the occasional cannon shot, the battlefield had gone quiet. 'Still, once Craufurd brought his fellows back into the main line I do not believe that they would have broken us, even if they tried.'

'Is the fighting over, then, sir?'

'My guess is yes,' Murray told him. 'Although the peer is saying nothing and will no doubt keep us all active for the rest of the day. I will have a word with him later on, but suspect that he will permit you to go back to Marshal Beresford tomorrow. Let us hope you will find the siege of Badajoz well under way by the time you get there.'

18

The hooded lantern offered only a poor light, although sufficient to recognise the figure waiting for them.

'It appears they could not provide us with a real engineer, sir,' Pringle announced.

'You may be right, Mr Pringle,' Lieutenant Colonel Fitz-William agreed, his teeth very white in the darkness as his own face split into a smile. 'Good evening, Mr Truscott.'

As the sun set two hundred men from the 106th had paraded without packs or muskets. They had drawn tools instead and spent the last two hours waiting to be led forward, and then two more tramping the five miles from the camp, sited because it was the only suitable place anywhere near the fortress. Some also carried empty sacks and another party were rolling gabions, wicker baskets taller than a man and twice as broad. Both bags and baskets were to be filled with earth to help build the first of the Allied batteries.

'Good evening, sir.' Truscott saluted, and then plucked out his watch and stared until he made out the time. 'We have five minutes before we should move.'

It was the night of 8th May, and the Allies planned to begin work on the trenches and gun positions around Badajoz. Their task was to start Number One Battery, facing the San Cristoval fort, but on the other side of the Guadiana; other working parties would cut trenches to threaten the Pardeleras and Picurina outworks. Those were diversions, and the main attack was to be directed at the San Cristoval.

While the colonel wandered along the lines of men,

encouraging and joking with them, Truscott asked after his brother.

'The young rascal is well, becoming ever closer to Derryck and his minions,' Billy said, 'so they are probably drinking or playing japes on each other rather than getting a good night's sleep like good Christians. He has not drawn a work detail until three nights' time.' Pringle lowered his voice. 'I suspect the colonel has ensured that only the older soldiers are called upon for this on the first two nights.'

Five minutes passed slowly, but eventually Truscott told the colonel that it was time, and then led them off.

'Right, lads,' hissed FitzWilliam, 'quietly now.'

None of them apart from Truscott had seen the ground in daylight, for it was clearly unwise to draw too much attention to the place. Sticks had been driven into the earth every thirty or so yards and bits of white rag tied around the tops to mark the route up to the ridge. Truscott went slowly, knowing that it would be easy for the column to break up into little groups. There was a covering party of fifty men with muskets and ammunition somewhere in the darkness. Pringle heard them once when Truscott halted this column, but he did not see them.

As they reached the top of the ridge, the cloud parted and the light of a crescent moon showed them the fortress of Badajoz, its shape a silhouette darker than the night itself. Two engineer officers were waiting, one taking charge of the men with gabions. The other took half of the work party, while Truscott led the rest. Pringle followed his friend down the slope until he stopped at a row of markers running in a long line across the hillside. The clouds had closed again, but he could make out the shape of the San Cristoval and guessed that they were some four hundred yards away from its ramparts. The engineer led the men rolling the gabions and had them set up in a row a few yards in front of the markers. Still empty, the wicker drums would offer no real protection, and yet Pringle did feel a warm illusion of security.

'Come on, lads, spread yourselves along the line.' His own voice sounded deafeningly loud, and surely the sentries pacing the wall would hear and give the alarm. The men, most of them his own grenadiers, filed past him. He had divided them into teams, one with a pick and two with shovels, and was pleased to see that each group had stayed together. The colonel had gone with the other group, and Billy wondered whether that was a mark of confidence or simply chance.

Sergeant Murphy passed him, and he thought he saw the man wink. He was pleased that he had managed to get Mary Murphy sent to Elvas, where Major MacAndrews' family had taken her under their protection. Dobson was at the rear of the column, and as always the presence of the man reassured Pringle that the company would cope, whatever task was set before them.

'When you start, pile the spoil in front or behind the trench. Only fill the gabions or sacks from the heap behind.' Truscott's instructions were precise, but Pringle had always felt his friend was inclined to be too detailed, and at times fussy. The men had been told, and the main thing was to get as deep into the earth as fast as they could. The French would spot them as soon as the sun came up, even if by some blessed good fortune they did not realise what the British were up too long before that. Then every gun that could bear would pound the work. He could remember watching the Spanish guns at Ciudad Rodrigo sending ball after ball and countless shells against the French besiegers as they toiled. It was no longer such a happy memory.

'Right, use the spades to cut the turf and then break it up with the picks before you shovel it out.' Pringle wished Truscott would just let the men work instead of spelling out each thing they were to do, and then he wondered whether his own nervousness was getting the better of him.

'Come on, then, lads.' That was Dobson, keeping it simple. Pringle stood beside the sergeant as he jabbed with the blade of his spade and cut down an inch or two, then did it again in a line until he had cut out a square.

'Roll it up, boy,' he told one of the redcoats, who kneeled down and grunted as he pulled the grass roots free and then rolled up the turf. 'Good. Put it over there by the marker. That's where you heap up the earth.' Pringle saw the veteran glance up and wondered whether he was explaining as much to his officer as to the men. He could not resist walking over and prodding the rolled turf with his boot. It was surprisingly solid.

Dobson cut out three more patches of turf, until they had cleared an area several square yards in size. All along the line men were doing the same, producing a low hubbub of whispers and grunts. Three lanterns rested on the ground to give a little light, their open side pointing away from the French.

'Now, Jenkins, put your back into it, lad.' The grenadier spat on to his hands and then grabbed the pick and raised it. He slammed it down – the dull thunk appallingly loud to Pringle's ears – and then raised it and struck again and again. The same chipping sound was repeated as other teams got to work. Once he had worked on one corner he moved on to the next and Dobson and the other man began to dig the earth out and fling it on to the row of turves. It did not look like much of a rampart.

Within five minutes men were taking off their jackets. No one had asked, but Pringle saw no reason to stop them, even though the white of their shirts seemed so very stark. He walked along the line, not bothering to say anything, for the men needed neither instruction nor encouragement. By the time he had got back to Dobson's group at the far left of the trench, he saw that Jenkins was back in the spot where he had begun. The ritual was the same. Lower the pick, spit on hands, grasp it again and raise it high before slamming it down. This time the sound was different, much sharper, and Pringle saw a spark fly from the strike. Jenkins raised it again, brought it down, and the crack was louder this time. The pick stuck in the hard soil and he had to struggle to wrench it out.

'Here, lad, let me have a go,' Dobson said, and took it from him. He did not bother to spit, and lifted the tool less high, before bringing it down with tremendous violence. The spark leapt high, the noise almost like striking against metal.

'Bugger, I was afraid of that.' The veteran looked up at Pringle.

'It's more stone than earth, sir. We'll have to chip it out bit by bloody bit.'

The other teams were making the same discovery, and the noise of rocks being struck and all the attendant grunts and curses rose.

'Quiet there, quiet as you can!' The senior engineer's voice was loud and nervous. 'Captain, can you not keep your men quiet!'

Pringle was about to reply that they were quieter than some fellow yelling, and then he noticed a figure appear beside the man. It was FitzWilliam, and even in the dark his shape conveyed the poise and calm of the aristocratic former Guards officer. Billy did not catch the words, but could guess their sense. The colonel had a knack for reassuring others.

Dobson launched a powerful assault on the hard ground, the point of the pick driving into the solid earth, clacking against stone with vivid flashes of light.

'Right, boys. Ten hits with all your might and then pass it on to the next man.'

Jenkins took back the pick and began to work again, his blows wilder than the veteran's. Then the third man took over.

'Get shovelling,' Dobson told Jenkins as the man finished, and the pair of them scooped out the dislodged lumps of earth, but almost every thrust of the spades grated on stone. When the looser earth was cleared away the corner of the pit did not look any deeper to Pringle.

He wandered along the line, and saw that most of the teams were working like Dobson's group, sharing the brutal work with the picks. A few had not, and men leaned on shovels as they watched the third man work, so he told them to take turns.

Time passed. Billy could not tell whether it was minutes or hours. He felt idle and useless, but when he finally decided to have a word with Dobson and suggest that he take a turn the answer was blunt.

'Beggin' your pardon, sir, but you won't be much damned use.'

'Thank you, Sergeant.'

The men laboured on, dim, distorted figures in the faint light of the hooded lanterns. Time after time they savaged the ground with picks and then scraped away the meagre clods of broken earth.

When the French sent up a blue light from the San Cristoval the brightness was dazzling.

'Down! Down!' Billy waited for the men to stop and crouch in the trench – if something little more than six or seven inches deep could be dignified with the name. At least the gabions offered some shelter if no protection.

He could hear the faint fizzing of the rocket, the strange flickering light showing him the gaunt faces huddled down as close to the earth as was humanly possible. As it faded, there was another flaring of light, red this time, as a flaming carcase of combustible material was flung from the rampart of the fort. The whole shape of the outwork was almost as clear as day, and Pringle could even see figures moving on top of the wall and hear their shouts. The French must have feared an attempt at escalade, because the burning carcase would make it hard for them to see much further into the dark until it went out.

'Get going, lads,' said Lieutenant Colonel FitzWilliam, before any of the engineers stirred.

Dobson was first up, and grunted with sheer effort as he drove the pick into the earth and then prised it back and forth to break up the heavy soil. Pringle watched him, but the glow of the carcase still filled his eyes and it was hard to see properly. He took off his glasses and rubbed them.

The French were silent for a while, and slowly the burning carcase faded until it was no more than a dull glow and the outline of the fort was barely visible in the night. They worked on, and Billy could tell that the pace was slowing. He walked back to where three of the battalion's drummers waited, each with the dozen canteens of water they had carried piled up beside them.

'Lads, take three canteens each and offer them to the men,' he said. One of the musicians was Dobson's son, a stocky, plump youth more like his poor dead mother than his massive father. 'Let them have two sips each and no more for the moment.'

Sergeant Dobson had suggested bringing the water to Pringle, who had in turn gone to the colonel and received his enthusiastic blessing.

They worked on, and the drink seemed to give them renewed energy, at least for a while. Yet Pringle could tell that the pace was slackening. Men were groaning more and more loudly with the sheer effort of driving the tools into the iron-hard soil. The picks still set off sparks, but the blows were less frequent and over time became weaker.

'Good work, boys,' he said, pacing along the shallow trench. He was about to suggest that the men with the gabions take a turn, but before he could the engineer set them to taking earth from the low spoil heap and starting to fill up the great baskets.

Truscott appeared. 'Slow work. No one realised that the ground was so hard.'

Pringle bit back the suggestion that perhaps someone ought to have checked. His friend had a tidy mind, resentful of mistakes and inefficiency, and was unlikely to welcome such an obvious comment.

'This is to be the main attack,' the acting engineer explained. Billy sensed that Truscott was as frustrated with watching and waiting as he was, and needed to talk simply to fill the time. 'The others are diversions. This will be the main battery. We knock a hole in the San Cristoval, storm that, and then put a battery there to breach the castle walls of Badajoz itself.'

'Might take a while,' Billy ventured. 'If the pace here is anything to go by.'

'It's worse than you think. I have seen the guns brought from the stores on Elvas.' Truscott sounded offended. 'You can see the dates when they were cast moulded on the barrels – half are from the seventeenth century.'

'Dear God.'

'We will need His help for certain if we are to have any chance at all. They are dreadful brass things, the bores distorted by age. The gunners have been sitting for days measuring shot with great care in the hope of finding enough to fit.'

Pringle tried to cheer his friend. 'It's all a waste. As I told you, what you clever engineers should really be doing is building a great wooden ...' He stopped, for out of the corner of his eye he caught a flash from the San Cristoval, followed by the dull thump. A gun had fired, and the thought that it must be a short-barrelled howitzer was confirmed when he caught a tiny spot of light high in the air and coming towards them.

'Down!' he shouted. 'Everyone down!' Pringle pushed his friend into the trench.

The men dropped tools and flung themselves into the pitiful scrape of a trench. The ones working on the gabions knelt behind them even though none had more than a few inches of soil in them.

Pringle was crouching, still following the flare of the shell's fuse. He noticed that the colonel remained upright.

'Best to take cover, sir,' he said with some urgency.

'I do not believe we are in danger,' FitzWilliam replied, 'but if I am wrong there will be time enough.'

The arc of the shell was now plainly to their left, and so Pringle half stood as he watched the sparking fuse trail through the air. It landed a good thirty yards away and a little behind them, spun crazily on the ground for a couple of seconds and then burst in a gout of flame, sending jagged pieces of its casing scything through the air. Lieutenant Colonel FitzWilliam sprang back a pace and peered down at something on the ground in front of him.

'Of course,' he said, 'at night it is quite easy to misjudge such things!'

Pringle heard men laugh at the antics of their commander. No more French guns fired, until several minutes later the howitzer went off with another dull thump.

'Get down!' Once again the workers dived for the little cover available.

The gun captain must have cut the fuse shorter because this time the shell burst in the air and some way short. A gabion was pitched over by a piece of whirling iron and another shook with the impact, but that was all the harm done.

'I do not believe they can see us too clearly,' Truscott suggested, as they stood up again, and the men went back to work. Once again FitzWilliam had not moved.

'Yes, they are trusting to luck, and trying to annoy us.' Pringle began counting under his breath, and had reached five hundred before the next shot was lobbed up high by the howitzer. This one was closer, and as he watched the line of the shell, the colonel took two paces forward and dived down into the trench. The shell landed only a few feet from where he had been standing and lay there, neither spinning nor with any trace of a burning fuse. Murphy bounded out, struck the metal sphere with the butt-end of his spade, so that the fuse flew out, flared for an instant and then went dim.

'Well, at least we know our enemy has a sense of humour,' FitzWilliam said, standing up and flicking dust from his jacket and breeches. 'My poor tailor's heart will be broken,' he added, and the men near by laughed. 'Sergeant Murphy, you are a brave fellow, but you should not take such risks.'

'It's fine, sir,' the sergeant told him in a loud voice meant to carry along the line. 'Everyone knows that you cannot kill an Irishman – you just make him mad!'

'Thought you were all ruddy mad in the first place,' Dobson called from the far end of the trench.

'Ah, well, a man digging a trench in hard ground while someone throws shells at him is sure to be the best judge of sanity!' Murphy yelled back. With the French firing at them, there was little point in keeping silent.

Pringle had started to count again, but it was almost twice as long before the French fired, this time dropping too short. The interval was never the same, and that made it worse because the shot could come at any time and no one knew where it would land. The seventh shell landed close enough to the trench for a piece of casing to strike a man in the shoulder and knock him flat. It did not seem to be too serious a wound, but he could not work and so was bandaged by one of the drummers and led away. The next shell plopped to the ground behind the gabions and burst, flinging the nervous engineer officer back several yards. He had wounds to the face and chest, but the worst was a gaping tear in his left thigh. They managed to stop the bleeding, and he was carried off, sobbing in pain at every step.

The men worked on, fighting against fatigue as well as the stubborn resistance of the stony ground. Some of the picks bent so badly that nothing could straighten them out, and the men using them took turns with the other tools. No more shells did any damage, and there were a few more jokes, even if no one had the energy to laugh as much as they had earlier on. Pringle realised that the shape of San Cristoval and the fortress on the far side of the Guadiana were both growing clearer. Dawn could not be far away.

There was a longer pause between shots from the howitzer, and this time its single thump was followed by the roar of half a dozen cannon. Two of the gabions were struck, and one was still too light to resist and so was flung down. An eight-pounder ball went through a gap between them and skimmed the low trench, striking the crouching figures, smashing through flesh and bone. When Pringle dared to look up, one man lay unmoving, with his head hanging to one side at an unnatural angle, and another was screaming.

The colonel took cover with everyone else, but the trench was barely eighteen inches deep. The line of gabions was spread thinly, with only half filled well enough to weight them down and offer protection from the enemy shot.

'Sandbags!' Truscott yelled. 'Fill the bags and stack them in front.'

Each French gun fired as soon as it was loaded, and so there were no more salvoes, and simply a sporadic fire pounding the position intended to form the battery.

'We need to have enough shelter for the covering party to stay!' Truscott called to him, and then he grabbed one of the sacks, dragging it along the ground. 'Follow me!' Murphy was beside him, hefting a tied-up sack over his shoulder, and so was

Dobson. Pringle was about to join them when a shot ripped through the air above him and he found himself cowering.

'That's right, build it up!' The remaining engineer officer was standing up, showing the men where to reinforce the gabions and form something like a parapet.

Pringle pushed himself up, went to grab a bag as men with shovels finished filling it, then saw gloved hands reaching for the same thing.

'My dear Pringle, after you,' Lieutenant Colonel FitzWilliam said, pulling his arms back. 'I shall have the next one.'

Pringle grasped the sandbag, was surprised at its weight, and staggered forward. The engineer officer was still shouting encouragement, and then a roundshot skimmed the top of the gabions and the man's head vanished in a spray of blood. Pringle felt something hot and wet slap into his cheek and one of the lenses on his glasses was covered in blood.

'I think you are in charge,' he told Truscott, hefting the bag and laying it down on the wall growing between the nearest gabions.

'We need this at least four foot high for a good twenty yards.' A strong picket of men from one of the brigade's Light Companies was to hold the position all day in case the French sallied out, hoping to fill in the small excavation that was all they had managed in a night's work. 'Oh, thank you, sir,' Truscott added, his tone full of surprise at seeing FitzWilliam laying a sandbag.

'Keep up the good work,' the colonel told him, and then ducked as a shot tore through the air over their heads. 'There is some advantage in not being too tall,' he added, but the laughter was thin.

A shell landed among the redcoats filling sandbags, the blast throwing men back. Murphy landed face down in the spoil heap. Jenkins helped him up, Murphy spitting out earth as he came.

'You cannot kill an Irishman,' he said, and then stopped because another grenadier was stretched out with the side of his face missing.

'That is the best we can manage,' Truscott said after five minutes more. The gabions were tall, but the wall of sandbags linking them was not much more than three feet high, and there were no more bags to fill. 'It ought be enough if they keep down.'

The covering party that had watched them through the night moved in behind the wall.

'Best if we go as fast as we can, sir,' Truscott said to the colonel.

'You give the order, Mr Truscott, since as acting engineer you have command. Mr Pringle, you will lead them off and I shall bring up the rear.'

'Pick up the tools as we need every one,' Truscott shouted. 'When I say go we run for the top of the hill. Stop when you are over the crest and we will form up there. Well done, lads, it was a fine night's work.'

The howitzer fired, and then two of the guns and a moment later another. The balls slammed into the makeshift rampart, which shuddered, but did not collapse.

'Go!' Truscott called, and Pringle bounded away, waving with his arm for the men to follow. He was tired, stiff from taking shelter, and his limbs did not want to move until a ball flicked through the grass ahead of him.

'Come on, boys!' The 106th swayed and sometimes staggered for they were all exhausted, but no one wanted to linger and they went up the slope as fast as they could. To his amazement, they lost no one. The colonel and Truscott were the last over the crest, and a ball rolling down the slope almost took the captain's foot.

'Look out!' Pringle yelled at them, and FitzWilliam realised the danger and shoved his companion aside.

'My apologies, my dear fellow,' he said, and perhaps it was the relief of getting into shelter, but the men were laughing again.

'Lead us back, Mr Truscott,' the colonel ordered. 'Smartly now, boys, do not let those fusiliers see us save at our best.'

The column formed up, picks and shovels shouldered like muskets. As they marched away, Truscott fell into step beside Pringle.

'You may be right, Billy, perhaps we should have just built a horse.'

19

'I make it at least one hundred and thirty English miles,' Dunbar said, his finger running down the list and doing the calculation again. 'Yes, at the very least.'

Williams had not made so precise a count, but his guess had been similar. The brigade had marched all that way in just eight days, and from the start the weather had been dry and the sun beat down on them. Colborne was no great stickler for the details of uniform, and he let the men replace their stiff stocks with any convenient piece of cloth. Even so they sweated in their thick woollen jackets, while dust from the road turned faces and uniforms alike as dusty brown as the Buffs' facings.

Three or four times they had seen small parties of French, patrols or foraging expeditions. Only twice had they come close enough to expend any powder, and even then the enemy soon retired. The French left in Estremadura were spread thinly, and so Colborne marched at them, changing his route time and again, but always advancing, so that the enemy could not guess how many men he had and where they were going. Unbalanced and confused, the French retreated, and so far they had not concentrated or mounted any serious resistance. All they left behind were little garrisons like the one outside this town. The plan was working well, and Colborne meant to keep on pressing them.

'Still a long way to go,' the colonel told them, 'even if much of it will be back the way we came. But for the moment, everyone can rest – well, everyone apart from us!'

The three men sat on their horses and waited in the shade of a tall house, for although it was barely an hour after dawn it was already getting warm. They were in the little town of Belalcazar, and the arrival of the redcoats had not caused the sleepy place to stir much from its slumbers.

A bleary-eyed man appeared on a balcony across the street and stared at them in silence. Dunbar raised his hat cheerily, but the man said nothing.

'I doubt it is a terribly wise thing for folk to stare too closely at the French,' Colborne commented. 'But we have not demanded food or the virtue of his daughter, so one would hope that counts for something.'

The man yawned, stretching his arms high and closing his eyes and then resumed his scrutiny. 'Inglés?' he ventured after a while.

'Sí,' Dunbar replied. 'English.'

'*Viva los ingleses!*' the man said, yawned again, and went back into his room.

'Not quite a Roman triumph,' Captain Dunbar said, and laughed. Colborne looked with some irritation down the street behind them, but saw no one and did not appear inclined to say anything.

'Remember when we marched through Campo Major,' Williams said after a while. 'Everyone was hanging from windows and calling out "*viva los franceses!*" until they realised who we were!'

Dunbar chuckled and the colonel gave a faint smile. 'Cannot blame 'em. They have been occupied so many times by the enemy that they have learned caution. It is surely for the best that they do not give us too warm a welcome here for we shall not stay long. Ah, at last.'

Two horsemen came up the street. One was a captain in the Portuguese cavalry and the other a trooper with a white handkerchief knotted on the tip of his sword as a rudimentary flag of truce. The officer reported that everyone was in place.

'Good,' Colborne said, enthusiasm returning, 'then let us be about our business.' He led them up the main street, keeping a tight rein on his horse as it tried to run up the slope. Williams was riding Musket and the horse continued to please.

They passed the last pair of houses and there was a hundred and fifty yards of open country rising up to the shelf on which the castle perched. It had high walls, reinforced by turrets elegantly decorated in the Moorish fashion, and a big tower twice as high in one corner. Its top was eight-sided and from this distance looked almost circular, carved with crests of long-forgotten nobles. There was a flagpole on its top, and as they rode towards the castle a tricolour flag rose up it, hanging down because there was no wind.

'At least there is somebody in,' Dunbar murmured.

'Two companies at least, if that priest was right,' Williams said. They had tried and failed to find the town's mayor, and then spotted a little boy who led them to the priest's house.

The challenge came as they walked the horses up the steep path on to the shelf around the castle. It must have sat on rock, for there was no sign of a moat. Up close it looked even more picturesque. Williams thought how much Hanley would have loved to sketch or paint the scene.

They halted, and Colborne called out that he wished to speak to the commander of the garrison. His French was good and clear, even if the accent immediately betrayed his true nationality. Williams glanced around as they waited. One of the battalions was formed up on each side of the little castle, standing in line about half a mile away. Half the Portuguese raced up and down behind them to throw up dust and give the impression of greater forces waiting to advance. That had been his idea, remembering a trick used by Sir Robert Wilson when he harried the French along the border with his Loyal Lusitanian Legion. Williams had seen the cavalier Sir Robert bluff a French garrison into surrender by pretending that a couple of companies were a whole battalion.

Colborne noticed him looking at the deployed brigade. 'It is a shame that we could not find a way of creating some great pieces of ordnance as you suggested.' That had been part of the same idea. Medieval walls like this were pretty things, but could not stand up to modern artillery. Yet all they had were the little Spanish pieces and they would not dent the stone. For over an hour the three of them had pondered various schemes to mock up something so that at a distance it looked like a heavy cannon. The only feasible plan required a cart and tree trunk and they had neither. 'We shall just have to hope the French assume that we come well prepared.'

Williams did not believe it very likely. Last year he had seen a small Polish garrison of an elderly fortification scorn two summons to surrender and then fight off a whole brigade with a few guns and support from the Navy. All that he had seen of Napoleon's men in the last years made him doubt that Frenchmen would prove any less resolute than their Polish allies.

'Taking his blasted time, ain't he?' Dunbar said, and then a little door creaked open beside the main gate. 'Good God,' he added in a low voice.

Two sentries had stepped out, each with a bayonet fitted to his musket, and with brasses polished and blue jacket well brushed. Behind them was a short, immensely fat man in a pale green dressing gown. The first breath of wind wafted round the walls and lifted up the flap of oiled hair combed to cover his bald pate.

The colonel raised his hat. 'I am General Colborne, of His Majesty King George's army,' assuming the rank since he genuinely possessed the responsibility.

'Major Legros.'

'A little obvious, don't you feel,' Dunbar whispered.

Colborne launched into a carefully prepared speech, telling the major that he was surrounded by a strong force of redcoats, and that two divisions of Spanish under General Blake would arrive by the afternoon. If the Spanish were forced to assault the castle then he could not prevent them from taking vengeance. Blake had sworn to put every man to the sword in punishment for the cruelty inflicted on his country. The Spanish general was senior, but if the gallant major was to surrender to Colborne then the British, and no less a person than Lord Wellington himself, would ensure that he and his garrison received honourable treatment as prisoners of war.

Williams had heard the colonel rehearsing his plea, but even so was impressed. As far as they knew Blake was fifty or sixty miles away, perhaps more, and moving in the opposite direction, but the mutual hatred of French and Spanish surely carried greater threat than anything else Colborne could say. It was a bluff, he thought, a *ruse de guerre*, and since the French had provided the name they could scarcely complain when such methods were employed against them. Yet the term did rather suggest that they might be naturally wary of such things.

Colborne finished with a flourish, inviting the brave Major Legros to spare them all unnecessary bloodshed.

The Frenchman let him finish, one hand rubbing his unshaven chin.

'*Non*,' he said, and gave a little bow. Then he turned on his heel and went back inside, followed by the two infantrymen.

'Oh well,' Dunbar sighed. 'That would appear to be that.'

Colborne turned his horse and led them away. A musket boomed from the high wall behind them. Then two more fired and Williams saw a ball strike not far in front of them. Each man prodded his horse and raced away as more shots followed.

'I believe we have offended them,' he called out to Dunbar.

'Must have interrupted the major's breakfast,' the captain replied. 'A fellow like that would take such things very seriously.'

They waited for most of the day, watching the castle from a safe distance, but there was no question of attempting an assault, for there were no ladders and even if these had been available it was not their task to fight.

'No sense in marching through this heat,' the colonel told them, and ordered small pickets to observe the garrison in the unlikely event that it showed any signs of coming out. The rest of the men had a chance to cook, to repair worn soles of boots and patch up their clothes, or simply to sleep. Just for once the colonel did not insist on a day of drill.

In the early evening they marched, following a road that soon began to climb and wind through the foothills of the Sierra Morena mountains. The temperature dropped as they went higher, the night closed in and they were happy to keep moving. Williams and some cavalry rode ahead to find a spot for the bivouac, and found one about twelve miles away. By the time the advance guard arrived and Dunbar waved happily in greeting, he had marked out each battalion's position and drawn a sketch map showing the alarm posts. The ritual was already a habit requiring little thought.

The next day Colborne drove the brigade hard. After just three hours' sleep the bugles and drums roused them. They set out at four o'clock and marched until noon before resting.

'Make sure they eat and do not simply fall asleep,' he ordered, sending Dunbar and Williams to prompt the unit commanders. The instruction was not a welcome one, and the Welshman could remember times when he had felt so exhausted that all he wanted to do was slump by the road, prop his head on his pack and sleep. As he rode past the companies he heard officers give orders, and the sergeants shouting to stir the men.

Colborne gave them two and a half hours and then ordered them up. They marched on under dull skies and steady drizzle through the afternoon and evening, and then kept going as night fell. The clouds had gone, and a bright field of stars made finding the way straightforward. Dunbar took a troop of Portuguese cavalry on ahead and so for a change Williams led the advance guard, leading his horse to show them that he was sharing the burden of this long march.

'Thirty-five miles in a day,' Dunbar told him when they arrived at the small town where they would stop. 'I have rarely heard of the like.'

'I am not surprised,' Williams told him. 'The men are quite done up.' It seemed the colonel was of the same opinion, for the next day they did not move, although he ordered an hour of company drill followed by another hour by each battalion.

The following day they did not go more than ten miles, although it was still hard because the road was bad and rose and fell through hilly country. The forty-three prisoners they had taken grew sullen, so Colborne posted half a dozen Portuguese cavalry to escort them. Fear of reprisals kept them moving.

'Did you hear what happened up north?' Dunbar asked Williams when the column halted for the five-minute break given regularly each hour. 'As Lord Wellington was chasing Masséna, they reached a village with the houses burned and people massacred. Some redcoats were leading a column of prisoners back past a Portuguese brigade. One of their light bobs suddenly runs out, shoots a Frenchman through the head, and then fixes his bayonet and runs amok. Killed three before they stopped him. But it turned out that it was his village and he had just seen the bodies of his parents lying dead in the street, the mother shamefully mistreated. Lord Wellington had the man released after a couple of days under arrest.'

Williams had heard the story several times, albeit with a steady increase in the number of prisoners cut down. It was a grim tale, and he tried to imagine seeing his own family lying slaughtered by the ruin of their burning house. The thought of Anne or one of the other girls violated brought on a horror and a rage that made him suspect that he might well act as the Portuguese soldier had done.

'I pray to God that the people of England never see just how horrible this war can be,' he said.

'Amen to that. Though it might make them take the business seriously and give us what we need to finish the job. By the way, have you found out any more from those rogues?'

They had taken seven prisoners wearing pale green jackets with yellow facings. None was French and they tended to stay together as a group, conversing in a strange mixture of half a dozen languages. The men confessed to be soldiers in the Irish Legion, and admitted that they were under the command of a Major Sinclair, but did not know where he was. They had caught them in a village, waiting at an inn. Three had fled and managed to escape by hiding in a nearby marsh.

'No,' Williams replied. 'I doubt that they know much more.'

He had told the colonel and Dunbar of the men's importance, and so a cavalryman had ridden back to the main army with a report for Baynes.

'Nasty-looking bunch,' Dunbar said. 'Don't think the other prisoners care for them too much.'

The pace quickened again the next day, but now they were heading back to join the rest of the army. The news once again refreshed spirits and the men stepped out with a will. For the first time in days they started to sing, the Buffs beginning with a spirited rendition of 'Confound our officers'.

Dunbar grinned at Williams when he heard the chorus. 'Nice to be appreciated.'

They kept moving, into flatter plains once again, and so the going become easier.

'Badajoz is under siege,' Colborne told them after speaking with a priest who had ridden to bring them news. 'And Marshal Soult has mustered an army and left Seville overnight in the small hours of the tenth of May.' That was two days ago, and no doubt the French would be moving quickly to relieve the beleaguered city.

It was Williams' turn to find a place for the night's camp, and when he rode on ahead he was pleased to run into an outpost of the 13th Light Dragoons. They were almost back with the army.

'I make it more than two hundred and fifty miles,' Dunbar concluded when the next afternoon they met up with the remainder of the Second Division, which was part of the force stationed to the south to screen the besiegers. 'It does seem rather a long way to end up pretty much where we started!'

'Well, that is the army for you,' Williams said.

'Gentlemen, if you do not have duties to perform then I will find something to fill your time,' Colborne told them, but his heart was not in the reproof, and instead he watched his men with a proud eye as they halted and were dismissed.

20

Battery Number One was ready, after a frantic night of dragging three twenty-four-pounder cannon and a couple of eight-inch howitzers into place. Truscott had supervised, aided by Major Dickson of the Royal Artillery, but currently attached to the Portuguese. The guns were all on old-fashioned solid and clumsy carriages, the metalwork rusty and some of the wood rotten. Two spokes on the wheel of one of the howitzers had snapped as they were hauling it up the slope behind the battery, and it had taken nearly an hour for the little Portuguese gunners to replace it. There were plenty of the stockier redcoats to help haul the pieces up, but Dickson had no experienced artillery artificers to speed the repair.

At first light Dickson's crews prepared to open fire on the San Cristoval. Three nights of hard slog had fashioned a reasonably solid position, with a rampart built mainly around the gabions and cut to make embrasures for the guns. Truscott watched the major polishing his spectacles as he waited to give the order to pull the sandbags out of the embrasures and allow the bombardment to commence.

'I must say I did not believe that we would be ready,' Dickson had said. A short man, his rotund shape belied a remarkable energy and talent for organisation. It was the major who had selected the guns and brought them from Elvas. Now he ran his fingers round the muzzle of the nearest and his expression was not one of fondness. 'You ought to have seen the ones I rejected,' he told Truscott. 'We must do our best. The angle is not ideal – too oblique to inflict the most damage – but at least we can see the base of the fort's wall. Yes, I believe we may do very well in spite of everything.'

The French had not made the work easy. The previous day they had done their best to slow the besiegers down, sending out a strong battalion and some cavalry to raid the trenches. They came from Badajoz itself, crossing the great bridge and streaming up the side of the valley. No one had been looking in that direction and the alarm was not given for some time. The enemy even brought a couple of light field pieces to support their attack.

Truscott had heard the shouting and then the discharge of muskets and cannon as he was making the long walk back to camp, and had immediately run back. With the weight of French fire, the main covering party lay back on the far side of the ridge, so the sortie had reached the battery position before anyone could stop them. A couple of men were wounded or captured, but they had not lost more than one or two spades.

'Dear heaven, I am beginning to think like an engineer,' Truscott muttered as the thought sunk in.

The French were soon evicted as the 40th Foot and some Portuguese companies came up in support of the covering party. They were driven out, but then the redcoats and their allies became excited and chased as far as the ditch outside the San Cristoval fort and stayed there for hours, engaged in a futile exchange of musketry. It had taken a while to drive the cavalry and guns back into the fortress, but in the end they were forced to retreat under the protection of the outwork covering the bridge. Throughout the day the guns in Badajoz pounded the battery position and trenches as the men toiled to repair the damage and extend them.

Truscott was told to assist one of the RE officers in laying out a new battery, which was designed to cover the bridge and threaten any fresh attack. They used flags to measure it out and mark the position, working in the open because it was set back a little, on a hummock near the top of the valley, and it was hoped that the distance was too great for accurate shooting. They had almost finished when a six-inch shell landed beside one of the redcoats working under their command. The man reached down to pinch out the fuse, but before he could the bomb went off, fragments ripping through his body and flinging him back. A tiny piece grazed Truscott on the cheek, but the engineer officer was struck in both legs.

They had begun the siege with nine Royal Engineers. By now two were dead and four wounded, which meant that there was even less rest for assistants like Truscott. He spent the remainder of the day supervising the men cutting a trench out from Battery Number One towards the site where Number Two would be constructed. The French fire never slackened, and throughout the day there was a steady trickle of casualties.

Truscott managed to get no more than a couple of hours' sleep, lying propped against the side of the trench and dozing in spite of the cannon fire. After that he went back to work, and kept on through the night as they armed the battery. When the sun came up he did not really expect relief, although he was so tired that he felt a dangerous fatalism coming on. The next strike by a French shot could not be predicted, and it was tempting to get on with things and accept whatever happened. The replacement of the work party with new men snapped him from his lethargy.

'Good morning, sir.' Sam was standing in front of him, hand raised in salute, and a broad grin on his face. 'The Light Company reporting as work party.'

Captain Headley was in hospital, struck in the face by stones and dirt thrown up when an eight-pounder shot hit the rampart just where he was standing. Truscott had a brief nightmare that his brother was in charge of the detachment, and then with relief saw two more officers and, best of all, Major MacAndrews striding up to see him.

'It looks as if the ball is about to begin,' the Scotsman said cheerily. Major Dickson was peering over the top, making his final calculations and then calling out instructions to his crews as to the charge and elevation required. 'Is not science a wonderful thing,' MacAndrews added. 'Now, where do you want us, Mr Truscott?'

He led them along the extension of the trench to the right of the battery. While he was doing so, Dickson must have ordered the embrasures to be uncovered because there was the sudden thunder of one, two and then a third shot from the big twenty-four-pounders. The gunners raised a cheer, and then the sergeants yelled at them to get back to work. A minute or so later the howitzers fired, and Truscott could not resist peering over the parapet and watching as the shells lazily sailed up and then dropped down on the fort. One struck the edge of the ditch, while the other almost passed over the fortification to fall on the other side. It was not such bad practice for inexperienced crews with antique guns.

Then the French showed them how it was done. Guns boomed from the San Cristoval, and then more than a dozen from the walls of the castle in Badajoz itself. The range was long, but these were big pieces, eighteen- or even twenty-four-pounders, and in a much better condition and far better served than the Allied guns. They were also aiming at the flank of the battery and could not be opposed by any of the besiegers' artillery. Truscott ducked as the gabion beside him shook from a violent impact. There were screams from one of the gun crews as a shell exploded above their heads, wickedly shaped pieces of metal spraying down on to the heads of the gunners.

The battle went on all day, but grew ever more unequal. Time and again French shot smacked into the sides of the embrasures and caused the earth to collapse so that it was impossible to fire out until it was cleared. Men died as they shovelled away to clear them, ripped to bloody shreds by the impact of heavy cannonballs flying with appalling force. The Portuguese worked hard, pulling aside the dead and wounded, and working the blood-spattered cannon, but they could not match the weight or the accuracy of the enemy fire.

After ten minutes one of the cannon was struck on the barrel, producing a strange ringing call and leaving the old bronze so bent by the impact that it was useless. One of the howitzers went next, its wheel – the new one fixed on with such labour during the night – was hit and shattered. All around them the parapet was crumbling from blow after blow. Both the other cannon were put out of action before noon, one hit squarely on the muzzle, bursting it open like the petals on a flower, and the other had its carriage broken. The remaining howitzer fired now and again, until the damage to the whole battery and the terrible losses to the gunners made Dickson abandon the effort.

'We shall have to repair as soon as we can,' he told Truscott as they stared at the shambles that had been Number One Battery.

'Not until nightfall,' the acting engineer replied, and wondered how much could be achieved even then. Until something was done to suppress the enemy fire Truscott suspected that the position was untenable. 'I'll keep the men working to extend the trench. That should be possible as they have more cover.'

The French fire slackened, but never ceased, and throughout the afternoon the party from the 106th dug, and tried not to show any part of themselves over the parapet. They worked hard and a slow, steady progress was made. Most of the shot fired at them hit gabions and earth and did no great harm. The shells were more dangerous for they could fall anywhere. One plopped down in the middle of the trench itself, sending Truscott, MacAndrews and all the nearest men diving down.

It fizzed, exploded and Truscott felt his body shake as if struck by a great gale, and yet when the smoke cleared and each man stood up, hands feeling for injury, it was discovered that no one was hurt.

MacAndrews found a couple of holes torn in the tails of his coat. 'That might have been unpleasant,' he said, examining them, and there were a few thin smiles.

Most of the time the men laboured in silence, breaking it only to curse. Truscott had seen the redcoats cheerful on long marches and in the middle of fierce battles and yet had never seen this sullen determination.

'They do not care for digging and labouring at the best of

times,' MacAndrews said when he asked the major about it. 'Think of it, a good half of them enlisted to get away from labouring. But it is more the lack of honour in this sort of business. They cannot fight back, do not know when the deadly shot may strike, and they are covered in filth all the time. I cannot quite say why, even though I feel it myself, but nearly all of them would far prefer falling in battle than being struck as they work here.'

The Scotsman was a tall man, and so bent his head down as he leaned against the wall of the trench beside Truscott.

'I fear they do not care too much for engineers,' he added after a few moments. 'At least not at times like this. They become the enemy, every bit as much as the French, for it is their orders which may see everyone killed. Oh, I know it is unfair, but you cannot blame them.'

'The engineers are doing their best,' Truscott said. 'Our best, I should say – and no one can claim they have not paid a high price.'

'Did I not say that fairness does not come into it. You are one of the family, so give them time and take them away from this and they will be as merry and willing as you please.'

Five men were wounded, all by pieces of shell. Young Samuel did not do anything foolish, and that was a relief. Truscott kept expecting the boy to climb up on to the parapet and jeer at the enemy.

'He is learning,' MacAndrews told him. 'In fact even as we speak.' The young ensign sat with his back to the side of the trench and read from a book. It was the gift his older brother had sent him as soon as the lad enlisted – *The Complete DRILL SERGEANT containing the PLAINEST INSTRUCTIONS for the DRILL, MANUAL, and PLATOON EXERCISE, according to the latest regulations* and so on – the immense title ran down the entire cover. He should have become thoroughly conversant with such things before the 2nd Battalion sent him out here, but the boy's memory had proved imperfect.

'I insist that he studies at every opportunity.'

'He is learning, as I say, and beginning to be accepted,' the major assured him. 'I know that it is an easy thing to say, but you should not worry. I believe the men are growing fond of him, and he has not done anything so very much more foolish than half the young idiots sent out to join regiments.'

They both ducked as a shell exploded in front of the parapet. Earth pattered down on their cocked hats.

'Do you know that the other subs have given him a nickname?' MacAndrews asked him.

'The Complete Truscott.' Billy Pringle had told him during that first night excavating. 'I cannot quite work out whether it refers to the book or my own shortcomings.'

'Both if I am any judge,' MacAndrews said, and looked at him with some concern. 'You really are quite fagged, my dear fellow. Get some sleep. I shall watch and make sure the work carries on.'

'It is my duty.'

'Captain Truscott, do you believe me incapable of making sure that the men dig a hole in a straight line! Sleep, man, sleep.'

Truscott felt himself blinking. He sank down, back against the rough wickerwork of the gabion, and the darkness came almost immediately.

21

Hanley took nine days to ride back to Elvas, changing horses regularly and going at what he thought was a good pace, even if it did not quite match the speed of Lord Wellington. Baynes did not let him have more than a short rest before he was given yet another mount.

'I had feared that you would not return in time,' the merchant told him when he arrived. 'Another day and it would have been too late. Perhaps it would not matter, but this is not something we can try too often. Get some food, for we leave in an hour.'

'We?'

'Yes, I shall come some of the way with you, at least as far as Marshal Beresford and the army at Albuera. We will have the hussars for protection and a couple of others who may prove useful. I will explain it all on the way. For the moment, eat, rest if you can, and be ready to go.'

'It would be nice to wash.'

'As you wish, but on a day as foul as this it will not make a lot of difference once we set out.'

Hanley thought for a moment of forgetting food, bath and rest and instead calling on Jenny Dobson, but before he decided he found that he was helping himself to the bread and ham laid out on the merchant's table. It tasted better than anything he could remember, and he ate with a fierce intent. Even the thought of standing up felt like too much effort, and a brief reflection made him suspect that his saddle-sore loins were scarcely up to vigorous activity.

The rain fell steadily as they rode out of the main gate on

the Badajoz road. Apart from the hussars, he was surprised to see Corporal Scott of the 60th wearing his greatcoat and looking uncomfortable astride a horse. Beside him was a dark, silent man in a drab uniform.

'I will tell you all later, but first I must have your own news from the north.'

Hanley told him as best as he could, sometimes having to raise his voice when the wind gusted hard so that the rain drove into them. He explained that the partisans had killed the captive before he arrived, but that he doubted that it was Sinclair.

'Your friend Williams captured a few men in the uniform of his Irish regiment. Did not see the fellow himself, but he is surely out there somewhere and up to no good. That is why we have to set out in such haste.' The merchant explained that he had fed information to Gutiérrez. 'I have asked him to meet with you and with the priest from Nogales outside the old convent of Santa Cruz near the village. He is to bring all the information that he has about Marshal Soult's army and also be prepared to find cattle to feed General Blake's divisions when they arrive. Even if nothing else comes of this business we shall at least fool them into thinking that the Spanish are several days' march away.'

'Are they not?'

'If all goes well Blake should join Marshal Beresford by sunset tonight – well, what passes for sunset on a day like this. That will give him at least ten thousand more men than the French. Who knows whether Soult may risk attacking at those odds? That is not our concern for there is no more that we can do about it.

'Gutiérrez will have reported to the French all that I have told him. I have given him a couple of pieces of entirely accurate information in the last fortnight. Too late for them to do the French any good, but it ought to have added to his credibility. So they should believe this and no doubt pay the fellow well, or even return his daughter, though somehow I doubt that. Be hard to get to her anyway, if she is still inside Badajoz.'

'Do you think Sinclair will come?' Hanley asked, struggling

to follow it all because he was tired, wet and cold and wanted only to sleep. 'Or Dalmas?'

'We would risk it, would we not, for the chance of taking one of those rascals? They may be elsewhere, may not get word in time, or any number of other things might stop them, but if they see such an opportunity then I doubt very much that they will not take the risk. That will give us our chance to take them as they try to trap us.'

'You mean as they try to trap me.'

'Oh yes, I am far too valuable – not to say far too old and corpulent to have any chance of escape if things go wrong. Thus it falls to Captain William Hanley to be our bait.' They rode ten yards ahead of the others, so that even when they had to shout to be heard it was doubtful that their escort could have made out one word in a dozen.

'I know that you would have preferred assistance from your own regiment. They would do it well, I am sure, but it is not possible to get them, at least not in time.' The merchant had sketched out his plan. 'Corporal Scott you know, and he strikes me as a good steady fellow and almost fully recovered from his wound. The other one is named Schwartz, and is from the Brunswick Corps. The provosts caught him and his brother lifting silver plate from a church and both are sentenced to hang. I offered him the chance to accompany you and promised that as long as his conduct met with your satisfaction then they would both be pardoned. His captain assures me that he is an excellent shot and a fine soldier even though he is a thief. That gives you two riflemen and that offers a distinct advantage, even if Sinclair brings the murderous Brandt.'

'You think it will be Sinclair?'

'Yes. I do not know why, but for some reason I do.'

'Then what if he comes with a squadron of dragoons – or a regiment?' Hanley felt that the scheme relied too much on guesses.

'You will see them coming. The hussars will come with you and you can trust them to spot any large force with plenty of warning. If he does that then more fool him, for you simply ride away and do not look back. Gutiérrez will lose some money – his life too if he makes them angry – and we will be no worse or better off than we were.'

'And Father Hernandez?' The priest from Nogales had proved a good source of information over the years.

Baynes shrugged. 'He is a wily one. I am sure he will find a way to escape. There is nothing I can do to change that. Nor can I leap the walls of Badajoz, sweep up Gutiérrez's daughter in my arms and carry her to safety on my white charger if that is what you want.' Baynes patted the thick neck of his heavy mare.

'There are risks, William,' he went on. 'I do not hide them.'

Hanley raised more questions, playing with the broader idea and every detail of the scheme, but knowing that he was growing more and more enthusiastic. It might work, and it was surely worth the attempt. After a while he raised his bigger concern.

'What if the whole thing has been a ruse? We assumed Bertrand had vital information. We assumed all those chests in the wagon had once contained money, but perhaps they wanted us to think that? Are they weak rather than strong, and so trying to bluff us into wasting all our time looking for an empty plot?'

Baynes brushed aside a damp lock of hair plastered over his forehead. He reined back and stared at Hanley with a fond smile. 'I know, William, I know, but how would we tell? We would be fools if we assumed that it was all a bluff and did nothing. So catch Sinclair and let us see if we can find out.' He clicked his tongue. 'Walk on, girl.'

'Of course, you may have an even bigger worry than all of these, my dear Hanley,' Baynes said after they had ridden in silence for a while.

'There appear plenty already.'

'Yes, but what if I am in the pay of the French!'

It was Hanley's turn to smile. 'I have considered that possibility.'

'I should be disappointed and offended if you had not. And what is your conclusion?'

'To keep an eye on you!'

Baynes roared with laughter, so loud that even their escort

could hear, and they stared at him with as much curiosity as anyone could muster during so soaking a ride. For a while the rain grew even heavier, the wind picking up and driving it into their faces so that no one bothered to talk. Later the wind fell and the rain slackened to drizzle and then stopped altogether. Hanley saw a dull red glow reflected off the clouds long before they could see the army's encampment, so the soldiers must have found enough dry wood to light fires. There was a murmur of conversation and even the odd snatch of song as they rode through the camp.

The mood at Marshal Beresford's headquarters was far less contented.

'The Spanish are late,' Colonel D'Urban told them. 'Blake was supposed to be here this afternoon, but he has not come. He says that he is on the way, but it is vital that he hurry. If you will excuse me, I must send another officer to hurry them along.'

The Fourth Division was still at Badajoz, covering the withdrawal of the siege guns and other precious equipment, a task made more difficult because the heavy rain had caused the River Guadiana to rise. 'I fear some of the regiments may be stranded on the wrong side and may not arrive at all. The remainder can scarcely be here before tomorrow morning,' an ADC explained. 'That leaves us with only the cavalry, the Second Division and the Portuguese, so we will be sorely outnumbered,' he said. 'It may mean that we shall have to withdraw. No one seems to know where Colonel Madden and his Portuguese cavalry have got to. He was supposed to join us, but there has been no word from him.' He hurried off.

There was constant bustle among the marshal's staff, a pervading air of nervousness and bickering. As far as Hanley could tell there were at most seventeen or eighteen thousand British and Portuguese soldiers to face twenty-three thousand French. Soult had arrived faster than they had reckoned.

'General Long and the cavalry came back far too precipitately,' D'Urban said. 'I fear he must be replaced before he can do more harm to our cause.' There was more than a hint of satisfaction in his voice, as if this confirmed his existing doubts.

They heard a different story from a captain of the Foot Guards who was on Long's staff and had come to seek new orders. 'We were told to come back with all speed and so we obeyed. Left to ourselves I am sure we could have held them longer, at least until their numbers forced us back.'

Hanley wondered whether more energy was being spent assigning blame than improving the situation. They waited for more than an hour, having brief snatches of conversation, and so learned that the French were to the east on the far bank of the little River Albuera. Cavalry and infantry had both been seen before darkness fell, and the rest of Soult's army was no doubt following them.

'Get something to eat and a little sleep,' Baynes told Hanley and the others after some time had passed. No one had shown any inclination to pay attention to them. 'From what I can tell the army is staying put because the Spanish will be here in a few hours – in fact they wanted to nab you so that you could act as one of the guides to take them to their assigned position. I refused, the marshal grew angry, but thankfully Colonel D'Urban knows me well enough to explain matters and insist that I would not act so other than with good reason. He promises to provide a guide for you, but I doubt that we will receive much more assistance.' The next words were whispered. 'It is my impression that affairs here are not dealt with as they would be if Lord Wellington were present. Still, there is one piece of good news. General Castaños is senior to Marshal Beresford, but he has most chivalrously stated that he will not be present in any official capacity and so command will stay with the marshal. That is surely for the best.' There was a slight trace of doubt in his voice.

The merchant woke them at two o'clock. 'You should go as soon as you are ready.'

Hanley struggled to stir, his limbs feeling stiffer than when he had lain down with blanket and cloak over him.

'Do not take unnecessary risks, William,' Baynes said. 'If there is a chance, then take it, but do not hesitate to give up the game if you sense something is wrong. Good luck.'

'They seem happy at such an unearthly hour,' Truscott said to Pringle as the 106th and the rest of the brigade prepared to march. Men talked and there was a fair bit of laughter before the sergeant major's booming voice called them to attention.

'Glad to see the back of this place, and of digging trenches while the French take pot shots at them.'

Truscott looked back at the brooding shape of Badajoz, just visible against the night sky. All the effort and death now seemed wasted. One of the brigades of the division was stranded on the far side of the river, but even they would follow on as best they could, and only a few token pickets would be left to guard the trenches and battery positions. If the garrison decided to come out then they would have to retire and so the French could demolish and fill in as quickly as they had men and tools to do the job.

'They do not usually care for retiring from the enemy,' Truscott said, feeling that others ought to share his own sense of failure.

'Well, there is the prospect of a battle, and they would prefer that to labouring. Especially my fellows.' Pringle's shoulders began to shake and his friend realised that he was in the throes of exercising his wit. No doubt if the light were better he would have seen Billy's face reddening and creases spreading from his mouth. 'After all, a tall grenadier has to make a deeper trench to shelter himself. You little chaps have a far easier time of it during a siege! I should call that... I should call...' Pringle was unable to continue.

'A tall order?' Truscott suggested, as usual unable to resist smiling at Pringle's delight.

Billy was doubled up with laughter, and only just able to recover a little when the sergeant major bellowed for silence.

The Fusilier Brigade was paraded behind several regiments of Spanish infantry, the remnants of the army almost destroyed by the French when they took Badajoz back in the winter. Truscott, relieved for the moment of his duties as engineer, had come past them on the way to rejoin his battalion.

'The poor devils have not a greatcoat between them, and I am not even sure that all have muskets,' he told Pringle once his friend had calmed down. 'I suspect this business will fall to us more than anyone else. Just like Talavera and Barrosa.'

'At least they are here. I would not discount them, but it is much to be lamented that Kemmis' brigade is not with us.'

'Well, at least MacAndrews has their light bobs,' Truscott said. 'Oh, did I not tell you. The three Light Companies from Kemmis' brigade were this side of the Guadiana, and so have been attached to the light battalion of our brigade. Old Mac will put them to good use.'

There was the sound of boots marching towards them with fixed intent. Sergeant Major Philips was formerly a guardsman and even in his greatcoat still managed to look smarter and more neatly pressed than anyone else in the battalion. A glance was enough to silence the two captains.

Philips turned to face the column, his boots slamming on to the ground. He filled his lungs.

''Talion will advance! Forward march!'

The drums rolled and their band struck up 'The Girl I left behind me'.

Pringle chuckled. 'I'd hardly call Badajoz a girl, but I am glad to see the back of the damned place!'

They marched into the night, and Truscott could not shake off his sense of despair at their failure. Young Sam was with MacAndrews and the Light Companies and no doubt he had not a thought in that empty head beyond his next meal and his excitement at the prospect of a battle. Truscott hoped that there would be a chance to see his brother before anything happened.

22

Williams watched as the shapes of the abandoned houses in the village of Albuera grew clearer. The brigade had stood to arms as usual, the drums and bugles rousing them at half past three in the morning. They were behind the village, and as the first and senior brigade of the Second Division they were on the right of its line. Next to them were the two other brigades – each with three battalions of redcoats. On their left were the Portuguese.

'Now they should not be there,' Dunbar said. The light was growing, a pale grey light for there was no hint of the sun and it looked as if the day would be cloudy and wet. The two staff officers had ridden up the gentle slope that hid their battalions from sight and were looking down at the village and the river beyond it. Williams could just see the dark shapes of columns of infantry over to their right and some way ahead.

'Only the Germans and the cavalry outposts should be ahead of us,' he agreed. The two battalions of greenjacketed KGL light infantry had the task of holding Albuera village.

Colborne joined them a few moments later, having returned from a brief meeting with General Stewart. 'It is the Spanish under Blake,' he explained. 'They were supposed to take up position level with us, but went astray in the darkness.'

Dunbar snorted and then noticed the colonel's disapproval.

'Just be glad that they are here. The Fourth Division is not.' Colborne looked at the dark shapes of the columns. 'They have over ten thousand men and this is too extensive a position to hold on our own.'

The main highway from Seville to Badajoz crossed the river at Albuera and on this side divided so that roads led off east and west as well as continuing north-west to Badajoz. Marshal Beresford had stationed his forces to block the route and to give himself the option of withdrawing along the main highway if he decided against risking a battle. The British and Portuguese were behind a low ridge, in truth little more than a fold of ground, gentle enough to walk up and down with ease. This continued to the south, rising slowly, and with a couple of knolls providing little crests a mile or more away. At the moment the Allies had nothing to cover this ground, and at the very least the Spanish would extend their line a little.

'From what I have heard,' Colborne continued, 'it is the Spanish generals who have urged us to fight, and so their arrival should add determination to our leaders.' Since Campo Major the colonel had avoided direct criticism of the high command, but it was clear from his comments that he disapproved of much they did – and just as obvious that he longed to hold such high responsibilities and demonstrate to all how things ought to be done.

Dawn came, and they could see that the Spanish battalions had stood to arms just like their allies.

'Not much sign of the enemy,' Williams said, as he scanned the plain on the far side of the river. It presented little obstacle, for even swollen by rainwater a determined man could cross it. There were two bridges in front of the village, a rather ugly old one and an elegant newer one, as well as a clear ford not far away from them. When Colborne had led them on a ride over the ground the previous afternoon they had found another one further to the south.

'No, probably taking their ease,' Dunbar suggested in an effort to lighten the mood. Colborne did not smile. There were several outposts of French hussars and infantry pickets a little to the rear.

'I suspect that soon the order will come to stand down,' the colonel said. 'Let the men have breakfast and ensure their firelocks are in a proper state. I have a feeling that they will need them before the day is out.' He lowered his glass and flicked the cover over the lens, but he kept staring past the Spanish and further to the right. Two tributaries met to form the River Albuera and the island between the two streams was covered in trees and scrub. 'I do wish that was not there, for they may form behind it without our having any idea of their intention. It appears we expect to be attacked straight at our centre, and if so we shall be in the thick of it soon enough. That is if we have read Marshal Soult properly. Yet I am not sure, not sure at all. I do not think that is the way I should attack this position, were I Marshal Soult, but then I am a mere lieutenant colonel so there is surely much I still have to learn of the art of war.'

Williams watched the trees. It was not an unbroken line, even if for the moment the shadows were too dark to penetrate. In full daylight it ought to be possible to see troops in the trees or moving behind them, even if it would be hard to tell their numbers or purpose.

Twenty minutes later one of General Stewart's ADCs brought the order to stand down and have breakfast. Soon afterwards the Spanish divisions began to re-form and march back until they were level with the rest of the army. There was a sporadic squibbing off of muskets all along the line as the men on picket duty tried to clear their loaded weapons. The easy way was to add a fresh pinch of powder to the pan and then pull the trigger in the hope that the main charge was still dry enough to go off. If it failed, and a persistently lazy soldier would often try two or three times, then all that was left was the hard way, yanking out ball and charge with the aid of a long rod, ideally hooked at the end. Williams had seen all sorts of contraptions devised by redcoats who swore that their own method was the best.

Sentries were posted by each company, and then the rest stripped off their drab grey greatcoats and set about lighting fires. There would be hot tea, at the very least, even if there was only cold biscuit to eat. Williams wondered how they managed to find the wood, because Albuera was little more than a ruin, roofs, doors and window frames long since stripped away by successive French armies that had marched through. Colborne and his staff enjoyed a pleasant breakfast with piping-hot tea, a thick porridge and several eggs and rashers of bacon.

'Found it, sir,' Dunbar's soldier servant said when questioned about the bacon.

'The man's a rogue, but invaluable,' the captain said when the private was out of earshot. Not even Colborne was inclined to take the matter any further, and little was said as they drank and ate in contentment.

At seven o'clock, well fed and as rested as they could be, the colonel decided that he had sat idle long enough. 'Dunbar.'

'Sir.'

'Stay here in case of orders. I doubt that there will be any for some time, but be here just in case I am in error. Williams and I will take a ride to see what is afoot.'

They went forward into the streets of Albuera with its unroofed houses. Marshal Beresford and his headquarters were in the few largely intact buildings nearest to them, and as they approached orderlies were waiting with horses for the commander and his staff.

'Good morning, sir.' Colborne saluted when the marshal appeared.

'Colborne,' the marshal replied with his accustomed bluntness, and without any trace of a smile. He glanced at Williams, but paid him no attention, and without more ado the big man climbed into the saddle and cantered off.

'We are going to see General Blake,' D'Urban explained. 'It is quite likely that with this reinforcement the French will not risk an attack.' Then he too clattered after his commander.

Colborne and Williams walked their horses through the village. The KGL light infantry were preparing to defend the far end, and as far as Williams could see it would be a hard business charging across the bridges to storm the place. If the French had enough men they might send some wading through the little river as well, but that would slow an attack down, and there was open ground for a musket shot in front of the houses. If they did get in it would cost them dearly.

They went around the village in a loop, passing some of the dragoon guards on outpost duty and exchanging pleasantries with Brigadier General Long before riding on. Yet Williams found his eyes continually drawn to the rolling country south of the Spanish infantry.

Colborne noticed. 'I do not care for it either, but if we had four or five times as many men we could not hold it all.' He rubbed his chin in thought. 'However, it will do no harm for you to take a ride down there. I shall return to the brigade and expect you back in half an hour.'

Williams gave Francesca a loose rein and let her rush up the smooth slope and then run along the top. He waved amicably at a few Spanish staff officers as he passed them.

It was soon clear that Colborne was right. The higher ground extended a long way south, all of it open with scarcely a tree or bush to be seen. It rose very gradually, with occasional dips and troughs, but there was no obvious point to anchor the entire position. About a mile south of Albuera, Williams came to a small knoll, which was perceptibly higher and then dropped away until it climbed to a second crest about five hundred yards away. That one was higher again, although not by much. Francesca rode down one slope and up the other side without the slightest hesitation, the going good at every stage. Even if not much of a ridge, this higher ground seemed very well drained. At the top of the second knoll he stopped and turned, and could see the village of Albuera and the entire Allied army in the distance. As the colonel had said, they did not have enough men to occupy all of this ground, but he did wonder what useful purpose the Portuguese served on the far left. The slope there was difficult, the river harder to cross, and an attack at that point seemed unlikely. Yet even if they were brought south they could not stretch the line this far without making it dangerously thin.

Williams rode back, and for a short while lost sight of the army as he went down into the little valley. When he reached the top things had changed. There were dark shapes of formations of French troops advancing towards the river – probably cavalry but impossible to tell at this distance. Much further away and to the north-west a shadow moved on the road from Badajoz, which he hoped was the Fourth Division and his own battalion. Williams wondered how his friends were, and inevitably Miss MacAndrews forced her way to the front of his mind. He had received no correspondence from her since his letter. Had she never received it or instead chosen not to respond? He stared off into the distance to where Elvas stood, too far to see, but close enough for a man to ride there in less than a day.

Would she be awake so early in the day? He pictured her lying in bed, a fan of red hair spread around her soft, peaceful face. The dream came of turning Francesca away from the armies and riding to her – just him, a knight riding to find his lady. He could bang on the door and demand entry, and then sweep her up in his arms.

It was only a dream, and not a serious one, even if a small voice whispered that such devotion might truly win her heart. At Barrosa he had fought knowing that the girl was not many miles away in Cadiz, and now it looked as if the same thing would happen again. In a strange way it was worse than if she were hundreds of miles away or even home in England. The thought that it was almost but not quite possible to see her made the prospect of an action worse. A vision came unbidden, but irresistible in its cruel irony, of lying bleeding out his life's blood, and thinking that Jane was not so very far away and yet might as well have been on the moon. He wondered whether there was time to write another note, and ask Dunbar to have it delivered if he fell, but dismissed such thoughts as indulgent.

Williams kicked his heels to race Francesca on as fast as she would go. This was not a time to think, but to try to be as busy as possible. No one had good thoughts before a battle, and the best a man could hope for was to have no thoughts at all. He had seen too much of battle not to know all the horrors that it held. Since being wounded the previous year some last piece of inner defence had crumbled. Before that, a naive part of himself had still believed that he could not be hurt. He was experienced enough to know that the odds of coming through were better than of being wounded or killed, but he no longer had quite the same assurance that he would always survive.

Instead of heading back straight towards the main Allied line, Williams decided to ride to where he had seen Brigadier Long and so be better placed to report to Colborne. It was an easier route, since it would not require him to thread his way between the Spanish formations, and he should be able to return well within the half-hour.

A cluster of mounted men ahead of him was surely the marshal and his staff, and rather than go through them he veered right and galloped along land sloping down to the river. Beyond the senior officers, four teams of horses pulled limbers and guns into position on top of the low ridge. There were several squadrons of cavalry in cocked hats and red jackets on the slope covering the new bridge and the main ford just to the south of it.

More French had appeared on the far side of the river. There were at least four regiments of cavalry, and their own horse artillery trotting up to deploy. Williams saw Long and headed to him, arriving just as the brigadier general angrily gave instructions to an ADC.

'Tell Marshal Beresford that I must have the Fourth Dragoons. Tell him that they are needed here and cannot be spared. Now go!'

'Back again, Lieutenant Williams?' There was no real anger in the general's voice and once again Long seemed pleased to see him. 'Some damned fool ordered the Fourth to the rear to tend to their horses and forage! Have you come from beyond our right?'

Williams nodded. 'Colonel Colborne asked me to take a look, sir.'

'We should have extended the line and at the least occupied those two low hillocks. Better yet have spent yesterday entrenching them and mounting batteries.'

'Sir, they are moving to cross at the ford!' One of Long's staff was pointing at a formation of cavalry in blue jackets and grey trousers walking their horses forward. Unlike other cavalry, their front rank carried tall lances and their red over white pennants fluttered as they moved.

'Are they French?' asked a captain with the blue facings of the 3rd Dragoon Guards. 'I thought only the Spanish had lancers?'

'They are Poles,' Williams said. 'The Legion of the Vistula, and they are fine soldiers.' Williams had seen the same uniform once before, back when he had held the bridge and protected the army's flank as it limped towards Corunna.

'Well, not as good as the Third I am sure – or any of our fellows,' Long declared. The captain looked pleased by the compliment.

The first of the Poles splashed through the ford and urged his horse up the little slope on this side. Half the formation came through and then divided into a line of skirmishers. The rest of the squadron came behind them as a formed reserve. Across the river dragoons in brass helmets, green jackets and high black boots manoeuvred to support them. The six guns of the French Horse Artillery battery deployed in a line to cover either this advance or fire at the village. Beyond them two regiments of chasseurs in green advanced towards the bridges.

'Well, they wish to draw our attention if nothing else,' Long said. 'Instruct Lefebure not to open fire without my express order,' he told an ADC, the Dutchman Williams remembered from Campo Major.

Williams spotted a column of infantry marching along the highway. They were in tan-coloured greatcoats with off-white covers over their shakos and they came with little pomp, but there was a sense of purpose about their movements.

'I imagine you should return to your own station, Mr Williams,' Long said, and then turned to the captain from the dragoon guards. 'Best drive those lancers back to their side of the water.'

Williams turned Francesca round and saw an officer in the scarlet jacket and lace of a major general accompanied by an

ADC coming to join them. It was General Lumley, the commander of one of the other infantry brigades in the Second Division, and he looked none too happy. Williams wondered whether his own presence had provoked the annoyance, but the general ignored him and reined in beside Long.

'Good day to you, my dear Long,' Lumley began. 'I do not enjoy the circumstances of this, but I am sent by Marshal Beresford to take command of the cavalry. At least one of the Spanish commanders is senior to you, and so it is thought better to appoint an Englishman of higher rank to ensure that the cavalry are not wasted.'

Long's horse stirred, throwing back its head, and Williams suspected that the rider had involuntarily jerked hard on the bridle. The brigadier general flushed, his mouth twitching at the corners, but he said nothing for a moment.

'I deeply regret this necessity,' Lumley said.

At length Long mastered his emotions. 'Well, sir, it is surely not the moment, but that is not in our hands. Be assured that I shall do my utmost to be of service to you in any capacity you wish.'

'I am most glad of it. I have not long arrived and had little chance to observe the ground. If you would be so good, I would have you at my side throughout the day.'

Williams trotted away before anyone remembered that he was there to witness such an awkward encounter. There was a cheer and he saw the dragoon guards turning their trot into a canter and raising their long swords. Ahead of them the Polish skirmishers gave way and scattered, for they could not hope to resist a formed body. The supporting half-squadron advanced in turn and as the two lines were about to meet some of the dragoon guards found their horses faltering. Even from this distance Williams could see the red and white pennants flickering and flapping with motion and he wondered whether this had frightened the beasts. There was a brief struggle, the flash of swords and the ripple of ranks intermingling, but the pace had gone from the British charge. The men in red retreated, chased by the lancers, until a second squadron of dragoon guards came forward, and this time they did not check. The Poles were sent in their turn flying back to the ford as Williams reached the top of the slope, still peering back over his shoulder.

The roll of many drums shocked him. The entire Allied infantry had formed up – the Spanish and Portuguese in two lines and the Second Division in a single line. Orders were shouted and they all marched forward towards him. There were ten battalions of redcoats in the centre, even more Portuguese in dark blue on the one flank, and Spanish in white, brown and light and dark blues on the other. With Colours unfurled and drums beating they stepped on with all the good order of a field day. It was an inspiring sight, and one that made him stop, but he was puzzled as to its purpose. Recovering himself, he went over to join Colborne and Dunbar as they walked their horses ahead of the brigade. Williams passed them, wheeled round and went with them.

'Wondering if you would turn up again!' Dunbar said in welcome. 'We are ordered to crown these heights.'

'Why?' Williams realised that his tone was impertinent from a lieutenant to a captain, let alone should the colonel feel that the question was directed at him. 'Forgive me, I am a little surprised, sir. Are we simply to occupy the higher ground or have we more to do?'

Colborne said nothing, so after a moment Dunbar replied. 'All we have been told so far is to take position where we can see the French and they can see us.'

'They have a lot of cavalry and half a dozen light guns, but as yet I have only seen a single infantry brigade advancing,' Williams said.

Dunbar grinned. 'Then we ought to give them a nasty surprise.'

The three horsemen were now close enough to see over the crest and were soon at its top. More French cavalry had appeared, but Williams could still see no more than five battalions of infantry, the leading units stationary and in line with their guns.

'Perhaps it is hoped that this display of our might will deter the enemy.' Colborne's tone was flat, not bitter but akin to that of a parent speaking with disappointment of a child. 'I am not sure that we are resolved to fight if it can be avoided.'

If it was a bluff then Williams doubted that it would work. His experience told him that the French never readily gave up a purpose, and he was sure that veterans like Colborne and Dunbar had just as much respect for their enemy.

The whole line crested the ridge and then orders were shouted for them to halt. Williams could see small groups of cavalry chasing the last of the Polish lancers back across the river before retiring to rally on their supports. More French cavalry, including several regiments of dragoons, had appeared and were formed on the far bank. Then he spotted a second brigade of infantry on the highway. It did not look as if Marshal Soult was ready to turn around and retire.

A row of puffs of smoke appeared, blotting out the French gun line, and a few seconds later they heard the dull reports. They were firing at the village. A few moments later the Royal Horse Artillery supporting the cavalry began to reply. Between their own brigade and the nearest Spanish, the guns attached to the Second Division moved forward to deploy. Before they were ready the French guns fired again. One of their infantry columns sent out skirmishers, who advanced towards the bridges.

'I do not believe that the enemy is deterred,' Lieutenant Colonel Colborne said with more than a hint of satisfaction, and Williams wondered whether it was pleasure in being proved right or at the prospect of commanding a brigade in a major field action.

23

Hanley started in the saddle when he heard the guns fire, and then told himself that he was a fool as the sound was from miles away. He was no longer sure that this was such a good idea and wished that Williams was with him, or even Sergeant Dobson. Rank mattered little to Hanley, and he would happily have let his friend or the veteran NCO decide how to do this. Pringle would have been a comfort, but the other two were what Baynes liked to call killers, and they understood fighting better than he ever would. They were also very good at it.

The high walls of the convent were ahead of him, a good three hundred yards away, looming up on the hilltop. Sinclair might be waiting there. Hanley remembered how the Irishman had tried to ambush him once before, with Brandt and his rifle lurking in the tower of a church. Yet that was when he had still believed Sinclair to be a British officer, so Hanley had gone to meet him and might well have died or been taken if he had not been warned.

Hanley was determined not to go inside the convent in case the enemy was waiting. Stay outside, he told himself, and he and the others would have a chance to move around, seek cover, or even escape. Would Sinclair think the same? There were trees on either side of the track, quite close on his left, and a hundred yards away to the right. On the right there was also a brook sunk into a little gully, and nearer to the convent a couple of low stone sheds with crumbling animal pens around them.

'Come on,' he said to the hussar riding behind him, and gestured for them to go forward. He nudged his horse, and then kicked harder and flicked it with his crop when the beast did not move. The animal's ears were flicking backwards and forwards.

It was about eight o'clock, the time Baynes had arranged for the meeting. Hanley's horse stopped again. Cannon rumbled on faintly in the distance. He scanned the trees to the right, and the nearest low wall, for it seemed to be something over there that was troubling the horse.

Hanley could not see anything wrong, and so made the horse walk on, the hussar following him. The corporal and the other two hussars were somewhere, scouting to make sure that there was no strong force of enemy near by. They had sent no word, and nor had he heard shots, so they had probably found nothing. Perhaps Sinclair was not coming, even if he was still alive.

There was movement up ahead, figures coming from one of the low sheds. Hanley let his crop hang on the strap around his wrist and drew the pistol tucked into his sash. A figure in black appeared, wearing a broad-brimmed hat, and he recognised the priest from Nogales. Gutiérrez emerged behind him. Neither man looked nervous or moved unnaturally, but that did not mean that there were not concealed enemies pointing guns at them. The convent was still a long musket shot away, a distance at which even a good rifleman like Brandt could not be sure of his mark. That was if they were there and not hidden somewhere else.

The priest waved, and Hanley responded, hoping that the pistol in his hand did not make him appear nervous. He and the hussar kept walking their horses forward. It started to spot with rain, the first drops pattering heavily on his hat.

Hanley was not looking at the two men, but scanning the huts and walls behind them, and happened to be staring directly at one of the pens when a man's head bobbed up. Three more were beside him in an instant and then they vanished behind dirty smoke.

The hussar gasped as a ball struck him in the chest. Hanley's horse staggered, then was hit a second time and reared, screaming in agony. He was thrown, landing heavily on his back, hat gone and the wind knocked from him, and for the moment he could only stare at the sky. The hussar was slumped forward in the saddle as his horse cantered away. Gutiérrez had run back to cover, but the priest was sitting on the grass, hands pressed to the wound in his belly.

Another shot, and there was a fierce stinging and a notch taken off the toe of his boot. Hanley tried to get up, felt the wind of a ball pass his shoulder, so he dived down behind his dying horse, placing a hand on its neck to calm the poor beast and keep it still. A ball smacked into the animal's flesh just inches from his hand. He felt it shudder at another strike and heard it let out a long sigh.

Hanley waited, trying to press himself as tightly to the ground as he could. He wondered where Corporal Scott and the Brunswick rifleman had got too, and regretted giving them his rifle. The pistol had fallen from his hand and was now several feet away. He stared at it, wondering what good it might do him, but relishing the thought of having some weapon in his hand. There was silence for several minutes, so he pushed himself up and scrabbled for the pistol. A shot came, striking the grass close by, but he had grabbed the pistol and then was turning to dive back into cover when something slammed into his left arm just above the elbow. He fell, managed to roll back behind the dead horse, but as he did so put his weight on the injured arm and felt a wave of pain.

Hanley lay on his back, sobbing in agony and trying to get his breath back.

'Give yourself up, Hanley,' a familiar voice called.

He did not answer.

'You haven't a chance,' Sinclair tried again. 'Give it up, man.'

There was another shot, not far from his holed boot, and Hanley realised that his foot was exposed. He pulled it in and rolled on to his side. Raising his head, he could just see over the dead animal.

'The father is in a bad way,' Sinclair shouted. 'Surrender and we will patch him up.' The priest was rocking gently back and forth as he sat on the grass. For a moment the rain hammered down and then as suddenly stopped. Hanley wondered whether the damp would stop the enemy from firing.

The answer came almost instantly as a musket flamed and Hanley ducked down as a ball drove into the side of the dead horse.

'You still alive, Hanley?' Sinclair called after a moment.

Hanley moaned, the cry growing stronger until he was sobbing with pain.

Sinclair called an order, but Hanley was pressed against the animal's corpse and could not see. The wound to his arm throbbed and as he shifted fresh pain shot through him and he cried out.

He heard the crack of a rifle and a grunt. There was a puff of dirty powder smoke on the edge of the wood to the left of the path. Someone screamed and the cry ended with a hiss. Another shot from the wood and then another – that was why he had given Scott his rifle, so that they would have a loaded weapon waiting for use.

Hanley peered out. A soldier in a light green jacket was on the ground, dark blood spreading across his coat's yellow front. Another was helping a man with a wound in his leg hobble to the animal pen. A fourth was clutching at his throat, his hands red with pumping blood, but the man's musket with bayonet fixed stuck up from the back of the priest. He could not see Sinclair, but a few minutes later there was another shout.

'Well, this presents us all with a little problem.' The Irishman sounded matter-of-fact, as if discussing a minor disagreement at a county fair.

'Give up!' Hanley called to him. 'You will never get away. I have a company of men who will be moving up now that they have heard the shots.'

' 'Tis a terrible thing for a man to lie so.' Sinclair had deliberately thickened his accent.

'Give up!'

'And that from a fellow with a bullet in him hiding behind a dead horse.'

A flurry of shots slammed into the corpse. Scott and Schwartz both fired, and he heard the sound of a ball striking the stone wall, but there was no cry.

'We have a prisoner,' Sinclair shouted. 'Senor Gutiérrez.'

Hanley did not reply.

'Be a shame if he came to harm,' Sinclair continued. Hanley raised his head and saw that one of the soldiers held the Spaniard's arms behind his back while Sinclair aimed a pistol at his head.

'You are not that sort of man, Sinclair,' Hanley shouted.

'Am I not? And do you think you know me?' The Irishman made a great show of pulling back the hammer on his pistol.

'I cannot stop you.' The habit of secrecy was too ingrained for Hanley to blurt out that he knew Gutiérrez was working for the French, but perhaps that would be some protection for the man.

'Stopping me is easy. Just give yourself up.'

'I cannot do that.'

'Then that's a shame, a real shame.' Sinclair straightened his arm and took aim, but then seemed to make a decision. He raised the pistol and slammed the barrel down on the Spaniard's head. Gutiérrez staggered, but the soldier still held him up. There was a nasty cut on his forehead.

'There is another way, but it is far less pleasant,' Sinclair called.

Hanley wished now that he had not told Scott and Schwartz to avoid killing the Irishman if they could. Sinclair was standing in the open gateway, and perhaps the simplest way to deal with this would be to shoot the man.

'We have the girl, Hanley,' Sinclair shouted, and then gestured behind him. There was a scream, a piercing and undoubtedly feminine scream.

'Do you want to see her? Gutiérrez's little daughter. A pretty thing she is and no mistake. Come on, lass.' Another of his greencoated soldiers appeared, pulling at the captive. The girl was quite tall, with thick black hair piled high on the top of her head. She wore a dark cloak, and her hands were down low and held together, so Hanley guessed that they must be tied.

'Is she not the perfect little darling?' The mock Irish brogue was back again. 'Be such a shame if she was to come to harm.'

'You would not!' Hanley shouted and hoped that he was right.

'Would I not?' Sinclair seemed amused. 'Do you remember Corporal Brandt? Well, Sergeant Brandt he is now, and as fine a son of Hibernia as most of the men in the legion. You know what sort of man he is. Do you remember?'

'Sinclair, you cannot!'

'I do not like to lose, Hanley. You had better show yourself, Sergeant. Let the nice gentleman see you.'

Brandt was limping and Hanley realised that he must have been the man wounded in the leg. There was the red stripe of a sergeant on the sleeve of his tunic and he thought that the face was familiar, but could not be sure. There was no doubting the hard look in the man's eyes, or the sharpness of the slim knife he held.

Shoot now, Hanley thought, as if his men would somehow read his mind. Knock over Sinclair and Brandt and we can rush the others.

Nothing happened, Sinclair jerked his head and the soldier dragged the girl back out of sight. Her father struggled to free himself and the Irishman hit him again with the muzzle of his pistol. Brandt ran a finger along the blade of his knife and then he too went back inside the pen.

'It is up to you, Captain,' Sinclair shouted. 'All you have to do is surrender. Your men can go if they lay down their arms. I do not care about them.'

One of the soldiers returned and held up a dark cloak, draping it over the wall. Gutiérrez struggled again until Sinclair aimed his pistol squarely between the man's eyes.

'The sergeant is not a pleasant man, but he does have his uses.'

A scream rent the air and for a moment Hanley forgot the throbbing pain in his arm. 'God damn you to bloody Irish hell!' he yelled.

Sinclair smiled. 'No doubt He will in His good time.'

The girl screamed again.

'Brandt likes women, although I suspect many of the ladies do not care much for him.'

The soldier returned, and placed a large piece of light-coloured cloth on top of the cloak. Hanley tried to think. The other hussars were out there somewhere, and the noise would surely have carried to them so they must know what was happening. He had told them to come back, but to approach with care. Sinclair might not know about them, but then he might have more of his own men hurrying to join him as soon as they heard the shots.

Hanley managed to tie his handkerchief around the wound. His arm still worked, although each move was painful. He had the pistol and his sword, but suspected that he would have to drop them if there was to be any chance of getting close. If he was here, Williams would think of a way, or at least get killed in the attempt. He tried to think of what his friend would have done. Hanley felt down and checked that the sheathed knife was tucked inside his boot. It was a trick he had learned from the partisans, although he had never before had occasion to make use of the slim stiletto.

Gutiérrez's daughter cried out, begging for mercy. Her father was sobbing.

'Give up, Hanley. You cannot win.'

It was not pleasant hearing a young woman being hurt, even when he did not know her and her father was in the pay of the enemy. Yet Hanley wondered why the sound did not bother him more. He tried to tell himself that it was pragmatism. It was not within his power to save her if Sinclair and Brandt chose to harm her, and so he tried to tell himself that he was simply facing the facts of the matter.

There was another shriek, and once again the man returned and piled another bit of material on the wall. As far as he could tell, they did not want him to think that they were doing more than slicing away her clothing. The thought reminded him of Jenny Dobson and her hussar uniform and he smiled. Would he be more worried if it was Jenny being held by the enemy, or was the girl right and he did not really care too much about anyone save himself?

'She is almost unveiled, Captain. And very lovely she is too. Soon there will be nothing else to cut apart from that smooth skin. Eventually that is. Be a shame to waste her charms too soon. Do you want this on your conscience?'

'What will you say to the priest, Sinclair?' Hanley yelled at him.

'I am no papist. You should know that.' Sinclair smiled. 'I do not believe in any God watching over us all and neither do you. I just believe in winning.'

The girl let out another scream, and something about it sounded odd.

'I shall count to ten and then let the sergeant enjoy himself. One.'

Gutiérrez managed to free himself from the soldier's grip and dropped to his knees, begging Sinclair to have mercy.

'Two.

'Three. Give up, man!

'Four.'

The girl screamed and Hanley made up his mind, hoping that he was right.

24

Baynes watched the French make another attempt to force the new bridge. Through his glass he could see the dark shapes of men who had fallen in their first effort. The column came rapidly, its frontage narrow so that it could fit across the bridge, but when it was halfway over it seemed to stagger. The formation rippled and men dropped. Baynes could see puffs of smoke from the garden walls and house windows of the village. A few Frenchmen kept running, but others slowed down and most stopped. Men started to fire back at their hidden opponents, and even from this distance he could tell that the attack had failed.

The merchant had tagged on to Marshal Beresford's staff, following when he went over to see General Blake. He knew quite a few of the Spanish officers and was pleased to see that servants were just bringing them breakfast. Before he could accept their offer to join them, he was drawn aside by Colonel D'Urban.

'I regret that we were unable to be of more assistance,' he said. 'But I hope that you were able to find all that you needed.' The colonel glanced to either side. 'Is there any news?'

'Not yet.' Baynes had told D'Urban a little of their plan, although not the details.

D'Urban nodded, and had the sense to say nothing more. Soon he was summoned to the marshal's side. Baynes wondered what was happening, whether Sinclair or Dalmas had come and whether Hanley had been able to seize his chance. It was ten past nine, and so long past the time they were supposed to meet, but still too early for worry to grow.

A German officer on the staff of General Zayas, commander of one of the divisions brought up from Cadiz, was beckoning to him to join them at their meal, Baynes accepted the offer with great readiness, for there was nothing for him to do and he preferred to chat rather than brood on what might be happening. The mood among the senior officers of all the Allies appeared to be good, for so far the battle was developing as Marshal Beresford had predicted and wanted.

They watched as the French prepared a more serious attack on Albuera. This time they would send a battalion over each of the bridges, while another waded through the river. More and more French cavalry gathered near the fords, hussars joining the dragoons and the lancers. The Allied cannon played on them, but the range was some seven hundred yards even for the closest battery and at such a distance their light guns did little harm.

'Here they come again,' one of the Spanish staff officers said, as the French cannon fired and their infantry columns started forward. The skirmish line ahead of them was thicker this time. 'They are learning,' the Spaniard added. 'Yet I do not think they can force us from this position.'

Baynes saw Beresford and D'Urban conferring. An ADC was summoned, given his instructions and then galloped away towards General Stewart and the Second Division.

The German officer had gone silent and was carefully scanning the woodland between the two streams feeding the River Albuera.

'Look there!' he said, grabbing Baynes by the arm. 'Here, take my glass.'

The merchant obeyed and focused on the trees, and at first saw nothing but green leaves. Then something glinted, and he caught movement. It was not clear, but he was sure there were soldiers there, although how many and what they were doing he could not tell.

'Do you see them?' the German demanded. 'That is where they are coming from and that is where they will deliver their attack!' The man's voice was deep, and he was inclined to shout even in ordinary conversation, and his strongly accented Spanish carried to the senior officers.

'What is this?' General Blake asked. He was thin, clean shaven and had a pale, sober countenance.

'Lieutenant Colonel von Schepeler is on my staff,' Zayas explained. He was stockier than his commander, red cheeked and with a luxuriant moustache. Born in the New World, his skin was deeply tanned.

'Well, Colonel?'

'The enemy are moving to threaten our right, sir. I can see men in the woods over there.'

'Numbers?' Zayas barked the question in his guttural voice.

'I cannot tell, sir.'

For a while no one spoke as they scanned the trees. The guns still thundered, and there was the distant rattle of musketry – the sound always reminded Baynes of a boy dragging a stick along an iron fence.

'It does not look like many,' General Blake said a few minutes later. 'This is a serious attack and the straight road to Badajoz, so I cannot believe that it is a feint. Yet we must be prudent. Colonel, you go and take a closer look.'

'Yes, sir.' Von Schepeler saluted and called for his horse.

'Ought we to apprise Marshal Beresford of this?' Zayas suggested.

'Yes, of course,' Blake said. 'Come.' They strode off to tell their news.

Down by the village the French had come across the river and were getting close to the houses. Some of their voltigeurs had driven the greenjacketed Germans back from an isolated garden and were now firing from behind its walls.

There was a murmur from in front of him and Baynes saw that French cavalry were crossing the river at the ford. An entire hussar regiment in brown led them, with dragoons and lancers behind. He watched as a horse was struck by a cannon shot and flung down, its rider falling into the muddy river. The cavalry did not stop and began to form in column on the near bank of the river. Impressed by their numbers, the British dragoons watched them from a distance.

'Colonel Colborne, Marshal Beresford's compliments and you are to advance your brigade to support the village.' Major General Stewart was today wearing his deep green rifleman's jacket, with its three rows of silver buttons. His manner was as cold as ever since their disagreement. 'Two Spanish regiments will be moving up on your right.'

'Sir.' Colborne saluted and turned to Dunbar. 'Captain, ride along the line and tell the battalions that we are to advance and that they are to wait for the order.'

The brigade was formed in its proper order, with the Buffs on the right, then the 2/48th, the 2/66th and the 2/31st. Each had all its ten companies, for the Second Division did not follow the common practice of grouping the Light Companies into a temporary battalion of their own.

Five minutes later, Colborne raised his hat and pointed it forward. Voices yelled in each of the corps, giving the necessary orders, and the entire brigade stepped off towards Albuera. The colonel waited for them to get nearer and then he and Williams walked their horses forward, a little in advance of the gap between the 2/66th and the 2/48th.

A four-pounder shot bounced some way ahead of them, skipped along for more than a hundred yards and then hit the ground again, popping up to pass over the heads of a file of soldiers in the 2/48th. The line marched on. Williams saw two columns on their flank, the closest wearing broad-topped shakos and dark blue jackets. From this distance they were hard to tell apart from the French, and he was glad that they had been warned about the Spanish infantry.

Dunbar was riding back to join them when his horse shied as another cannonball threw up a spout of mud as it buried itself in the ground. He pulled hard on the reins, making the animal buck, but he kept a tight grip and used his whip each time the beast kicked out with its hind legs. Williams had changed mounts and was now riding Musket, and the gelding seemed disturbed by the sight.

He patted its neck. 'Steady, boy.'

A shell exploded almost underneath Dunbar's horse, hurling it up in the air as jagged pieces of casing drove into the poor animal's belly. The captain managed to free his feet from the stirrups and spring away, rolling as he landed on the grass. His horse was on its side, its tongue lolling out as its head writhed, great coils of pale innards spilling from its torn stomach. Dunbar managed to open the saddle holster and fish out a pistol. Williams looked away, and even so shuddered a little when he heard the shot. An orderly brought another horse and the captain joined them. No one said anything.

The brigade marched on, and more and more shot fell among them. A man in the front rank of the 2/48th lost his foot when a four-pounder ball came skimming across the grass looking no more lethal than a well-hit cricket ball. His rear rank man was lucky, the shot passing between his legs. The sergeant walking behind jumped out of the way.

'Close up!' he shouted as the ranks parted to go around the wounded soldier. 'Wait for the bandsmen, boy,' he added, leaning down to pat the man on the shoulder as he stared mutely at the mangled end to his leg.

As they came up behind the village an ADC from General Stewart brought new orders.

'You are to wait here, ready to advance in support of the KGL when needed.'

'Pass the word, Dunbar,' Colborne said, 'and tell the battalions to lie down.' They were not the principal target of the French gunners, but some shots missed the troops around the village or flew high and so fell among them.

The brigade halted, and the men were allowed to lie down in their ranks. Officers paced up and down beside them, for an officer was not permitted to take shelter in the open field. A bouncing shot took half the arm off a young ensign from the

2/66th, who screamed for only a moment before he was carried off.

'Brave lad,' Dunbar muttered.

'Keep moving! Quickly there, keep moving!' The sergeants harried the men as sergeants always did, and only a few had time to tuck the long tails of their coats up before they ran across the ford. A line of skirmishers from the voltigeur companies was already extended along the top of the slope above them.

Dalmas found a place where the bed of the stream looked solid enough and took his horse down the bank into the water. He did not want to slow down the infantry going through the ford. The big horse did not hesitate and the water came no higher than its knees.

'Over there, form on the markers.' An officer pointed to men standing holding the little flags or fanions carried by each company of infantry. 'Quickly now.'

The leading regiment was forming up in column of companies on the gentle slope ahead of him. It was a narrow formation, each of the five companies deploying in a line three deep one behind the other while the voltigeurs were out skirmishing. Such a formation moved quickly and kept its order, and if necessary could deliver a charge against the enemy, as long as that enemy was weakened and unlikely to stand the sight of bayonets coming through the smoke.

They were good soldiers, these men, almost all of them moustached veterans, and they moved with spirit in spite of the long march they had made to get here. Dalmas remembered the army that had trained at Boulogne and then crossed half of Europe to shatter the Austrians and Russians at Austerlitz. He doubted that there would ever be regiments quite so good as those, where every man was a veteran and they had had years to train. Even so the sight of these men gave him confidence.

Dalmas let his horse run up the slope until he was among the skirmishers and then knew that they had done it. The low rolling ridge stretching to the north towards the village of Albuera was empty of soldiers. Marshal Soult had let the enemy see what they expected, sending a single brigade across the river at the Allied centre. The feint was delivered with force to keep their attention there, and all the while two entire divisions of infantry and most of the guns were marching to hook around the enemy right. Another brigade had made itself visible behind the diversionary assault against Albuera, but it too was now marching to come up as a reserve for the flank attack. Dalmas had discovered the route the flanking force had taken, riding it as darkness fell the night before, and he had led the vanguard this morning.

Four regiments of French cavalry were already across the river and formed on the Allied bank, and several more were coming. They faced the Allied positions and helped to add to their sense of meeting a frontal attack. As Dalmas watched, the closest regiment wheeled towards him and set off down the road running parallel with the stream. They would move to this position, cross in front of the infantry and form up covering their left flank – the right would be protected by the stream. When that was done Marshal Soult would have concentrated three-quarters of his army ready to deliver a massive hammer blow to the Allied flank.

As he rode back to report, Dalmas spared only a brief thought for Sinclair. The Irishman was off trying to capture the exploring officer Hanley. He was a prize, but what truly mattered was the fight about to flare into a battle. Dalmas thrilled at the prospect, for at heart he was a soldier, and if he could not prove his worth in the sight of the Emperor then at least he would do it with a marshal of France as witness. One British officer really did not matter so very much when they had a chance to cut an entire army to pieces.

Dalmas saluted as he joined the group of officers, sitting watching the infantry crossing the stream and forming up. 'The heights are empty, Your Grace.'

A squall of rain blew in, clattering noisily against his helmet and breastplate.

'Unoccupied?' Marshal Soult's face was eager, making him look younger than usual. The last few days of manoeuvring the army seemed to have brought the man to life. If he revelled in administration, meetings and lists, Jean-de-Dieu Soult remained a soldier at heart.

'There are no enemy formations much beyond half a mile from the village. The higher positions on the ridge are quite empty.'

'We have them,' said General Girard, the commander of the leading division of infantry and also acting commander of the V Corps. If Dalmas had a concern, it was that since they had left Seville the army's command structure had been thrown into confusion. La Tour-Maubourg was relieved of command of the corps and put in charge of the cavalry and replaced by Girard. This was one of several changes, and with the Army of the South's headquarters as well as V Corps headquarters there were almost too many staff officers and not enough clarity over responsibility.

'How are the enemy formed?' This was from Gazan, the chief of staff and until recently commander of the army's second infantry division.

'The Spanish are closest,' Dalmas explained, 'the English in the centre and the Portuguese on their far left. There are a few cavalry squadrons behind the line.'

'How many Spanish?' Soult asked. 'Has Blake arrived?' They had seen the colourful Spanish regiments in the enemy line, but did not know whether they were the remnants of the often defeated army of Estremadura or the fresh regiments from Cadiz.

'I cannot say, Your Grace,' Dalmas confessed. 'I would guess at two divisions.' That probably meant that they were outnumbered, even if many of the Spanish were most likely raw troops and the Portuguese not much better. Everything else was in their favour.

'Well, their weakest soldiers are here at the point of most danger,' General Girard said. He had a beak of a nose and with an unusually short neck his head rested on his collar and made him seem even more bird-like. 'The Spanish can never manoeuvre.'

'Do they know we are here?' Gazan asked. 'Is there any sign of retreat?' A prudent general would withdraw when outflanked so completely. Turning a whole army to face while the enemy pressed was a recipe for disaster.

'They are not moving, sir.' Dalmas did not bother to say that the enemy would soon realise what was happening even if they had not already done so. The movement of La Tour-Mauborg and the cavalry would give the game away.

'Gentlemen, it does not matter.' Marshal Soult passed a hand across his face to rub the rainwater from his eyes. 'If they stay we will smash them, and if they run we will cut them to pieces. 'General Girard, how long to form your leading division?'

'Another twenty minutes, Your Grace.' The wind and rain were making him duck his head repeatedly, and Dalmas thought of a little sparrow, even though he knew the general's reputation as a fighter. 'The first brigade is already in position.'

'Excellent. We move as soon as you are ready. The Second Division is to follow and form behind you.'

The rain stopped and just for a moment the clouds parted and a beam of sunlight speared through to warm them. It was ten minutes to ten o'clock and the Emperor's soldiers were about to march to triumph.

25

'We cannot let this go on, sir!' Corporal Scott shouted from the edge of the wood. Hanley saw that he was standing up, rifle held down low. He stepped out of the shade, the red collar and cuffs still bright on his faded and patched green jacket. 'We cannot stand by and let the lass be violated.'

Schwartz appeared alongside him, his face full of doubt.

'Listen to them, Hanley,' Sinclair called out. 'You do not have a choice. Now where is the third of your men?'

Hanley stood, his right hand held up with the pistol pointing into the air. 'I do not like this, Corporal.'

'Isn't much choice, sir.' Scott's tone was flat, and once again Hanley wished that he had Dobson or Murphy or someone else he knew better.

'He is right, Hanley old fellow. There is not much choice. Now where is the other man? We heard three shots so do not try anything foolish.'

'There are only two of us, Your Honour.' Scott sounded as confident as any NCO reporting to a superior officer. He nodded to Schwartz. 'Show him, lad.'

The Brunswicker took his own rifle in his left hand and then unslung the other from his shoulder.

'Do you see, Your Honour, three guns, but only two of us.'

'Lay them down, Corporal,' Sinclair told him.

'Begging your pardon, Your Honour, but not until we see that the lass is safe. Otherwise ...' Scott shifted only slightly, and his rifle did not move in his hands, and yet his posture now suggested that he could raise it and fire in a moment. 'Let us see the girl, sir.'

Hanley had a familiar feeling that an NCO was taking charge, his tone making it clear that no sane officer would try to challenge him.

Sinclair levelled his pistol at Hanley. 'No tricks. That would be most unwise. Bring her out, boys,' he ordered.

The rain started again, as one of the soldiers brought out the girl. She was still wearing a shift, but her hair was loose and there was a bruise swelling around one eye. Hanley was surprised, for he had suspected that they were simply making her cry out, but that Sinclair would not actually let her be harmed. He had decided to call the Irishman's bluff before Scott had come out. It still seemed a reasonable plan, and he could only hope that the corporal had some idea beyond surrender.

Brandt limped as he came behind, and Hanley thought that there was something odd about the musket he carried.

'Drop your weapons, lads,' Sinclair said, his aim never wavering. 'You too, Captain.'

Hanley threw down the pistol.

'The sword too.'

Hanley reached down slowly and gripped the handle. It resisted his tug, and he had to yank it out with some violence. He kept his left arm hanging limply at his side, the bandage obvious.

Sinclair grinned. 'How do you English ever beat anyone? You have lost, old fellow, and from all that I hear your army will be crushed before the day is out. Soult is not coming the way you expect, do you know that? He will surprise you just as we did and the French will slice through your men like a scythe through grass. It's a shame I shall not be there in time to see the redcoats running. But this is pleasure enough, I suppose.

'Now, Corporal, drop your rifle. You too, my German friend.'

'Do as he says,' Hanley told them.

Scott took a pace forward. 'First let the lass go, sir.'

'You are not in any position to make demands.' Sinclair sounded more weary than annoyed. 'Perhaps this would persuade you.' He shifted the pistol so that it pointed at the girl. She was shivering, her shift growing wet with rain.

Gutiérrez scrabbled along the floor, bending down to kiss the Irishman's boots and beg him to spare his daughter. The priest moaned softly, still doubled up on himself with the bayonet and musket sticking from his back. Hanley had assumed that the man was dead, and he saw Sinclair turn in surprise.

There was a shout, the sound of horses galloping as the three KGL hussars burst out from the trees near the convent, curved sabres raised high. Hanley ran forward, yelling as loud as he could. Scott raised his rifle in a fluid motion and fired, but Gutiérrez had grabbed Sinclair by the knees, and so the ball took the Irishman in the shoulder instead of the middle of his chest.

Schwartz had his rifle held low at the hip, an awkward posture, but it was levelled at Brandt. He pulled the trigger and the hammer sparked, but the powder in the pan must have got wet because it did not fire. He dropped it and pulled the slung rifle from his shoulder.

Brandt had his gun raised, and Hanley realised that it had two barrels. The German switched his aim from target to target. First Hanley, then Scott, but then he saw Schwartz and he fixed on him. His shot struck the Brunswicker in the belly, flinging him back. Gutiérrez still had a firm hold around Sinclair's legs, and one of the greenjacketed soldiers thrust down with his bayonet into the Spaniard's side. His daughter screamed, louder than ever before. When he did not let go the soldier wrenched the blade free and stabbed down again.

Hanley ran on. One of the soldiers was helping Sinclair away, but he ignored them and went for the one who was grappling with the shrieking girl, pulling her away. Brandt pulled back the hammer on the second barrel and pointed it at him, but the hussars were close now and he switched his aim to them. Another soldier appeared inside the animal pen and fired at the horsemen, who rode on unscathed. Hanley slammed his shoulder into the man dragging the girl away, wincing because it was his wounded left side. The soldier reeled back, tearing her shift as he grasped it. Hanley punched him in the face and he let go and staggered away from the shelter of the walled pen. The noise and smell of the horses filled Hanley's nostrils.

A musket boomed, the ball driving into the neck of one of the horses, making it swerve away and block the path of the corporal. The third hussar came on, slicing down into the shoulder of the man Hanley had pushed away. He yelled, dropping his musket and raising his good arm protectively over his face. The German's horse reared, hoofs flailing and knocking the man down. Hanley shied away from the beast, took the girl around the waist and dived against the bottom of the wall, covering her with his own body.

Sinclair and his men were inside the shelter of the walls, and as the hussar urged his mount through the open gate bayonets thrust up at him, piercing his thigh, and then a pistol fired and the ball struck him in the mouth. The German's head was flung back, his arms spreading wide, and he rolled down out of the saddle.

'Come on, sir!' Scott yelled. 'Run!'

Hanley hauled himself and the señorita up, accidentally widening the rent in her damp shift as he pulled her, and started to run. The girl saw her father lying bleeding into the grass and stopped, hands pressed to her mouth, but no sound coming from her. Hanley took her arm and hauled her with him.

'Look out!' Scott was kneeling, the only loaded rifle at his shoulder. There was a shot, the sound lighter than a musket, and Hanley guessed it was a pistol ball that flicked through the girl's long hair.

Scott fired, there was a satisfying cry of pain from behind, but then another pistol fired and red blood blossomed on the corporal's kneecap. Scott hissed in agony as he fell to the side, rifle gone and his hands clutching at the wound. Not far away, Schwartz lay groaning.

'Down!' Hanley said, forgetting to speak in Spanish, but he pushed the girl off her feet so that she sprawled on her front, grunting as she hit the ground hard. He dropped alongside her, vaguely noting that her ragged shift was almost transparent from the rain, but more concerned with scooping up Scott's rifle.

'Cartridge,' he called.

The hussar corporal sat on his horse some twenty yards back from the pen. Not far away, the wounded horse had slumped down on its knees and the other German stood beside it, loading his stubby carbine.

Scott reached out, blood from his hand on a cartridge he had fished out of his pouch.

'Careful, sir,' he whispered. 'Use your hand to shield the pan when you put the powder in.'

He could see the heads and light green coats of Sinclair and his men above the stone wall of the pen, riding mounts they must have hidden in the animal shed. The KGL corporal saw them too, and brought his sabre up into the regulation high guard. Hanley was loading as fast as he could, not having time to wrap the leather patch around the ball so that it fitted snugly into the barrel, gripping the spiralled grooves that gave the rifle its deadly precision.

With a shout Sinclair and his men surged out of the gateway. There was a dark patch of blood on the Irishman's jacket, and he let one of the soldiers go a little ahead of him. Brandt and the other man came next, and they urged their horses out so that the four formed a ragged line.

The German corporal set his horse off in a canter straight at them.

'Bloody hell,' Scott said with admiration.

The dismounted hussar fired, the ball driving through Brandt's cheek, smashing teeth and bursting out through the other cheek. The sergeant shook in the saddle, but did not fall. Hanley drove the ball and charge down the barrel of his rifle as the rain hammered against his face. As he worked he stared at the girl's shape, but his admiration was slight in comparison to his desire to finish loading.

'Get the sod!' Scott yelled in encouragement as the hussar corporal and Sinclair's men closed. With a slash the leading infantryman was chopped from the saddle, his neck sliced through so that his head hung down at an unnatural angle. Sinclair stabbed before the corporal had recovered his guard, driving his blade hard into the neck of the German's horse, so deeply that the blade stuck and the major was almost pulled from the saddle before he could free his hand of the wrist strap. The dying horse pitched forward, flinging the rider high over its head.

Hanley was sitting up, resting the rifle on his legs so that he could use one hand to shield the pan as Scott had suggested. With care he emptied the last bit of powder from the waxed paper cartridge into the pan. The paper ought really to have gone in with the main charge, but he had saved it in the hope of keeping his priming dry. He closed the pan, brought the hammer back to full cock and knelt, raising the rifle to his shoulder. Then he waited, steadying his breath.

'Remember, sir, squeeze the trigger, do not yank it,' Scott told him.

The dismounted hussar had run forward, sabre drawn, to rescue the corporal, but the three riders ignored the downed man and rode on. A dash brought him close enough to slash at the last of them, Brandt, cutting him across the side before he passed. The sergeant's jacket was already covered in blood from the wound to his face. Hanley saw the man slump in the saddle, almost fall, but then he recovered and rode on.

Hanley waited, muzzle trained on Sinclair. For a moment Brandt blocked his path, and he was tempted to fire because the man undoubtedly deserved killing, but he knew that Sinclair was more important. The Irishman appeared, then vanished again behind the other rider. By the time the three spread out and he had a clear shot the distance was well over one hundred yards.

He fired and to his relief the powder in the pan went off and the main charge exploded, the butt slamming back into his shoulder. Smoke blotted Sinclair and the others from sight, and when Hanley ran to the side he saw that all three men were still riding away.

'You hit him, sir.' Scott told him. 'Saw the bugger shake from the blow. Reckon you got him in the body. That's not bad, sir, not bad at all, especially at this range and riding away.'

Hanley said nothing, but undid his sash and began to take off his jacket. The girl was sitting now, shivering again and hunched up as she tried to cover herself. He passed her his scarlet coat. The wool was wet, but it should still be warm, even if it dwarfed her slim figure. Sinclair was wounded, perhaps twice, and that was something, but even so he felt the weight of failure. They had learned very little, still did not know whether the French plot was real or an empty bluff, and on top of that he and most of his men were wounded or dead.

'You need to warn the army, sir.' Corporal Scott interrupted his thoughts. He was tying a piece of cloth around his leg. 'That Irish bugger said that the French were going to surprise them. You have heard the guns going off for hours now. It might be too late, but then it might not.'

The German corporal came up, looking dazed. 'He is right, sir. If any of the horses are left you should ride to the army. We can take care of things here until you send help.'

Once again it seemed that the NCOs were taking over. Hanley's arm ached, but he could move it well enough. The ball through his boot did not seem to have touched his foot, although no doubt there was a bruise. They had the horses the two riflemen had tethered behind the wood. Not the best animals, but good enough.

'I will send aid as soon as I can. Take care of the girl,' he added. 'The poor child has been through enough.' Gutiérrez still lived, but his breathing was laboured and he was unlikely to last long.

'No fear, sir. She will be safe with us.' Hanley wondered about that, decided that it was probably true and that even if it was not the NCOs were right and he needed to ride back to Baynes and the army. He took the remaining hussar and left the two corporals to tend to the wounded.

'Schwartz needs a surgeon,' Scott told him before he left. 'He did well, sir, very well, and I hope you will tell them as much whatever happens.' Hanley had forgotten the sentence hanging over the Brunswicker and his brother.

'Of course,' he replied.

Scott used his rifle as a crutch and managed to stand up. 'Good luck, sir.'

Hanley rode off, his sash retied around the waist of his loose white shirt. The rain had stopped and ahead of him he heard a steady rumbling of guns.

26

General Blake still had his doubts. 'One of the attacks is a feint, that much is clear, but I suspect their aim is to draw strength away from our centre so that they may pierce it more easily.'

Von Schepeler had reported French columns crossing the stream to their south, and then they had all seen the cavalry coming across the ford and riding in that direction. Baynes had been pleased to see that the Spanish commander immediately sent the information on to Marshal Beresford, yet otherwise he had done nothing.

'If they come at us from the flank in strength then there will be the devil to pay, sir,' General Zayas said.

'As there will be if we all start running around to face south and then they hit us here. Damn those trees, we cannot see where their real strength lies. If they are waiting behind that woodland they could be back crossing the bridge and fords in half an hour, before we could turn again to face them.'

The other generals and staff officers watched their commander weighing up the decision.

'Don José.'

'Sir,' General Zayas replied.

'Turn one of your brigades to face southwards in case the attack there is real. The others are to remain in position and wait. Gentlemen, the regiments on your extreme right may adjust their position to support Don José's new line, but no others. Do you understand?'

'Yes, sir.'

'Good. Move them immediately. I am going to take a closer look at the attack on the village and then I shall find Marshal Beresford and discover his intentions.' Baynes could see that the French now held some of the buildings on the edge of Albuera, but from this distance it was impossible to tell more.

Five minutes after Blake left, Beresford arrived, looking for the Spanish commander.

'Damn the man, what is he about?'

Baynes hoped that none of the Spanish staff officers near by spoke English, although only the most dense would fail to recognise his anger.

'Ah, Baynes. Perhaps you can give me a straight answer?'

'I shall do my best, sir, you may be sure of it.'

'Some of the Spanish are moving. Is General Blake turning in force to face the French on our flank?'

'A brigade is forming to face them, supported by a few regiments.'

Marshal Beresford was resting his right hand on his hip, an oddly elegant gesture for such a burly figure. Baynes noticed that his fingers were drumming against the air.

'Damn it, not enough – not nearly enough! What is the fellow thinking?'

Baynes wondered at the ease with which the Allied commander had altered his conviction that the main French effort would come from the front.

'No, it will not do.' The marshal spoke so loudly that it was almost a shout, startling some of the Spanish officers, and frightening Baynes' horse.

'We must move the Second Division to meet the attack and drive it back,' he said in a more controlled voice. 'Come, let us find General Stewart. You come along too, Baynes,' he added.

'I am at the marshal's service,' the merchant replied with a beaming smile, growing more than a little concerned at the commander's agitation. It would be best to be present in the hope of smoothing any offence he might cause to the Allies.

'It looks like they have caught us on the hop,' D'Urban whispered as they trotted away.

Behind them, General Zayas led some of his men into a new position on the nearer of the two knolls. They went in column of march, wheeling into line so that they stood at a right angle to the rest of the Allied army. His men were good soldiers, who had spent much of the last year training at Cadiz. On the right were the Irlanda regiment, a few still the sons and grandsons of Catholics who had fled from persecution in Ireland. Their jackets were light blue, with yellow fronts, collars and cuffs. Over half wore the bicorne hat of the pre-war army, and the rest had a motley selection of forage caps and shakos. Only a couple of the officers still had the white regulation breeches, and the men wore brown, grey or white trousers, usually patched or with gaping holes at the knees.

Next to them were two battalions of Royal Guards in deep blue jackets with red facings, and blue trousers. All save the senior officers wore wide topped shakos much like those worn by the French. There was a wide gap between the battalions, into which drivers urged the mule teams pulling a battery of guns – the only ones with Blake's army. They were small pieces, four-pounders, their carriages painted blue, but the gunners who crewed them unlimbered the cannons and deployed ready to fire with a smooth efficiency.

General Zayas kept his remaining battalion, the brown-jacketed Navarra regiment, in closed column behind his right flank, ready to support the others and to provide some protection should enemy cavalry threaten his flank, which at the moment was wide open save for a few distant squadrons of Spanish horsemen.

His men were forming well, and already skirmishers were going forward just as he had taught them to do in the long weeks and months of drilling at Cadiz. Over on his left, two battalions from the other divisions, one in the traditional white of the old army – now much faded and patched – and another in brown, extended his line. He could not yet see the enemy, but he had six battalions and half a dozen guns to stop whatever was coming from behind the higher knoll to the south of his position.

The thirty-nine-year-old General Don José Pascual de Zayas y Chacón uttered a silent prayer, crossed himself, and prepared to do his duty.

'It seems God is against us,' one of the staff officers shouted at Dalmas.

The French attack had formed up and begun to advance when the sky grew so dark that it seemed like evening rather than an hour or so before noon. Driven by a strong, cold wind, the rain swept in, slamming down on the tops of shakos and into faces. A moment later it turned to hail, and the grass turned white as the stones landed. Such was the violence of the onslaught that everyone stopped, the infantrymen as one turning round away from the wind, hunching their heads down into the collars of their greatcoats. There was not a single enemy in sight, but for the moment the attack had stopped.

Seeing the ground white and the greatcoated men sheltering, Dalmas thought back to the freezing slaughter at Eylau. The hail rattled against his armour, some of the blows strong enough to shake the helmet, and he remembered the great charge, Murat at its head with a riding crop instead of a sword, as thousands upon thousands of cuirassiers, dragoons and Guard Cavalry trotted in one vast column and rode down the Russians.

'I though the Emperor had settled things with the Pope!' the officer shouted again, and the words had a magical effect for hail turned back to rain, and then slackened, the wind dropping.

'*En avant!*' General Girard shouted, and the cry was taken up by officers and NCOs in each regiment. Drums struck up the steady beat of the advance and the columns turned about, straightened ranks, and stepped off once more. Two regiments were in the lead, each with two battalions in column one behind the other. Four companies of voltigeurs went ahead of them, half as a chain of skirmishers working in pairs and the rest as formed supports. A pair of four-pounder guns was driven along

243

on the flank of each regiment. More artillery followed with the second brigade.

Muskets popped from the top of the southern knoll. There were enemy light infantry there, but they did not seem to be in great strength. Dalmas saw one of the voltigeurs fall and roll back down the gentle slope. Another was helped to the rear by a comrade until a sergeant ran up and told the helper to return to his duty. The wounded skirmisher was lowered to the ground, where he sat, one hand pressed to his shoulder.

'Is that the highest point, Dalmas?' Marshal Soult asked, pointing at the knoll.

'Yes, Your Grace. It is the key to the whole position.'

That key was soon in French hands. The voltigeurs were veterans and they outnumbered the defenders. The Spanish had done better than most Spanish skirmishers had ever done in the past, but they could not hold back their French counterparts, let alone the formed columns coming on steadily behind them. Dalmas watched as the right-hand voltigeur company's supports charged forward, bayonets lowered. The Spanish ran, leaving a dozen crumpled blue bodies on the grass behind them. Voltigeurs chased them, their tall yellow and green plumes bobbing as they went. Through his glass Dalmas could see the yellow epaulettes which they insisted on attaching even to greatcoats to mark them out as the battalion's elite. The columns marched steadily forward behind them, and soon their front ranks were going over the crest.

Marshal Soult reached the top of the knoll and took in the situation with one quick sweep of his delighted eyes.

'I want guns up here, as many as we have, to cover the attack.' The senior artillery officer galloped off to turn wishes into actions. Ahead of them the leading four battalions and their skirmishers had halted in the dip between the two knolls. The other two regiments from the division followed them until they too halted, one hundred yards behind. Their voltigeur companies ran forward to join the skirmish line.

Higher than the enemy, Dalmas and the French senior officers could easily see the thin line waiting on the crest of the other knoll. He counted three battalions, with perhaps another on the flank. Two more lines were deploying at a painfully slow pace on the left flank of the others. He saw men in shades of blue, as well as white and brown.

'No redcoats,' General Girard commented. 'Just Spanish.' The words carried the satisfaction of a man who had led his soldiers to rout many a Spanish army. Their soldiers were sometimes brave, but never well led.

Behind the thin lines of Spanish were more Allied formations, a mix of lines and columns and all facing towards the river. There was movement among them, but no clear pattern showing that the enemy understood their peril and were trying to meet it.

'British dragoons, Your Grace.' Dalmas was looking to the left, across the flat valley bottom to the west, where a regiment or so of horsemen in red coats was forming. There were more brightly uniformed cavalry beyond them – surely Spanish and so unlikely to be of much account.

'La Tour-Maubourg will watch them,' Marshal Soult said, dismissing the enemy horsemen. Adding the British and Spanish together they did not have even a third of the numbers the French had massed on their left.

Drivers flogged horse teams up to the top of the knoll. Most of the batteries with the army had lacked the animals to bring more than a fraction of the guns they should deploy, but they had made sure that the ones they brought were drawn by strong teams in good condition and served by large crews. The nearest guns looked a little odd, and Dalmas realised that they must be the mountain howitzers, designed so that they could be broken down and carried on the backs of mules instead of being towed.

In ten minutes there was a line of a dozen guns spaced along the top of the knoll, a mix of howitzers and eight-pounders. A pair of the heavier twelve-pounders, the only two with the army, were further back somewhere in the column following behind them.

'Your Grace, shall I deploy my leading battalions?' General

Girard asked. 'I should prefer to press on, for I doubt that these fellows will detain us for long.'

The marshal was of the same mind. 'Attack now, General Girard. They will not stand.'

An ADC set off at a gallop down into the little valley. A few minutes later the heavy skirmish line went forward.

Soult made a sign to the commander of the artillery.

'Fire!' Battery commanders repeated the order and the gun captains touched burning matches to fuses. The guns belched flame and smoke, leaping back on their trails – Dalmas noticed that the mountain howitzers almost bounced up into the air as they recoiled on their stubby carriages.

On the knoll, Spanish soldiers began to die. The lines were three ranks deep, with sergeants, drummers and a few officers standing behind them. One of the first balls bounced just in front of the 2nd Royal Guards, smashing the knee of the first man to bloody ruin, ripping the man behind completely in two at the waist, flinging entrails and blood on all sides, and smashing the chest of the man in the third rank. The head of a drummer standing at the rear vanished in a spray of blood and bone, his body standing for a moment before seeming to fold down on itself. Sergeants dragged the dead and wounded out of the way, and bellowed at men spattered red by the carnage to close up and fill the gap.

The voltigeurs were within range now, and as the pairs of men advanced, one would kneel, take aim and fire. His comrade covered him while he reloaded and then he too would present his firelock and pick a target. An officer from the Irlanda regiment gasped as he was hit by a ball, the yellow front of his tunic darkening as he bled. Not far away a soldier was struck in the belly and screamed in agony, until a drummer pulled him back from the ranks and a sergeant said quietly that it was not too bad and he should not make a fuss.

'Fire!' The French guns once again slammed back. Shells from the howitzers burst all along the other crest. A moment later there was a great gout of orange flame and black smoke spreading up into the sky like some giant sprouting plant.

'A caisson,' General Girard said approvingly.

The Colours in the centre of the 4th Battalion of Royal Guards dipped for a moment, the young officers carrying them wounded by the fragments of a shell. A sergeant held one up again, until he was hit in the thigh by a musket ball, but soon the flags rose proudly once more.

'Fire!' By now the gun teams were each going at their own pace, so instead of one great salvo, a steady ripple of fire came from the gun line. Shot tore through the Spanish formations, and shells landed to throw up gouts of earth and fling wickedly sharp pieces of casing through the air. All the while the voltigeurs nibbled away at the lines, dropping men here and there, and trying their best to pick off the officers. The Spanish skirmishers replied as best they could, but there were not enough of them. The formed lines remained in place, waiting silently with their muskets still on their shoulders.

'They won't take much more of this,' a colonel from the staff of V Corps announced with confidence.

Others clearly agreed and now the four battalion columns of the leading regiments stood to attention. Drums rolled, orders were shouted and Dalmas could hear the great cheer even over the roar of the cannon.

'*Vive l'empereur!*'

The columns marched forward, one regiment aiming at the centre of the line dressed in light blue coats and the other making for the battery of guns. Dalmas and the others had all seen this so many times before. Skirmishers and guns flayed the enemy, stripping away their confidence as they took the lives of some of their men. It was a horrible thing to stand still under fire, as comrades fell all around, some of them appallingly mutilated. The voltigeurs kept searching for the leaders, dropping the men there to give instructions and inspire confidence.

'*Vive l'empereur!*'

The columns cheered every time the drummers paused before repeating the rhythm of the charge. Marching with muskets resting on their shoulders, the right hand tucked over them to hold the weapon upright, the men in their light brown greatcoats shouted as loud as they could.

At last the Spanish cannon opened fire, blanketing the front of the battery in smoke. Most of the balls went high, missing the leading battalion. A few struck the column behind, carving bloody furrows through the ranks.

'*Vive l'empereur!*' The regiment did not check, and they were now well within musket range of the defenders. Weakened by guns and skirmishers, it was an even more terrible thing for an enemy to wait as the formed infantry bore down on them. Dalmas and the others had also seen this many times. The defenders would be stung into firing too soon, and even if they still had good enough order to deliver a volley and not simply shoot individually, then the volley would be too high and at too long a range. It would not stop the column, which would keep coming on, the drums and the shouting getting closer and closer until the column charged and the enemy line fell apart like rotten wood.

'*Vive l'empereur! En avant!*'

The columns were within a hundred yards of the waiting infantry and still the Spanish held fire. A cannonball skipped at waist height into the Irlanda regiment, cutting a file of men in two. Shells exploded, making the lines quiver as men fell. One burst in front of a Spanish four-pounder and swept away half of the crew. Still the Spanish waited.

'*Vive l'empereur!*'

The voltigeurs ran back into the gaps between the columns, for their job was done for the moment. Grenadiers led each of the columns, and the colonel of the regiment on the right had ignored regulations and kept the old bearskin caps. The other regiment boasted shakos, but with the rim and chevrons on the side decorated in red, and all four companies had tall red plumes and red epaulettes. They were the biggest men in the regiment, all of them picked veterans, with long moustaches and thick side whiskers. On they marched, muskets tucked into their shoulders so that no one would be tempted to halt and fire. Officers capered in front, waving their swords and urging the men on, and the drums beat and the men cheered. On the southern knoll the guns kept firing, the shape of the valley allowing them to shoot over the columns at the Spanish lining the crest. Dalmas knew that no one liked any artillery, even their own, firing over their heads, but the men would be glad of the havoc wrought against the defenders.

General Girard was sitting up, almost standing, in his stirrups as he watched his men approach the enemy. Even from this distance they could see the light and dark blue Spanish lines seem to ripple like a flag in a wind and they knew that soldiers were bringing muskets to shoulders. A wild volley would not stop these veterans, these 'old moustaches', and it was always more difficult to fire down a hill rather than up one because the instinct was to fire high.

'*Vive l'empereur!*'

At last the French guns stopped. The howitzers which lobbed their shells up to drop down on the target kept firing, but the gouts of smoke they threw up were blotted out when the Spanish infantry fired and a dirty cloud covered the whole line of the crest. Alongside the infantry the four-pounders boomed, each gun loaded with canister, metal tins which shattered as they left the muzzle and sprayed musket balls out like giant shotguns.

The fronts of the columns quivered like live things as men fell.

'Now, go on, finish them!' General Girard urged his men, as if his will alone was enough to give them victory.

The grenadiers charged, but the Spanish did not run. The Royal Guards and the Irlanda were busy loading their muskets, and they stood in their ranks, not terrified by the big grenadiers as they ran forward. A few of the French kept going, led by an officer on a grey horse, until one of the four-pounders, firing a little after the others, aimed a canister at them. Horse and rider were peppered with dozens of balls, and three of the men following pitched back. It seemed to take the heart out of the attack.

Some grenadiers ran back a little way to re-form on the company following them in the column. Others stood their ground and brought their muskets up to their shoulders and fired. Men fell in the Spanish lines, and then they began to reply, each man shooting as soon as he was loaded.

'*Merde!*'

Dalmas was not sure which of the generals spat out the word. The attack had stalled, for the despised Spanish were not running.

'Come on!' General Girard beckoned to his staff and set off down into the valley to get things moving. General Gazan looked at Soult, waited for the curt nod, and then followed.

'Not you, Dalmas,' the marshal said as the cuirassier's instincts made him start walking his horse after them. 'I want you to ride to General La Tour-Maubourg. Tell him to watch the enemy horsemen, but to be ready to charge in support of our infantry if there is a good opportunity. Stay with him, Dalmas. Come back only if there is something I need to know.'

As he rode away Dalmas heard the guns firing again, and that meant the high tide of the French advance had flowed back a little and let the gunners see the enemy without fear of hitting their own men. They pounded the Spanish lines, and soon another wave would surge forward. The enemy could not stand for ever, but if the infantry failed to shift them then the cavalry would do the job. On that happy thought, Dalmas rode to join the massed squadrons.

By the time the Fusilier Brigade halted the firing was a continuous rumble from the south and ahead of them by Albuera itself. Pringle stood with Truscott and they stared at the high ground more than a mile ahead of them and tried to make sense of the battle.

'Looks like they have hooked around our flank,' Pringle said. All around them the 106th were taking off their greatcoats and rolling them up. They had marched for more than nine hours, losing their way in the dark and having to double back, so that the sixteen miles turned into twenty, but at long last the Fourth Division had arrived.

'Wonder where they will want us,' Truscott said. The brigade had marched left in front, which suggested that someone had either felt creative when writing the order or expected them to deploy to the left. It made little difference to the 106th, for as the junior corps in the brigade their place in the line was always in the middle between the other two battalions.

'Hopefully they will want us to eat something first.'

'What? Food before glory? Have you no soul, Billy?'

'I have a deep hunger,' Pringle announced, aware that quite a few of his grenadiers were watching, so performing for the audience, 'and also a raging thirst. Any more of this and I shall waste away.' He patted his ample girth.

Lieutenant Colonel FitzWilliam and the adjutant trotted back along the column.

'We are in reserve, boys,' the colonel called out. 'So get something inside you and have a little rest, for they are sure to need us later.'

'Someone of authority evidently has a deep respect for your stomach, old boy,' Truscott said when they had passed.

The 106th settled down to rest and eat, the sound of battle throbbing away in the distance.

27

I took time to bring the brigade back from its station just behind Albuera.

'I hope that the Spanish can hold out,' Colborne said with doubt in his voice, as the noise of cannon fire became so frequent that it could be heard even over the sound of the guns closer to them.

Major General Stewart was ordered to take the Second Division to the south to meet the French flank attack, and the general did not want to set out until his three brigades were in the proper order. Colborne's was the strongest, with four battalions, and it was also the senior brigade in the division, so it should lead the formation and then deploy on the right. That was the way the entire division was used to forming and fighting, and it was sound enough to want to act in this way in the chaos and confusion of battle, but it did take time, and Williams wondered whether it might not have been better to send the other two brigades on ahead in case the enemy broke through.

They needed thirty minutes to explain matters to the battalions and then bring them back to their original position, and then another ten to form into column of march. The Grenadier Company was at the head of each battalion, then the eight Centre Companies and the Light Company bringing up the rear. At long last they were ready, and a relieved Dunbar rode up and reported to the colonel.

'Proceed, Colonel Colborne,' Stewart told him, before galloping off to instruct his other brigade commanders.

The Buffs led, the wind stirring their flags so that Williams could see the dragon at the centre of both the King's and

Regimental Colours. He kept meaning to ask why one of the oldest corps of the line had this most Welsh of symbols on their flags, for officially this was the East Kent Regiment. The other regiments all had variations on a shield with their number in Roman numerals surrounded by a wreath of roses, thistles and shamrocks, although sadly nothing representing Wales. Each Colour was six foot high and six and half feet wide, each side almost always taller and wider than the young ensigns carrying them. When the 2/48th followed the Buffs, he saw two young lads struggling to manage the heavy flags as the breeze caught them. The four sergeants marching behind them as protection for the precious flags were older, bigger men, each carrying a sturdy half-pike taller than the young officers. Next were the 2/66th, their Regimental Colour with a greenish yellow field to match their facings rather that the pale buff of the other three battalions. The 2/31st brought up the rear, and behind them was a brigade of KGL artillery, with six guns towed by teams of horses and the gunners jogging alongside them.

A stray shot fired at the troops near the village bounced high, struck again not far from the colonel and his staff and then hit a company of the 2/66th, smashing one man's shoulder into a pulp and taking the head off the redcoat next to him. It plucked the shako off the next man and flew above the rest of the rank.

'Keep going!' a sergeant bellowed, as the men stepped around the dead soldier and let the wounded man sink to the ground.

The leading battalions were already sheltered by the ridge line as they followed the road running behind it. Soon they climbed and went along the high ground, though still behind the crest which was lined with formations of Spanish soldiers.

'Tell the Third Foot to steady their pace!' Colborne said to Dunbar, and the major cantered away. If the leading troops went at a brisk pace, the men at the rear would soon find themselves running to catch up.

Ahead they could see the Spanish lining the nearer of the two knolls, and through the clouds of smoke around them they could just glimpse the higher crest some way beyond. Williams was sure he spotted the flash of the first enemy gun and soon afterwards saw the faint dot of a shell that seemed to be coming directly at him. He forced himself to keep Musket walking straight and not to duck, and at last realised that the missile was running a little to his right. It dropped beside the Buffs, exploding almost instantly and flinging two men aside like rag dolls. Another was clutching at his eyes, his face a sheet of blood.

'Don't stop! Keep going.'

Two more shells went off harmlessly, although the second made the horse of one of the officers from the 2/48th bolt back halfway down the column. The major riding it eventually calmed the beast and returned, looking rather shame faced.

'I have put this horse under arrest,' he called to his battalion, and the men grinned.

Another shell landed, this time at the feet of a captain walking along beside his company, and as he leaned down to pinch out the fuse it exploded, throwing him back, his clothes scorched and torn from more than a dozen pieces of the casing.

'Leave him! Keep going.'

Dunbar had returned, but they soon noticed that the Buffs were going faster again, the regulation pace forgotten.

'I doubt we can stop them now,' Colborne said. 'Tell the other battalions to double.'

'Water, water,' pleaded the badly wounded captain as Williams rode past. He said the same thing to the redcoats as they went by, all of them avoiding his gaze. 'For the love of God, please give me water.'

The rest of the brigade set off at the double, jogging along, their equipment bouncing and rattling as they tried to keep up with the Buffs.

'Water, please water,' the captain begged. Another shell landed a few feet away, fizzed, but then failed to go off. A roundshot skimmed across the 2/66th, smashing two men's heads into a spray of blood and bone that soaked their comrades.

'Close up! Keep going!'

'Dear God, shoot me, please shoot me,' the captain begged as

Williams rode back to the colonel. He kicked Musket to make him run, but found himself staring straight into the eyes of the poor man.

The Buffs and the rest of the brigade were past the worst of the cannon fire by now, the 2/31st catching most of it until they got far enough forward and the gunners began to strike at the artillery and the next brigade.

'Dunbar, stay at the head of the column. Williams, come with me and we will find out where we are to deploy.' Colborne set off towards the line of embattled Spanish soldiers, now less than a quarter of a mile away.

When they got close Williams could see the dozens of wounded dragged back behind each of the lines. There were dead as well, lying in strange, unnaturally twisted shapes. The Spanish lines were ragged, but as they came closer he could see that they were standing firm, firing and reloading again and again. Closest was a regiment in dark blue coats and wearing shakos, and as he looked at them he saw a shot shatter the legs of all three men in one file. Sergeants dragged the injured soldiers back and pushed the ranks to close up again.

They could not see the French until they were almost on the crest itself, riding into one of the gaps between the shrinking battalions. There were several columns ahead of them, the closest ones now little more than shapeless masses of men, but they were also firing as fast as they could, and because of the slope men behind the first three ranks could point their muskets up and shoot over the heads of the men in front.

A shell exploded behind them, cutting down a drummer who was carrying fresh cartridges to the men in the firing line. Colborne paid no heed, his focus entirely on reading the battle.

'Come on,' he said, and Williams followed him as he rode to the flank of the Spanish position, going behind a battalion in pale blue. Once past them they could see a little better. Williams guessed that at least half a dozen French columns had come up the slope and perhaps there was a full division. There were not the usual wide gaps between each battalion, allowing it room to form line and deliver a greater weight of fire. He guessed that supporting units had instead come forward in between the leading columns, but that they too had failed to close those last twenty yards or so and drive the Spanish back.

'French cavalry, sir,' Williams said, glimpsing several squadrons some way off on the shallow slope of the high ground.

'I see them, Lieutenant,' Colborne replied, the slightest trace of irritation in his voice.

They went back, Colborne searching for a senior officer to give him his orders. There was no sign of Marshal Beresford, and then suddenly Stewart and a couple of ADCs appeared through the drifting smoke.

'Sir,' Colborne said as he saluted. 'Shall we form a second line and let the weary Spanish withdraw through us if needed?'

The general did not seem to hear. His face was glowing with enthusiasm.

'We have them, Colborne, we have them!' It was the most friendly he had been since Campo Major. Two soldiers in pale blue uniforms limped by, the one with a ball in his leg leaning on the other, whose left arm was hanging bloodstained and useless. A shell from one of the French mountain howitzers went off behind and a little above, knocking them over. A piece of casing had smashed open the back of one man's head, and more had peppered his comrade's back. Flecks of blood splashed over them, dotting the general's light bay horse.

'Poor fellows.' The general looked at them with mild pity and not the slightest trace of fear.

'Colborne, we shall take the French in the flank. Extend to open column and then march your brigade past the Spanish right. Keep going until you can form a line and have the enemy in enfilade. Give them a few volleys and then a taste of cold steel and we will sweep them away!' Major General Stewart clapped his right hand into his left as it held the reins. His bay stirred with surprise and he calmed it.

'Yes, sir,' Colborne replied. It was a bold plan, very bold, Williams thought, but boldness could often succeed. He followed the colonel back to the head of the brigade, and they started to lead the Buffs so that they would continue past the flank of the Spanish. The battalions were ordered into open column, each company waiting for there to be a gap equal to their frontage in a two-deep line before they stepped off to follow the company ahead of them. That way forming into line to face the flank would be a simple matter of each company wheeling to the left.

They had not gone far when Stewart and his staff joined them. The sky was darkening again, so that the general's green jacket looked almost black and the silver buttons on it gleamed brightly. This was Stewart's plan, and until a few months ago this had been his brigade, and it was clear that he could not resist leading it into this attack.

'Come on, double time!' he called, and the Buffs began running. Williams glanced back and knew that by the time the units following them realised what had happened they would struggle to keep up.

It started to drizzle, and perhaps this and the smoke drifting across the crest stopped the French from seeing the danger for some time. They rode at the head of the redcoats, and Williams kept looking to the left and staring at the French columns as they drew level with them and then began to go past.

The gunners were the first to see them. A shell burst above the Buffs' Light Company and bits of casing rattled on the barrels of their shouldered muskets, knocked off a couple of shakos, but only left a scratch on one man's face. The column doubled forward, ranks wavering and the intervals between companies stretching as they went. A roundshot took the arm off one of the sergeants in the Colour party and then cut the soldier behind him in half, flinging his torso so that it knocked down two men in the next rank and drenched them in blood and entrails.

'Form here!' General Stewart halted and yelled at the Buffs' Grenadier Company as they doubled up behind him. 'Wheel to the left and form on me! The other companies to extend to your right.'

Williams was surprised that he had stopped so soon.

'Halt!' their captain shouted, but then he looked uncertain. This was an unusual order, for the grenadiers' place was on the far right of the line. The battalion's lieutenant colonel appeared.

'Do you wish us to form a clubbed line, sir?' he asked. It was the slang term for a line in reverse order. Williams had heard that the rifle regiment Stewart had raised and led often deployed on any other companies, but this was rarely done by line battalions.

Colborne interrupted before the general could reply. 'Sir, with your permission I will take the Third Foot on a little further and form them in column at quarter-distance to guard our flank.' A close column made it changing into square far faster.

'Column, sir? No, sir. We need a line to attack.'

A cannonball broke the shaft of his half-pike and then glanced against the leg of the sergeant standing on the flank of the company, smashing the flesh and muscle and breaking the bone so that he fell moaning.

'But there are French cavalry out there, sir,' Colborne said, stung by the abruptness of the general's reply.

Stewart frowned, puzzled that anyone could fail to understand. 'Too far away to trouble us. If we deploy and advance quickly we can break them in ten minutes.' He turned to the Buffs' commander. 'Deploy your battalion as ordered, Colonel.'

The Grenadier Company wheeled so that they now faced the flank of the French. As the first of the Centre Companies arrived, they waited until they were past the grenadiers and then made their own quarter-wheel and came level with them.

The general struggled to contain his enthusiasm. 'We have them, we have them!'

Williams looked back and to his eye there did not seem enough space to the left of the steadily growing line to deploy the rest of the brigade.

'Come on, boys, advance with me!' The major general was waving his cocked hat in the air. Only three companies of the Buffs were in line and the fourth just starting its wheel, but already Stewart was taking the formation forward.

'At the double!' the captain of the wheeling company yelled

at his men in the hope of catching up. There was an explosion, and three redcoats dropped to shell fragments. Another was shot through the body by a musket ball, for a few Frenchmen were at last aware of the threat and had begun to open fire.

'Williams, help the Buffs to form up. I shall ride to the Forty-eighth,' Colborne told him. 'Dunbar, you take the Sixty-sixth. Tell them to hurry, but not to lose their order.'

The fourth company had sprinted and almost caught up with the small line the general was taking forward, although its men had spread out or bunched up as they ran. The next company followed by the Colour party was jogging forward to come alongside them. That meant that half the battalion, one of its two wings, was almost deployed.

'Form on me!' he shouted as the next one came up. 'Form and wait for the rest of the battalion to extend on you.' He managed to get two companies in line, but then they heard the sound of a volley as General Stewart's little force halted and began to engage the French.

'We must join them!' a major shouted. 'And form as best we may once we get there!' He had some respect for an aide-de-camp as the instrument of his brigadier, but that would not last long once the divisional commander and the rest of his own corps were engaged.

'It will not take long to form the rest of the left wing,' Williams said, hoping to delay a little. Another company was up and beginning to wheel.

'We cannot, sir,' the major said, his tone courteous but firm, and then raised his voice. 'The Third will advance. Forward march!'

With that the two companies stepped off, and the third abandoned its wheel and simply hurried as individuals in an effort to catch up. Shouting until his voice was hoarse, Williams managed to form the last of the Centre Companies and the Light Company together before they too went forward. He rode behind the line. Ahead most of the rest of the Buffs were halted, thick smoke in front of them as they poured fire into the enemy. The 2/48th and 2/66th were advancing as well, but they too were broken up into several sections rather than a continuous line. He could not see the 2/31st and guessed that they were still in column.

It was a hasty, disorganised advance, but for all that the general had brought well over fifteen hundred redcoats against the French flank and was pressing them hard. The smoke made it impossible to see, but from all he could hear the Spanish were still gamely holding their ground, and so the enemy would be taken on two sides.

'Make ready!' The two companies had come up so that they were roughly at the far right of the battalion's line – albeit a line that was not straight and had several gaps in it. At the order the one hundred and thirty-six men in the two ranks brought their muskets from their shoulders and held them upright in front of them, right hand on the small of the stock and the left holding it higher up.

Williams could see the mass of a French column some fifty or sixty yards ahead of them, the officers beating men with the flats of their swords as they forced them round and managed to form a rough line facing towards the redcoats.

'Present!' Each man's left hand slid upwards as he brought the musket down level, butt firmly into his shoulder and right hand on the trigger.

One of the men in the front rank gasped as a ball drove through his ribs. His musket clattered to the ground and he slumped forward.

'Fire!' Each redcoat pulled the trigger. None of the muskets failed to spark or to set off the main charge and a thick wall of smoke spread to cover their frontage and blot out the enemy. The men brought the firelocks down ready to prime and then right hands reached for cartridges. Williams noticed that all of the light bobs had pulled their pouches round to the front of their hip to make it easier to get at them.

A shell exploded behind them, close enough for Williams to feel the gust of hot air wash over him, blowing dirt and bits of powder smoke into his eyes. The smoke in front of the company was thinning, and he could see the French formed up, the men in the first rank kneeling and two more behind. Then they fired, vanishing behind their own cloud. A redcoat's head was flung back, a neat hole in his forehead. Another doubled up, shrieking, blood bright on his fingers as he pressed his hands around his groin. Behind him his rear rank man shuddered as first one and then two more balls struck him in the body.

'Make ready!' The companies were loaded again, but Williams noticed that the Light Company's captain and one of his lieutenants were behind the end of the line and looking away to the south.

'They are lancers,' he heard the captain say as he rode over to them. 'They must be Spanish.'

'Then what are they doing there, sir?' his subaltern asked.

Williams asked them what they had seen and then tried to find the distant figures moving away to the flank. It took a while, but he spotted the shape of a horseman just as the companies fired their second volley. The noise made Musket flick his ears back and pull away. Around them the evil, rotten-egg stench of powder was growing.

There was a cavalryman a good five hundred yards away where there was less smoke. It was too dark to see the details or colour of his uniform, but it was clear that he carried a slim lance.

'He is Polish, in the French service,' Williams told them. For the second time today he was surprised that scarcely anyone else had ever seen a French lancer.

'Just one or two of them prowling about at the moment,' the captain said, and Williams was not sure that the man was convinced. 'Probably no more than outposts.'

'Keep a good watch,' Williams said. 'The French have a whole regiment of them and plenty of others besides.' Part of him wondered about ordering these companies to angle back and form a line facing any horsemen that tried to roll up the brigade.

A roundshot took a front rank man in the chest, tearing away his right arm and half his shoulder before ripping open the whole side of the stomach of the man behind him. The soldier standing next to him was knocked over by the severed arm. He stared at it, holding it up, and screamed.

'Quiet!' a sergeant shouted from his place behind the formation, and when the man kept on yelling he slapped him hard. 'You're not the poor bugger who is hurt. Get back in the ranks.'

'Cease fire!' the loud voice of Major General Stewart called. 'Cease fire!'

Officers took up the call. The group of companies to their left fired a rolling volley, but then their captains yelled out to stop firing.

'Prepare to advance. Fix bayonets!'

'Fix bayonets!' the captains repeated all along the Buffs' staggered line. Men slid their right hands up to hold the musket nearer the middle, and the left reached back to grab the top of the bayonet. They drew the triangular blades, each eighteen inches long, slid them over the muzzles and then turned them to click into place.

A man was flung back, gasping for breath. His rear rank man managed to dodge out of the way, but looked down in horror at his mate stretched on the ground. Then he grinned.

'You're a lucky devil, Charlie.'

The man felt the great dent in the plate on his cross-belt where the ball had struck. He groaned as he pushed himself up, still struggling for breath.

'Pick up your musket, you lazy bugger!' a sergeant shouted, and then grinned.

'Prepare to charge!' Williams drew his sword. The redcoats held their muskets across their bodies. He could remember that moment, and how the weapon felt odd, the balance changed by adding the steel spike.

'Forward march!' The companies went forward into the smoke. Williams was on the end of the line and had to rein Musket in to stop the horse bounding ahead. A musket ball hummed through the air and took the top off his tall white plume. He could see the French again, in a rough line more than a hundred men strong and with the mass of the rest of the battalion behind. Some of the greatcoated figures fired, not in any order, but as soon as they were able. One of the Light Company fell, hissing because there was a bullet in his calf, but the line kept on.

'Charge!' The general's voice seemed to echo along the ridge.

'Charge!' Officers took up the shout and Williams found himself bellowing the order and finally giving Musket his head. The men were already dashing forward, the front rank lowering their bayonets to reach for the enemy. They cheered as they ran, throats already a little dry from biting off cartridges.

Some of the French were running. Others went back more slowly, still facing the enemy. A few stayed, and Williams saw an officer pulling men by the collar and trying to keep them in line. He wrestled with one of his soldiers and then the man broke free, and he left him, instead raising his sword. Williams was ahead of the line, carried on by his horse, and he steered Musket so that he would pass to the left of the man. The gelding responded, and he wondered how often the animal had done the same thing for the dragoon sergeant.

At the last minute Musket almost leapt forward, his stride longer, so that he surprised the officer, who cut too late. Williams thrust at the man, felt the tip of his blade grate on rib bone before sliding through the muscle, then he turned his wrist and let momentum pull the sword free. Musket reared as he reined him in, and he saw the officer fall, wounded, but still breathing. Next to him the redcoats reached the few Frenchmen to remain. Only one of the enemy made an effort to fight, clubbing a Light Company man with the butt of his musket and knocking him down. Another redcoat ran his bayonet into the Frenchman's stomach, twisting it with savage glee. Two more greatcoated men were stabbed. The rest were told to drop their muskets and then were pushed to the rear.

Most of the French halted ten yards away, rallying on another company, and the charge stopped, its force for the moment spent. British and French soldiers alike began to reload.

Williams rode behind the rough line, searching for Colborne. As far as he could tell the 2/31st had yet to arrive or could not find room to deploy. The other two battalions were in the same rough and scattered line as the Buffs. He was surprised to see small groups of Spanish skirmishers in some of the gaps in the redcoated line. They were eagerly loading and firing as rapidly as their allies, but it would do nothing to help them restore some sort of order.

Colborne was with Dunbar behind the 2/66th, their own battalion. As Williams rode up he saw the yellow-green Regimental Colour fall. It was raised again in a moment, but he saw a badly wounded young ensign being carried back and laid down behind the line. By the time he joined the colonel, the King's Colour fell and another young officer was brought back to lie beside the first. Other men fell to musketry, and now and again a ball or shell scythed through the ranks.

Major General Stewart appeared just as Williams told them about the lancer he had seen.

'No time for that,' he declared. There was a graze on his cheek and the same burning excitement in his eyes. 'Colonel Colborne, we need to charge again. Stay here and they will whittle us away, so we must drive them off. Tell the regiments to cease firing and I will lead them forward.'

Colborne nodded. 'Captain Dunbar, kindly take command of the Sixty-sixth.' Their commander, wounded three times but refusing to leave his post, had just been shot through the heart.

'I shall go to the Forty-eighth,' the general said, once again unable to resist playing a direct role. 'When they charge, the others are to join them.'

'Williams, come with me and we will tell the Buffs,' Colborne said, and at least that would place them on the far right of the line should their fears prove grounded. 'Come on!' Colborne galloped along behind the brigade, his horse quickly more than a length ahead of his ADC.

They could hear shouting, officers taking up the cry and telling men to stop firing and prepare to charge. Williams did not see or hear the shell that burst just as it landed a couple of feet from Musket's hind legs. The blast flung him and the horse to the side, and he struck the ground hard.

The world went black.

28

Once upon a time, Jean–Baptiste Dalmas had been a school-master in a sleepy town where nothing much ever happened. Nearly all of his pupils were dull, unreasoning brutes, and so he flogged them and hoped that some little knowledge could be driven into their empty heads. Then a magistrate jealous of the favour shown by his wife to the tall schoolmaster had added Dalmas' name to the following year's list of conscripts. The army had saved him from boredom and given a purpose to his life. As he rose through the ranks he encountered many men as stupid as the children he had tried to teach, but others with that spark or talent and skill that reflected some of the dazzling genius of the Emperor. General La Tour-Maubourg was just such a man.

'The Lancers of the Vistula and the Second Hussars are to advance and attack the English infantry,' the general said to one of his ADCs. 'Tenth Hussars to support.'

A Polish officer had come in with the report, and while Dalmas rode forward to confirm that the British really had committed so grave an error, orders went out for the light cavalry to prepare to advance. The six dragoon regiments would be more than enough to ward off the Allied cavalry on the far side of the valley, but the general wanted to make sure that there was enough power in his attack.

Dalmas coughed and the general smiled. As his name suggested the general was an aristocrat, one of those who had been willing to serve as an ordinary soldier and fight for the Revolution, and had since risen on merit. 'Very well, Dalmas, you may take command of the escort squadron. Leave a dozen troopers with me, but have the rest. See what you can do to help.'

As commander of the cavalry of the entire army, La Tour-Maubourg was entitled to the protection of a squadron of picked men drawn from the regiments under his command. He had selected sixty, all of them from the elite companies of the dragoons. Half wore bearskin caps like some of the grenadiers in the infantry, the rest a red plume in their helmets, and all had red epaulettes on their shoulders. They were all veterans, mainly big men, and if they were not cuirassiers then Dalmas knew that they were still a formidable force.

Dalmas drew his long sword and raised it in salute. 'Thank you, sir.'

The lieutenant in charge of the escort was almost as tall as Dalmas and had a thick black beard. His voice sounded as smooth as a barrel rolling on cobblestones, and there was no doubt that he was a man the army and the Emperor had raised from the gutter to command. He looked pleased that they were to join the charge and angry that someone else had arrived to lead.

'Do not worry, Gillet, you give the orders until I say otherwise,' Dalmas said. 'There will be plenty of English for us all.'

The beard parted in what was probably a grin. Dalmas led them forward, past the 10th Hussars in their sky-blue braided jackets. The regiment was formed in column of squadrons. Some way ahead of them was a similar column formed by the 2nd Hussars in their brown jackets and overalls. To the right and a little in advance, the lancers had two squadrons in line and two more a hundred yards behind them. Dalmas brought his small squadron level with the brown hussars. He could see the top of the knoll wreathed in smoke, and now and then glimpse the dark shapes of the Spanish up there. The redcoats were out of sight for the moment, hidden behind a fold in the ground, but he had seen them clearly when the general sent him to check the report. There were three or four battalions, their formations broken in their haste to attack the flank of V Corps' leading division. None of the Spanish or English cavalry was near enough to shield their open flank, and that meant that the English were very brave, very stupid, or badly led. Dalmas suspected that all three were true.

A trumpet sounded, warning the men to prepare to advance. All of the horses, Dalmas' big black horse included, pricked up their ears at the familiar notes. The animal snorted, and even pawed its front hoof on the ground like a bull.

'*En avant! Promenez!*' He heard the strongly accented shout of the lancers' colonel, and listened as the order was repeated by his squadron commanders. The Poles would be able to see the enemy, for they were a little higher, and the others would follow their lead. All four squadrons walked their horses forward. Red and white pennants fluttered from the lances of the front rank, but the men in the second rank of each squadron carried a carbine as well as a sabre instead of the eight-foot spears. Their square-topped *czapka* hats were covered with dark oilskins to protect them from the weather, and today the Poles had buttoned their jackets to cover their yellow fronts. Had it not been for the swallow-tailed flags on each lance, their uniform would have been very plain.

'*Promenez!*' The hussar's commander and his captains echoed the order.

'*Promenez!*' Gillet's accent sounded more barbarous than that of the Polish officers, and Dalmas wondered where the man came from. He did not sound like an Alsatian, and his skin must have been quite swarthy before the sun of Andalusia dulled it even more.

It was getting dark, very dark indeed, and as they walked forward the rain grew heavier, blowing in on the strengthening breeze. The dragoons had rolled their cloaks and wore them over their left shoulders, just like the hussars, a protection against all but the strongest sword-cut. Dalmas had tied his to the blanket behind his saddle. He was sure that there must already be a little rust on his cuirass and a day like this would make it worse. Now the rain tapped against it just as it spattered on his helmet and those of the dragoons.

The trumpet sounded again. '*Au trot, marche!*' The Polish

colonel gave the order and it was repeated as before. Men bobbed up and down in the saddle, hips working in the familiar rhythm as the horses trotted forward. A thin line of officers and NCOs rode behind each squadron to make sure that no one tried to drop out of the ranks, but today Dalmas could not see any signs of reluctance. The dressing remained good, each squadron in two main ranks of fifty or sixty men.

By now they were where the lancers had begun the advance, crossing a higher fold on the side of the heights. The weather was closing in quickly, but even so he could glimpse groups of men in red through the mist of rain and the clouds of smoke. The English were pushing forward, driving their infantry back, but the French had not quite given way. If anything it would make the enemy even less prepared to meet the charge. Dalmas guessed that they were eight or nine hundred yards away.

Gillet crossed himself, and then uttered a string of the vilest oaths – and a few in languages Dalmas did not understand. He heard some of the men behind him laughing and guessed that this was a familiar ritual. It reminded him of the infantry general who used to strip to the waist and then command from among the leading voltigeurs, advancing in all his bare-chested, very hirsute glory. The Emperor did not care as long as a man won battles for him. Only victory mattered.

Even a steady trot ate up the distance surprisingly quickly. On the wet ground the horses' feet yanked up clumps of grass and earth. They dipped down into another shallow trough and for a while the enemy vanished. Wind whipped the rain into their eyes and men instinctively bowed their heads into it. Dalmas had often seem them do the same useless thing when under enemy fire.

Once again the trumpet called, and this time he did not catch the lancers' commander shout the order, but he heard it repeated through the formation and saw the Poles accelerate.

'*Au galop, marche!*' Gillet roared the words, spraying flecks of water caught in his beard. Dalmas needed only the slightest pressure from his heels to set the big horse racing forward. It snorted in excitement, running in its wonderfully smooth motion, its big feet pounding the ground. The lines of horsemen became less neat.

For a moment the torrent of rain was so savage that Dalmas blinked, and when he opened his eyes he could not see far so that even the foremost lancers were invisible. Then it cleared as instantly as it had come and he saw all of the cavalry and ahead of them the infantry in their red coats. A big British flag and another that was mostly very pale brown stood in the centre of the nearest battalion, and they were now very close. He saw men at the far end of the line turning, pointing at them, and could imagine their cries. As a soldier he knew something of the horror that struck a man when he realised that he was in a hopeless situation. As a cavalryman he exulted in the sight of a helpless enemy waiting to be slaughtered.

The trumpet sounded those last intoxicating notes. '*Chargez!*' There was a glitter even in this dull light as the lancers in the second rank of each squadron drew their curved sabres and kicked hard at their horses' sides to urge them to one great effort. Many officers liked to wait until this minute because it raised the spirits and also made it hard for the enemy to know whether or not the charge was a feint until it was too late. There was no point in concealment, so Dalmas drew his long sword and Gillet ordered the squadron to do the same. Like the hussars they waited for a dozen heartbeats before giving the order.

'*Chargez!*' Gillet growled. This was the last great rush, giving their horses their heads and no longer caring about order. Faster horses raced ahead of the rest, the riders with swords held up, wrists twisted so that the blade pointed forward and down. They splashed through a patch of muddy ground, flinging filthy water and muck on the men and horses behind them.

The British broke. Their lines were ragged after a hasty attack and because they were fighting hard against a stubborn opponent. Worse still, they were facing the wrong way. Someone seemed to be trying to turn men on the far right, but it was too late and too confused to make a difference. There was no solid line of men waiting to fire a volley at point-blank range and send horses and riders tumbling, just three battalions stretched thinly, and when the men on the far right saw the cavalry coming fast through the rainstorm it was too late for anyone to gather enough men to stop them. Some of the redcoats ran. Others clustered together back to back and prayed that the enemy riders would hunt for easier prey. Further up the line, most still did not know what was happening and just kept loading and firing into the smoke.

The leading lancers were among the redcoats by now, leaning to put all their own weight and the momentum of their charging horse behind the razor-sharp tips of their slim lances. Dalmas heard the screams as they rode down the surprised or fleeing men. Some of the British dropped their muskets, and perhaps they were trying to surrender, but the moment a charge struck home was no time for such niceties and the Poles speared them, let their own speed free the lance, and then rode on. The second ranks chopped down with sabres to finish the men they had missed.

'That way!' Dalmas pointed. The nearest English battalion had lost all order as the leading Polish squadrons rode through them. They had no chance of recovering and their destruction would be completed by others as the supporting lines came up.

'Come on, boys!' Gillet grunted and the two officers led their squadron behind the British line to strike at the other battalions.

A redcoated officer on horseback boldly turned to face the lancers, slim sword raised across his body. He urged his horse at the oncoming Poles, but the animal wanted to run with the herd and so it started to turn. Desperately he swivelled, and tried to flick the point of the lance aside with his blade. The first lancer swerved and avoided him, just as a second, slightly behind, drove his lance through the man's back with such force that the spear-point and a good six inches of shaft erupted through the front of his jacket and the officer was hurled from the saddle.

Some men fought. A redcoat standing alone raised his musket and waited until the lancer was just yards away before shooting. The ball drove through the horse's skull and the beast was dead even as it ran a few more steps and then slid down, knocking the soldier over and breaking his leg. The lancer rolled free and a comrade jabbed down to stab the screaming Englishman in the belly.

The second battalion in the line was scattering just like the first as the Poles reached it. Gillet pointed his sword at the two Colours surrounded by a knot of redcoats. Plenty of men made their names by taking a standard from the enemy. Reward was certain, whether it came as a decoration, money or promotion, and perhaps all three. Better yet it made a reputation, and the rest of the army would know that a man who took such a trophy was a real soldier, a man to admire, respect and fear.

Dalmas shook his head. 'Ours is the next one!' he yelled. 'Come on!' There were already lancers clustering around the two flags, but the leading Polish squadrons were spread out and many had slowed or stopped to fight. Dalmas reckoned that his squadron would be the best-formed unit by the time they reached the next English regiment.

Men were running all around them, some crossing their path. Gillet thrust the tip of his sword into the back of a man's neck as they rode down a couple of soldiers with red jackets and buff facings. The other turned, saw Dalmas bearing down and flung himself to the floor. Perhaps the hoofs broke bones as the squadron passed over him or perhaps he was lucky.

The third battalion in line broke apart just like the others, as a swarm of fugitives and the first cavalry ran among them.

'There!' Dalmas yelled, seeing a British flag and another with a yellow-green field. 'That's ours!'

A man in pale blue, so a Spaniard, got in their path, and one of the dragoons sliced down diagonally and cut the artery in his neck. Blood fountained over the man and his horse as the Spanish soldier fell, barged one way and another as the cavalry passed.

The English flags were close now, no more than twenty yards.

'*Vive l'empereur!*' Dalmas yelled, and the squadron took up the cry.

29

Williams opened his eyes, the sound of firing growing louder and louder as he came back to consciousness. Raindrops slapped down on him. His face was pressed into the grass and there was salty taste on his lips. He pushed up, and then there was half-dried blood around his mouth. His nose felt sore, but he did not think that it was broken. Musket lay a few yards away, the poor beast still breathing faintly, even though a mound of pale, reeking entrails had spilled from the horrible gash in his belly. One of his rear legs was bent back the wrong way, obviously broken. The gelding raised his head, tongue lolling from the side of his mouth. There were more wounds on his neck and chest.

The officer stood, patting himself down. He did not seem to have been hit. Colborne was nowhere to be seen, but with the drifting smoke and rain it was hard to see very far. The line of redcoats was a little further forward than it had been, so he guessed the charge had been launched. It must have won a little ground, but not managed to break the enemy's will to fight on.

Williams walked over to his horse, and when Musket looked at him he felt his own eyes moistening, and not from the weather. He pulled his pistol out of the saddle holster, cocked it, aimed and fired before the rain could spoil the powder. Musket jerked once and then was still. Williams licked his lips, realising that the lower one was split when he felt a little jab of pain. He tucked the empty pistol into his sash, not bothering to reload in this foul weather. It took an effort to pull the holster on the other side enough to open it, for the dead horse seemed impossibly heavy. Somehow he managed and retrieved a few essentials and the boarding axe. Hefting it in his hand made him think of Hanley, and he wondered where his friend was, and that set him to thinking about the rest of the 106th. The Fourth Division was supposed to be on their way, but he had no idea whether they had arrived.

A man limped towards him, right trouser leg torn, bandaged, and using his musket for support.

'Forty-eighth?' he asked.

'Yes, sir. Wounded, sir.' The man seemed nervous, as if the strange officer would accuse him of deserting his regiment.

'You will be fine,' Williams told him. 'Keep going and find the surgeons.'

'We're beating them, sir,' the soldier said. 'They cannot hold the Forty-eighth.'

'I know, I saw you at Talavera.'

'That's right, sir, that's right. Now that was a day.'

Williams had been on the other wing at Talavera, too far away to see, but he knew the story of the 48th standing firm and was sure it would please the man to be reminded of it.

'Good luck,' he said. 'They will soon sort you out and have you dancing again!'

Colborne had been heading for the Buffs on the right, so Williams walked in that direction, hoping to find him. He wondered where Stiles was, for he would be of little use as an aide until he found another horse. It was hard to tell where the dispersed firing line of the 2/48th ended and that of the Buffs began, for even from quite close the uniforms were similar. Then he stopped and stared, because a nightmare was emerging from the pouring rain.

Horsemen, hundreds of horsemen, were sweeping down from behind the brigade's open right flank. In the lead were the Poles he had seen earlier in the day. Pennants waved brightly as lances were lowered.

'Cavalry!' he yelled, his lips hurting as he opened his mouth wide to shout as loud as he could. 'French cavalry behind us!' He ran towards the Buffs, not quite knowing what he was doing, and kept shouting until his boots slipped on the wet grass and he fell flat on his face.

Williams got up, and already dozens of men were running, and then the first began to cry out in fear and pain as the lancers caught them. He saw the Colour party of the Buffs and ran towards them. A few mounted officers galloped past, but one was slower than the others and screamed as he was speared through the back and flung down. A drummer dropped his heavy drum and fled. The first lancer misjudged his attack and did no more than drive the lance into the musician's epaulette and rip it off, sending the man staggering. He was knocked aside when he hit the chest of the second lancer's horse, and then speared in the arm by a third man, blood spreading darkly on the buff sleeve of his jacket. A Pole from the second rank drew alongside and cut back, slicing into the man's face. The drummer fell, sobbing because he could not see.

'Form on me, I shall be your pivot!' The voice was high-pitched, and he saw a young ensign trying to gather a group of men, and then the lancers were on them. Men screamed as the spearheads drove into them, and in an instant the redcoats split up.

Williams ran on, managing to dodge so that a Pole passed him on the wrong side and could not swing his lance around quickly enough. The smell of wet horse and old leather filled his nostrils, and he swung the axe, felt it sink into the man's back, heard the lancer cry out. The Welshman tried to pull him from the saddle, but the horse kept going and he lost his grip.

'Mercy! Mercy!' a man kept yelling as he ran, hands clasped protectively on top of his bare head. A lancer drove the point of his weapon into his side, pulling it free as he went on, but then turned his horse and came back.

'Mercy!'

Another thrust, this time to the thigh, made the man yelp in pain. A second Pole arrived, sabre raised.

'Mercy!' It was more of a gasp this time, and then the sabre flashed down in an arc and sliced off one of the man's hands and bit into his skull. The redcoat staggered, almost fell, but tried to keep going, and then the lancer speared him in the stomach and he dropped. The other horseman urged his mount to trample the fallen man.

Williams shifted the axe to his left hand and drew his sword, winding the knot around his wrist so that he would not lose it. He pressed on, barging past a score of fleeing men. A Pole was among them, hacking down again and again with his sabre, and Williams could hear the man grunting with the effort, but his victims were oddly silent, mouths open and faces locked in a mask of terror.

He came through that group, and then slipped again on the grass, rolling as he fell, and so just avoiding the hissing lance-point that would have taken him in the back. The horse's hoofs, looking very large, trod inches from his face and he hunched up like a baby as he lay. The spear jabbed down, cutting through the damp wool of his jacket, and he felt a stinging pain as it grazed the skin. Then the horseman rode on, looking for new victims.

Two sergeants had managed to gather three others around them, and so Williams pushed up and went towards them. The Poles had already seen the group and half a dozen lancers spurred at them. One of the Buffs raised his musket, and pulled the trigger, but the flint sparked on damp powder and it did not go off. Another tried to jab at the oncoming horsemen with his bayonet, but at full reach he could not match the long lance and before he could prick the horse's nose its rider had taken him in the throat. It was over in moments, just a succession of skilful thrusts, and all five men were down. The Poles rode their horses round in a circle stabbing again and again until the movement and the moaning stopped.

The Colours were close now, and so Williams went to them, drawn by the great flags even though he knew that the enemy would desire these more than anything else.

'*Vive l'empereur!*' He heard the shout as a fresh wave of lancers charged over the ground where the Buffs had stood. Hussars in brown jackets and overalls and with black shakos came behind them.

There was already a pile of bodies of men in red coats with

buff facings around the flags. A little ensign, his face that of a pink-cheeked child, was wrestling with the Regimental Colour, its nine-foot-ten-inch pole almost twice his size. 'Rally, men, rally!' the lad shouted in the same high-pitched voice Williams had heard before. He had it in both hands and was swinging it, the big standard with the union flag in the top corner and a buff field with a dragon in the centre flapping heavily, not really under his control. A tall sergeant stood beside him, his leg bandaged, shako gone and a cut to his cheek, but still gamely jabbing with his half-pike to keep the horsemen at bay. A quick thrust and one of the horses wheeled back, blood seeping from a wound to its neck.

A Polish officer switched his sabre to his left hand, holding the reins as well as the weapon, and drew a stubby pistol. His men baited the sergeant, nicking him from behind before he could turn to face them with his own long spear.

'Save the Colours!' Williams yelled. 'Save the dragons!' He did not know where the words came from, but knew that all that really mattered was the tone. Men responded to the sound more than the meaning, or they did not respond at all.

A lance turned, and through sheer luck Williams was on his left so the man had to turn his spear over the neck of his horse. The Welshman hooked his axe head over it, catching in the pennant, and spun so that the beautifully balanced sword in his right hand drove up and pierced the man's neck. The lancer gurgled as blood gushed from his neck and mouth. Up so close Williams was surprised at how small the lancers' horses were. Then the man slid from the saddle, falling on him, and Williams was on the ground again, trying to push the dying man off.

A shot rang out, loud over the other noise, and between the legs of the horse he saw the big Regimental Colour fall, covering the body of the ensign.

'Bastard!' The sergeant bounded forward, thrusting his pike at the officer, whose horse reared, turning. Williams felt an appalling weight as the riderless horse panicked and bounded away, treading heavily on its former master, who still lay on top of the Welshman.

Lances thrust, taking the sergeant in the back, both arms and then the neck. Somehow the man was still standing, flailing round with the pike so that the blade seemed to scar the air and the Poles drew back from his rage, all apart from the officer, who dropped his pistol and took his sabre back in his right hand even as his mount reared. The hoofs struck the sergeant in the face, knocking him back, and a few moments later the sword-point took him in the eye, driving deep into his brain.

A corporal and a private from the Buffs appeared from nowhere, running up and standing to block the pathway to where another ensign, an older, thicker-set man, held the King's Colour. A lieutenant joined them, his face handsome even under the grime of battle. He raised a pistol and the two soldiers levelled their muskets. Flints snapped down and to Williams' amazement both the muskets fired, and the officer's horse was rearing again, and then fell, landing across the legs of the lancer lying on top of him. The officer rolled easily free and yelled at his men to cut the English down.

Williams' face and chest were covered with the warm blood of the lancer, who had stopped writhing, but was pinned on top of him by the wounded animal. He tried to push him off and could not, so could only watch the last act of the tragedy. The lancers closed on the little group of redcoats, joined by half a dozen hussars in braided brown jackets and oilskin-covered shakos. The Polish officer strode up on foot to join them, and some French infantry appeared from out of the smoke.

The corporal took a lance in the chest, and then was hacked down by sabres. One of the infantrymen shot the ensign in the body, but before the Colour fell the lieutenant flung his useless pistol at one of the lancers and grabbed the staff with his left hand. The private gave an appalling scream of agony as a lance drove into his stomach, just before another took him in the chest.

A hussar sergeant stood in the stirrups, hacking down with all his might to shear through the lieutenant's arm as it gripped the shaft of the Colour. The redcoated officer did no more than gasp, as a gout of blood sprayed from the severed stump. He flung his sword away and grabbed the King's Colour, shaking it as he tried to bring it upright and making his hand and attached piece of arm fall off.

'Give it up!' One of the hussars spoke English and all of the horsemen were yelling at the man.

'Only with my life!' Williams heard the words and made a renewed effort to push the corpse off him. When that failed he tried to squeeze out from underneath, but he could not move at all.

The hussar sergeant cut down again, just as the lieutenant turned his head, and so instead of carving through shako and skull, the well-sharpened blade sliced through his nose, which hung down on a great flap of peeled-off skin. The officer shouted, but the words were no more than noises. Blood flowed from jabs to his body and limbs, and yet the redcoat swung the heavy Colour one-handed, a horrible, unearthly sound coming from him. The French gave back a little.

A lancer came cantering up, eager to join the fight, and although his comrades yelled at him he drove his horse on, pushing them aside, lance-point lowered. The lieutenant saw him coming, let the Colour fall back against his shoulder and grabbed hold of the silk flag, starting to tear it free. Then he was lifted off his feet, hurled yards back as the spearhead sank deep into his groin. Most of the flag tore off, gripped tight in his hand, and as the body rolled it covered the crumpled and bloodstained silk.

One of the hussars caught the staff, only a quarter of the banner still attached and raised it high in triumph.

'*Vive l'empereur!*' More hussars arrived, some of them in sky blue, and they took up the shout.

'*Vive l'empereur!*'

Williams heard the sound of French victory and then a great drumming of hoofs. Whether or not horses liked treading on flesh, there were so many dead and wounded lying strewn across the grass that they had little choice. He gasped as a great weight pressed down on him. Something hard struck the side of his head and once again there was only darkness.

30

'Dear God.' Truscott whispered the blasphemy, but he could not lower the telescope and watched as a brigade died.

'Poor devils,' was all that Pringle could think to say. They were a good three-quarters of a mile away and even with the magnification they could not see the detail. It was simply that there had been several straggling lines of men in scarlet pouring fire into the smoke and the vague masses of French beyond them. They might have been going forward, and certainly were not going back.

Then the cavalry had swept along the ridge, glimpsed now and then through the rain, and as the weather cleared the red lines were gone, simply gone, and the only trace was little scarlet dots in the distant green.

'Who are they?' Ensign Samuel Truscott asked in horrified awe.

'Better ask who they were,' Pringle said, 'for there will be precious few of the poor fellows left.'

Truscott lowered his glass at last and stared at his friend. He had rarely heard Pringle speak with such brutality.

'Are they dead?' Samuel asked, his voice quavering.

'What do you damned well think!' Truscott was surprised to realise that he had said the words. 'Sorry, Sam,' he added. 'It's never nice to see the French doing well, but do not worry, we will have them by the hip by the end of the day.'

'Shall we advance soon?' There was not quite the usual enthusiasm in the lad's question. He might have been pale, although even his brother found it hard to know with his skin covered by so many livid spots.

'When they need us. Now you had better go back to your company. Good luck, brother.' He passed the glass to Pringle and then offered the boy his hand. He had never done that before, not even when the lad arrived. Samuel smiled, then did his best to look earnest. Some of his high spirits were returning.

'Good luck, sir,' he said, and walked back towards the spot where the collected Light Companies sat and waited.

Truscott wondered whether he would ever see the boy again.

'Those poor, poor devils,' Billy repeated, scanning the distant slope.

Around them the men of the 106th waited. Some kept looking at the distant battle, while others pretended to pay no heed. They rested, ate and waited. Men cleaned their muskets, adjusted their belts, and there was a steady scrape as they sharpened bayonets.

'I wonder if a few are starting to think that life might be safer in a trench,' Truscott said.

Gillet raised the flag high in the air. His wild beard shook as he waved his head and roared in delight. The British Colour was big, mostly a greenish shade of yellow and a good chunk of it torn away, but Dalmas could still read the numerals LXVI in gold on the red-wreathed shield in the centre.

It had been a short, vicious fight, the redcoats holding out with savage desperation until they were all cut down. Dalmas had killed one and left two wounded on the ground, and he had let the lieutenant take the flag even though he could have reached it first. A Pole took the other Colour, with its big union flag.

'Go back!' he told the lieutenant.

Gillet shook his head, said something incomprehensible and handed the awkward flag to one of his men to take back to the general.

'Don't forget that it's mine,' he barked at the man, and then straightened his bearskin cap.

'Come on, then,' Dalmas said.

'*Au trot, marche!*' Gillet bawled, and they set off. There were a good thirty dragoons still with them, in no sort of formation beyond a swarm, with Dalmas and the lieutenant at their head. That was always the way in a charge. Everything happened so fast that men simply vanished, most to turn up later, and all you could hope was that they were doing something useful. It might have been five minutes since the charge began, perhaps less, even if enough had already happened to fill many hours.

There were fugitives ahead of them, horsemen riding in the crowd and cutting or thrusting at will. Others chivvied prisoners to the rear, most of them wounded, often several times. Dalmas saw the leading lancers and hussars getting among an artillery battery caught in the act of deploying.

'That way.' He pointed his long straight sword, blood on it drying and dulling the polished steel blade.

'*Au galop, marche!*' Gillet ordered, and they sped forward again.

Hordes of fleeing redcoats poured through the battery first. Their muskets were gone, often their packs, and any other equipment the men had managed to fling off in the hope of running just a little faster. The fugitives streamed between the six guns as the KGL were just unhitching each piece and rolling them into place in the gun line.

The first French horsemen were only just behind. A lancer speared a redcoat in the back, whirled his lance free and then impaled a gunner pushing at the wheel of one of the six-pounders. Another Pole shot one of the drivers with his carbine, and then rode on to club another from the saddle.

Artillery officers and NCOs shouted at the men, warning them, for until now few had realised the danger. The gunners did not panic, but there was no chance of loading or firing their cannon. Many grabbed anything they could find as crude weapons, for their muskets were stored in one of the brigade's wagons far in the rear. A bombardier with a huge chest swung a trail spike as if it were a toothpick, knocking two horses down, and bludgeoning one hussar unconscious until a lancer stabbed him through the mouth.

More and more French reached the battery, Dalmas and the dragoons arriving just as a fresh squadron from the 10th Hussars swept in. He saw gunners trying to hitch the nearest cannon back on to the limber to get it away and headed for them.

Gillet cut down a limping redcoat officer as they passed, and then one of the few soldiers still carrying a musket turned round and raised the weapon. Dalmas saw his terrified face, watched as the muzzle still with heavy bayonet attached wavered in the air, and then there was flame and smoke. The ball punched through Gillet's beard and the lieutenant slumped in the saddle as his horse rode on. Dalmas leaned over, and thrust his sword into the redcoat's throat at almost exactly the spot where his shot had hit the dragoon officer.

A gunner with a jacket styled the same as the English infantry but blue with red collar and cuffs and yellow lace came screaming at them, waving a rammer. He swung, struck Dalmas' breastplate, the force making him jerk back. The cuirassier sliced down, destroying one of the artilleryman's eyes and cutting through to his jaw. He pressed on, but another gunner appeared, wielding a short sword. The man slashed the blade through the air, almost catching the head of Dalmas' horse and making the beast shy away.

Some of his dragoons were by the limber and team now, chopping the drivers from their seats. Dalmas feinted a cut, let the man raise his little blade to parry, and then kicked the horse so that it bounded forward and barged the gunner aside. As they passed he cut back, felt a moment's resistance as the steel met bone, and then the blade sank into the man's shoulder.

They were behind the Spanish line now. Ahead was a red-coated battalion, its march column closed up on the flanks to form a crude square, and Dalmas doubted that any of the cavalry were still fresh enough to risk charging it. A swarm of people on foot had followed the horsemen, some of them infantry from the embattled V Corps, but many more women and other followers eager for plunder. Even after so many years of campaigning

Dalmas remained amazed at how quickly such people appeared and then vanished.

'Keep those bastards off!' Dalmas screamed at the nearest dragoons as two women and a soldier in the grey of the supply train dashed up to the horse team, knives in their hands ready to cut the traces and steal the precious animals. One of the dragoons struck a woman in the face with the flat of his sword and snarled at her to keep away.

'Kill the bitch if she tries that again,' said a sergeant with a beard almost as thick as Gillet's.

Dalmas stood as tall as he could and looked around. Four of the guns were captured, but already the looters were carrying off most of the draught horses. Two more teams were being driven away by the Germans, but as he watched carbine and pistol shots brought a couple of the horses down on the nearest one. An infantryman raised his musket and fired, plucking one of the drivers off the other team, but a bold fellow in a dark blue jacket sprang off his own horse and rode the other, taking the team to safety. There were fresh lines of redcoats approaching and no point in pursuing.

The charge was spent. He could tell by all that he saw and by how he felt. Men and horses were tired, scattered, and even the supporting regiment had no more energy left for a fresh charge. They had saved their own infantry, slaughtered the English, destroyed an entire brigade and captured a battery of guns, all with just three regiments of light horsemen, but now it was over. Fresh enemy reserves were advancing, there were no more helplessly exposed battalions to massacre, and so it was time to go back. It was over, although some of the fools did not realise it. Dalmas could see several dozen Vistula lancers galloping along behind the Spanish regiments.

'Get that piece hitched up,' he told the sergeant. Now that he had time to look he could see that it was a stubby-barrelled how-itzer and had a twin trail unlike the usual single-block trail the English used. 'You and you.' He pointed at two of the dragoons. 'Act as drivers. Sergeant, get a man to lead their horses. And take poor Gillet's as well.' The lieutenant was still in the saddle, but his head was bent down against the beast's neck and the scarlet front of his green tunic was dark with his blood.

'And well done, everyone, that was the most perfect charge I have ever seen.' He smiled and they grinned back.

'*Vive l'empereur!*' someone shouted, and they all joined in the cheer.

Baynes was with Marshal Beresford and his staff when the commander appeared back behind Zayas' Spanish.

'Where is Blake? Where is the damned man?' The marshal made no attempt to hide his anger. The merchant saw looks of annoyance and a little distrust from the handful of Spanish staff officers.

General Zayas said something to one of his aides. 'I believe General Blake is with General Ballesteros,' the man said in very good English.

Beresford grunted, and then peered forward.

'Your men fight well,' the marshal said, the words a little less brusque than his usual manner. 'Be kind enough to tell General Zayas.' He repeated the compliment in Portuguese, in case that might help.

'What is happening?' Baynes had joined Colonel D'Urban. For all his frequent protestations of military ignorance, the merchant had witnessed several battles and was generally able to understand what was happening. Today in the smoke, rainstorms and chaos, he really had no idea what was going on and whether or not things were going well. The agitation of Marshal Beresford was scarcely encouraging.

'Well, it appears...' D'Urban began and then Baynes saw the colonel's stare widen in surprise. 'Look out!' he called, and tried to grab the reins of the merchant's horse. At the same instant Baynes felt a terrible pain in his thigh.

D'Urban led go of the reins and whipped out his own sword. Baynes turned, but could not move his leg, and there was another appalling surge of agony. A man was a few feet away, dressed in a dark blue tunic and grey overalls and with an odd-shaped hat. He was holding a lance and the point was driven into the merchant's leg so far that it had come out the other side and stuck in his saddle. The lancer struggled to free it, until a Portuguese ADC raised a pistol and shot the man through the head.

Two more lancers rode in among the staff officers. One stabbed at a major, giving him a wound to the side and pitching him from his horse. The other rode at Marshal Beresford, leaning as he aimed the eight-foot spear.

Beresford yelled, a great bear-like bellow of anger. Dropping the reins, his huge left hand moved with remarkable speed, fastened round the spearhead and pushed it aside. His horse did not move as the lancer came at them, and then the army commander had the Pole by the throat and lifted him bodily out of the saddle. He shook the man as if he were no heavier than a rag doll and then hurled him on to the grass.

'Goddamned cheek,' he said, as one of his staff leaned over and shot the man dead.

The last Pole took some killing, two of the officers hacking at him until another produced a pistol and finished the job.

'Stop them! Stop them!' General Zayas shouted. Another straggling group of lancers was riding along behind his men. One of the redcoated battalions advancing in support saw the enemy and either did not see or did not care about their allies because they halted and fired a volley.

Baynes groaned. D'Urban tried as gently as possible to free the lance.

'For God's sake, fetch a surgeon,' he ordered, and an ADC galloped away.

'Hold on, old fellow,' the colonel said as soothingly as he could.

Beresford galloped off, yelling with even more than his usual anger at the redcoats and telling them to stop firing.

Williams stirred as the weight above him shifted. There was a shot, close by, and a convulsive jerk shook the corpse lying over him. He pushed as hard as he could and to his surprise the dead lancer rolled off him. The man already felt cold to the touch, even though Williams suspected he had not lain there for more than a few minutes.

His amazement was as nothing to that of the French infantryman who had just shot the wounded horse to put the animal out of its misery. Its final death throes must have shifted its weight off the dead lancer.

Williams rose from under a corpse, his face and chest smeared in dark congealed blood. As he stood he grabbed the axe and the hilt of his sword.

The Frenchman ran, dropping a bag of plunder he had gathered from the dead and wounded. Williams ignored him, for just ten yards away three horsemen in dark blue and with square-topped hats surrounded a tall man in a red coat with yellow-green facings. It was Colborne and he was obviously a prisoner. Further off parties of redcoats were being shepherded to the rear and other horsemen were drifting back towards their own army. Some British heavy dragoons in red jackets and cocked hats appeared lower down the slope and their presence made the French retire more quickly.

Williams jumped over the dead horse and charged straight at them. The sword felt light in his hand and he whirled the axe to loosen his wrist.

There was a cry, and one of the Poles, a junior officer judging by the silver epaulette on his left shoulder, was pointing and shouting at his men. The nearest one turned, trying to urge his horse into a canter, but there were too many bodies in front of it and the animal refused, stepping to the side and only walking forward.

Williams yelled, his lips hurting and blood and spittle spraying from his mouth. The horse did not like this strange sight and tried to pull away. Williams bounded forward, smacked the animal in the face with his sword and blocked the sabre-cut with the shaft of his axe. The beast bucked, surprising its rider and lashing out with its hoofs so that the mount of the second Pole sprang back out of the way. As the rider struggled for balance, Williams thrust the sword into his stomach, twisted the blade free and ran on.

The second Pole had a carbine. He calmed his nervous horse and the beast responded. The muzzle looking very big as Williams ran on, still screaming, and he saw the man settle his aim. The rider squeezed the trigger, the hammer snapped down, but there was justice in the world for the flint did not spark well and perhaps the powder was also wet because it did not fire.

Williams slashed with his axe because it was closest, felt the head sink into the man's leg, and then he thrust up with the sword, striking the man's belt plate with enough force to un-balance him. The Pole lost a stirrup, was leaning heavily to the left, and Williams wrenched the axe free and hit him twice in the side with it until the man fell off. There was more blood on the Welshman's face.

The officer looked at him, then at Colborne, and turned his horse round to flee. Several heavy dragoons chased him, but failed to catch up.

The lieutenant colonel stared down at his ADC.

'Where did you get to, Mr Williams?' he asked with a wry smile, but his face was ashen pale.

Williams clambered on to the wounded Pole's horse. The colonel still wore his sword, which suggested that his captors had accepted his word as a gentleman that he would not try to escape. Well, he had not, and there was no obligation to remain a prisoner if freed.

'Dear God, my brigade,' he said, staring at the corpses, the wounded and in the distance the hundreds of prisoners.

For the moment the colonel seemed too stunned to move.

'Let us go, sir,' Williams said in as kindly a way as he could manage. At the same time he wondered whether the battle was already lost.

31

The rain slackened, the sound of drops falling on leaves diminished, and Hanley strained to hear the guns. He stopped for a moment, and gestured to the hussar to do the same. There was a faint sound, but nothing compared to the intensity of an hour ago. They had gone a good two and half miles, and should be getting closer.

The KGL hussar tapped him on the arm and then raised a finger to his lips for quiet. He gestured through the thinning trees towards the field beyond, and Hanley saw horsemen. There were only four of them, but the shape of the brass helmets and long horsehair crests left him in no doubt that they were French. They would have to find another way. Hanley and the hussar doubled back the way they had come and began to loop around to the west.

On another road, perhaps a dozen miles away, a small party of horsemen also noticed that the sound of cannon was quieter than it had been.

'What do you think it means?' Esther MacAndrews asked the officer, while her eyes flicked towards the sergeant and indicated that she would value his opinion.

'May be all over, worst luck,' Cornet Lillie said. Mrs MacAndrews was well aware that the seventeen-year-old had not seen any service.

'Maybe, sir,' the sergeant said, 'but they are more likely shifting position before they have at each other again.'

The officer was in nominal command of a draft of replacements and returning convalescents for the 4th Dragoons. Hearing that there would most likely be a battle – the rumour had spread quickly in Elvas – Esther and her daughter had secured permission from the regiment's commander to accompany the party as it went to join the army.

'You must go, Mrs MacAndrews,' the colonel's wife had insisted. Mrs Dalbiac followed her husband everywhere on campaign, and was now nursing him back to health after a bout of fever. 'I could not bear the thought of not being there if Colonel Dalbiac were in danger, and I am sure that your sentiments would match my own. Do not worry, the colonel will arrange everything.'

Jane was keen, even if she suspected there was more to it than simply the desire to see that her father was safe – or, if it came to the worst, to tend to him as best they could. Mrs MacAndrews did not bother to ask Jenny Dobson whether she wished to join them. The lure of an estranged father was a weak one, and Miss Dobson, or the widow Hanks or whatever the woman was called, showed no sign of wishing to leave her comfortable lodgings. Esther also doubted that Hanley and her other keepers would be willing to let the woman roam. It was hard to say just what plans they had, but so far she and Jane had done nothing untoward. They tried to add a little polish to Jenny's manners and appearance. Jane had spent several happy days with Miss Dobson discussing clothes and putting in orders for materials. Esther liked Jenny, but that did not mean she altogether trusted her, or indeed the schemes of Hanley and the others. Yet she was grateful that he had arranged for them to come to Elvas, since this now gave them the chance to go to the major's side.

It was a good twenty mile ride, but with the escort of the subaltern, sergeant and a dozen troopers they ought to make good time and be safe. The weather was foul, but both she and Jane were experienced riders. They would make it. She just hoped that her husband was safe and sound when they arrived. At least they carried some good news. Yesterday Mrs Murphy was delivered of twins, a boy and a girl, and the mother and babies were doing well.

★

The sergeant was right, and there was simply a lull over the battlefield as the armies reformed and prepared to fight again. The Spanish regiments had held up the entire French army for almost an hour. They had stood when all save one of Colborne's battalions were slaughtered on their flank. They had even stood when some of the oncoming redcoats from the rest of the Second Division had fired into the straggle of lancers and the Spanish battalions beyond them.

The Spanish had held their ground and given the rest of the army a chance, but they were weary and low on ammunition. There was little trace of formal lines, or of ranks and files. Men had clustered together, closing up to the centre as casualties mounted, and each battalion had become a mass of a few hundred stubborn men loading and firing as fast as they could. General Blake and Marshal Beresford at last found each other and ordered them to withdraw behind the approaching six battalions of redcoats. At the same time Marshal Soult gave orders for his second division to advance through the battered leading division, and so for a short while the fighting stopped.

Colborne and Williams arrived at the improvised square of the 2/31st just as the new British battalions opened out to let the Spanish retire through them.

'Know that we are ordered to do this!' a young Spanish officer called out to them as he passed, leading fifty or so powder-stained men who had become detached from the other survivors of the battalion.

Captain Dunbar was with the 2/31st, his hat gone and his hand bandaged, but otherwise unscathed.

'You look like Banquo's ghost,' he said to Williams with thin humour, but his face looked as strained as the colonel's. Their own battalion had been one of those slaughtered, its Colours snatched by the French.

Some of the Spanish would not withdraw. Several dense clusters of men refused to retreat, and so as the two remaining brigades of the Second Division advanced their line became broken. Closest to them was Major General Houghton's brigade, the general himself riding at their head and still wearing a green frock coat. The 1/29th was on the right, next to them, and the much-flogged Steelbacks of the 1/57th in the centre, both battalions with yellow facings and a yellow field on their Regimental Colours. On the left was the 1/48th, and Williams wondered whether they had heard of the grim fate of their second battalion. He could just glimpse the other brigade in line beyond them, commanded by Major General Lumley until this morning and now presumably led by the senior lieutenant colonel.

Colborne sent Williams to Major General Houghton. Shells began to fall as he cantered his captured horse across the slope. A shot struck the 1/29th, ripping off the leg of a front rank man and smashing the foot of the soldier behind.

'Close up!' called the sergeant standing behind the company.

Williams had to wait as another group of Spanish infantry shuffled to the rear. One of them dropped as a musket ball slammed into the square of his back. A few voltigeurs were on the crest given up when the Spanish were ordered to retire.

A ball whipped past Houghton's round face as Williams rode up and reported. There were grim expressions as he told the general and his staff what had happened to the three battalions. 'Lieutenant Colonel Colborne wishes to say that he will keep the Thirty-first in close column to guard your flank in case the cavalry should return.'

Houghton nodded. 'Are they steady?'

'As a rock, sir,' Williams said. For all the horror at the devastation they had witnessed, he had seen more anger on the faces of the 2/31st. Men were saying that the Polish lancers had killed redcoats as they surrendered and stabbed even those prisoners they had taken.

'They were all drunk,' one man had said.

'They were promised gold for every man they killed,' another claimed. Williams could never understand how such rumours sprang up and spread like the fires that had burned through the dry grass at Talavera and scorched the wounded.

'No quarter to those buggers,' several men had said.

'You need have no fear for your flank, sir,' Williams added, remembering their savage expressions.

'Good.' The major general's servant appeared, bearing his scarlet uniform coat with its blue collar and cuffs and gold lace. Houghton passed the man his cocked hat, began to unbutton his jacket, and for a few moments stood out in his white shirt.

A shell burst near the centre of the 1/57th, flinging four men down. Another reeled out of the line, the right side of his face a mangled ruin. The battalion's commander was busy adjusting the dressing of the line, which had become a little untidy as they deployed, one company ending up behind another instead of alongside it. As he rode along the line a fragment from another shell hit his horse in the head. It sank down to its knees, but the lieutenant colonel remained upright, standing on his own feet once they touched the ground. Still giving orders to re-form the line, he stepped free.

Major General Houghton slipped one arm into the sleeve of his uniform coat and pulled it on. With a slap a musket ball struck the chest of his ADC's horse. The beast gave a sigh and the rider sprang off, calling for another mount.

Stewart rode up, bandaged on the arm and around his ankle. Houghton had just put on his hat and now raised it in greeting.

'Now, boys, those French blackguards think that they can beat true Englishmen!' Stewart raised his voice and waved his sword in the air. A shell exploded near by and muck pattered down on the rump of his horse, but the general ignored it. 'We shall show them the error of such notions and drive them off that ridge!' He pointed his sword at the crest. 'Now is the time – let us give three cheers!'

The response was immediate, the three battalions yelling out their challenge to the enemy. Williams joined in, his lips painful. With all the Spanish back behind them, apart from a few stubborn groups still firing on the crest, the six battalions of redcoats marched up the gentle slope. The voltigeurs fired a few more shots as they came and men dropped, but then the French skirmishers fell back down the far slope. As the British advanced, more and more of the enemy guns on the further knoll were able to see them.

A shell wounded both ensigns carrying the flags of the 1/29th and killed one of the sergeants protecting them. The other NCOs held the Colours aloft until new officers arrived to hold them. The heavy ball from a twelve-pounder struck a man from the 1/57th in the chest, destroyed his shoulders and much of his arms, flung his head into the air, and then went on to decapitate his rear rank man.

'Close up! Close up!'

The lines reached the crest.

'Battalion, halt!'

There were French columns no more than thirty yards down the slope, most of them fresh troops from the supporting division, although several of the battalions that had fought the Spanish had refused to retire. In front of Houghton's brigade the ground was especially crowded, columns packed together too closely to deploy into line, and four-pounder cannon or voltigeurs in the few gaps they had left.

'Make ready.'

French cannon fired from the higher knoll to the south, the four-pounders sprayed blasts of canister from close range and the infantry fired up the slope, many of the men in the rear ranks pointing their muskets over the heads of those in front. Men slumped forward or were flung back by the force of flying metal, but there were so many cries of pain that they merged into the roar of fire.

The British lines staggered as they were flayed with this deluge of fire, and now bodies in red coats dropped among the layer of Spanish dead and wounded.

'Steady, lads, steady!' officers told their men.

'Close up, close up!' Sergeants shoved men to cover the holes torn by the enemy.

'Present!' Muskets came up to shoulders all along the three lines. Williams guessed that the other brigade was engaged just as heavily, but he could not see them. Thick smoke wafted up the slope, making it hard to see the French.

'Fire!' The sound always made him think of some strong man ripping apart heavy cloth or canvas. More smoke added to the clouds, and he could only imagine the devastation as fifteen hundred heavy lead balls slammed into the French columns.

The redcoats reloaded. A roundshot bounced in front of the 1/29th, only brushing against the thigh of one of the captains but ripping his leg open and snapping the bone. Behind him a corporal lay on the grass, clutching at his stomach.

'Close up!'

Two drummers helped the captain to the rear, one of the men a tall negro. Williams knew that the 29th were very proud of their band.

The British were firing platoon volleys, sections of each company shooting in turn so that fire rippled along the line. Every now and again the wind parted the cloud to reveal the enemy columns still there and still firing, but most of the time each side blazed away at an invisible menace beyond the smoke.

Williams did not think that he was needed and so watched, as if this would somehow help the men slowly being consumed in this slaughter yard. The redcoats loaded and fired, loaded and fired, the routine an unthinking habit, and within a few minutes the ordered platoon volleys degenerated into a free fire as each man worked at his own pace. They did not speak, barely noticed what happened around them, but simply raised their firelocks, shot into the thick smoke and reloaded.

'Steady, lads!' The officers had little to do apart from set an example and show calm. A young ensign was dragged back behind the line, both legs gone beneath the knees and pieces of white bone sticking out from the stumps. He was little more than a boy and tears streamed down his face.

'My sword, I must have my sword,' he pleaded with the drummers pulling him back.

'Close up! Close up.'

Williams watched the battalions shrink away in front of his eyes. When men fell, others stepped or were pushed into their places and the lines closed towards their Colours in the centre.

Each time the line became shorter, and the gaps between battalions widened.

'Steady. Pour it into them, boys!'

Major General Houghton kept calling out encouragement to his men until he was struck by a blast of canister from a four-pounder. He shook in the saddle, arms waving like those of a man having a fit, and his horse collapsed under him. Williams was near by and jumped down to help the ADC and some redcoats who clustered around the fallen general.

The ADC stared at him, his face pale, and shook his head. There must have been a dozen holes torn in the general's coat, the material around them turning a deeper red as they watched.

'Colonel Inglis,' the general moaned, and then passed out. As they carried him back, the ADC rode to find the lieutenant colonel of the 1/57th and tell him that he was now in command of the brigade.

Some of the French guns on the higher knoll began to fire heavy canister, a dozen or so larger balls that had a longer range, even if they spread less widely.

Williams saw an officer of the KGL artillery coming across the slope.

'Who is in command? the man asked. 'Where shall I place my cannon?'

There was no sign of General Stewart in the drifting smoke. Lieutenant Colonel Inglis was already down, sitting behind his own battalion as a surgeon bandaged an awful wound in his neck.

'Anywhere you can find a gap!' Williams told the man. 'Just fire at the enemy.'

As the man rode off a shell exploded, cutting down two drummers helping a wounded captain to the rear. Two of the 57th were cut down by the same cannonball, and the broken stump of one of their muskets impaled another redcoat in the chest.

'Close up! Close up!'

The whole crest seemed to be carpeted with dead and wounded men, but only in the rare lulls in the firing could Williams hear the soft moaning of the terribly injured. He was not sure how long he had stayed watching the action, but decided that he ought to report back to Colborne, although with the colonel and the brigade major as well as the 2/31st's officers he doubted that there was much for him to do.

Thick smoke drifted slowly across the slope and he realised that he had gone too far to the right. Suddenly Marshal Beresford was close by, and the big man was riding past him, dragging along a Spanish officer by his golden epaulettes. Behind stood a column of infantry with yellow fronts to their brown jackets and wide-topped shakos like those of the French.

'Will you not advance, you rascal!' the marshal bellowed, and then let go of the officer. It was the colonel of this regiment and the man seemed too stunned to speak. His soldiers looked horrified and angry.

'They will not advance, Williams,' Colonel D'Urban said, appearing alongside. 'It is quite shameful. We need to bring up fresh troops, but they refuse to go.'

Williams wondered whether the marshal had been less wild when he appeared and gave the order. Few men were likely to obey an instruction given in such a manner.

'Have the Fourth Division arrived, sir?' Williams asked.

'They are here, but we cannot risk committing them in case ...' D'Urban did not finish and Williams wondered whether he meant in case they were needed to cover a retreat. From all he had seen the remainder of the Second Division was being devoured back on the crest.

'Come, the Portuguese must do what the Spanish will not!' Beresford shouted angrily, and then spurred away. D'Urban and the handful of other officers followed him.

Williams turned back more to the left, and managed to glimpse a redcoated battalion in close column which must be the 2/31st. He had never before seen an army commander appear so agitated, and D'Urban's face had been drawn and gloomy. It seemed that the battle was truly lost.

32

The Fourth Division began to advance, even though no order had come instructing them to do so. Major General Sir Galbraith Lowry Cole had waited, watching the dreadful struggle unfold on the ridge ahead of them, but no word came and the hours had passed. His two brigades were rested and ready, but they were not summoned, so they could only wait. No word came from Marshal Beresford, except to tell them to move to support the cavalry and to stay in that position. They went forward a short distance and then waited, watching the low ridge ahead of them and following the battle as well as they could through the thick smoke.

A staff officer arrived without orders from the marshal, but with the suggestion that the Fourth Division should attack. Yet the responsibility was Cole's and so was the decision, and if he was wrong it might well end his career. The general, who had once competed for the hand of Kitty Pakenham and lost to the then Sir Arthur Wellesley, was too much the soldier to place his own fears before what he knew was right. He made up his mind, gave the orders, but then it took time to deploy the battalions, so it was at almost precisely one o'clock that the advance began.

Dalmas saw the British and Portuguese soldiers forming up and immediately went to report to Marshal Soult. Finding him was not easy, for the marshal had gone forward to urge on the men of V Corps. Two divisions, all told more than eight thousand men in eighteen battalions, had marched over the southern knoll, gone down into the little valley and attacked the lower knoll. Over a third were now dead or wounded, including all the generals and most of the colonels. Girard and Gazan were both back with the surgeons.

The cuirassier rode through the gun line on the knoll and then between clusters of soldiers, the remnants of the leading battalions withdrawn back from the firing line. It was hard to see much pattern as he went forward. Men stood in masses or as loose skirmishing lines, and there were half a dozen four-pounders among them. All those close enough fired into the smoke again and again, and sometimes they dropped as balls came out of the gloom and found a mark. The French infantry were not giving way, but neither were the English. He passed a brigade commander, propped up against his dead horse and supported by a weeping ADC. The general had at least three severe wounds to the chest and as he tried to call out encouragement to his men he coughed up blood. A Polish officer with a few of his lancers was riding between the groups of men, showing them the six Colours they had taken in the great charge and telling them that the redcoats would crack if only they pushed on.

Soult was unscathed, and had a distant look on his face. He was listening to a report from one of his staff.

'Tell the grenadiers to advance and press the enemy on the right.' Soult pointed, even though it was impossible to see the ground through the smoke.

'The enemy are committing their last reserves,' Dalmas reported. 'Seven or eight battalions, some English and the rest Portuguese. They are forming to attack across the plain and strike our left. If we can smash them then the day is ours. General La Tour-Maubourg asks for orders, Your Grace.'

The dragoon regiments had done little. The hussars and lancers were not as fresh, but had recovered enough to play their part once again.

Soult said nothing. A bullet whipped past between Dalmas and the marshal, and neither man blinked. Four soldiers in greatcoats were carrying a moaning officer to the rear.

'Who is that?'

'Chef de battalion Astruc,' one of the men said. The number sixty-four was painted on the light grey cover of his shako.

Dalmas doubted that the officer would reach the surgeons alive.

'Your Grace, the plain offers us excellent ground for manoeuvre. With support the cavalry can cut the English to ribbons as they did before.'

A staff colonel glared at him. A mere major did not speak to a marshal of France in such an intemperate way.

Soult did not appear concerned. He stared intently into the smoke, and just for a moment a gap appeared and they glimpsed a few redcoats on the crest. Dalmas knew that if the French had suffered so much then the English must be bleeding as well. General Werlé's strong brigade of nine battalions remained in reserve. Attack with these fresh infantry and the might of the cavalry at the same time and the new enemy attack could be shattered.

'No,' Soult said suddenly, as if hearing Dalmas' thoughts. 'We cannot rout this enemy. The Spanish have joined them in force and so we are outnumbered.' That had not been a concern earlier in the day. 'We will hold what we have. Tell General Werlé to bring his nine battalions and oppose the new British attack. Tell him that he is to defend and not to attack. We will hold here and let the enemy break themselves on us.' The marshal turned to the cuirassier officer.

'Dalmas.'

'Your Grace.'

'Go to General La Tour-Maubourg, and tell him that he may attack if he sees an opportunity.'

'Yes, Your Grace!' It was not quite what he had wanted, but this was something. If the cavalry could ride down the enemy, then the day might still be theirs.

The 106th were formed with their nine companies in column ready to advance. Lieutenant Colonel Myers, the brigade commander, walked his horse along in front of them, waving his hat in the air.

'Come on, my brave lads, this will be a great and glorious day!'

Pringle's grenadiers at the head of the column cheered him with great enthusiasm. They were in the centre, with the 1/7th Fusiliers on their left and the 1/23rd on their right. Enough space was left between each column for them to form line when they were closer to the enemy and so deliver the greatest weight of fire. Lines moved slowly, for in so wide a formation the dressing was bound to become ragged and disordered, so that it needed to stop and reform at frequent intervals.

'This will be a glorious day for the fuzileers!' Pringle heard Myers call out to the 1/23rd, his own battalion, and heard them reply with a great roar. The battalions were formed in echelon, with the 1/7th some way ahead, then the 106th, and the 1/23rd back from them. The Portuguese brigade was to their right, and their four columns were also staggered. It meant that if necessary they could readily form a continuous line facing to the right, towards the French cavalry. More protection was offered to the vulnerable right by MacAndrews' temporary battalion formed from the Light Companies. These would march in hollow square on the right of the Portuguese. Beyond them were the six guns of the KGL artillery attached to the division and four more from the Royal Horse Artillery. General Lumley's heavy dragoons and some Spanish squadrons came forward and covered the flank of the guns. On the less vulnerable left wing, a battalion of the Loyal Lusitanian Legion, Portuguese light infantry and the most experienced of the Allied units in the division, were to the left of the Fusilier Brigade in close column.

'The brigade will advance.' Myers shouted the order, warning them that they were about to go forward.

'The One Hundred and Sixth will advance.' The sergeant major's voice carried easily to the men at the very rear, but even so each company commander repeated the instruction.

'At the quick step, march.' Lieutenant Colonel FitzWilliam shouted the order as the entire division began its advance. They were aiming at a stretch of the ridge somewhat to the right of the dirty smoke blanketing the high ground. Pringle reckoned

that they had over a mile to march in this complicated formation. With his company at the head of the 106th, he could see
the squadrons of French cavalry waiting over to the right. If
the Fourth Division lost its good order, or anyone panicked or
became confused, then the French would ride them down and
slaughter them like sheep.

Some of the grenadiers looked pale as they marched, muskets
on shoulders, towards the distant enemy. Their destination looked
no closer, and it seemed as if they were walking in soft sand or
through thick mud. Pringle's legs felt heavy and sluggish, each
movement a great effort. It would change when they got closer,
but waiting was always terrible, especially when the enemy was
in sight.

A horseman appeared, riding across the front of the brigade
until he came up to FitzWilliam. Pringle heard a whisper run
along the front rank and then realised that it was Williams.

The Welshman saluted, touching his battered hat, the plume
no more than a broken stub. For some reason Williams seemed
able to ruin the smartest new uniform in a remarkably short time.

'Lieutenant Williams asks permission to fall in, sir.'

The colonel returned the salute. 'Certainly, Mr Williams. It is
a pleasure to see you.' FitzWilliam offered the subaltern his hand.

A cheer went up from the grenadiers, spreading to the companies behind, even if they had no idea what it was about.
Williams walked his horse around the two ranks of Pringle's
marching men. He freed his feet from the stirrups and then
jumped down, slapping the beast on the rump so that it walked
off. Pringle noticed that its tail was undocked, which meant that
it was a French horse, but he could see that it was smaller than
the one Williams had had before.

'Where did you get that?'

'Took it from a lancer who did not need it any more,' Williams
replied.

'Damned pirate,' Billy told him.

Dobson was in place behind the company and grinned broadly.
Pringle could sense that the distraction and the arrival of a

familiar face had lifted the spirits of the grenadiers. Williams beamed at them happily.

'Have you deserted your post, young Bills?' Pringle asked.

'The colonel did not need me for the moment, and when I saw you fellows advancing I asked him if I might ride over to join you.' He raised his voice. 'Thought you might need a hand.'

'On the run from the magistrates more like.' The voice came from the ranks.

'I believe that we are all aware of the adage about a bad penny!' Truscott called. His company was directly behind Pringle's.

Williams bowed, then had to step quickly to catch up. Like the other battalions in the brigade, the 106th was in column at quarter-distance and stepping out at the quick pace of one hundred and eight paces a minute. The sky had gone dark once again, and flurries of rain kept blowing into them. They could no longer see the high ground, but they could see Lieutenant Colonel Myers. FitzWilliam followed him and they followed FitzWilliam.

A lieutenant should be behind the two ranks formed by the company, but for the moment Williams strode alongside Pringle. Billy could see his friend's scarred uniform and thought it better not to ask too much about what had happened.

'We are holding them,' was all Williams would say. 'But it will take the Fourth Division to break them.'

Pringle did not press him and for a while they marched on in silence. A horse trotted across the field ahead of them, most of its jaw gone and blood on its haunches. Even at fifty yards Pringle could see its huge eyes and felt that they were watching him.

'Someone shoot the poor beast,' one of the grenadiers hissed.

'Quiet in the ranks.' Pringle was not sure which of the sergeants had spoken, but suspected that it was the officious Fuller rather than Murphy or Dobson. Thankfully the poor creature ran on and he no longer had to witness its agony.

The rain slackened and they could see the ridge ahead of them. Up on the knoll the French artillery saw them coming and the batteries shifted the gun line, the crews wheeling each piece into a new position.

At three-quarters of a mile the first shot struck them. One twelve-pound ball bounced a few yards from Pringle and then sped on so that it struck Truscott's company, cutting a redcoat in two at the waist. Its path was at an angle so it missed his rear rank man, but ripped the arm off the soldier next to him and then disembowelled the sergeant marching as file closer.

'Dear God,' gasped another sergeant as he stared in horror at his friend. 'Close up! Close up!' he shouted quickly, and rubbed off the gore and fragments of flesh spattered across his face.

They marched on.

Another shot shattered the heads of two grenadiers just as Pringle was casting his eye along the line. One moment the men were marching, the man in the rear grinning at some joke told to him by his neighbour, and then there was a smear of bone, flesh and inner matter spraying across the men around them. The company marched on, but the two headless corpses stood for what seemed an age, even if it cannot have been much more than a second or so. The one in the rear fell first, dropping back, and then the other slumped forward. Pringle found himself wondering why in an effort to ignore the horror. He had seen such things many times, but it only made it a little easier.

'Close up!' That was Murphy this time.

Another grenadier stepped out of the ranks, blood pouring from his cheek, which had been struck by several teeth and part of the jawbone of one of the dead men.

A shell burst and flung muck on to FitzWilliam, but the aristocrat rode on, flicking debris from his sleeve with an elegant gesture.

Williams was still walking alongside Pringle. 'I had better go to my station.'

'I would not have dared make the suggestion to a staff man,' Pringle said, and then the urge came to him to speak because he wondered whether he would ever get another chance. 'Before you go, old fellow, there is something I must say.'

'If it is that my plume is sorely hurt, then I already know,' Williams replied cheerfully.

'No,' Pringle said, 'it is not that.' A little voice said that he should not bother, for either or both of them might be dead in half an hour and so it would not matter, but his mind was made up. He must speak, even if these were some of his last words – indeed, perhaps especially if that proved so.

'Mr Williams,' he began, for this ought to be done properly. A shell interrupted him, a big piece of metal flying through the air and embedding itself in Private Jenkins' chest. The grenadier staggered, his face going pale. His musket dropped to the ground with a clatter.

'Close up!'

'Mr Williams,' Pringle repeated, and he could see that his friend was puzzled. 'I wish to inform you that it is my intention to seek your sister's hand in marriage.'

'Oh,' Williams said, looking genuinely startled, and failing to match the solemnity of the question. 'Which one?' He must have seen Pringle's expression. 'Oh, it must be Anne.'

Shells exploded in the companies behind them and they heard the screams.

'Close up, close up!'

'Have you expressed your ambitions to Anne?' Williams asked.

Ahead of them they could see French infantry moving forward to face them. They looked fresh and in good order, and there seemed to be plenty of them. They could see the cavalry more clearly now, with a front line formed of dragoons in green jackets facing the Portuguese.

'Not in as many words,' Pringle confessed. 'I felt it only right to seek your blessing first.'

A roundshot flung up a plume of earth as it struck the ground in front of them and bounced high, striking the barrel of one of the grenadier's muskets and flinging it from his grip. By the time it landed the stock was broken and the barrel itself twisted and bent.

'Move to the rear rank, lad,' Dobson said as the man massaged his hands. 'There'll be another to pick up soon enough.'

Lieutenant Colonel Myers was down, but then they saw his slim figure get up again and call for another horse. Until it arrived he marched at their head.

'I suppose I shall have to weigh the matter with great care.' Williams was now more sober than Pringle, but Billy thought he saw amusement in his friend's eyes. 'Yes, great care, and I must keep a close scrutiny of your conduct.'

'Get back to your post, damn your eyes!' Pringle knew that he was grinning.

'I am not sure that cursing will help your cause,' Williams said with mock solemnity.

Even at the quick pace they seemed to crawl across the plain. After ten minutes they stopped to redress the ranks, and then did the same again after a similar interval. The Portuguese were falling further behind than they were supposed to be, but otherwise they were coming on boldly enough. Their four battalions had seen no real service, but were well-trained and eager.

Slowly the Fourth Division advanced and the French guns killed men by ones and twos, and occasionally by fours and fives. Drummers helped the wounded to the rear, but there were soon too many of them to be carried, and so they added to the trail of red bundles left behind by the Fusilier Brigade. They were leading and so the guns on the knoll concentrated their malice on them.

Pringle's ensign had his thigh shattered by an eight-pound shot, and that made Billy all the more glad that he had Williams there. The men marched on, heads bowed, and Pringle found that it took real effort to keep his own upright and looking at the enemy. There were three distinct columns ahead of them, with more troops behind. Some of the guns were firing canister now, which meant that they were at long last getting closer. The hail of balls rattled and pinged off the muskets of his company. Then a burst came lower and three men were flung back, bodies twitching from the strike of missiles bigger and heavier than a musket ball.

Billy wondered when they would form line. The French liked to advance in column, and often tried to barge through the defending line without bothering to change formation. That only worked against unsteady troops and risked leaving it too late. If it came to a contest of musketry then the narrow-fronted column was at a severe disadvantage because fewer men could fire their muskets compared to a battalion in line.

A shell exploded, the force staggering him, and there was a pain in his right arm and blood on his sleeve. Williams ran to him.

'It's nothing,' he said, for he could see that the gash was not deep. 'Back to your station, you pirate.' Williams nodded and went back. Pringle glanced around and waved to Truscott. His friend looked drawn, but then he doubted his own appearance would be any better. They had been marching for almost half an hour and most of that time under fire. Only a fool would relish something like that, and the thought brought young Sam to mind. Truscott had plenty to worry about.

Truscott's company had been ordered to fall back a little, for the battalion needed longer gaps between companies if it was to deploy into line.

'Brigade will halt!' Myers had remounted.

'Halt!' This time FitzWilliam had the sergeant major deliver the order since his voice needed to be heard over the cannonade.

The 1/7th were little more than one hundred yards away from the French. Pringle's grenadiers were some fifty yards behind them and the 1/23rd a similar distance again. Fortunately the French infantry were still busy moving into position. Pringle could see them up the slope, three battalions with blue jackets and trousers, so probably a regiment of light infantry. They were in a column of divisions, with a frontage of two companies, and as yet had not had time to send out skirmishers.

The 106th began to form line on the centre company, which meant that Pringle had to wheel his grenadiers, take them to what would be the far right of the line and then have them about-face. The minutes spent with his back to the enemy as they marched into position were wearing, but he had to concentrate on the task in hand for any error would upset the whole manoeuvre and place the battalion in danger. He tried not to imagine the greencoated dragoons spurring their horses into a charge.

A cannonball passed so close that he was buffeted, and then it ripped off the backpack of one of his men, hurling him down, before it tore the arm from another. The man knocked over screamed, until Murphy went over and dragged him to his feet.

'You're not hurt, you idiot!'

The line was formed, so Pringle could pay attention to the enemy once again. He did not understand why the French had watched them and could only assume that they were also busy. One of the three columns was squarely in front of the 106th, the others facing each of the fusilier battalions.

'The brigade will advance!' Myers sat on his horse looking as calm as a man out for a leisurely hack.

'The One Hundred and Sixth will advance,' the sergeant major boomed. 'March!'

Then the French dragoons began to trot their horses forward.

33

Major MacAndrews was pleased with the way his little battalion was behaving. The three companies from Kemmis' brigade had been attached only a few hours ago, and it had taken a little thought to work out how the temporary formation would form and manoeuvre. In the end he decided to have two companies forming the front and rear of the square, one on each side, and let the Brunswickers skirmish. If pressed the 'Owls' would run back to shelter under the bayonets of the square. He formed the Light Companies each in four ranks, the sides effectively marching in column, for it would be a simple matter to turn them if needed.

It was a long march, and as they were the unit on the far right and held furthest back it was a while before they began to go forward. A square, even an open one like this, usually offered a target no gunner could resist, but today they drew little fire. One shell exploded and cut down two men from the 23rd's Light Company, and a stray roundshot took the foot off one of the Brunswick riflemen, but in the main the French artillery concentrated on the rest of the Fourth Division and especially the fusiliers.

'Why are they always uphill?'

'Sir?' His acting adjutant, a lieutenant from the Royal Fusiliers, looked puzzled.

'My apologies, Mr Carson, I was merely thinking aloud. But on the last two occasions I have fought the French they have always held the high ground and we have had to drive them off it. That is a most unnatural feeling for a Highlander – we expect to be the ones up a mountain!'

'Halt!' The Portuguese brigade formed line a good one hundred yards back from the Fusilier Brigade.

'Face front!' MacAndrews had improvised the command and now the men at the sides and the rear turned to face outwards. Only one man turned the wrong way and had to be pushed into place by the sergeants.

'First and second ranks kneel! Fix bayonets!' They were level with the right-hand battalion of the Portuguese brigade and now offered a solid block shielding them from an attack on their flank.

'Here they come,' Carson said. MacAndrews had already spotted the squadrons of enemy dragoons moving forward.

'Steady, boys, wait for the orders.'

Two regiments of dragoons were advancing, and their walk turned into a trot. MacAndrews counted the front rank of one squadron, multiplied it, and came up with a force of at least six hundred men. There were two squadrons with red fronts to their dark green jackets, coming one behind the other, and to their left three squadrons with yellow collars and fronts.

'Wait, boys, wait.'

The French were aiming for the blue-coated Portuguese standing in two deep lines. Most of them were young, and all were small, and in the early years of the war French horsemen had swept aside battalions like this with ease.

'Steady, lads, wait.' MacAndrews watched but saw no sign that any of the squadrons was coming for his square.

He heard a trumpet sound and the French horses began to come on, closing the distance fast. If the Portuguese fired too soon then the helpless sense of holding an empty musket might well panic them. MacAndrews held his breath.

'Well done,' he whispered as the young soldiers in blue jackets waited just as they should.

'Third and fourth ranks, make ready!' he ordered. The sound of flints being pulled back came from all sides of the square.

'Front face only,' he added, making his order more specific this time. 'Present!'

Steel glinted as the dragoons drew their long swords and the trumpet called again. MacAndrews could see the horses as they threw up clods of earth, their mouths open and yellow teeth bared. The riders were shouting, and beneath the long moustaches he saw the men's mouths gaping almost as wide as their mounts' great jaws.

Flame and smoke spouted all along the bluejacketed line and the sound of the volley reached him almost immediately. MacAndrews saw horses and men tumbling.

'Front face fire!' he called, and then the enemy were lost behind the smoke.

From horseback he could look over the heads of his men, so when the smoke thinned just a little he saw the dim shapes of French horsemen pressing on, as their reserve squadrons came up.

A second volley split the air and MacAndrews remembered thinking that the first was not as loud as he expected. The Portuguese must be firing as platoons or as half companies, so that they kept up a steady, rolling fire.

In less than a minute the French dragoons were going back, leaving thirty or so horses and a score of men on the ground. For the moment the other enemy cavalry remained where they were, watching the British and Spanish squadrons to see who would make the first mistake. Alongside the square, the KGL and British artillery began to set up their gun line.

MacAndrews felt happy. The Portuguese were doing well, and now the Allies had guns of their own. Then the sound of great rolling volleys came from the Fusilier Brigade and he knew that none of this would matter if the redcoats could not break the enemy. In the end, it was always the infantry who decided matters. MacAndrews had faith in his own battalion and the others, but before he lost sight of them in the smoke he could not help thinking that the odds were against them.

'They're always damned well uphill,' he said to himself.

★

The three battalions of redcoats were now in line level with each other. Canister from the French guns continued to flay them, snatching groups of men from the companies and flinging them back. Truscott saw a single burst kill one of his front rank and wound the man on either side, knocking over the men behind as well. One cursed, but shrugged off the nick to his face and trudged on. Another limped to the rear. The rest lay moaning or sobbing in pain.

'Close up!'

'Steady, lads,' he said. He was on the end of the company, next to Pringle's grenadiers, and as he turned he saw Sergeant Dobson, as always carrying a musket rather than the regulation half-pike. The sergeant winked at him.

At ninety yards the front of the French column vanished behind a bank of smoke. Musket balls snapped through the air above his head. One of his men fell, blood jetting from his throat, and several more were down.

'Steady,' he said.

'Close up there, close up!'

They marched on, no longer at the quick step, but the ordinary rate of seventy-five paces per minute. As the smoke cleared, he could see the enemy better. They were from a light infantry regiment, and he thought he could glimpse its eagle standard somewhere in the centre of the column. Each man was busily reloading, even though only the three ranks of the leading companies could fire. The men were not in jackets, but wore their long sleeved blue waistcoats instead.

A shell burst overhead and something slapped into his left shoulder, causing a stab of pain. He tried to twist his head round and managed to see a quarter-inch fragment of shell casing sticking through his jacket.

'Are you wounded, sir?' his ensign called.

'It is nothing,' he said, for the pain was now less and he did not think that it should slow him down much. Yet why did the French have such a strong dislike for his left side?

At forty yards he saw a ripple of movement from the enemy

column as muskets came up to shoulders. Officers were shouting at their men, trying to wheel out companies to extend the line, but the men did not move willingly. He had seen the same reluctance at Barrosa.

The volley struck the companies nearer the centre of the 106th. Truscott saw the line shake like a flag in the wind.

'Halt!' The sergeant major's voice rang out. They were little more than twenty yards away now and the artillery fire slackened because they were so close to the enemy. As the smoke thinned Truscott could see their faces, some staring at the redcoats, others trying to ignore them as they set about reloading. All seemed to have moustaches and it made them look older than the clean-shaven redcoats.

'Make ready!'

French officers tried again to bring the supporting companies out from behind the shelter of the front of the column, but they were having to drag men one by one.

'Present!'

Lieutenant Colonel Myers had dropped back so that he was in the gap between Pringle's grenadiers and the left-hand company of his own Royal Welch Fusiliers. FitzWilliam was sitting on his horse in front of the 106th's Colours.

'Fire!' The noise was appalling, even though he had known what to expect. All three battalions fired, not bothering to use sophisticated platoon fire, but both ranks shooting as one.

'Fix bayonets!' Truscott drew his sword as the men slotted the long spikes on to the muzzles of their muskets.

Myers was struck in the thigh by a ball. For a moment Truscott was sure that he would fall, but then he seemed to recover.

'Charge, my boys, charge!' he yelled.

'Charge!' FitzWilliam called out. The men cheered, three hearty hurrahs, and at the last the front rank brought their long bayonets down ready to thrust at the enemy.

'Come on!' Truscott ran forward, not bothering to look because he knew that his men were following. They ran through their own smoke and the clouds left by the enemy volleys. Soldiers in blue waistcoats and trousers lay stretched on the ground, many moaning and some still. A handful were standing, and these screamed as the bayonets took them. Truscott saw one of his men, a quiet, rather slow lad called Jackson, twisting his blade with wild frenzy as he held his victim down with his boot.

They ran forward, Truscott nearly tripping on a body that called out in agony as he trod on the poor man's wounded belly. The French light infantry had fled, but they did not go far, and he could see them clustering around another column some fifty yards back. These men had white waistcoats, so were infantry of the line, and as the last of the fugitives cleared their front they raised muskets to their shoulders.

'Halt! Reload, reload!' Truscott began to shout, and then his shouts were blotted out by the rolling deluge of shots. Jackson fell, hit in the arm and knee, and he sobbed as he lay. Another man was struck in the forehead, a look of fixed surprise on his face. The artillery could see them now and a roundshot came through the smoke and took the leg off a corporal who screamed until a second ball shattered his body.

'Reload!' Truscott shouted. Myers was carried back by his staff, one of their sashes managing to hold back a little of the blood flowing from his leg.

Men fired as soon as they were loaded, not waiting for the orders. The French were doing the same, and so there was an almost constant banging of muskets and frequent roars from the cannon.

'Close up! Close up!'

The 106th's line was ragged, but it was still a line. As men fell they were pulled out of the way and the others shuffled together. Truscott thought that half of his company had already gone, and there seemed no end to the dying.

'Steady, lads,' he called until his voice was hoarse. The stench of gunpowder filled his nostrils until there was no other smell in the world apart from the offal stink of mutilated bodies.

'Close up, there, close up!'

A redcoat had his jaw shattered, and ran around, making

313

appalling sounds. He grabbed Truscott by the shoulders, sending a stab of pain through him, and the fellow's eyes begged for understanding and relief from pain.

'Back, man! Back to the rear.' He could not think of anything to say, and then a ball hit the man in the back, knocking him and the officer over. A sergeant helped Truscott out, and as he was lifting him he took a ball through the body, so that he dropped his captain.

'I am so sorry, sir,' he said. His hand wavered as he grasped Truscott's hand. 'So sorry.' The sergeant fell to his knees and then keeled over to the side.

'Cease fire! Cease fire!' That sounded like the sergeant major's voice.

'Prepare to charge!' FitzWilliam joined in the shouting. With difficulty Truscott sat up and then pushed himself to his feet.

'Cease fire!' He stuck his sword into the ground so that he could tap men on the shoulders. 'Stop firing!' Sometimes he had to yell to men just inches away and they frowned as if he were speaking another language. One of the company nodded his understanding and then was flung back by a ball driving deep into his side.

'One Hundred and Sixth, follow me, charge!' He saw the colonel, hat gone, waving his sword as he rushed at the enemy.

'Charge!' He took up the cry, pulled his sword out of the earth and went forward. Men on either side of him dropped, but the survivors ran on, bayonets reaching for the enemy.

The French gave way. Truscott slashed at an officer who was trying to keep his men in place, hacking into the man's arm.

'Prisoner!' he bellowed as the man's sword fell to hang by its wrist strap.

'*Oui*.' The Frenchman was a veteran, scars on his cheek, and suddenly Truscott noticed that he had an empty right sleeve. He smiled at the absurdity of it all, two one-armed men coming to blows, and then more than a third of the forty-one balls from a tin of heavy canister struck as a cluster and flung them both twitching to the ground.

34

MacAndrews was summoned to assume command of the
106th because FitzWilliam had taken over the brigade,
the second replacement for the grievously wounded Myers. His
Light Companies remained in square, the Portuguese still in
line and facing off the French cavalry. These had tried a second
charge, but it was a half-hearted affair compared to the first and
stopped as soon as they saw the determination of the blue-coated
infantry waiting for them. MacAndrews' men had suffered no
other casualties, so at least he would be able to tell Captain
Truscott that his young brother was safe.

By the time the Scotsman reached his regiment he found that
he was now brigade commander. FitzWilliam had taken a ball
in the hand and a much nastier wound to the neck, and so had
been carried to the rear. MacAndrews was the senior major left
on his feet; in fact, as far as he could tell, he was the only major
left on his feet.

Billy Pringle commanded the 106th as the senior remaining
captain, with Williams in charge of the Grenadier Company. The
Welshman had picked up a musket and was now standing in the
ever thinning line of men. He pulled the trigger, felt the butt
push back hard against his shoulder, adding more smoke to the
clouds surrounding them. He did not know what time it was,
how long they had been engaged, for the battle now seemed to
have raged for days. He did not know how many men he still
had, and had no idea whether the balls he fired found a mark.

Slide the left hand to the middle of the musket. Drop the
butt, and with right hand reach into pocket for a new cartridge.

There was only one left after this, which meant that he would soon have to search in the pouches of the dead and wounded for more. Put the paper cartridge to the mouth, bite off the bullet, making that bitter, salty taste of saltpetre all the stronger. Flick open the cover to the pan, sprinkle in a little powder, then flick the cover shut. Butt falls to the ground, then pour the rest of the powder into the muzzle. Stuff down the empty cartridge, and spit the ball after it. Then slide out the ramrod, thrust down firmly once. Withdraw the ramrod and slide it back into its hoops. Raise musket to the shoulder, pull back the hammer to full cock, settle, aim and then fire.

The noise was constant, so that it was hard to tell whether it was real or just in his head. A grenadier was on all fours in front of him, vomiting blood. There were some French in white and blue scattered among his own men, for this was where the second charge had brought them. Dead and wounded alike shook when blasts of canister churned up the ground. Dobson had taken a couple of balls in the leg, but swore that it was nothing and had bound them up. He stood beside Williams and loaded and fired, and it was almost as if three years had not passed and they were still front and rear rank men.

'Close up!' The cries were less common now. Not because fewer men fell, but because it was an unthinking reaction. Red-coats dropped on either side, and the survivors edged closer together.

Truscott was hit – badly from what Dobson had said. Sergeant Murphy had lost a leg and might lose the other, but sat behind the grenadiers, telling them that he was just getting angry with the French.

Williams found himself wondering whether there had ever been a battle where everyone died. Talavera had been a hard fight, but it had not gone on as long as this. Then he jumped as something hit his shoulder.

'Sorry!' Pringle said, smiling and lifting up his hand. 'We need to charge again. Get the men to stop firing.'

316

'Cease fire!' Pringle shouted. 'We have to drive these fellows off.'

'Stop firing, stop firing!' Williams' throat cracked as he tried to yell. Dobson took up the cry and then pointed to the right.

'Cavalry!'

Williams could barely see the shapes through the smoke.

'Close up, lads, close up!' He started shoving men together so that the remnants of the company formed a two-deep line. 'Front rank, kneel!'

'Bayonets!' Dobson called, and took his place at the far end of the line.

'Second rank present!' Williams did not know how many of the men were loaded. His own musket was ready, even though he could not remember loading it. Still, for the moment it was more important for him to give orders than to fight.

The weight of the charge was heading towards the 1/23rd and he heard a ripple of fire, but could not see much in the gloom. The silhouettes of a dozen or more lancers were coming at the grenadiers, led by a tall officer on a big horse. As they came close Williams saw the red and white pennants and the glinting armour of their leader. It was Dalmas.

'Wait for it.' Williams had eleven men in the front rank and twelve in the second rank.

The lancers came on, so close now that even their short mounts looked like tall monsters. Pennants rippled as they brought them down into the charge. Williams could hear the drumming of their hoofs even over the general din of the battle.

'Second rank, fire!' he shouted. Two muskets misfired, but the enemy were only fifteen yards away. Three of the horses were down, one sliding to a halt just a couple of feet from the front rank. Another was without a rider. Dalmas rode on.

'Lucky sod,' Dobson said, recognising the man.

The cuirassier was just yards from them, but his horse slowed as it saw the row of bayonets of the kneeling front rank. Dalmas was yelling curses at them, trying to force the big horse closer

317

so that he could make it rear and let its feet clear a path. The remaining lancers had faltered, but now came on again.

Williams raised his musket, steadied his aim and squeezed the trigger. He saw the ball strike the front plate of Dalmas' cuirass, and there was a dull metallic thunk as it punched a hole in the metal. The Frenchman shook with the impact, and was struggling to stay upright as his horse wheeled away. He rode off, the lancers going with him, and the grenadiers cheered as loudly as parched throats allowed.

'The One Hundred and Sixth will prepare to charge!' Mac-Andrews rode along behind the line.

'Mr Williams, take command of the battalion,' he called to the Welshman. 'You will charge on my order.' He must have seen Williams' concern. 'Pringle is hit in the leg. I do not believe it is serious. Now take command, sir, and do your duty.'

'Sergeant Dobson,' Williams said, turning to the veteran.

'Sir.'

'You have the Grenadier Company.'

'Yes, sir.' Dobson smiled. 'Bloody hell, sir.'

'The army's going to the dogs,' Murphy jeered, his face as white as a sheet.

Williams ran to the centre of the battalion, struggling to believe that all the captains were down. He suspected several of the companies were led by sergeants. He found the Colour Party, and saw Derryck and young Truscott holding the flags. How the lad had got here from the flank was a mystery. The standard poles had been broken by musket balls and in some ways that made it easier for the boy to manage the Regimental Colour with its red cross on a white field. The silk was torn and filthy from powder smoke. A headless corpse lay on the ground behind the line, and it was only when Williams saw the four white chevrons on the sleeve that he realised that it must be the sergeant major. He pushed his way past the others to stand in front of the line.

'Are you in charge now, Williams?' Derryck said. He chuckled. 'At this rate I shall be a colonel by tomorrow!'

Williams filled his lungs and then shouted as loud as he could. 'Prepare to charge!'

MacAndrews rode back along the front of the line, and then his horse was struck and he fell, rolling as he hit the ground. He stood up, and then drew his sword.

'We're going to charge, lads. So let those blackguards hear you!'

The cheer was thin, but that was surely because so few were left to raise it.

'Follow me, charge!' MacAndrews dashed forward.

'Would it not be a jape if none of us followed,' Derryck said quickly.

'Charge!' Williams ignored him. He dropped his empty musket as he ran, drew his sword and then pulled the axe from his sash for good measure.

The French quit. As they went through the smoke they saw figures in white waistcoats turning and running and any that moved too slowly were clubbed or stabbed to the ground. There were bodies everywhere. Williams knew that if the French had managed to charge it would probably have been the battered redcoats who ran.

Marshal Soult's last reserve was broken, and his entire infantry began to run. The 106th and the rest of the Fusilier Brigade charged for thirty or forty yards before exhaustion hit them and from then on they could only trudge forward. Up on the ridge the remnants of the Second Division advanced and so did the few knots of Spanish soldiers who had refused to retire or to give in. They walked forward as men in a dream, eyes staring at some far horizon, but they went forward because they would not give in.

Williams saw what looked like a company of men in line around their Colours, the Regimental Flag a yellow field. Marshal Beresford appeared, the first time he had seen the commander for what seemed like an age.

'Stop, stop the Fifty-seventh.' Williams thought the marshal sounded on the verge of tears and yet his words carried. 'It would be a sin to let them go on.'

319

The French artillery did not run, but they did begin to retire, half of the guns pulling back while the others fired a few more shots. A shell from one of the mountain howitzers pattered on to the ground near Williams and rolled towards the Colour Party. The fuse was fizzing and then it erupted. He was flung hard on to the ground and felt something slap him on the rump.

'Oh dear God, I cannot see.' Derryck – irrepressible, laughing Derryck – put a hand to a face that was a sheet of blood from where a large fragment of casing had sheered across at eye level. The sergeant standing behind Sam Truscott was struck on the forehead and the jagged metal tore through his shako and blew off the top of his skull. The young ensign was smeared with blood from both men, but did not seem to be hurt. He was shaking so that the flag in his hands quivered.

'It is all right, lad,' MacAndrews said, appearing from nowhere. 'Take the lieutenant to the surgeons,' he said to a couple of the men, who helped Derryck away. The last of the sergeants with the party took charge of the King's Colour.

'Are you hurt, Mr Williams?'

The Welshman stood up. 'I have a small piece of shell casing in the behind,' he said. He thought how Pringle would laugh when he heard, and then he remembered poor Truscott. It would all be so absurd if it was not at the same time so heartbreakingly sad.

'That seems careless. Are you fit enough to continue in command of the battalion?'

'As long as I do not sit down, sir.'

'Splendid. The brigade will halt here. Call the roll and we can begin to take more thought for the wounded.' MacAndrews began to stride away, but then turned. 'And Mr Williams, please tell the men that I have never in my life seen such gallant conduct.'

At two o'clock Hanley's luck ran out. Every time he and the German hussar had tried to find a way around the French they met up with a patrol. Twice they were chased, the second time by a dozen dragoons. His horse was struggling, for it was not in the best of condition, and he wished that he was still on one of his own mounts. The hussar pulled ahead, but looked back, and the man was clearly wondering whether to turn. It could not be anything more than a gesture, for two men on weary horses had no hope against twelve.

'Go on!' he shouted. 'Leave me and take word back!'

The German nodded and then found some reserves of strength in his horse because he pulled away. Almost immediately the animal Hanley was riding gave a shudder. He whipped it on, still hoping for some miraculous escape, but then it shuddered again and stopped. Its breath was laboured and it sank down to its knees.

Hanley sprang off, landing badly and hurting his ankle. When he stood it was more painful than his wounded arm.

'I surrender.' He raised his hands, but the leading French dragoon had his sword up and cut as he passed. Hanley dodged out of the way, but the second man thrust and gave a deep graze to his side.

'I am an English officer and I surrender.' There was an officer with the patrol and when Hanley repeated his words in French the man barked at the dragoons to stop. Hanley offered the man his sword.

His horse rolled over on to its side. Hanley felt a brief pang of guilt for riding it into the ground, but for the moment was more worried about what would happen to him.

'Your name, sir?' the man said as he took the sword. At the present there was no offer of parole.

'I am Captain Hamish Williams of the Fourth Dragoons, and I am your prisoner, sir.' Hanley hoped that Baynes' subterfuge would work, but for the moment there was nothing else he could do. An exploring officer would be a great prize for the French, and so he had chosen this false identity in the hope of being able to escape. With luck Sinclair was finished, but he could not be sure. There was no knowing where Dalmas was or whether the cuirassier would be able to recognise him. Hanley did not believe anyone else would know who he was.

321

An hour later he was herded along with hundreds of other prisoners, most of them British and many of them wounded. They limped and staggered along as the French army retreated. It seemed from what the prisoners said that the Allies had won the battle. As Hanley struggled along the muddy track, his ankle very painful, he did not feel that it looked much like victory.

EPILOGUE

Williams' command of the battalion lasted for barely three hours, but long enough for the rumble of cannon fire to fade away. The French guns had deployed on the far bank of the Nogales stream and fired with such speed and accuracy that the Allies gave up the pursuit. It was five in the afternoon, and the rolling fields around Albuera had gone quiet save for the soft moaning of thousands of wounded men, the buzzing of countless flies and the ecstatic crowing of the carrion birds.

Pringle returned, his leg bound and walking with the aid of a stick.

'Oh no,' Williams said, and grinned in relief to see that his friend was not badly hurt.

'I regret that your elevation proved so temporary,' Billy said. 'Next time I shall try to suffer a more serious wound. That way your ambitions will be given free rein and I shall spend weeks in idleness.'

'Lazy devil.'

Major MacAndrews remained in charge of the brigade, although it was unlikely to be permanent.

'Colonel FitzWilliam is seriously hurt, but they hope for recovery,' Pringle told him. 'They say Myers has little chance, poor fellow.'

'Truscott?'

Pringle shook his head. 'It is bad.'

Others were hobbling back to rejoin the battalion, men with minor wounds treated or ones who had gone astray in the confusion. At the end of the fighting Williams reckoned that there were barely one hundred men around the Colours, the only officers another lieutenant and two ensigns, including Sam Truscott. Now, as he drew up a list of the 106th's strength for Pringle to take to MacAndrews, he saw that the numbers had grown.

'One captain – that is poor old Hamilton – killed,' Williams read from the list, 'along with a lieutenant, the sergeant major, a sergeant and forty-six men. The colonel, four captains and ten subalterns wounded, along with sixteen sergeants, two drummers and two hundred and sixty-nine men.'

Pringle had taken off his glasses and was rubbing the lenses on his sash. Williams could not bear to look him in the eye and so focused on the paper. 'Total losses sixteen officers, eighteen sergeants, and three hundred and seventeen other ranks. Fit for duty, twelve officers and about two hundred others.'

'About?' Pringle's tone was harsh.

'I am sorry, sir, but several of the men report seeing others who have not yet come in.' Williams stared at the figures. He had a nasty feeling that he had miscalculated.

When he took the list to the acting brigade commander, MacAndrews made it clear that the appalling losses were typical of the brigade.

'Both of the fusilier battalions have lost at least half their strength,' the major said. The Portuguese had been less heavily engaged, but by all accounts the Second Division had been hit even harder. 'I hear the Buffs have barely eighty men left out of more than seven hundred,' MacAndrews said.

It was easy to believe, for Williams could remember the lancers and hussars riding down the redcoats. The long ridge was strewn with bodies, thousands upon thousands of bodies. Most lay white and pale, stripped of their clothes and anything else of value by looters.

'Do you need to go back to your brigade, Mr Williams?' MacAndrews asked.

'I doubt there is much of it left, and I am needed here.'

'Better send word or make sure that you have permission, but of course we are glad to have you.'

Williams led Dobson and a party of thirty fit men to search for wounded, and as luck would have it ran into Captain Dunbar. It was clear that the stories the major had heard were not exaggerated.

'The Buffs are virtually destroyed, and the Forty-eighth and Sixty-sixth not much better. Houghton's brigade is as bad, and Abercromby's losses would be called serious on any other day.'

'The colonel?' Williams asked.

'Bearing up. He knows that it was not his orders that led to disaster, but does not know what the world will say. Six Colours taken and three battalions cut to ribbons! Dear God, it could scarcely be worse, and you know how easily great men pass the blame to others.'

Williams did not have the energy to launch into an attack on the army's commanders. 'Does he need me to return, sir?'

'He told me to say that there was no need, for he was sure that you were keeping busy and that your own corps would need you.' Dunbar looked around at the men lying across the grass. 'I do not know how we will deal with them all. Well, good day to you, Williams. Do you know it is still the sixteenth of May? It feels like a year has passed.'

Williams and his men began to do what they could for the wounded, carrying back any that could be moved. Yet there were so many, often with terrible wounds. In just five minutes he saw a dozen men missing a leg, three with both legs gone and half a dozen with great gashes to the stomach and their innards showing. The flies were thick in the air, their buzzing a constant hum.

The looters kept their distance, but he was amazed at the speed with which they worked. Some were soldiers, and many more camp followers, often women with children in tow. Even more numerous were the peasants, and he did not know where they had come from because Albuera itself had seemed to be abandoned. They stripped the Allied soldiers as well as the French corpses, but the Spanish and even the dead English were laid out tidily, with hands folded across their chests.

Wounded Frenchmen begged the redcoats to carry them

away and not leave them to the mercy of the Spanish, whether soldiers or civilians. There was little he could do, even though they spotted several bodies of injured enemies who had clearly been stabbed to death where they lay.

'Is it not wonderful that the enemy trust the British to be merciful and kind,' he heard an officer with yellow facings say. The man was leading a party from his own regiment on a similar task.

'Perhaps.' The speaker was a staff officer in Spanish uniform, but his accent sounded German or Swiss. 'But what would that same mercy say about you if your homes had been burned by the French, your folk murdered and raped. What would that make you – Christians or unfeeling fiends?'

Williams did not want to think. Perhaps the years had helped the memory to fade, but even the carnage at Talavera had not seemed so appalling. At least then they had known that they had won, and there was no sense of bungling and mismanagement.

After the third trip he had only a dozen men left.

'They're done up, sir,' Dobson said firmly, as they stood among the other survivors of the 106th. It was not yet sunset, but many slept or sat huddled by fires and did not speak. Women tended to their husbands or wept because they were widows. 'They'll fall down if we don't let them sleep.'

There were simply too many fallen men and not enough fit ones to care for them. Williams could see fewer and fewer men moving across the field to care for the wounded.

'We will get back to work tomorrow,' he said. His vision was blurring, not with tears, but sheer exhaustion. 'Thanks, Dob. I do not know how you keep going.'

'A few years ago I would have said best brandy, sir. Now I reckon it's not being bright enough to quit. That and the love of a good woman.'

'You should find her.' Mrs Dobson had managed to travel out from England and join the regiment before it left Cadiz.

'You should get a surgeon to take a look at that, sir.' The sergeant pointed at Williams' backside.

'It only hurts if I sit down,' he said, his heart not in the joke, and then he saw something and knew that it must be a trick of his drained mind and spirit. He rubbed his eyes, realised that he was smearing dried blood into them and across his face, and so shook his head to clear them.

Then he ran, using his last strength.

'Well I'm buggered,' the sergeant said, and then saw and understood. 'He is a lucky sod and no mistake.'

Miss MacAndrews was walking her horse towards them. There was a whoop of almost boyish joy as the major and his wife met and embraced. A sergeant of heavy dragoons grinned and then led his little party of three away, their escort duties done.

Jane was in a stained riding habit, and she looked tired and very pale, even for someone of such fair skin. Her smile was thin when she saw the lieutenant running towards her. Mother and daughter had seen battlefields before, but the sheer scale of Albuera was new even to old soldiers like Dobson or the major.

'Mr Williams,' she said, 'I am pleased to see that you are unharmed. Do you know where Sergeant Murphy is? He is the father of twins!'

Williams ran on.

'Mr Williams,' the girl gasped in surprise as he reached up and grabbed her waist, pulling her from the horse. One boot slipped from the stirrup, but her leg was hooked around the side-saddle's horn. 'Please, Mr Williams!' she cried, losing her balance, and caught between amusement and anger.

He pulled her backwards, but managed to take her in his arms and all would have been well had he not stepped back and lost his footing in a patch of grass wet from rain mingled with blood.

Williams fell heavily on his behind, the girl landing squarely on his lap, until the pain from his wound shot through him. Without thinking he yelled and pushed up, spilling the girl.

'You fool!' she yelled angrily. Men began to stir, and some of those around the fires were watching them and laughing.

As so often in his meetings with Miss MacAndrews, Williams found himself apologising. He began to explain that he was wounded, soon realised that he could scarcely talk about that part of his anatomy and so launched into more apologies.

Williams helped Jane up, managing to tread more mud on to her skirt in the process, but at least realising before he tore it.

Miss MacAndrews laughed, a sound of simple mirth, strange and precious in a place like this. The more he apologised the more she laughed.

'I really never know what to expect when I meet you, Mr Williams,' she said, her expression serious for a moment. 'All I know is that I shall be surprised – and probably mauled and muddied about.' She laughed again, her joy golden and pure.

Williams did not know what to say, but they were close together, so he took her in his arms, lifting the small young woman off her feet, so that she gasped again and went on laughing. A row of bodies laid out and covered in greatcoats or blankets was only a few yards away. Williams smelt her hair and some faint scent as well as the odour of her wet riding habit, but could not blot out the stench of death.

'Mother has arranged shelter for the colonel,' she said, and then said no more because he kissed her and the soreness of his lips did not matter. After a wonderful moment Jane pulled away.

'You are a fool,' she said. 'But I rather think you are my fool.'

'Always.'

They kissed again and Williams lowered her feet to the ground, his arms still enfolding her. Then he began to weep.

HISTORICAL NOTE

Whose Business is to Die is a novel, but the story is based on real events and the reader is entitled to know how much is truth and how much is fiction. The central characters such as Williams, Hanley and the other officers and men of the 106th Foot are inventions, as is the regiment itself. A regiment with that number did not exist at the time of the Peninsular War, although the number was used briefly in the 1790s and again later in the nineteenth century. I have done my best to make the officers and men of this fictional battalion act, speak and function like their real counterparts. Moving the 106th so quickly from fighting at Barrosa outside Cadiz in *Run Them Ashore* to join Marshal Beresford's army further north is a piece of artistic licence, but a fairly minor one. In reality it would probably have taken a few weeks longer, but I wanted them involved from the start of the book.

Apart from the skirmish involving Hanley and his handful of men, all of the fighting described in the book actually happened, and I have done my best to describe these events faithfully, in particular the charge at Campo Major, the siege of Badajoz and the Battle of Albuera. As usual, a detailed list of the sources I have consulted appears on my website – http://www.adriangoldsworthy.com/ficsources.htm – and there is more information on the page devoted to this story.

In 1811 the situation in the Iberian peninsula still looked grim for Britain and her allies. Lord Wellington had prevented the French from taking Lisbon, and, as the story begins, had chased them out of Portugal altogether. The line of fortifications on the heights of Torres Vedras, supported by his own army reinforced by substantial numbers of the re-formed Portuguese army, was the key to his success, but had cost the public purse a vast amount of money by the standards of the day – as Baynes says in the book, the total was over nine million just for 1810. There was every reason to expect a fresh attempt at invasion by the French as soon as they had rebuilt their strength.

In early 1811 Wellington had managed to avoid losing the war, but to many it was hard to see any prospect of winning it. Nearly all of Spain was under French control, with just a few Spanish armies stubbornly continuing the struggle in spite of defeat after defeat. French success still appeared to be just a matter of time, for Napoleon was at peace in the rest of Europe and could continue to reinforce his armies in Spain.

The war in Portugal and Spain was not popular with many people in Britain, especially the leaders of the Whigs – currently in opposition, although many expected the Prince Regent to ask them to form a new government. Some of this hostility came from simple party rivalry. Others genuinely believed that wealth and resources – and lives, although as usual this came low down the list – were being spent for no significant gain in what was probably a doomed cause. Wellington repeatedly made fresh requests for more troops, more supplies, and ever more money to pay them, fund the remodelled Portuguese army, aid the Spanish and support the wider war effort. To opponents he was a Tory general, intimately linked to the government in which his older brother served, and his demands were reflections of his own lust for glory. He was not yet the national hero of later years, and any perceived mistake or failure on his part was ammunition with which to attack the government.

This was the context of the operations in 1811. Wellington remained heavily outnumbered, under-resourced and unsure of how long his supporters would remain in power in Britain. The capture of Badajoz by Marshal Soult left three out of the four key border fortresses in enemy hands, making it much easier for the French to attack Portugal again. Retaking these towns was essential, but the Allies did not have the resources to do the job properly, and so they improvised, took chances, and hoped for luck to run their way.

It meant dividing the army into two, and inevitably entrusting command of one of the groups to someone else, since Wellington could not be in two places at once. With Lieutenant General Hill on leave in Britain, Marshal Beresford was given command of the force sent against Badajoz. The natural son of an Anglo-Irish peer, the one-eyed Beresford was an experienced soldier and a highly gifted administrator. He directed the reorganisation, training and supply of the Portuguese army, without which Wellington would simply not have had the numbers to campaign at all. Large, ill mannered and quick tempered, he was not always an easy man to be around, but he got the job done. By 1811 the Portuguese infantry and artillery were well on the way to becoming every bit as effective as their British allies. It takes longer to produce good cavalrymen, who not only have to be soldiers, but skilled in caring for their mounts as well, and to the end of the war the Portuguese mounted troops proved to be somewhat erratic. At Campo Major one regiment charged boldly, while the other broke and fled just as described in the book.

As a general Beresford did not shine. It is worth remembering that for all his time in the army, his experience of high command was limited and of mixed fortunes. In South America his initial success turned to defeat when he was forced to surrender to the Spanish. Under Sir John Moore he led a division, only to see discipline fall to pieces during the retreat to Corunna – a fault shared by most of the army, but scarcely encouraging. From the beginning of the 1811 campaign his actions were hesitant and he appeared too inclined to be overwhelmed by difficulties. It should be said in his defence that acting as a subordinate to Lord Wellington was a daunting prospect for anyone. Beresford was given strict instructions, and in particular was warned not to suffer serious losses among his cavalry. Wellington had few horsemen in proportion to the size of his army, and distrusted the enthusiasm of their officers as likely to lead to them charging too far, too fast and suffering losses when they inevitably fell into disorder.

Beresford and his staff lacked experience of commanding an army of some twenty thousand men in the field – and even less when they were joined by the Spanish and numbers increased to some thirty-five thousand. It is also fair to say that quite a few of his subordinates were similarly inexperienced, and three out of the four British brigades at Albuera were led by the senior battalion commanders because no one of general rank was available. Major General Stewart had taken over the Second Division only a few months before. He was a very brave man, a gifted regimental officer, but needed a tight rein to restrain his recklessness and so was not suited for independent command. Brigadier General Long comes across as an agreeable man in his letters. As in the book, he arrived to take command of the cavalry only a few days before Campo Major. His equipment and his chosen ADC had not yet arrived, hence his having to ride a troop horse on the day. He was also suffering from stomach trouble, and may not have felt at his best. There had been little time to get to know his new command or the men serving as staff officers.

The action at Campo Major with which the story opens began an increasingly bitter feud between Long and Marshal Beresford. In time almost every aspect of the campaign became controversial as the commanders blamed each other for failures and disappointments. In later years a war of pamphlets was waged over the key events, the controversies stoked by the historian Napier, who was deeply critical of Beresford. This does mean that there is a good deal of information about each action in the campaign, but also that many decisions and actions are disputed. I have done my best to present what I believe to be the most plausible version and have tried to be fair.

At Campo Major the Allies outnumbered the French, but manoeuvred clumsily. The 13th Light Dragoons charged and broke the French 26ième Dragoons and perhaps some squadrons of hussars, and then pursued them for some eight miles, reaching

Badajoz itself. Wellington issued the biting criticism mentioned by Major Morres. It was believed that he later changed his opinion when he learned the truth, but made no public statement to that effect. Lord Wellington was not a man to make public admission of an error.

Somehow Beresford received reports that convinced him that the 13th Light Dragoons had not routed the enemy, but had in fact been surrounded and captured. He was not in a position to see the truth, unlike Colborne, who saw the charge from higher ground. That the marshal was not in the right place to observe and did not bother to find out what had really happened to the light dragoons says a lot about his inexperience in high command and his lack of confidence. Perhaps this was a legacy of the defeat in South America, producing a readiness to believe bad news. As a result he halted the heavy dragoons and made no real use of the advanced elements of Colborne's brigades. The French column marched away, recapturing the siege train taken by the 13th Light Dragoons, who were too blown and scattered to oppose them. As an aside I have no direct evidence for a conscious attempt to capture the French guns, but they would certainly have been a great asset to the Allies.

Apart from the bickering between members of the high command, the events at Campo Major testify to an army whose staff were learning as they went along and made plenty of mistakes. This was even more true of the loss of Major Morres and an entire Troop of the 13th Light Dragoons a few weeks later. They believed that they were screened by a line of outposts when there was a large gap in the line. This was not the fault of the Portuguese cavalry, but whoever issued the orders and did not check to ensure that the screen was in place.

Wellington rode south to issue directions for the siege of Badajoz, but after he returned it was conducted with the same caution and inadequate staff work seen in the earlier operations. Having said that, the resources were utterly inadequate for the task and so success was always unlikely. The heavy guns were the best that could be found in Elvas, but that best was little enough and almost all were at least a century and a half old – one had been cast in 1620. Not enough engineers and the supplies they needed were available, and so they could not copy the French plan of attack and bombard sections of wall so recently breached and repaired. The idea of attacking the San Cristoval and then placing batteries there to strike at the old castle walls had some merit given the limited resources. Yet it is hard to see how the objective could have been achieved before Marshal Soult came north with an army. Wellington's prediction of at most sixteen days to take the fortress proved accurate. Success in such a short period was always improbable, especially given the skilful and well-equipped defence mounted by the French. After Albuera the siege was resumed with a stronger force, but the same inadequate siege train and basic plan. It failed.

Lieutenant Colonel Colborne would later become famous as commander of the elite 52nd Light Infantry, part of the Light Division, in the rest of the Peninsular War and at Waterloo. He was widely liked and admired in the rest of the army, not least by Napier, who claimed that he possessed a 'singular talent for war'. Tall, fair haired, self-confident and a pious man not given to strong language or heavy drinking, he is in many respects the prototype for my fictional Williams. As far as I can tell, he did not have an ADC while commanding the brigade in these months, and so this offered a perfect opportunity to slip Williams into this post.

The manoeuvring of Colborne's brigade at the end of April and in early May fooled the French into thinking that they were facing a much bigger advance, making them give ground faster than was necessary, so keeping them well away from the force besieging Badajoz. There is no doubt that Colborne was a very gifted officer, but it should be said that admiration for him was not universal. Some of his seniors felt that he had too high an opinion of himself and his troops, and that this was not always justified. His formidable personality was no doubt another factor in the often uncomfortable working relationship between the senior officers of Beresford's army. His disagreement with Stewart occurred much as described in the book, the general taking offence at the lieutenant colonel's criticism, even though it was not directed at him.

The Battle of Albuera was very nearly a great French victory, and to some extent this was because the British commanders did not perform well together. Beresford blamed Long for retreating too quickly, although once again this was probably in obedience to a direct order and a reflection of poor staff work. He did indeed replace him as cavalry commander on the morning of the battle. The ostensible reason was that Long was inferior in rank to some of the Spanish cavalry officers and so ought to come under their authority. Lumley was senior to them and so had a right to command all of the Allied cavalry. Long had suggested the arrangement some days before, but was understandably annoyed to be supplanted when the action had actually begun. It should also be said that it was a tall order for Lumley to take over regiments he did not know and immediately lead them in a major battle. To his credit Long stayed beside him for the rest of the day and did his best to assist.

Marshal Soult arrived sooner than expected, and it is hard to see Beresford's order for the entire infantry to show themselves on the heights as anything other than an attempt to deter the French from attacking by this display of Allied numbers. It took urging from the Spanish commanders – even the threat that they would fight alone if the British and Portuguese retreated – to stiffen Beresford's resolve to fight. Wellington believed that he did so unwillingly.

The French were outnumbered by more than ten thousand men, although they did have a marked advantage in cavalry. Soult attacked anyway, and skilfully feinted an attack on the village of Albuera before slipping around the exposed Allied right. Masséna had done the same thing on the second day of fighting at Fuentes de Oñoro and caught Wellington off guard. The scene where the French emerge from the mist and surprise Don Julian Sanchez and his partisans comes from Captain Brotherton's memoirs. Wellington was soon on the spot, seeing for himself, and then came the famous action by the recently returned Craufurd and the Light Division to cover the withdrawal to a new position.

Wellington was wrong-footed at Fuentes de Oñoro, but quickly understood his error and reacted to deal with the threat. At Albuera Beresford took longer to recognise the threat to his flank and dealt with it clumsily. The army was saved by the stubborn resistance of Zayas' regiments and the other Spanish troops, who faced off the main French attack on their own for more than half an hour. This was the finest performance by Spanish soldiers in sight of their redcoated allies throughout the entire war. It clearly surprised the French, who were hurrying forward and expecting the defenders to cave in.

Beresford ordered the Second Division to march to the aid of the beleaguered Spanish, but appears to have left the execution of this order entirely to Stewart. The latter led Colborne's men to march past their allies along the French flank and to hit them from the side. Stewart directed this in person and did not grant Colborne's request to keep the Buffs in close column to guard the flank from enemy cavalry. Perhaps he was carried away in the moment by the prospect of such an opportunity, or believed that they could break the French infantry before any cavalry intervened. The general was certainly in a hurry, ordering the battalions to form 'left in front' or 'clubbed' – the opposite to their normal formation – and then rushing them forward before they were ready. Even so, this hurried attack did begin to make headway. Combined with the stubborn resistance of Zayas' regiments it took all the momentum and energy from the leading French division.

The charge by the Lancers of the Vistula and 2ième Hussars supported by the 10ième Hussars was the greatest success won by French cavalry over the British in the entire war. General La Tour-Maubourg's escort squadron does appear to have joined the attack, so there is justification for involving Dalmas and the dragoons. Stewart had left the flank of the infantry completely open. The downpour gave the redcoats even less chance of resisting the onslaught of the cavalry, but even so they were very poorly placed. In ten minutes or so the horsemen rode down Colborne's brigade and overran the KGL artillery. A few of the horsemen continued on behind Zayas' infantry, prompting the redcoats coming up in support to fire on them. A couple of lancers got among Marshal Beresford and his staff and the story of the marshal bodily plucking a Pole from the saddle is true. Beresford was a big man and no one ever had reason to doubt his physical courage. Some British sources claim that the Polish lancers were drunk and particularly brutal, stabbing again and again at wounded or captured men. It is hard to say whether this went beyond the normal excitement of cavalry riding down a broken enemy, but it did result in ill feeling.

Colborne's brigade was destroyed as a fighting force, with the exception of the 2/31st who were able to form some sort of hasty square – a drill the regiment continued to practise for several decades. Even they lost a third of their strength in the course of the day. The Buffs suffered 85 per cent casualties, the 2/48th lost 76 per cent of their men and the 2/66th some 66 per cent. These figures do not include some lightly wounded men who returned to duty within a day or so, or others scattered in the fighting who did not reappear until after the battle was over. Actual numbers with the Colours in the later stages of the fighting were probably significantly lower.

The 2/48th and 2/66th both lost their King's and Regimental Colours. Substantial parts of the flags from the Colours of the Buffs were later found on the battlefield, and so the battalion was able to claim that it had not lost them. For the British Army, it was the silk flags that had value. The French placed most importance on the staffs carrying them, both of which they carried off. Thus as far as they were concerned they had captured six Colours. The British claimed that only four or five had been lost. Most of the Buffs' King's Colour was torn off by Lieutenant Matthew Latham – the man Williams sees defending it and suffering a series of terrible wounds. Latham lost his arm, much of his face and nose and was stabbed in the body, but somehow managed to conceal the flag under him. It was found later in the day, the men assuming that the mangled lieutenant was dead. Later it was discovered that he was still alive, and he eventually recovered to continue serving with the regiment. Surgeon's drawings reveal the horribly disfiguring nature of his wounds.

After the destruction of Colborne's brigade, the other two brigades of the Second Division engaged in a prolonged and bloody firefight with the French infantry. Neither side was able to charge and break the stalemate and so the men stood and mowed each other down with musketry, with the French artillery in particular adding to the carnage. The three battalions of Houghton's brigade each suffered some 60 per cent casualties – hardly any of them missing – and the 1/57th or 'West Middlesex' gained the nickname 'the Diehards' to add to their existing one of the 'Steelbacks'. The name certainly dates to Albuera, but there is no contemporary evidence for the story that it came from their commander, Lieutenant Colonel Inglis, calling out to them to die hard as he lay badly wounded. It is possible that the story is true, although the ball of heavy canister that struck Inglis in the neck is today on display in the National Army Museum in London, and it does seem unlikely that he was able to shout to his men. What is not in doubt is the courage of their commander or the battalion, and the name was surely well earned.

The Second Division was slowly being ground away. Its other brigade suffered losses of around a quarter of its strength – something that would be considered severe in any other battle. Beresford knew that he needed to reinforce them, but clearly wanted to keep the Fourth Division as a reserve to cover a retreat should that prove necessary. He did ride up to a Spanish regiment and manhandle its colonel when the man refused to advance. This is normally told as an indication of the poor quality of the Spanish army, and it is true that the regiment in question consisted of survivors of a defeat earlier in the year. Yet more probably it is an indication of the marshal's state of mind, and it is possible that he did not issue the order in as clear or proper a manner as he should. At the very least he was not tactful in dealing with an ally, and may all too quickly have grabbed the regiment's commander rather than finding a senior Spanish officer to give the necessary orders.

Around the same time, Soult hesitated. He still had the fresh dragoon regiments and the re-forming lancers and hussars as well as the strong brigade of infantry under Werlé. It is more than possible that a strong attack by these forces working together would have won the battle. Willing or not, many of the Spanish regiments were not well enough drilled to manoeuvre and Beresford does seem to have been close to admitting defeat. We can never know what would have happened, but it is worth remembering that the French were heavily outnumbered. If Soult had attacked again and been defeated then it would have been hard to withdraw without suffering very heavy losses. In particular he would need his cavalry in good condition to cover his withdrawal. Very heavy losses not only risked his reputation, but could threaten French control of Andalusia. Subsequently he used the presence of Blake's Spanish as an excuse for not pressing the attack, but he knew that some or all of the Spanish were there from the early morning and yet had advanced anyway. Many people felt that Soult was a better strategist and organiser than he was a battlefield commander. It probably did not help that so many of his senior officers had already fallen.

Major General Lowry Cole on his own responsibility ordered his Fourth Division to advance. He was urged to act by some of Beresford's staff, but this was contrary to the marshal's orders. His two brigades had to cross a wide plain ideal for cavalry and then deploy into line to attack the infantry. It could easily have gone wrong, but instead the complicated manoeuvre went well. The inexperienced Portuguese regiments stood and saw off the French dragoons, aided by the presence on their flank of infantry in square – in this case the British Light Companies. This was close to what Colborne had requested permission to do. Afterwards the Fusilier Brigade attacked Werlé's infantry and after a ferocious combat broke them. It won the day for the Allies, but only at tremendous cost. Overall the Fusilier Brigade lost more than half its strength. By the closing stages it was under the command of a major – in reality Major Pearson of the 1/23rd rather than the fictional MacAndrews. In the story the 106th take the place of the 2/7th Foot or Royal Fusiliers. After the battle with its appalling losses, the two battalions of the 7th were merged into one and the 1/48th joined the brigade. I have anticipated this by attaching the 106th before the battle.

Albuera was one of the bloodiest day's fighting in the entire Peninsular War. Beresford lost almost six thousand men, two-thirds of them British. All in all, almost half the British infantry to see action became casualties. Spanish losses were comparably heavy for Zayas' division and the other heavily engaged regiments. Soult's losses were similar, but concentrated mainly among the infantry of V Corps and Werlé's brigade. All sides fought with great courage, whether it was the Spanish holding off the French attack, the Portuguese standing firm against the cavalry, the French advancing doggedly into the appalling firefight or the redcoats marching to meet them. Albuera was very much a soldier's battle, and the Allies won in spite of the errors of their commanders, but the cost was appalling.

Afterwards Beresford seems to have fallen prey to a deep depression and the dispatch he sent to Wellington was extremely gloomy. Fearing that this 'whining report ... would drive the people in England mad ...' and provide plenty of ammunition for the Opposition, the commander of the army declared, 'This won't do, write me down a victory.' This was duly done, and even though there was widespread criticism of Beresford in the army, this was concealed at home. However, the marshal was never again given a major independent command. Long continued in charge of a cavalry brigade until he was sent home in 1813. Stewart remained in charge of the Second Division until he was badly wounded two years later, but survived to become a lieutenant general.

Albuera was a victory, for Soult's attempt to relieve and re-supply Badajoz was stopped and the French forced to retreat. It was not won by the brilliance of the Allied high command, but by luck, the bold action of Lowry Cole, and most of all the stubborn fighting of the Allied infantry, which in the end overcame the courage of their French counterparts. If the French had matched the Allied numbers then it is possible that the result would have been different.

It is very easy to criticise decisions made by senior officers, without placing them in the context of the immense pressures they were under. Little in his previous career had prepared Beresford for command of an army of some thirty-five thousand men comprised of formations from three different nations – not including the King's German Legion, who were fully integrated with their British colleagues. It should therefore be no great surprise that the marshal did not shine in the role, for it would have been amazing if he had done so. Things might have been very different had the more experienced Hill been present, but none of the British senior officers apart from Wellington had experience of command on this scale.

As we have seen, the Second Siege of Badajoz failed, but Fuentes de Oñoro and Albuera were hailed as victories and did go a long way to saving Portugal from the immediate prospect of fresh invasion. The Prince Regent decided not to ask the Whigs to form a government and so support for Wellington and the war effort was maintained. His army grew slowly, but steadily, and in time he was in a better position to attack. For the men of the 106th there was still a long way to march and many battles to fight, but although they might not realise it, the tide of the war was turning.

CAST OF CHARACTERS

Names underlined are fictional characters.

The 106th Regiment of Foot

Captain Billy PRINGLE – Born into a family with a long tradition of service in the Royal Navy, Pringle's short-sightedness and severe seasickness led his father to send him to Oxford with a view to becoming a parson. Instead Pringle persuaded his parents to secure him a commission in the army. Plump, easy going and overfond of both drink and women, Pringle has found active service easier to deal with than the quiet routine and temptations of garrison duty in Britain. Through the battles in Portugal, and the arduous campaign in Spain, Billy Pringle has won promotion and found himself easing into his role as a leader. Part of a detachment whose ship was driven back to Portugal after being evacuated from Corunna, Pringle served in the 3rd Battalion of Detachments at Talavera and was wounded in the last moments of the battle. After a brief spell in Britain, he returned to Spain, serving at Ciudad Rodrigo and the River Côa in 1810, and then at Barrosa in 1811.

Lieutenant William HANLEY – Illegitimate son of an actress and a banker, Hanley was raised by his grandmother and spent years in Madrid as an aspiring artist. His father's death ended his allowance, and reluctantly Hanley took up a commission in the 106th purchased for him many years before. He served in Portugal in 1808, suffering a wound at Roliça. Since then his

342

fluency in Spanish has led to periodic staff duties. Even so, he was with Pringle and the Grenadier Company throughout the retreat to Corunna. Captured by the French, he escaped and has found himself involved in intelligence work. He was wounded at Talavera. In 1810 and 1811 he was once again employed on detached service, gathering intelligence and often operating behind French lines.

Lieutenant Hamish WILLIAMS – Williams joined the 106th as a Gentleman Volunteer, serving in the ranks and soon proving himself to be a natural soldier. He was commissioned as ensign following the Battle of Vimeiro. During the retreat to Corunna, he became cut off from the main army. Rallying a band of stragglers, he not only led them back to the main force, but thwarted a French column attempting to outflank the British army. He was praised by Sir John Moore for his actions, and was beside the general when the latter was mortally wounded at Corunna. In 1809 he was promoted to lieutenant and commanded a company in the 3rd Battalion of Detachments and fought with distinction at Talavera. Returning to Spain, he was left in charge of a small party of redcoats and Spanish infantry when the French besieged the frontier town of Ciudad Rodrigo. He also saw action in several border skirmishes and at the River Côa, and took part in landings along the southern coast of Spain. Wounded and left behind at Fuengirola, he spent several months with a band of *guerrilleros*, before serving at Barrosa. Fervently in love with Jane MacAndrews, Williams' cause seems to be continually thwarted by her unpredictability and his clumsiness, and most recently by her acquisition of a considerable fortune.

Captain TRUSCOTT – A close friend of Pringle, Hanley and Williams, the slightly stiff-mannered Truscott was wounded at Vimeiro and suffered the loss of his left arm. A slow recovery kept him from participating in the Corunna campaign. He served in the 3rd Battalion of Detachments and by the end of the Battle of Talavera was its commander. He returned to Spain with the battalion at the end of 1810 and fought at Barrosa.

Ensign Samuel TRUSCOTT – The younger brother of Captain Truscott, Sam is inexperienced, naive and prone to wild enthusiasm.

Ensign MESSITER – Young officer in the battalion.

Major Alastair MACANDREWS – The fifty-one-year-old Mac-Andrews first saw service as a young ensign in the American War of Independence. A gifted and experienced soldier, his lack of connections or wealth have kept his career slow. Raised to major after decades spent as a captain, he took charge of the 106th at Roliça, and led the battalion throughout the retreat to Corunna. Given the temporary local rank of lieutenant colonel, he led a training mission sent to Spain and became involved in the border fighting in 1810, fighting with distinction at the River Coa. At Barrosa he commanded a temporary battalion composed of Flank Companies, and fought with such distinction that he was praised in the dispatch and promised a brevet lieutenant colonelcy. This has not yet been gazetted. In the meantime he has returned to the battalion as a major and its second-in-command.

Lieutenant Colonel FITZWILLIAM – The commander of the 106th, fresh from the Guards. He led the battalion into action at Barrosa and is widely respected and liked.

Lieutenant DERRYCK – The senior ensign in the battalion, he served in Portugal and Spain in 1808–09, and gained his promotion to lieutenant at Barrosa.

Sergeant DOBSON – Veteran soldier who was Williams' 'front rank man' and took the volunteer under his wing. The relationship between Dobson and the young officer remains quietly paternal. However, at Roliça he displayed a ruthless streak when he killed an ensign who was having an affair with his daughter Jenny. Repeatedly promoted and broken for drunken misbehaviour, he has reformed following the accidental death of his first wife and his remarriage to the prim Mrs Rawson. He was wounded at Talavera, and served with Williams at Ciudad

344

Rodrigo and at the River Côa, and in the south, including the Battle of Barrosa.

Sergeant Tom EVANS – NCO in the Light Company, Evans is an experienced, but somewhat surly, soldier.

Private JACKSON – A soldier in Captain Truscott's company.

Private JENKINS – Young soldier in the Grenadier Company.

Sergeant MURPHY – A capable soldier, Murphy and his wife suffered a dreadful blow when their child died during the retreat to Corunna. He fought at Corunna, and was with Williams at Ciudad Rodrigo and at the Coa, and then in the south.

Their families

Jenny DOBSON – Older daughter from Dobson's first marriage, Jenny has ambitions beyond following the drum and flirted with and let herself be seduced by several of the young officers. During the winter she abandoned her newborn son to the care of Williams and Miss MacAndrews and left in search of a better life. She is currently the mistress of a French officer.

Mrs DOBSON – Herself the widow of a sergeant in the Grenadier Company, the very proper Annie Rawson carried her lapdog in a basket throughout the retreat to Corunna. The marriage to Dobson has done much to reform his conduct.

Jacob HANKS – Son of Dobson's daughter Jenny. His father killed and his mother run off to seek her fortune, the baby was protected by Williams and Jane. He is now being raised by Major MacAndrews' family.

Mrs Esther MACANDREWS – American wife of Major MacAndrews, Esther MacAndrews is a bold, unconventional character who has followed him to garrisons around the world. More recently, she managed to sneak out to Portugal, bringing her daughter with her, and the pair endured the horrors of the retreat to Corunna. In 1810 they once again travelled to Spain in the hope of joining her husband and the battalion.

Miss Jane MACANDREWS – Their daughter and sole surviving child, the beautiful Jane has a complicated relationship with Williams. During the retreat to Corunna, she was cut off from the main army and rescued by him, becoming involved in the desperate fight he and a band of stragglers fought to defend a vital bridge against the French under Dalmas. There is now talk of an understanding between Miss MacAndrews and Pringle's older brother Ned.

Miss Anne WILLIAMS – Oldest of Williams' three sisters, Anne is an intelligent and prudent young woman, and Pringle's affection for her has grown into something stronger.

Mrs Kitty GARLAND (neé WILLIAMS) – The middle sister, Kitty is bright, but impulsive and her marriage to the light dragoon Garland occurred only after Pringle had fought the cavalryman in a duel. Garland subsequently died of wounds received in the summer of 1810.

Captain Edward PRINGLE – Until recently master and commander of HMS *Sparrowhawk*, Edward is Billy Pringle's older brother and has followed the family tradition of going to sea. Smaller than his brother, and more sober in his manner, he has risen to command his own vessel by the age of twenty-eight. However, professional success has been marred by personal tragedy and a few months ago his wife died in childbirth. He has just been promoted post captain and given command of a frigate. There are rumours of a proposal to Miss MacAndrews.

The British

Mr BAYNES – A merchant with long experience of the Peninsula, now serving as an adviser and agent of the government.

Marshal William Carr BERESFORD – the forty-three-year-old

Beresford was appointed the commander of the Portuguese Army in 1809 and has spent the last few years industriously reforming and rebuilding it. He is the natural son of Lord Waterford, a prominent Anglo-Irish peer, who has assisted his career. In spite of the loss of sight in one eye after a hunting accident, he has served around the globe. In 1806 he led an expedition to capture Buenos Aires and after initial success was forced to surrender. Beresford is a big, powerful man with an abrupt manner and quick temper.

Colonel MURRAY – As quartermaster general, Murray served Wellesley in 1808, Sir John Moore in 1808–09, and returned with Wellesley in the spring of 1809. He contributed a great deal to making the headquarters of the army function, in particular developing a far more effective system for the collection and processing of intelligence.

Lieutenant General Viscount WELLINGTON – After several highly successful campaigns in India, Wellesley returned to Britain and several years of frustrated ambition before being given command of the expedition to Portugal. He managed to win the battles of Roliça and Vimeiro before being superseded. Along with his superiors, Wellesley was then recalled to Britain following the public outrage at the Convention of Cintra, which permitted the defeated French to return home in British ships. Cleared of responsibility, Wellesley was given command in Portugal and honoured with a title for his victory at Talavera. In 1810 he won a defensive battle at Busaco, and then retired behind the shelter of the lines of Torres Vedras. The French were unable to break through the lines and after several months retired.

Lieutenant General Thomas GRAHAM – Born in 1748, Graham became a soldier in his forties after the coffin carrying his late wife was desecrated by French revolutionaries claiming to be searching for weapons. He served as a volunteer at Toulon in 1793, raised a regiment at his own expense – the 90th Foot – and saw considerable service, notably in Egypt in 1801. A close friend of Sir John Moore, he served on the latter's staff in Spain. He has recently been appointed to command the British and Portuguese troops at Cadiz and in March won a victory at Barrosa.

Brigadier General Robert CRAUFURD – Born in 1764, Craufurd was a serious soldier who studied his profession and spent several years with the Austrian and Russian armies on the continent of Europe. In spite of this, he found little opportunity to distinguish himself and his rise was slow. In 1807 he was given charge of a brigade in the disastrous expedition against Buenos Aires, where through no fault of his own he was forced to surrender. Even so, in 1809 Wellington asked for him and gave him the plum command of the Light Brigade – later the famous Light Division – over the heads of officers who were senior to Craufurd in the army list. At first unpopular with his officers, the ordinary soldiers respected and liked their tough commander from the start. He is currently on leave in Britain.

Colonel Benjamin D'URBAN – British staff officer attached to the army in Portugal, who in 1809 acted as observer with Cuesta's Spanish Army of Estremadura. He is Marshal Beresford's quarter master general and has worked hard to assist in reforming the Portuguese army. A capable officer, he is also fiercely loyal to his chief.

Major General the Hon. William STEWART – Born in 1774, he is the fourth son of the Earl of Galloway, and has had a distinguished military career. He was instrumental in forming the experimental corps of riflemen and later commanded them when they became the 95th Foot. Popular with the men, who nicknamed him 'Auld Grog Willie' from his habit of issuing more than the standard allowance of rum, he is brave, but impulsive.

Lieutenant Colonel William MYERS – The commander of the 1/23rd Foot or Royal Welch Fusiliers, Myers is currently in charge of the entire brigade.

Major General Daniel HOUGHTON – Commander of the second brigade of the Second Division.

Brigadier General Robert LONG – Lately arrived in Portugal, Long has received command of the cavalry with Marshal Beresford's army. In the past he served on the staff with Sir John Moore. A few months after Albuera he wrote this mock obituary for himself – *The Thanks of the Country to ROBERT LONG, Major-General and Cabbage Planter, who had luck enough to do his public duty, Sense enough to know when he had done it and WISDOM enough to prefer Cabbage Planting to DEPENDENCE upon Princes or Power for More Substantial Happiness.*

Lieutenant Colonel John COLBORNE – Currently in command of the first brigade of the Second Division in place of Major General Stewart, Colborne serves in the 2/66th. He owed his step to lieutenant colonel to the recommendation of the dying Sir John Moore. Colborne is a highly gifted soldier and has immense confidence in his own abilities. Williams is currently acting as his ADC.

Captain William DUNBAR – Colborne's brigade major and a fellow officer in the 2/66th.

Major General William LUMLEY – Commander of the third brigade of the Second Division, Lumley was originally a cavalryman.

Colonel Michael HEAD – Commander of the 13th Light Dragoons.

Major MORRES – Commander of a detachment of the 13th Light Dragoons.

Cornet MACREA – Junior officer in the 13th Light Dragoons.

Corporal STILES – A wounded member of the 23rd Light Dragoons now employed as servant and groom by Williams.

Corporal SCOTT – Experienced soldier from the 5/60th Foot who trains Hanley to fire a rifle.

Private SCHWARTZ – Rifleman from the Brunswick Oels Jaeger.

Captain VON WACHHOLTZ – Commander of the Brunswick rifle company attached to the Fusilier Brigade.

The Spanish

Captain-General Francisco CASTAÑOS – The senior Spanish general and the man credited with the great victory at Bailén in 1808. Although present at Albuera, he waived his seniority and accepted Marshal Beresford's command on the basis that his main force was further north in Galicia.

General Joaquín BLAKE – One of many descendants of Irish exiles to rise to high rank in the Spanish army, Blake commands the army in the south. He is also a member of the Regency Council. Although his commitment to the cause is unquestioned, there is less confidence in his military ability and he has suffered a string of defeats. However, like the Spanish army in general, he continues to recover and renew the struggle.

General José Pascual de ZAYAS – The commander of one of the divisions of Spanish soldiers brought up from Cadiz. During their time in the south, the general has written a drill manual for his soldiers and had time to train them well. He was born in Cuba.

Lieutenant Colonel Andreas von SCHEPELER – A Westphalian officer serving on the staff of General Zayas.

Don Julián SANCHEZ/El CHARRO – One of the most famous of the guerrilla leaders, El Charro operated from Ciudad Rodrigo. A former soldier who had served in the ranks of the Spanish army, over time his band has developed into a regiment of irregular lancers.

GUTIÉRREZ – A farmer who supplies information to Baynes and Hanley.

The French

Capitaine Jean–Baptiste DALMAS – A former schoolteacher, Dalmas was conscripted into the army and took readily to the life of a soldier, serving in most of the Emperor's great campaigns and winning promotion. Since 1808 he has served as a supernumerary ADC to Marshal Ney and proved himself to be both a brave and an intelligent officer. The only blemish on his career has been his failure to seize a bridge so that the French could outflank Sir John Moore's British army as it retreated towards Corunna. On that occasion he was repulsed by a ragtag band of stragglers led by Hamish Williams. In 1810 he was tasked with capturing or killing Hanley. The British officer escaped, but during the pursuit Dalmas uncovered the vulnerability of General Craufurd's Light Division and helped Marshal Ney drive the British back across the River Coa. After that he was sent to Marshal Soult's staff and in early 1811 he helped to arrange the capture of the fortress of Badajoz.

Sergeant BRANDT – A Pole who has served in many different uniforms, he was discovered by Williams attempting to rape the wife of a partisan leader. Arrested, Brandt escaped, deserting to the French and enlisting with them. He is a savage man and a crack shot with a rifle.

Major James SINCLAIR – A United Irishman who refused to give up the struggle, the man who calls himself Sinclair serves as an officer in Napoleon's Irish Legion. For more than a year he acted as a spy, pretending to be a British officer so that he can infiltrate partisan bands. Williams and Hanley unmasked him, but he remains at large.

Major Emile BERTRAND – An engineer officer and the current keeper of Jenny Dobson.

Captain GILLET – Dragoon officer commanding General La Tour-Maubourg's escort squadron.

Major LEGROS – French garrison commander.

Marshal Jean-de-Dieu SOULT, Duke of Dalmatia – Born in 1769, he served in the ranks of the Royal Army before rising rapidly in the Revolutionary Army and was a general by 1799. He served in Italy and on the Rhine, and was chosen as one of the first batch of marshals in 1804. He played a distinguished role at Austerlitz, Jena and Eylau, before being sent to Spain. He led the pursuit of Sir John Moore's army, but was evicted from Portugal by Sir Arthur Wellesley later in 1809. In 1810 he led the invasion of Andalusia, and has been placed in command of the French armies in the south.

General Honoré-Theodore-Maxime GAZAN – Divisional commander and acting chief of staff to Marshal Soult.

General Jean-Baptiste GIRARD – Acting commander of V Corps under Marshal Soult, he is an experienced and gifted soldier, but this is his first taste of command at this level.

General Marie-Victor Nicholas LA TOUR-MAUBOURG – Formerly in charge in Estremadura and then the commander of the cavalry in Marshal Soult's army. As an aristocrat he had made his way through the ranks of the Revolutionary and Imperial armies by his own achievements.

General François-Jean WERLÉ – Commander of a strong brigade in Marshal Soult's army and an old friend, the general had risen from the ranks.

KING JOSEPH Bonaparte – As Napoleon's older brother, Joseph has reluctantly been moved from the comfort of his kingdom in Naples to Spain, where he finds himself less welcome. A man of strong literary and philosophical tastes, he has done his best to win popularity. Recently he has lifted a ban on bullfighting imposed by the chief minister of his Spanish predecessor.

Marshal Andrea MASSÉNA, Prince of Essling, Duc de Rivoli – Born in Nice in 1758 (which was then part of the Kingdom of Sardinia and not in France), Masséna was the son of a shopkeeper and served in the ranks of the French army for fourteen years, but did not become an officer until the Revolution. From then on, his rise was rapid, and he was a general by 1793. He served with great distinction, particularly in a succession of campaigns fought in Italy. Napoleon dubbed him the 'spoiled favourite of victory' and was willing to trust him with independent commands. In 1809 he helped to stave off utter defeat at the Battle of Aspern-Essling. The rigours of campaigning and an unhealthy lifestyle made him appear even older than his sixty-one years, and Masséna hoped to retire to the comfort of his estates. Alongside his reputation as a soldier, he had earned another as a rapacious plunderer, and loot has supplemented official rewards to make him an extremely wealthy man. Although perhaps past his best by the time he came to Spain, Wellington had immense respect for Marshal Masséna's skill. After capturing Ciudad Rodrigo and Almeida, he advanced deep into Portugal, but was stopped at the lines of Torres Vedras and eventually forced to retreat.

Marshal VICTOR, Duke of Belluno – Victor originally served in the ranks of the artillery, and then won rapid promotion during the Revolutionary Wars so that within three years he led an entire division. He has fought and beaten the Austrians, Prussians, Russians and recently the Spanish and is a capable, if extremely aggressive, commander. However, at Talavera and Barrosa his divisions were defeated by the British.